D1388084

THE YEAR OF THE DEATH OF RICARDO REIS

"This is a major political novel, which also throws a sharp light on one of the oldest and apparently most eroded of themes: the intimacies between the creation of poetry and death"

"*The Year of the Death of Ricardo Reis* shows Saramago to be a novelist of the grandest sort ... A dramatic work of great philosophical weight, filtered through a refined contemplative intelligence ... the novel is always moving between delicacy and indelicacy, between lofty abstractions and knock-about humour ... Not many novels in recent years have been able to bind spells with anything like this alliance of wit and seriousness. Maybe this is what masterpieces are made of, who knows?"

"One of the masterpieces of the 1980s – one of the best novels I have ever read"

"A rare, old-fashioned novel – at once lyrical, symbolic and meditative – by one of Europe's major writers"

"An engaging, impressive and moving literary novel ... The density and poise of its descriptions of Lisbon in 1936 recall Flaubert's description of Paris in 1848 or Joyce's Dublin in 1904 ... Full of precisely-observed physical, historical and political details and themes, and rich psychology"

JOSÉ SARAMAGO was born in 1922, in a small farming community north of the Alentejo. When he was still young his family moved to Lisbon, where, after leaving school at the age of 16, he worked as a mechanic, a draughtsman, in the social services and in publishing. He first wrote a novel at the age of 25, but after a long interlude his writing career really began when he was 44, by which time he was working as a translator and a journalist. He wrote three volumes of poetry and several short prose works, before publishing a second novel, *Manual of Painting and Calligraphy*. It was not until *Baltasar and Blimunda* was published in 1988 that his work was brought to the attention of an English-speaking readership. His next novel, *The Year of the Death of Ricardo Reis*, won him the *Independent* Foreign Fiction Award. His subsequent works, *The History of the Siege of Lisbon*, *The Stone Raft*, *The Gospel according to Jesus Christ*, *Blindness* and *The Cave* have earned him a world-wide following. In 1998 he was awarded the Nobel Prize for Literature.

GIOVANNI PONTIERO, formerly Reader in Latin-American Literature in the University of Manchester, was, until his death in 1997, Saramago's regular English translator. His translation of *The Gospel according to Jesus Christ* was awarded the Teixeira-Gomes Prize for Portuguese translation. He was also the principal translator into English of the works of Clarice Lispector.

José Saramago

THE YEAR OF
THE DEATH OF
RICARDO REIS

*Translated from the Portuguese
and with an introduction by
Giovanni Pontiero*

THE HARVILL PRESS
LONDON

First published in Portuguese with the title *O Ano da Morte de Ricardo Reis* by
Editorial Caminho, SARL, Lisbon, 1984

First published in Great Britain in 1992 by Harvill, an imprint of HarperCollins*Publishers*

This paperback edition first published in 1999 by The Harvill Press

11

The Harvill Press
Random House, 20 Vauxhall Bridge Road, London SW1V 2SA

Addresses for companies within The Random House Group Limited can be
found at: www.randomhouse.co.uk/offices.htm

The Random house Group Limited Reg. No. 954009

A CIP catalogue record for this book is available from the British Library

ISBN 9781860465024

The Random House Group Limited supports The Forest Stewardship
Council® (FSC®), the leading international forest-certification organisation.
Our books carrying the FSC label are printed on FSC®-certified paper.
FSC is the only forest-certification scheme supported by the leading
environmental organisations, including Greenpeace. Our
paper procurement policy can be found at
www.randomhouse.co.uk/environment

Printed and bound in Great Britain by Clays Ltd, St Ives PLC

The Portuguese Heritage:
José Saramago's
The Year of the Death of Ricardo Reis

GIOVANNI PONTIERO

Wise is the man who contents himself with the spectacle of the world.

—RICARDO REIS

To choose ways of not acting was ever the concern and scruple of my life.

—BERNARDO SOARES

If they were to tell me that it is absurd to speak thus of someone who never existed, I should reply that I have no proof that Lisbon ever existed, or I who am writing, or any other thing wherever it might be.

—FERNANDO PESSOA

José Saramago suggested in a recent interview that his major novel, *The Year of the Death of Ricardo Reis* (1984), might be fully appreciated only by someone who is Portuguese. In effect, the novel demands considerable knowledge of Portugal's history and culture from the stirring times of glory and empire up to the first ominous chapters of dictatorship under Salazar. Like most novels of substance, *The Year of the Death of Ricardo Reis* can be interpreted in various ways.

Ricardo Reis was one of the pseudonyms exploited by the Portuguese poet, Fernando Pessoa (1888–1935), and the frequent dialogues between Pessoa and Reis throughout the novel constitute a comprehensive and perceptive account of the life and work of Portugal's most famous poet since Camões. Pessoa argued that his three main pseudonyms (Alvaro de Campos, Alberto Caeiro and Ricardo Reis) were not mere aliases, but evidence of the multiple personalities we all possess, contrasting facets of our innumerable selves. Inspired by what Pessoa defined as 'a constant and organic tendency towards depersonalization and make-believe', Saramago ingeniously exploits the relationship between Pessoa and Reis by allowing the alter ego to outlive his creator by nine months, while summoning Pessoa from his tomb to renew friendship with Reis, who has returned to Portugal after sixteen years of political exile in Brazil.

The physical portrait of Pessoa is accurate in every detail: he is a slight, scholarly figure, with gold-rimmed spectacles, a small moustache above a tiny mouth and pointed chin; invariably courteous, somewhat nervous in manner, fastidiously dressed and with a distinctive gait. Pessoa never married, and despite at least one brief love affair with Ophélia Queiroz, there were vague hints of sexual ambivalence. He clearly found companionship preferable to love because it was ultimately less demanding and painful. Saramago captures the complexity and sense of mystery that contributed to Pessoa's obscurity during his lifetime and have attracted so much attention in recent years. Pessoa's interests were encyclopaedic: poetry, crime fiction, politics, astrology, theosophy, occultism, magic and freemasonry; a natural anti-conformist, his political views were controversial, his philosophical ideas eclectic and unsystematic, his literary theories influenced by the European avant-garde, by the experiments of the Neo-Socialists, Cubists and Futurists among others. Pessoa even elaborated his own poetic manifesto which he defined as *Paulismo*. Intent upon greater interaction between things abstract and concrete, between the poet's inner feelings and material reality, Pessoa expounded and practised *Paulismo* in his contributions to modernist journals published in Lisbon, notably *A Renascença*, *Centauro* and *Orpheu*. The lasting image of Pessoa as conveyed by Saramago is that of guarded privacy, unresolved contradictions of mind and spirit, and an unassailable awareness of his inner solitude, a poet who confided to his friends: 'I do not know who I am, nor what soul I possess.'

Ricardo Reis represents a vital aspect of Pessoa's nature, a fictitious character who gives utterance to Pessoa's thoughts, rather as an actor brings a dramatic text to life. Saramago builds on the factual details about Reis provided by Pessoa himself. Ricardo Reis was born in Oporto in 1887 and educated by the Jesuits. He graduated in medicine, became a general practitioner while writing poetry on the side, and opted for political exile because of his monarchist sympathies. Predictably, Reis betrays certain affinities with Pessoa's other two important pseudonyms, Campos and Caeiro, but Reis's radical scepticism is much more pronounced. An aesthete who tries to reconcile the clarity of reason and the obscurity of the dream world (at times on the fringe of madness), Reis confronts the unknown and the unknowable with total equanimity. A freethinker and fatalist, he is openly hostile in his attitude to orthodox Christianity because of its exclusive nature. Reis believes in Christ, but no more and no less than in all the other gods. *Freedom* he defines as the illusion of being free, *happiness* as the illusion of being happy. Truth, he declares, cannot be known, perhaps not even by the gods. Reis's deepest conviction is the omnipotence of Fate; the wise man enjoys each moment as if it were his last, advocating a state of calm acceptance rather than one of active enjoyment.

In short, Saramago invites us to contemplate Portugal and the world during the turbulent thirties through the eyes of Ricardo Reis alias Fernando Pessoa: a decade blighted by Fascist regimes and monstrous tactics as nations struggled for supremacy. Saramago combines factual documentation with idiosyncratic commentaries provided by Reis and Pessoa. And the author's sardonic asides add a further dimension to this reappraisal of Portugal's fortunes. Unlike Reis, Saramago is not content simply to contemplate the world. Guided by intuition, he is out to question its values. The interpretation they offer of Portugal's chequered history reveals a deep commitment to humanitarian ideals but without attempting to disguise their own political and social prejudices. Author and characters attest in their own way the glaring contradictions which are inherent in the Portuguese nation, the oscillating moods of bravado and self-effacement, the inherent mysticism. Key lines from Pessoa's odes attributed to Reis are worked into the text, often in mid-dialogue with recurring echoes of existential anguish in the face of the enormity of life and its constant betrayals.

The love theme which develops in the novel is not so much a subplot as a deepening analysis of human relationships. Two sharply contrasted women attract Ricardo Reis. First, the lowly hotel chambermaid Lydia, who provides sexual reassurance and exemplary housekeeping at no cost. Undemanding, energetic and forthright, she could not be more different from the idealized, incorporeal Lydia invoked by Reis in his *Odes*. Then there is his relationship with the anguished, circumspect Marcenda, a girl of aristocratic background, whose hopes of a normal life have been dashed by the embarrassing disfigurement and incurable symptoms of her withered arm. Lydia and Marcenda represent the gulf between man's carnal desires and the irresistible appeals of an unattainable ideal. Neither woman can resolve the conflict Reis experiences between his private inclinations and social proprieties, a conflict further aggravated by his own inadequacies as a lover who is ever cautious, egoistical and unwilling to enter into any firm commitments. Reis's troubled thoughts go to the very heart of the male versus female debate in tradition-bound Portugal in the thirties.

Poetry and philosophy overlap in this novel. The issues debated by Fernando Pessoa and his alter ego Ricardo Reis help to clarify the even more ambivalent relationship that exists between Saramago and Ricardo Reis. The novelist has confessed his admiration for the intellectual rigour and formal discipline to be found in the odes of Reis; he also identifies with the poet's stoicism and scepticism. What he cannot accept, however, is Reis's avowed indifference when confronted with the spectacle of the world, an indifference uncomfortably close to apathy. The tense dialogues engineered by Saramago between Pessoa and Reis expose the points of convergence and divergence in their perceptions of art and life. The discussions are wide-ranging and dialogue is used here as an effective means of insistent probing and spiritual catharsis. Pessoa and Reis explore mental labyrinths which closely resemble those of Borges's *Ficciones*. The influence of the Argentinian writer is manifest in recurring references to Herbert Quain's *The God of the Labyrinth* and in Saramago's choice of metaphors: mirrors, the river of time and eternal flux, the chessboard, mystical numerology, games of chance and hazard, and a mythology dominated by perverse and cunning gods. Like Borges, Saramago undermines certainties in favour of possibilities. To walk the labyrinth is to journey at random through time and space, a human adventure which demands courage and imagination.

The vision of mankind presented here is complex and total. Saramago's protagonist is a precarious entity, inhabited by alien voices, driven by desires, tainted by self-interest, a creature at once prodigious and tragic. Every human being is unmistakably individual even while resembling every other human being. We are all unique, yet *innumerable*. Saramago's gods, too, are innumerable, and never one, undivided God. This multiple personality exacerbates the problem of self-identity and accentuates our fragmentation. As Saramago puts it: 'We all suffer from some malaise, from some essential malaise, inseparable from what we are, a malaise which makes us what we are: it might even be more accurate to say that each of us is our own malaise, because of that malaise we are so little, because of it we succeed in being so much.'

Like some great book of life, *The Year of the Death of Ricardo Reis* rakes over the issues no thinking man or artist can ignore: truth, motivation, transience, solitude and nothingness. Pessoa and Reis progressively sink into infinite weariness as they struggle to come to terms with human destiny, the novel's leitmotif: 'No one escapes his destiny,' the dead Pessoa warns Reis, and who better qualified to confirm the thin divide between the traumas of life and death? The poet assures Reis: 'The wall that separates the living, each one from the other, is no less opaque than the wall that separates the living from the dead.'

Portugal in the thirties was already reduced to an insignificant role in Europe. Saramago refers to 'the timid voice of Portugal', timid perhaps, but strikingly individual, predictably low-keyed yet aware of her past glories and enduring worth. The example and spirit of Portugal's heroes, saints, visionaries and poets live on, this is the land of Camões, of the giant Adamastor, of Dom Sebastião. As Saramago reminds his readers: 'The history of Portugal is not that of Europe, but the history of Europe would be unimaginable without that of Portugal.' Dwarfed by powerful neighbours, her colonies depleted, Salazar's 'New State' dragooned the nation into a harsh regime based on xenophobia as opposed to healthy nationalism, which was doomed to end in repression, and crippling isolation. Saramago observes: 'It is, indeed, true that the definitive virtue of patriotism absolves all excesses and justifies all contradictions.' Yet the final impression is that of a resilient people, patient and hard-working, a people endowed with inner resources of courage and faith, qualities which make them natural pioneers and emigrants.

Political events in the thirties dramatically changed the face of Europe. Portugal had cause for concern when civil war erupted in Spain, and the upsurge of Fascism gathered momentum in Italy and Germany. Confining his narrative to the years 1935–6, the author reconstructs from news bulletins of the period the atmosphere of frustration and uncertainty which fostered Salazar's ambitions. Surrounded by threatening nations and dubious allies, Portugal, like the giant Adamastor, felt herself to be embedded in rock and trapped by hypocrisy and fraud. Portugal's 'timid voice' went largely unheard in the tragic farce that ensued.

This is the atmosphere to which Ricardo Reis returns after sixteen years in exile. In visual terms, Lisbon has barely changed; the same landmarks, the same familiar echoes reconnect Reis with his youth. Saramago's Lisbon is not merely a backdrop but the very nerve-centre of Portugal. In the company of Reis, we move across the city from the elevated Alto de Santa Catarina to the animated streets of the Baixa below. With Reis, we explore a city dominated by its port and the waters of the Tagus, a city rich in historical monuments, churches, theatres, restaurants and cafés, a city in which the eye continually travels from sky to sea, the twin forces of attraction and repulsion throughout the novel. Their horizons are infinite, both promise routes to a new existence, to a brighter future, but they can also mislead and destroy us.

Saramago sees the world as a great theatrical arena in which we fulfil our multiple destinies. Drama and the dramatic are stressed throughout the novel. Ricardo Reis frequents Lisbon's theatres and cinemas with avid curiosity. Both art forms enhance reality with the resources of imagination. At the same time, the author is anxious to remind us that in Portugal there is as much drama on the streets as in any auditorium. This, after all, is a nation much given to parades and processions, festivals and feast-days, a country where even the distribution of alms to the poor assumes all the trappings and excitement of solemn festivities. Market-place, carnival, a pilgrimage to Fátima, military manoeuvres, mock air-raids, clandestine subversion, the activities of Salazar's secret police and political rallies all represent different aspects of the collective national drama, just as the Hotel Bragança, a doctor's surgery, the public park, and the bedroom in Reis's apartment become the stage-sets for intimate scenes of tragedy and black comedy.

An astute observer of human nature, Saramago takes us through the ages of man with some memorable descriptions of infancy and old age, the innocence and spontaneity of children standing in sharp contrast to the fears and furtive obsessions of the elderly. Every human utterance, gesture and facial expression conveys its own mood and shade of feeling. Eyes and lips are particularly expressive, even a simple kiss becomes an erotic ritual. His touch is infallible where he describes the inner turmoil engendered by hatred, fear, mistrust and self-doubt. The characters in *The Year of the Death of Ricardo Reis* bare their souls in a succession of soliloquies and dialogues while genuinely interacting and influencing each other. Human relationships are fraught with contradictions and misunderstandings, egotism and hypocrisy all too frequently destroy any real friendship or love. The author constantly reminds us: 'Human nature is not to be trusted.' In this context, a simple, almost illiterate hotel chambermaid has more to offer in terms of selfless devotion and loyalty than the shrewd urbane Reis. Ironically, it is the undemanding and much exploited Lydia who clearly possesses the freer spirit. Her very lack of sophistication helps her to accept life with an inner tranquillity unknown to Reis.

In matters of technique, *The Year of the Death of Ricardo Reis* reveals an individual combination of traditional and contemporary elements. When the philosophical probings become particularly dense, Saramago draws upon the eloquence and subtlety of post-Renaissance prose; elegant conceits, frequent circumlocutions, symmetrical phrasing and pungent satire are exploited to the full. The author's impressive erudition and wide range of cultural references permit him to move with ease from past to present and the registers and modulations of discourse are adjusted accordingly. His impressive grasp of historical and political developments enable him to evaluate and compare situations, to unmask the ironies of circumstance, and vagaries of fate. As with all great satirists, his observation of the world is conducted with disarming honesty and an unsparing eye for the sham and hypocritical. Things human and divine are dispassionately examined and boldly reviewed.

Saramago, like Borges, is out to persuade us that: 'There is no more elaborate pleasure than that of thought.' Technically secure and intensely poetic, Saramago passes effortlessly from description to commentary, from subtle speculation to popular wisdom, from elaborate metaphors to simple human statements.

Working on a broad canvas, he strives for a rich pattern of interwoven themes. The abundant soliloquies and dialogues revive traditional concepts of novel form yet elsewhere he chooses to adopt the experimental techniques associated with twentieth-century fiction, arbitrary shifts of time and location, multiple focus, flashback, collage, linguistic pastiche and stream of consciousness. Ultimately, mood and atmosphere are as essential to the narrative as plot or action. Throughout the novel there is a prevailing note of imminent changes, a clear hint of menacing forces and encroaching doom. The feelings and impressions experienced by the characters are deeply influenced by the elements, by the incessant rain and moments of tempest, by the blazing sun and the torpor of the sweltering dog days. Symmetry and counterpoint are the basic stylistic features. The suggestive opening phrase: 'Here the sea ends and the earth begins' finds its response in the closing lines: 'Here, where the sea has ended and the earth awaits'. The nine months granted to Fernando Pessoa to wander from the grave are balanced against the last nine months of Ricardo Reis's existence. There is futher correspondence between the nine months that elapse from conception to birth and the nine months that strip Pessoa of any vestige of life. Symmetry and counterpoint are also observed in the relationship between public and private events, between epic crowd scenes and those of quiet intimacy. Remarkably vigilant, the author interpolates key phrases and recurring motifs almost as if he were orchestrating a score. Images, too, spark off unmistakable associations: when Lydia unexpectedly drops a plate, which smashes into smithereens, the incident immediately evokes the shattering discovery that she is pregnant.

As this is primarily a novel of ideas, discourse prevails throughout the novel. The speech forms encompass every level of cultural and social background. Linguistic features range from verbal parrying of the utmost refinement to crude banalities, from poetic statements to repartee reminiscent of the picaresque, from classical diction to the slovenly exchanges of the lower orders.

Like most important novels, *The Year of the Death of Ricardo Reis* also tells us a great deal about the craft of fiction and the demands of creative prose. As an experienced linguist and translator, Saramago devotes much thought to the problem of language, its limitations and inadequacies. His comments on the writer's struggle with words are instructive. He observes: 'Man has been endowed with words to disguise his thoughts.' He finds words exasperatingly perverse, even misleading, conveying truth and lies in the same breath. Bridging the gap between expression and meaning can cause endless frustration. The inauthenticity of words haunts him and even names can become meaningless if divorced from a human content. He claims: 'We are not what we say, we are the credence others give us,' and at one point, he even reaches the provocative conclusion that: 'The best words of all are those that say nothing.' Nonetheless, even the mute cicadas in the novel create their own unmistakable song. Portuguese, like Spanish, tends to be a verbose language, generous and flamboyant, rich in emotions, yet these same characteristics can be self-defeating and render it conceptually woolly and inexact. Saramago shines among a new generation of Portuguese writers who convey unusual insights without any loss of clarity or precision.

The problems Saramago poses for the translator are considerable. Disregarding conventional syntax and punctuation, he favours an uninterrupted sequence of extended paragraphs. Pauses are invariably indicated by commas and full-stops. All other forms of punctuation, such as colons, interrogation or exclamation marks, are ignored. At one point, punctuation is dispensed with altogether. The conjunctions *and* or *but* are rare. Adverbs, on the other hand, denoting uncertainty or speculation, abound. Tenses can be problematic with unorthodox shifts backwards and forwards from past to present. The unpunctuated dialogues also switch unexpectedly from first to second to third person, or from direct speech to inner monologues.

The novel incorporates a vast range of specialized vocabulary: everything from church liturgy to strategic warfare, from political propaganda to the finer points of all-in wrestling. The translator has to learn to distinguish between the intellectual and pseudo-intellectual, the educated and the primitive, the speech of the living and ghostly voices, to find suitable equivalents for the innumerable proverbs, puns and ingenious examples of word-play. The oscillations between serious introspection and droll asides, between lofty rhetoric and pithy colloquialism, call for subtle adjustments if the translator hopes to match the fluency and nimble pace of the original.

Finally there is the all-important question of sound-patterns. For Saramago, colour, temperature and music are as important as ideas. His distinctive voice has created his own 'word music', mercurial, pliant and unfailingly expressive.

Convinced that the function of anyone who writes is 'to enlarge the world', Saramago enhances our vision of nature and mankind, and goes even further, by pricking our conscience and touching our heart. In the end, we care passionately about 'the timid voice of Portugal' and endorse its plea to be heard in a universal context.

Here the sea ends and the earth begins. It is raining over the colorless city. The waters of the river are polluted with mud, the riverbanks flooded. A dark vessel, the *Highland Brigade*, ascends the somber river and is about to anchor at the quay of Alcântara. The steamer is English and belongs to the Royal Mail Line. She crosses the Atlantic between London and Buenos Aires like a weaving shuttle on the highways of the sea, backward and forward, always calling at the same ports, La Plata, Montevideo, Santos, Rio de Janeiro, Pernambuco, Las Palmas, in this order or vice versa, and unless she is shipwrecked, the steamer will also call at Vigo and Boulogne-sur-Mer before finally entering the Thames just as she is now entering the Tagus, and one does not ask which is the greater river, which the greater town. She is not a large vessel, fourteen thousand tons, but quite seaworthy, as was demonstrated during this crossing when, despite constant rough weather, only those unaccustomed to ocean voyages were seasick, or those accustomed but who suffer from an incurably delicate stomach. On account of the homey atmosphere and comforts on board, the ship has come to be affectionately known, like her twin the *Highland Monarch*, as the family steamer. Both vessels are equipped with spacious decks for games and sunbathing, even cricket, a field sport, can be played on deck, which shows that for the British Empire nothing is impossible. When the weather is fine, the *Highland Brigade* becomes a garden for children and a paradise for the elderly, but not today, because it is raining and this is our last afternoon on board. Behind windowpanes ingrained with salt the children peer out at the gray city, which lies flat above the hills as if built entirely of one-story houses. Yonder, perhaps, you catch a glimpse of a high dome, some thrusting gable, an outline suggesting a castle ruin, unless this is simply an illusion, a chimera, a mirage created by the shifting curtain of the waters that descend from the leaden sky. The foreign children, whom nature has endowed more generously with the virtue of inquisitiveness, are curious to know the name of the port. Their parents tell them or it is spelled out by their nurses, *amas*, *bonnes*, *Fräuleins*, or perhaps by a passing sailor on his way to some maneuver. Lisboa, Lisbon, Lisbonne, Lissabon, there are four different ways of saying it, leaving aside the variants and mistaken forms. And so the children come to know what they did not know before, and that is what they knew already, nothing, merely a name, causing even greater confusion in their childish minds, a name pronounced with the accent peculiar to the Argentinians, if that is what they happen to be, or to the Uruguayans, the Brazilians, the Spaniards. The latter, writing Lisbon correctly in their respective versions of Castilian or Portuguese, then pronounce it in their own way, a way beyond the reach of ordinary hearing or any representation in writing. When the *Highland Brigade* sails up the straits early tomorrow morning, let us hope there will be a little sunshine and a clear sky, so that the gray mist does not completely obscure, even within sight of land, the already fading memory of those voyagers who passed here for the first time, those children who repeated the word Lisbon, transforming it into some other name, those adults who knitted their eyebrows and shivered with the general dampness which penetrates the wood and metal, as if the *Highland Brigade* had emerged dripping from the bottom of the sea, a ship twice transformed into a phantom. No one by choice or inclination would remain in this port.

A few passengers are about to disembark. The steamer has docked, the gangplank has been lowered and secured, unhurried baggage handlers and stevedores appear below, guards emerge from the shelter of their huts and sheds, and the customs officers begin to arrive. The rain has eased off and almost stopped. The passengers gather at the top of the gangplank, hesitant, as if in some doubt as to whether permission has been granted to disembark, or whether there could be a quarantine, or perhaps they are apprehensive about those slippery steps. But it is the silent city that frightens them, perhaps all its inhabitants have perished and the rain is only falling to dissolve into mud what has remained standing. Along the quayside grimy portholes glow dimly, the spars are branches lopped from trees, the hoists are still. It is Sunday. Beyond the docksheds lies the somber city, enclosed by façades and walls, as yet protected from the rain, perhaps drawing back a heavy, embroidered curtain, looking out with vacant eyes, listening to the water gurgling on the rooftops, down the drainpipes to the gutters below, and onto the gleaming limestone of the pavement to the brimming drains, some of their covers raised where they have flooded.

The first passengers disembark. Their shoulders bent under the monotonous rain, they carry sacks and suitcases and have the lost expression of those who have endured the voyage as if in a dream of flowing images, between sea and sky, the prow going up and down like a metronome, the waves rising and falling, the hypnotic horizon. Someone is carrying a child in his arms, a child so silent it must be Portuguese. It does not ask where they are, or else it was promised that if it went to sleep at once in that stuffy berth, it would wake up in a beautiful city where it would live happily ever after. Another fairy tale, for these people have been unable to endure the hardships of emigration. An elderly woman who insists on opening her umbrella has dropped the green tin box shaped like a little trunk that she was carrying under her arm. The box has crashed onto the pebbles on the quayside, breaking open, its bottom falling out. It contained nothing of value, a few souvenirs, some bits of colored cloth, letters and photographs scattered by the wind, some glass beads shattered into smithereens, balls of white yarn now badly stained, one of them disappearing between the quayside and the side of the ship. The woman is a third-class passenger.

As they set foot on land, the passengers run to take shelter. The foreigners mutter about the storm as if we were responsible for the bad weather, they appear to forget that in their beloved

France or England the weather is usually a great deal worse. In short, they use the slightest pretext, even nature's rain, to express their contempt for poorer nations. We have more serious reasons for complaint, but we remain silent. This is a foul winter, with whatever crops there were uprooted from the fertile soil, and how we miss them, being such a small country. The baggage is already being unloaded. Under their glossy capes the sailors resemble hooded wizards, while, down below, the Portuguese porters move swiftly in their peaked caps and short jackets weatherproofed and lined, so indifferent to the deluge that they astonish all who watch. Perhaps this disdain for personal comfort will move the purses of the passengers, or wallets as one says nowadays, to take pity on them, and that pity will be converted into tips. A backward clan, with outstretched hand, each man sells what he possesses in good measure, resignation, humility, patience, may we continue to find people who trade in this world with such wares. The passengers go through customs, few in number, but it will take them some time to get out, for there are many forms to be filled in and the handwriting of the customs officers on duty is painstaking. It is just possible that the quickest of them will get some rest this Sunday. It is growing dark although it is only four o'clock, a few more shadows and it will be night, but in here it is always night, the dim lamps lit all day long and some burned out. That lamp there has been out for a week and still hasn't been replaced. The windows, covered with grime, allow a watery light to penetrate. The heavy air smells of damp clothing, rancid baggage, the cheap material of uniforms, and there is not a trace of happiness in this homecoming. The customs shed is an antechamber, a limbo, before one passes on to what awaits outside.

A grizzled fellow, skin and bones, signs the last of the forms. Receiving copies, the passenger can go, depart, resume his existence on terra firma. He is accompanied by a porter whose physical appearance need not be described in detail, otherwise we should have to continue this examination forever. To avoid confusing any-one who might need to distinguish this porter from another, we will say only that he is skin and bones, grizzled, and as dark and clean-shaven as the man he is accompanying. Yet they are both quite different, one a passenger, one a porter. The latter pulls a huge suitcase on a metal cart, while the other two suitcases, small by comparison, are suspended from his neck with a strap that goes around the nape like a yoke or the collar of a religious habit. Once outside, under the protection of the jutting roof, he puts the luggage on the ground and goes in search of a taxi, they are usually here waiting when a ship arrives. The passenger looks at the low clouds, the puddles on the rough ground, the water by the quayside contaminated with oil, peelings, refuse of every kind, then he notices several unobtrusive warships. He did not expect to find them here, the proper place for these vessels is at sea, or, when not engaged in war or military maneuvers, in the estuary, which is more than wide enough to give anchorage to all the fleets in the world, as one used to say and perhaps still says, without bothering to see what fleets they might be. Other passengers emerged from customs, accompanied by their porters, then the taxi appeared, splashing water beneath its wheels. The waiting passengers waved their arms frantically, but the porter leaped onto the running board and made a broad gesture, It's for this gentleman, thus showing how even a humble employee in the port of Lisbon, when rain and circumstances permit, may hold happiness in his meager hands, which he can bestow or withhold at a moment's notice, a power attributed to God when we talk of life. While the taxi driver loaded his luggage into the trunk, the passenger, betraying for the first time a slight Brazilian accent, asked, Why are warships moored here. Panting for breath as he helped the taxi driver lift the heavy suitcase, the porter replied, Ah, it's the naval dock, because of the weather these ships were towed in the day before yesterday, otherwise they would have drifted off and run ashore at Algés. Other taxis began to arrive. Either they had been delayed or else the steamer docked an hour earlier than expected. Now there was an open-air market in the square, plenty of taxis for everyone. How much do I owe you, the passenger asked. Whatever you care to give on top of the fixed fare, the porter replied, but he did not say what the fixed fare was or put an actual price on his services, trusting to the good fortune that protects the courageous, even when the courageous are only baggage handlers. I have only English money, Oh, that's fine, and he saw ten shillings placed into his right hand, coins that shone more brightly than the sun itself. At long last the celestial sphere has banished the clouds that hovered oppressively over Lisbon. Because of such heavy burdens and deep emotions, the first condition for the survival and prosperity of any porter is to have a stout heart, a heart made of bronze, otherwise he will soon collapse, undone. Anxious to repay the passenger's excessive generosity, or at least not to be indebted in terms of words, he offers additional information that no one wants, and expressions of gratitude that no one heeds. They are torpedo boats, they are ours, Portuguese, this is the *Tejo*, the *Dão*, the *Lima*, the *Vouga*, the *Tâmega*, the *Dão* is that one nearest you. No one could have told the difference, one could even have changed their names around, they all looked alike, identical, painted a drab gray, awash with rain, without a sign of life on the decks, their flags soaked like rags. But no disrespect is intended, we know that this destroyer is the *Dão*. Perhaps we shall have news of her later.

The porter raises his cap and thanks him. The taxi drives off, Where to. This question, so simple, so natural, so fitting for the place and circumstances, takes the passenger unawares, as if a ticket purchased in Rio de Janeiro should provide the answer to all such questions, even those posed in the past, which at the time met with nothing but silence. Now, barely disembarked, the passenger sees at once that this is not so, perhaps because he has been asked one of the two fatal questions, Where to. The other question, and much worse, is Why. The taxi driver looked into his rearview mirror, thinking the passenger had not heard him. He was opening his mouth to repeat, Where to, but the reply came first, still indecisive, hesitant, To a hotel. Which hotel, I don't know, and having said, I don't know, the passenger knew precisely what he wanted, knew it with the utmost conviction, as if he had spent the entire voyage making up his mind, A hotel near the river, down in this part of the city. The only hotel near the river is the Bragança, at the beginning of the Rua do Alecrim. I don't remember the hotel, but I know where the street is, I used to live in Lisbon, I'm Portuguese. Ah, you're Portuguese, from your accent I thought you might be Brazilian. Is it so very noticeable. Well, just a little, enough to tell the difference. I haven't been back in Portugal for sixteen years. Sixteen years is a long time, you will find that things have changed a lot around here. With these words the taxi driver suddenly fell silent.

His passenger did not get the impression that there were many changes. The avenue they followed was much as he remembered it, only the trees looked taller, and no wonder, for they had had sixteen years in which to grow. Even so, because in his mind's eye he could still see green foliage, and because the wintry nakedness of the branches diminished the height of the rows, one image balanced out the other. The rain had died away, only a few scattered drops continued to fall, but in the sky there was not a trace of blue, the clouds had not dispersed and they formed one vast roof the color of lead. Has there been much rain, the passenger inquired. For the last two months it has been bucketing down like the great flood, the driver replied as he switched off his windshield wipers. Few cars were passing and even fewer trams, the occasional pedestrian warily closed his umbrella, along the sidewalks stood great pools of muddy water caused by blocked drains. Several bars were open, side by side, murky, their viscous lights encircled by shadows, the silent image of a dirty wineglass on a zinc counter. These façades are the great wall that screens the city, and the taxi skirts them without haste, as if searching for some break or opening, a Judas gate, or the entrance to a labyrinth. The train from Cascais passes slowly, chugging along at a sluggish pace yet still with enough speed to overtake the taxi, but then it falls behind and enters the station just as the taxi turns into the square. The driver informs him, The hotel is that one as you enter the street. He halted in front of a café and added, You'd better ask first if they have any rooms, I can't park outside the door because of the trams. The passenger got out, glanced fleetingly at the café, which was named Royal, a commercial example of monarchical nostalgia in a republican era, or of reminiscences of the last reign, here disguised in English or French. A curious situation, one looks at the word without knowing whether it should be pronounced *rôial* or *ruaiale*. He had time to consider the problem because it was no longer raining and the road went uphill. Then he imagined himself walking back from the hotel, with or without a room, and no sign of the taxi, it has vanished with all his luggage and clothes, his papers, and he wondered how he could exist deprived of these things and all his other worldly goods. Climbing the front steps of the hotel, he realized from these musings that he was exhausted, that he was suffering from an overwhelming fatigue, an infinite weariness, a sense of despair, if we really know what despair means when we say that word.

As he pushed open the door of the hotel, an electric buzzer sounded. At one time it would have been a little bell, ting-a-ling-a-ling, but one must always count on progress and its improvements. There was a steep flight of stairs and on the post at the bottom stood a figurine in cast iron holding aloft, in its right hand, a glass ball. The figurine represented a page in court dress, if the expression isn't redundant, for who ever saw a page not in court dress. It would be clearer to say a page dressed as a page, and judging from the cut of his costume, he was of the Italian Renaissance. The traveler went up endless steps. It seemed incredible that one should have to climb so far to reach the first floor, it was like scaling Mount Everest, a feat which continues to be the dream and utopia of every mountaineer. To his relief, a man with a mustache appeared at the top of the stairs offering words of encouragement, Up you come then. The man did not say these words but that was how one might have interpreted the look on his face as he leaned over the landing to investigate what fair winds and evil times had brought this guest. Good evening, sir. Good evening, he has no breath left for more. The man with the mustache smiles patiently, You need a room, the smile becomes that of someone apologizing, There are no rooms on this floor, this is the reception desk, dining room, lounge, and through here is the kitchen and pantry, the rooms are upstairs, and to inspect them we must go up to the second floor. This room is no good, it is small and gloomy, nor this, it looks onto the back, and these are already occupied. What I wanted was a room with a view of the river. Ah, in that case you will like room two hundred and one, it was vacated only this morning, I'll show it to you right away. The door at the end of the hallway had a little enameled plate, black numerals on a white background. If this were not a humble hotel room without any luxuries, and the room number were two hundred and two, and if the guest were called Jacinto and like Eça de Queirós's hero owned an estate in Tormes, then this episode would be set not in the Rua do Alecrim but on the Champs Elysées, on the right as one goes up, just like the Hotel Bragança, but that is the only detail they have in common.

The traveler approved of the room, or rooms to be precise, for there were two of them connected by a broad archway, on that side the bedroom, which once upon a time would have been described as an alcove, and on this side the sitting room, living quarters as satisfactory as in any apartment, with dark furniture in polished mahogany, drapes over the windows, and lampshades. The traveler heard the harsh screeching of a tram going up the street. The taxi driver was right. It seemed ages since the traveler had left the taxi waiting, and he smiled inwardly at his fear of being robbed. Do you like the room, the manager asked with the voice and authority of his profession but ever courteous, as befits someone negotiating a rental. It's fine, I'll take it, How long are you staying, I can't tell you, much depends on the time it takes to settle my affairs. It is the usual dialogue, the exchange one expects in such situations, but on this occasion there is an element of falsehood, because the traveler has no affairs to settle in Lisbon, no affairs worthy of the name, he has told a lie, he who once declared that he despised inaccuracy.

They descended to the first floor and the manager summoned an employee, a messenger and luggage porter, whom he sent to fetch the gentleman's suitcases. The taxi was waiting in front of the café and the traveler went down with him to pay the fare, an expression that harks back to the days of the horse-drawn cab, and also to check that there was nothing missing, but his mistrust is misguided, undeserved, the driver is an honest fellow and wishes only to be paid what is on the meter plus the customary tip. He will not share the good fortune of the baggage handler at the docks, there will be no further distribution of silver coins, for the traveler by now has changed some of his money at the reception desk, not that we disapprove of generosity, but enough is enough, too much ostentation is an insult to the poor. The suitcase weighs a great deal more than money, and when it reaches the landing, the manager is waiting to supervise its transportation. He moves forward to help by placing his hand underneath, a symbolic action, like someone laying the first stone, for the load is carried up on the errand boy's shoulders. A boy by profession rather than age, and he is beginning to feel his years as he carries up the heavy suitcase, supported on either side by futile gestures of assistance, for those made by the guest are not much help as he looks on in distress at the man's exertions, One more flight to go and you are there. It is room two hundred and one, Pimenta. This time Pimenta is in luck, he does not have to climb to the upper floors.

Meanwhile the guest returns to the reception desk, somewhat out of breath after all that effort. He takes the pen and enters the essential details about himself in the register of arrivals, so that it might be known who he claims to be, in the appropriate box on the lined page. Name, Ricardo Reis, age, forty-eight, place of birth, Oporto, marital status, bachelor, profession, doctor, last place of residence, Rio de Janeiro, Brazil, whence he has arrived aboard the *Highland Brigade*. It reads like the beginning of a confession, an intimate autobiography, all that is hidden is contained in these handwritten lines, the only problem is to interpret them. And the manager, who has been craning his neck to follow the linking of words and decipher their meaning at the same time, thinks he knows more or less everything. He introduces himself, beginning, Doctor. This is not intended as flattery but rather as a sign of respect, the acknowledgment of a right, a merit, a quality, which warrants immediate recognition even when not made known in writing. My name is Salvador, I am in charge of this hotel, should you require anything, Doctor, you need only tell me. At what time is dinner served. Dinner is at eight, Doctor, I hope you will find our cuisine satisfactory, we also serve French dishes. Doctor Ricardo Reis concedes with a nod that he shares that hope, retrieves his raincoat and hat from a chair, and withdraws.

The porter was waiting for him in the open doorway of his room. Ricardo Reis saw him there as he entered the corridor and knew that the man would hold out a hand, servile yet nonetheless imperious, demanding according to the weight of the luggage. As he proceeded, he noticed something he had failed to observe before, there were doors only on one side of the corridor, on the other side was the wall that formed the well of the staircase. He thought about this as if it were an important matter that must be borne in mind, really feeling very tired. The man hefted the tip rather than look at it, from long experience, and was satisfied, so much so that he said, Many thanks, Doctor. We cannot explain how he knew, for he had not seen the register of arrivals. The fact is that the lower orders are every bit as shrewd and perceptive as those who have been educated and lead a privileged existence. All that bothered Pimenta was the wing of his shoulder blade, for one of the straps reinforcing the suitcase had not been adjusted right. One would think that he did not know how to carry luggage.

Ricardo Reis sat on a chair and looked around him. This is where he will live who knows for how many days, perhaps he will rent a house and open consulting rooms, or he might decide to return to Brazil. But for the moment the hotel will do nicely, a neutral place requiring no commitment. He is in transit, his life is suspended. Beyond the smooth drapes the windows have suddenly become luminous, an effect created by the street lamps. Already so late, this day has ended, what remains hovers in the remote distance over the sea and is fast escaping. Yet only a few hours ago, Ricardo Reis was still sailing those waters. Now the horizon is within arm's reach, embodied by walls, pieces of furniture that reflect the light as a black mirror, and instead of the deep vibration of the steamer's engines he can hear the whispering, the murmuring of the city, six hundred thousand people sighing, calling in the distance. Then cautious footsteps in the corridor, a woman's voice saying, I'm coming at once. These words, this voice, it must be the maid. He opened one of the windows and looked outside. The rain had stopped. The fresh air, damp with the wind that was sweeping over the river, pervaded the room and cleared away the musty smell, the smell of dirty linen forgotten in some drawer. He reminded himself that a hotel is not a home, smells of one kind or another linger, the perspiration of insomnia or of a night of love, a drenched overcoat, mud brushed from shoes at the hour of departure, the maids who enter to change the beds and sweep the rooms, the odor peculiar to women, unavoidable smells, the signs of our humanity.

He left the window open and went to open another. In his shirt sleeves, refreshed, his vigor suddenly restored, he began to unpack his suitcases. Within half an hour he had emptied them and transferred his clothes to the chest of drawers, his shoes to the shoe rack, his suits to the hangers in the closet, his black suitcase with the medical instruments to a dark recess of a cupboard. The few books he had brought with him were placed on a shelf, some Latin classics which he had got out of the habit of reading, some well-thumbed editions of his favorite English poets, three or four Brazilian authors, less than a dozen Portuguese authors. Among them he found one from the library of the *Highland Brigade*, a book he had forgotten to return. If the Irish librarian notices the book is missing, grave and grievous accusations will be made against the Lusitanian nation, a land of slaves and brigands, as Byron once quipped, and O'Brien will concur. Insignificant local transgressions often give rise to resounding and universal consequences. But I am innocent, I swear it was merely forgetfulness on my part and nothing more. He placed the book on his bedside table, intending to finish it one of these days, *The God of the Labyrinth* by Herbert Quain, also Irish, by no unusual coincidence. But the name itself is certainly most unusual, for without any great variation in the pronunciation one might read Quain as the Portuguese for Who. Take note, Quain, *Quem*, a writer who is no longer unknown because someone discovered him on the *Highland Brigade*. And if that was the only copy, and even it is now missing, all the more reason for asking ourselves Who. The tedium of the voyage and the book's evocative title had attracted him. A labyrinth with a god, what god might that be, which labyrinth, what labyrinthine god. In the end it turned out to be a simple detective story, an ordinary tale of death and investigation, the murderer, the victim, and finally the detective, all three accomplices to the crime. In my honest opinion, the reader of a mystery is the only real survivor of the story he is reading, unless it is as the one real survivor that every reader reads every story.

There are also documents to be stored away, handwritten sheets of verse, the oldest of them dated the twelfth of June, nineteen fourteen. War was about to break out, the Great War, as they were later to call it, until they experienced one even greater. *Maestro, placid are the hours we lose, if in losing them, as in a vase, we place flowers.* And then it finished, *Tranquil, we depart this life, feeling no remorse at having lived.* The most recent sheet of all is dated the thirteenth of November, nineteen thirty-five, six weeks have passed since he wrote it. Still fresh, the lines read, *Innumerable people live within us. If I think and feel, I know not who is thinking and feeling, I am only the place where there is thinking and feeling*, and, though they do not end here, it is as if everything ends, for beyond thinking and feeling there is nothing. If I am this, muses Ricardo Reis as he stops reading, who will be thinking at this moment what I am thinking, or think that I am thinking in the place where I am, because of thinking. Who will be feeling what I am feeling, or feel that I am feeling in the place where I am, because of feeling. Who is using me in order to think and feel, and among the innumerable people who live within me, who I am, Who, *Quem*, Quain, what thoughts and feelings are the ones I do not share because they are mine alone. Who am I that others are not nor have been nor will come to be. He gathered together the sheets of paper and put them into a drawer of the little writing desk, closed the windows, and went to run the hot water for a bath. It was after seven.

As the last stroke of eight echoed on the pendulum clock that adorned the wall above the reception desk, Ricardo Reis descended punctually to the dining room. The manager, Salvador, smiled, raising his mustache above his teeth, which looked none too clean, as he hurried forward to open the double doors. Their glass panels, engraved with the initials H and B, the B entwined with curves and countercurves, with appendages and floral elongations, stylized acanthuses, palm fronds, and spiraling foliage, bestowed dignity on this otherwise modest hotel. The maître d' led the way. There were no other guests in the dining room, only two waiters who had finished setting the tables. Noises could be heard coming from behind the pantry door, which bore the same monogram. From that door soup tureens, covered dishes, and platters would soon make their entrance. The furnishings were what you might expect, anyone who has seen one of these dining rooms has seen them all, a few dim lights on the ceilings and walls, immaculate white cloths on the tables, the pride of the establishment, freshened up with bleach in the laundry, if not in the Caneças, which only uses soap and sunshine, but with so much rain for days on end, it must be well behind with its work. Ricardo Reis is now seated. The maître d' tells him what is on the menu, soup, fish, meat, unless the doctor prefers something lighter, that is, another kind of meat, fish, soup. I should advise the latter until you get used to your new diet, since you have just come back from the tropics after an absence of sixteen years. So even in the dining room and kitchen they know all about him. The door leading from the reception desk was pushed open in the meantime and a couple entered with two young children, a boy and a girl, both of them the color of wax though their parents were florid, but both legitimate, to judge from appearances, the head of the family in front, guiding his tribe, the mother pushing her children forward from behind. Then a man appeared, fat and heavy, with a gold chain crossing his stomach from one little waistcoat pocket to another, and almost immediately after him came another man, very thin, with a black tie and a mourning band on his arm. No one else arrived for the next quarter of an hour. The noise of cutlery could be heard against the plates. The father of the children, authoritative, struck the knife against his wineglass to summon the waiter. The thin man, his mourning disturbed and good breeding offended, gave him a severe look, but the fat man calmly went on chewing. Ricardo Reis contemplated the blobs of grease that floated on his chicken broth. He had chosen the lighter meal, following the maître d's suggestion out of indifference rather than conviction, for he could see no real advantage to it. A ruffling sound against the windowpanes told him that it had started raining again. These windows do not face onto the Rua do Alecrim, what street could it be, he cannot remember, if he ever knew, but the waiter who comes to change his plate informs him, This is the Rua Nova do Carvalho, Doctor, before asking, Did you enjoy your soup. From the waiter's pronunciation, which is good, one can tell that he is Galician.

Through the door now entered a middle-aged man, tall and distinguished in appearance, with a long, lined face, along with a girl in her twenties, if that, and thin, although it would be more correct to describe her as slender. They made their way to the table facing Ricardo Reis and it suddenly became clear that the table had been awaiting them, just as an object awaits the hand that frequently reaches out and takes possession. They must be regular clients, perhaps the owners of the hotel. It is interesting how we forget that hotels have an owner. These two, whether the owners or not, crossed the room at their leisure as if in their own home. Such details you notice when you pay attention. The girl sat in profile, the man with his back to Ricardo Reis, and they conversed in a whisper, but she raised her voice as she reassured him, No, Father, I'm fine. So they are father and daughter, an unusual pairing in any hotel nowadays. The waiter came to serve them, solemn but friendly in his manner, then went away. The room was silent again, not even the children raised their voices. How strange that Ricardo Reis cannot remember having heard the children speak, perhaps they are mute or have their lips stapled together with invisible clips, an absurd thought, since they are both eating. The slender girl, finishing her soup, puts down the spoon, and her right hand starts to caress her left hand as if it were a little lapdog resting on her knees. Surprised by this, Ricardo Reis realizes that her left hand has never moved, he remembers that she used only her right hand to fold her napkin, and now she is holding the left and is about to rest it on the table, very gently, like the most fragile crystal. There she leaves it, beside her plate, a silent presence at the meal, the long fingers extended, pale, inert. Ricardo Reis feels a shiver, no one is feeling it for him, his skin shivers within and without, as in utter fascination he watches that hand, paralyzed and insensible, ignorant of where it should go unless taken, resting to catch the sun or listen to the conversation or be seen by the doctor who has just arrived from Brazil. A tiny hand which is left on two counts, left because it is lying on the left side and left because it is a gauche, disabled, lifeless, and withered thing that will never knock on any door. Ricardo Reis observes that the plates for the girl come from the pantry already prepared, the fishbones removed, the meat diced, the fruit peeled and cut into segments. It is clear that the daughter and father are well known to the hotel staff, they may even live in the hotel. He finished his meal but lingered a while, to allow time, but what time and for what. At last he got up, drew back his chair, and the noise he made, too loud perhaps, caused the girl to turn around. Seen from the front, she looks older than twenty, but in profile her youth is immediately restored, her neck long and fragile, her chin finely molded, the entire restless line of her body insecure, unfinished. Ricardo Reis got up from the table, headed for the glass-paneled door with the monograms, where he was obliged to exchange courtesies with the fat man who was also leaving. After you, sir, Please, after you. The fat man went out, Thank you, kind sir, a somewhat obsequious use of the word *sir*, for if we are to take all words literally, Ricardo Reis would have passed first, for he is innumerable men, according to his own understanding of himself.

The manager Salvador is already holding out the key of room two hundred and one. He makes a solicitous gesture, as if about to hand it over but then slyly drawing back. Perhaps the guest wishes to slip out quietly in search of Lisbon by night and its secret pleasures, after so many years in Brazil and so many days crossing the ocean, although the wintry night makes the cozy atmosphere of the lounge seem more enticing, here at hand, the deep high-backed armchairs in leather, the chandelier in the center of the room so rich in crystal pendants, and that big mirror that encompasses the entire room and duplicates it in another dimension. This is no simple reflection of the common and familiar proportions the mirror is confronted with, length, width, height, they are not reproduced in it one by one and readily identifiable. Instead they are fused into a single intangible apparition on a plane that is at once remote and near, unless there is some paradox in this explanation which the mind avoids out of laziness. Here is Ricardo Reis contemplating himself in the depths of the mirror, one of the countless persons that he is, all of them weary. I am going up to my room, I'm exhausted after my journey, two whole weeks of the most awful weather, have you by any chance some newspapers, I'd like to catch up on the national news until I'm ready to fall asleep. There you are, Doctor, help yourself. Just at this moment the girl with the paralyzed hand and her father passed into the lounge, he in front, she behind, one pace apart. Ricardo Reis had already picked up his key and the newspapers, the color of ashes, the print blurred. A gust of wind caused the front door to bang downstairs, the buzzer sounded. There is no one there, only the storm which is gathering. This night will bring nothing more of interest, only rain, tempest over land and sea, solitude.

The sofa in his room is comfortable, the springs on which so many bodies have reclined form a human hollow, and the light from the lamp which stands on the writing desk illuminates the newspaper at the correct angle. This is like being at home, in the bosom of one's family, by the fireside I do not possess and perhaps never will. These are the newspapers of my native Portugal, they inform me that the Head of State has inaugurated an exhibition in honor of Mousinho de Albuquerque at the Colonial Office, one is not spared imperial commemorations or allowed to forget imperial personages. There is cause for anxiety in Golegã, I can't even remember where it is, ah yes, in the province of Ribatejo, that the floods may burst the dike known as Vinte, a most curious name, where could it have come from, we shall see a repetition of the disaster of eighteen ninety-five. In ninety-five I was eight years old, naturally I don't remember. The tallest woman in the world is Elsa Droyon, two and a half meters tall, the water won't rise that much. And that girl, I wonder what her name is, that paralyzed hand, so limp, it might have been an illness or perhaps some accident. The fifth national contest for beautiful babies, half a page of photographs of infants, stark naked, their rolls of puppy fat bulging, nourished on powdered milk. Some of these babies will grow up to become criminals, vagabonds, and prostitutes, after being photographed like this, at such a tender age, before the lewd eyes of those who have no respect for innocence. The military operations in Ethiopia continue. What news from Brazil, nothing new, everything destroyed. General advance of the Italian troops. There is no human force capable of stopping the Italian soldier in his heroic onslaught, what can the Abyssinian rifle achieve against him, the inferior lance, the wretched cutlass. The lawyer of a famous woman athlete has announced that his client has undergone a major operation in order to change her sex, within a few days she will be a man, as if from birth, do not forget to change her name too, what name, Bocage, before the Tribunal of the Holy Office. A painting by the artist Fernando Santos, the fine arts are cultivated in this country. At the Coliseu they are showing *The Last Wonder* with Vanise Meireles, a statuesque figure clad in silver, a Brazilian celebrity. Funny, I must have missed her in Brazil, my fault. Here in Lisbon one can get a seat in the gallery for three escudos, a seat in the stalls costs five escudos and up, there are two performances daily and matinées on Sundays. The Politeama is showing *The Crusades*, a spectacular epic. Numerous contingents of English troops have landed at Port Said, every era has its crusades, these are the crusades of modern times, it is rumored that they are making for the borders of Italian-occupied Libya. A list of the Portuguese who have died in Brazil during the first half of December. These names are unknown to me, I don't need to express my sympathy or go into mourning, but clearly lots of Portuguese immigrants die down there. Charity fêtes with free dinners for the poor throughout the country, the quality of food has been improved in the hospices for the poor, the elderly are so well treated in Portugal, not to mention abandoned children, little flowers left on the streets. Then this item of news, the president of the city council in Oporto sent a telegram to the Minister of the Interior, At today's session the council over which I preside resolved, after discussion of the decree which will provide assistance for the poor throughout the winter, to congratulate Your Excellency on this admirable enterprise. Other news, polluted drinking troughs full of cattle dung, smallpox is spreading in Lebução and Fatela, an outbreak of flu in Portalegre and typhoid fever in Valbom, a sixteen-year-old girl has died of smallpox, a pastoral flower of bucolic innocence, a lily cruelly severed from its stem and so prematurely. I have a foxhound bitch, not a purebred, who has already had two litters and on both occasions she was found eating her young, not one escaped, tell me, dear editor, what should I do. In reply to your question, dear reader, the cannibalism of bitches is generally due to malnutrition during the period of gestation. The dog must be well fed with meat as her staple diet and supplemented with milk, bread, and vegetables, in brief, a well-balanced diet. If this does not change her habits, there's no remedy, either destroy the dog or do not allow her to mate, let her put up with being in heat or you can have her spayed. Now let us try to imagine what would happen if women suffering from malnutrition during pregnancy, starved of meat, bread, and green vegetables, which is fairly common, were also to begin eating their infants. After trying to imagine it and having confirmed that such crimes do not occur, it becomes easy to see the difference between people and animals. The editor did not add these comments, nor did Ricardo Reis, who is thinking about something else, a suitable name for the bitch. He will not call her Diana or Lembrada, but a name to throw light on her crime or motives, and will the wicked creature die from eating poisoned food or from a rifle shot fired by her own master. Ricardo Reis persists and finally finds the right name, one which comes from Ugolino della Gherardesca, that most savage, lusty nobleman who ate his children and grandchildren, there are testimonies to this in the *History of the Guelphs and Ghibellines*, also in the *Divine Comedy*, chapter thirty-three of the *Inferno*. Therefore let the bitch who eats her young be called Ugolina, so unnatural that her heart suffers no compassion as she tears the warm and tender skin of her defenseless brood with her jaws, slaughtering them, causing their delicate bones to snap, and the poor little pups, whining, perish without realizing who is devouring them, the mother who gave them birth. Ugolina, do not kill me, I am your offspring.

The page which calmly narrates these horrors falls onto the lap of Ricardo Reis. He is fast asleep. A sudden gust of wind rattles the windowpanes, the rain pours down like a deluge. Through the deserted streets of Lisbon prowls the bitch Ugolina slavering blood, sniffing in doorways, howling in squares and parks, furiously biting at her own womb, where the next litter is about to be conceived.

After a night of severe winter, of violent storm, the latter two words, violent storm, have been linked together since their inception, the first pair not quite as much, but both phrases are so pertinent to the circumstance that they spare one the effort of having to invent new words, the morning might well have dawned with bright sunshine, blue skies, and joyful flutterings of pigeons in flight. But there was no change in the elements. The swallows continue to fly over the city, the river is not to be trusted, the pigeons scarcely venture there. It is raining, but tolerably for anyone going out with a raincoat and umbrella, and in comparison with the gales earlier this morning, the wind is a mere caress on one's cheek. Ricardo Reis left the hotel early, he went to the Banco Comercial to change some of his English money into escudos, and for every pound sterling he received one hundred and ten thousand reis. A pity those pounds were not gold, otherwise he could have changed them for almost double that amount. Even so, the returning traveler has no real cause for complaint, seeing as he leaves the bank with five thousand escudos in his wallet, a small fortune in Portugal. From the Rua do Comércio, where he finds himself, the Terreiro do Paço is only a few meters away, but Ricardo Reis will not risk crossing the square. He looks into the distance under the protection of the colonnades, the river dark and choppy, the tide high. When the waves rise offshore, one imagines they are about to inundate and submerge the square, but that is an optical illusion, they disperse against the wall, their impact broken by the sloping steps of the wharf. He recalls having sat there in days gone by, days so remote he doubts whether he really experienced them. It may have been someone on my behalf, perhaps with the same face and name, but some other person. His feet are cold and wet, he also feels a shadow of gloom pass over his body, not over his soul, I repeat, not over his soul. The impression is physical, he could touch it with his hands were they not both gripping the handle of his umbrella, which is needlessly open. This is how a man alienates himself from the world, how he exposes himself to the jesting of some passerby who quips, Hey mister, it's not raining under there. But the man's smile is spontaneous, without a hint of malice, and Ricardo Reis smiles at his own distraction. Without knowing why, he murmurs two lines from a poem by João de Deus, well known to every child in nursery school. Under this colonnade one could comfortably spend the night.

He came here because the square was so near and in order to verify in passing if his memory of the place, clear as an engraving, bore any resemblance to the reality. A quadrangle surrounded by buildings on three sides, a regal equestrian statue in the middle, a triumphal arch which he cannot see from where he is standing. But everything is diffuse and hazy, the architecture nothing but blurred lines. It must be the weather, the hour of day, his failing eyesight. Only the eyes of remembrance remain, as sharp as those of a hawk. It is almost eleven o'clock, and there is much activity under the colonnades, but activity is not the same thing as haste. This dignified lot move at a steady pace, all the men in soft hats, their umbrellas dripping, few women are in sight at this hour, the civil servants are arriving at their offices. Ricardo Reis walks on in the direction of the Rua do Crucifixo, resisting the insistent pleas of a lottery-ticket vendor who tries to sell him a ticket for the next draw. It is number one thousand three hundred and forty-nine, the wheel will spin tomorrow. That is not the number and the wheel will not be spinning tomorrow, but this is how the soothsayer's chant goes, a licensed prophet with a badge on his cap. Do buy a ticket, sir, if you refuse to buy, you will live to regret it, believe me, it's a winner. There is menace in this imposition. Ricardo Reis enters the

Rua Garrett, goes up the Chiado, where four porters lean against the plinth of the statue, paying no heed to the drizzle. This is the island of the Galicians. Farther ahead it has actually stopped raining. There is a white patch of light behind Luís de Camões, a nimbus. That is the trouble with words, *nimbus* signifies rain as well as cloud as well as halo, and since the poet is neither God nor saint, the rain stopping was merely the clouds thinning out as they passed. Let us not imagine that these are miracles like the ones at Ourique or Fátima, not even the simple miracle of the sky turning blue.

Ricardo Reis goes to the newspaper archives. Yesterday he made a note of the directions before going to bed. There is no reason to believe he slept badly, that he found the bed or country strange. When one awaits sleep in the silence of a room that is still unfamiliar, listening to the rain outside, things assume their real dimension, they all become great, solemn, heavy. What is deceptive is the light of day, transforming life into a shadow that is barely perceptible. Night alone is lucid, sleep, however, overcomes it, perhaps for our tranquillity and repose, the peace of our souls. Ricardo Reis goes to the newspaper archives, where everyone must go who wishes to know what has taken place, for here in the Bairro Alto the entire world passes, leaving footprints, broken twigs, trampled leaves, spoken words. What remains is this necessary invention, so that of the aforesaid world a face may be preserved, a look, a smile, a mortal agony. The unexpected death of Fernando Pessoa caused much sadness in intellectual circles. The poet of *Orfeu*, an admirable spirit who not only composed poetry in original forms but also wrote cogent critical essays, died the day before yesterday, in silence, just as he had always lived. Since no one can earn a living in Portugal by writing literature, Fernando Pessoa found employment as a clerk in a commercial firm. Some lines further on, his friends left wreaths of remembrance beside his tomb. This newspaper gives no more information. Another reports the same facts with different words, Fernando Pessoa, the extraordinary poet of *Mensagem*, an ode of patriotic fervor and one of the most beautiful ever written, was buried yesterday, taken unawares by death in a Christian bed at the Hospital of São Luís during the late hours of Saturday night. In his poetry he was not only Fernando Pessoa but also Alvaro de Campos, Alberto Caeiro, and Ricardo Reis. There you are, an error caused by not paying attention, by writing what one misheard, because we know very well that Ricardo Reis is this man who is reading the newspaper with his own open and living eyes, a doctor forty-eight years of age, one year older than Fernando Pessoa when his eyes were closed, eyes that were dead beyond a shadow of doubt. No other proofs or testimonies are needed to verify that we are not dealing with the same person, and if there is anyone who is still in doubt, let him go to the Hotel Bragança and speak to the manager Senhor Salvador, ask him if there is not a gentleman in residence there called Ricardo Reis, a doctor, newly arrived from Brazil. He will say Yes, the doctor said he would not be back for lunch but would almost certainly be dining here this evening, if you would care to leave a message, I shall see that he receives it. Now who will dare impugn the word of a hotel manager, an excellent physiognomist and well practiced in establishing identities. But rather than satisfy ourselves with the word of a man whom we cannot claim to know intimately, here is another paper which has reported the news on the page under obituaries. It outlines his career in detail, Yesterday there took place the funeral of Fernando António Nogueira Pessoa, bachelor, forty-seven years of age, forty-seven, take note, born in Lisbon, studied literature at an English university, became established as a writer and poet in literary circles, on his coffin were placed sprays of wild flowers, worse luck for them, as they wither so quickly. While he is waiting for the tram that will take him to Prazeres, Doctor Ricardo Reis reads the funeral oration delivered at the graveside, he reads it near the place where a man was hanged, as everyone knows, almost two hundred and twenty-three years ago, during the reign of Dom João V, who is not mentioned in the *Mensagem*. They hanged a Genoese swindler who for the sake of a piece of cloth killed one of our countrymen, stabbing him in the throat with a knife, then doing the same to the dead man's mistress, who died on the spot. He then inflicted two wounds on their servant, which were not fatal, and put out another's eye as if he were a rabbit. The murderer was arrested, and sentenced to death here, since it was near the house where he committed the crimes, in the presence of the crowd that had gathered to watch. Scarcely comparable with this morning in nineteen thirty-five, the month of December, the thirtieth to be precise, the sky overcast, and only those who cannot avoid it out walking in the streets, even though it is not raining now as Ricardo Reis, leaning against a lamppost at the top of the Calçada do Combro, reads the funeral oration. Not for the Genoese swindler, who did not receive one, unless you count the insults of the rabble, but for Fernando Pessoa, poet and innocent of any murders. Two words about the poet's earthly passage. For him two words suffice, or none. Indeed silence would be preferable, the silence that already enshrouds both him and us and which is in keeping with his temperament, for what is close to God is close to him. Yet those who were his peers in extolling beauty should not, could not have allowed him to descend into the earth, or rather ascend to the final horizons of Eternity without voicing their protest, calm yet aggrieved at this departure, the companions of Orpheus, more brothers than companions, who pursued the same ideal of beauty, they could not, I repeat, abandon him in this final resting place without having showered his gentle death with the white lilies of silence and suffering. We mourn the man whom death takes from us, and the loss of his miraculous talent and the grace of his human presence, but only the man do we mourn, for destiny endowed his spirit and creative powers with a mysterious beauty that cannot perish. The rest belongs to the genius of Fernando Pessoa. Come now, come now, exceptions can fortunately still be found to the normal rules of life. Since the time of Hamlet we have been going around saying, The rest is silence, in the end it's genius that takes care of the rest, and if this genius can do it, perhaps another genius can too.

The tram has come and gone, Ricardo Reis has found a seat all to himself. The ticket cost seventy-five centavos, in time he will learn to say, One at seven and a half. He resumes his reading of the funeral oration, unable to convince himself that it is dedicated to Fernando Pessoa, who must be dead if we look at the press reports, because the poet would not have tolerated such grammatical and lexical bombast. How little they must have known him, to address him and speak of him in this way. They take advantage of his death, his feet and hands are bound. They call him a despoiled lily, a lily like a girl stricken by typhoid fever, and use the adjective *gentle*. Such banality, dear God. Since gentle means noble, chivalrous, gallant, elegant, pleasing, and urbane, which of these would the poet have chosen as he lay in his Christian bed in the Hospital of São Luís. May the gods grant that it be pleasing, for with death one should lose only life.

When Ricardo Reis reached the cemetery, the bell at the gate was ringing, its peals filled the air with the sound of cracked bronze like the bell of some rustic villa ringing out in the drowsy heat of the siesta. About to disappear, a bier was carried by hand, its funeral valances swaying, the women's faces covered with black shawls, the men attired in their Sunday best, purplish chrysanthemums in their arms, more chrysanthemums on the upper ledges of the coffin, not even flowers enjoy a common destiny. The bier disappeared into the depths and Ricardo Reis went to the registry office to inquire where he might find the grave of Fernando António Nogueira Pessoa who died on the thirtieth day of last month, buried on the second of this month, laid to rest in this cemetery until the end of time, when God will command poets to awaken from their temporary death. Realizing that he is in the presence of an educated man of some standing, the clerk carefully informs him about the road and the number, for this is just like any city, sir. In order to make quite certain that his instructions are clear, he comes around the counter, accompanies him outside, and points, Go straight down the avenue, turn right at the bottom, then straight ahead, it's on the right-hand side about two-thirds down the path, look carefully, the tomb is small and you could easily miss it. Ricardo Reis thanks him for his assistance. The winds that come from afar over sea and river, he does not hear them wailing as one might expect in a cemetery, there are only these gray skies, these damp marble stones glistening after the recent rain, the dark-green cypresses darker than ever. As instructed, he starts to descend the road lined with poplars, in search of the grave numbered four thousand three hundred and seventy-one, a number which was drawn in the lottery yesterday and will be drawn no more, drawn by destiny rather than fortune. The road slopes gently downward, one is almost strolling. At least those remaining few steps were not difficult, that final walk of the funeral procession, for nevermore will Fernando Pessoa be accompanied, if during his lifetime he was truly accompanied by those who brought him here. Here is the corner we must take. We ask ourselves why we came, what tears remain to be shed, and why, if we did not shed them before. Perhaps we were more shocked than grieved, the sorrow came later, dull, as if our entire body were a single muscle being crushed internally, no black stain visibly locating our grief. On either side, the chapels of the family tombs are locked, the windows are covered with curtains made of lace, the finest linen like that of handkerchiefs, the most delicate flowers embroidered between two plants, or in heavy crochet made with needles like naked swords, or saying *richelieu* or *ajour*, Gallicisms pronounced God alone knows how. It reminds me of those children on the *Highland Brigade*, now far, far away, sailing northward over seas where the salt of Lusitanian tears is that of fishermen amid the waves that claim their lives and of their families crying on the shore. The threads of this embroidery were made by the Coats and Clark Company, Anchor Brand, so as not to stray from the disasters of maritime history. Ricardo Reis has already proceeded halfway along the path, constantly looking to the right. Eternal regret, Sad remembrance, Here lies in loving memory of, we would see the same inscriptions if we looked on the other side, angels with drooping wings, lachrymose statues, fingers entwined, folds carefully arranged, drapes neatly gathered, broken columns. Perhaps the stonemasons cut them like that, or delivered them in perfect condition so the relatives of the deceased could break them as a token of their grief, like those warriors who marked the death of their leader by solemnly smashing their shields. Skulls at the foot of the crosses. The evidence of death is the veil with which death masks itself. Ricardo Reis has gone past the tomb he was looking for. No voice called out, Hello, it's here, yet there are still those who insist that the dead can speak. What would become of the dead if there were no means of identifying them, no name engraved on a tombstone, no number as on the doors of the living. A good thing they taught us how to read, for you can imagine some illiterate needing to be led by the hand and told, The tomb is here. He will look at us suspiciously, because should we mislead him, either out of error or malice, he would find himself praying to Capuletto instead of Montecchio, to Gonçalves instead of Mendes.

These are titles of property and occupation, the tomb of Dona Dionísia de Seabra Pessoa inscribed on the front, under the overhanging eaves of this sentry box where the sentinel, a romantic touch, is sleeping. Below, at the height of the door's lower hinge, another name and nothing more, that of Fernando Pessoa, with the dates of his birth and death, and the gilded outline of a funeral urn that says, I am here. Ricardo Reis repeats the words aloud, He is here. At that moment it starts raining again. He has traveled so far, all the way from Rio de Janeiro, days and nights on the high seas, the voyage seems so recent and yet so remote, now what is he to do, alone in this road, among graves, his umbrella open. Time to be thinking about lunch. In the distance he could hear the hollow sound of a bell tolling, the sound he had expected to hear upon arrival, when he touched these railings, his soul gripped by panic, a deep laceration, an inner turmoil, like great cities collapsing in silence because we are not there, porticoes and white towers toppling. In the end nothing but a gentle sensation of burning in one's eyes, no sooner felt than gone, not even time to think about it or be troubled by the thought. There is nothing more to be done in this place, what he has done is nothing. Inside the tomb is a mad old woman who cannot be left to roam at will. Under her watchful eye is also the decomposing body of a composer of verses who left his share of madness in the world. The great difference between poets and madmen is the destiny of the madness that possesses them. He felt afraid, thinking about grandmother Dionísia lying in there, and about her afflicted grandson Fernando, she keeping vigil with eyes wide open, he with eyes averted, looking for a gap, a breath of air, a glimmer of light, his uneasiness turned to nausea as if he were being assailed and suffocated by a great sea wave, he who throughout the fourteen days of the voyage had not once been seasick. Then he thought, It must be my empty stomach, and he was probably right, for he had eaten nothing all morning. The rain came pouring down, arriving just in time. Now Ricardo Reis will have his answer ready if anyone questions him, No, I didn't spend much time there, it was raining so heavily. As he started to climb the road, walking slowly, he felt the nausea pass. All that remained was a slight headache, perhaps an emptiness in his head, like an absence, a piece of brain missing, the piece relinquished by Pessoa. He found his informant standing in the doorway of the registry, and it was obvious from the grease on the man's lips that he had just finished eating lunch. Where, right here, a napkin spread out on his desk, the food he brought from home, still warm because wrapped in newspapers, or perhaps reheated on a gas flame, there at the far end of the filing cabinets, interrupting his chewing three times to file. So I must have spent more time there than I thought. Then you found the tomb you were looking for. I found it, Ricardo Reis replied, and as he went through the gate he repeated, Yes, I found it.

Famished and in a hurry, he gestured toward the row of taxis. Who knows if he can still find a restaurant or eating house prepared to serve him lunch at this late hour. The driver was methodically chewing a toothpick, passing it from one corner of his mouth to the other with his tongue. It must have been with his tongue, since his hands were occupied with the steering wheel. From time to time he noisily sucked the saliva between his teeth. The sucking sound, the intermittent warbling of digestion, made two simultaneous notes like birdsong, Ricardo Reis thought to himself and smiled, but at the same moment his eyes filled with tears. Strange that such a sound should have such an effect. Or it might have been the sight of a little angel being carried to its grave on a white bier, some Fernando who did not live long enough to become a poet, some Ricardo who could not become a doctor or poet. Perhaps the reason for this outburst of weeping is simply that the moment had come for the release of pent-up emotions. These physiological matters are complicated, let us leave them to those who understand them, particularly if it should prove necessary to follow the path of sentiment into the tear glands themselves, to determine, for example, the chemical difference between tears of sadness and tears of joy, almost certainly the former are more salty, which explains why one's eyes smart so much. In front, the driver pushed the toothpick between his canine teeth on the right. Silently he moved the toothpick up and down, respecting the passenger's sorrow, something he is used to doing when he picks up people at the cemetery. The taxi descended the Calçada da Estrela, turned at the Cortes, heading toward the river, and then, reaching the Baixa, went up the Rua Augusta. As it entered the Rossio, Ricardo Reis suddenly remembered, Stop at the Irmãos Unidos, the restaurant just ahead, draw up on the right, there is an entrance at the back, in the Rua dos Correeiros. One can be sure of a good meal here, the food is excellent, the atmosphere traditional, because the restaurant is situated on the very spot where the Hospital de Todos os Santos once stood many years ago. You would think we were narrating the history of another nation. An earthquake comes along, and behold the result, but whether we change for better or for worse depends on how alive we are and hopeful.

Ricardo Reis lunched without worrying about his diet. Yesterday had been an act of weakness on his part. When a man comes ashore after an ocean voyage he is like a child, sometimes seeking a woman's shoulder on which to rest his head, at other times ordering one glass of wine after another in some tavern until he finds happiness, provided happiness has been poured in that bottle beforehand. At other times it is as if he has no will of his own. Any Galician waiter can decide what he should eat, I'd suggest a little chicken if you are feeling queasy, sir. Here no one wishes to know whether he disembarked yesterday, whether tropical dishes have ruined his digestion, what special food will cure his nostalgia for his native land, if that is what he suffers from. If not, why did he come back. From the table where he is sitting, between the gaps in the curtains he can see the trams pass outside, he can hear them creaking on the turns, the tinkling of their little bells, a liquid sound in the rain, like the bells of a submerged cathedral or the strains of a harpsichord echoing ad infinitum within a well. The waiters hover patiently, waiting for this last customer to finish his lunch. He arrived late and pleaded with them to serve him, and his request was granted, although the kitchen staff was already clearing away the pots and pans. Now he's done, he thanks the waiters, politely wishing them a pleasant afternoon as he leaves by the door to the Rua dos Correeiros, which opens onto that Babylon of iron and glass, the Praça da Figueira. Still bustling with activity, the market is calm by comparison with the morning hours, when the noisy cries of the tradesmen grow louder and louder. One inhales a thousand pungent odors, kale trampled and wilting, the excrement of rabbits, the feathers of scalded chickens, blood, bits of flayed skin. They are washing the benches and the alleyways with buckets, hoses, and brooms with tough bristles. From time to time you can hear the scraping of metal, then a sudden boom as a shutter is rolled down. Ricardo Reis went around the square from the southern side and turned into the Rua dos Douradores. The rain almost over, he could now close his umbrella and look up at the tall, grimy façades. Rows of windows at the same height, some with sills, others with balconies, the monotonous stone slabs extending all along the road until they merge into thin vertical strips which narrow more and more but never entirely disappear. Down in the Rua da Conceição, appearing to block the road, rises a building of similar color with windows and grilles of the same design or only slightly modified. All exude gloom and humidity, releasing into the courtyards the stench of cracked sewers, with scattered whiffs of gas. Little wonder that the shopkeepers standing in their doorways have an unhealthy pallor. Dressed in their smocks or aprons of gray cotton, their pens stuck behind one ear, they look disgruntled, because this is Monday and Sunday was disappointing. The road is paved with rough irregular stones, the gravel almost black where the metal wheels of the carts have bounced as they passed. It used to be that in the dry season, which this is not, the iron shoes of the mules gave off sparks when the loads they hauled exceeded the strength of man and beast. Today only lighter freight is carried, such as those sacks of beans which appear to weigh about sixty kilos and are now being unloaded by two men, or should one say liters when referring to beans and seeds. Since the bean by its nature is light, every liter of beans weighs approximately seven hundred and fifty grams, so let us hope that those who filled the sacks took this into account and reduced the load accordingly.

Ricardo Reis started walking back to his hotel and suddenly remembered the room where he had spent his first night like a prodigal son under a paternal roof. He remembered it as if it were his home, not the one in Rio de Janeiro, nor in Oporto, where we

31

know he was born, nor here in Lisbon, where he lived before sailing off to exile in Brazil, none of these, even though they had all been homes to him. A strange sign, and of what, a man thinking of his hotel room as if it were his own home. Disquieted, uneasy at being out for so long, since early morning, he murmured, I'll go back at once. He fought down the urge to hail a taxi, allowed a tram to pass that would have dropped him almost at the hotel door, managed in the end to quell this absurd anxiety, to force himself to be simply someone going back to his hotel, unhurried yet without any needless delay. He may see the girl with the paralyzed arm in the dining room this evening, it is a possibility, like that of seeing the fat man, the thin man in mourning, the pale children and their ruddy parents, who knows what other guests, mysterious arrivals from an unknown place enshrouded in mist. Thinking about them, he felt a consoling warmth in his heart, a deep sense of reassurance, Love one another were the words once spoken, and it was time to begin. The wind blew with force, channeled into the Rua do Arsenal, but it was not raining, all that fell on the pavements were some heavy drops shaken from eaves. Perhaps the weather will change for the better, this winter cannot last forever. For the last two months there has been nothing but heavy showers, the taxi driver told him yesterday, in the tone of one who no longer believes that things will improve.

A sharp buzz as he opened the door, and it was as if he were being welcomed by the statue of the Italian page. Pimenta looked down the steep flight of stairs from the landing above, waiting to greet him, deferential and punctilious, his back slightly stooped, perhaps the result of those loads he is constantly carrying. Good afternoon, Doctor. The manager Salvador also appeared on the landing, saying the same words but in a more refined tone. Ricardo Reis returned their greetings. No longer manager, hotel porter, and doctor, they became simply three men smiling, pleased to be seeing one another again after such a long time, not since early that morning, just imagine, and such nostalgia, dear God. When Ricardo Reis entered his room and observed how carefully it had been cleaned, the bedspread neatly arranged, the washbasin shining, the mirror spotless despite the dents it had collected over the years, he sighed with satisfaction. Changing his clothes and getting into slippers, he pulled open one of the bedroom windows, the gesture of someone who is glad to be home, then settled in the armchair. It was as if he had fallen into himself, a sudden violent fall inside. And now, he asked, And now, Ricardo Reis or whoever you are, as others might say. In an instant he understood that the real conclusion of his voyage was this precise moment, that the time which had elapsed since he set foot on the quay at Alcântara had been spent, so to speak, in the maneuvers of berthing and dropping anchor, probing the tide, throwing the cables, because this was what he'd been doing when he looked for a hotel, read those first newspapers, then visited the cemetery, lunched in the Baixa, strolled down to the Rua dos Douradores. That sudden longing for his room, the impulse of indiscriminate, universal affection, the welcome extended by Salvador and Pimenta, the immaculate bedspread, and finally the wide-open window, its net curtains fluttering like wings. And what now. The rain has started up again, making a noise on the rooftops like sand being sieved, numbing, hypnotic. Perhaps during the great flood God in His mercy put men to sleep in this way so death might be gentle, the water quietly penetrating their nostrils and mouths without suffocating them, rivulets gradually filling, cell after cell, the entire cavity of their bodies. After forty days and forty nights of sleep and rain, their bodies sank slowly to the bottom, at last heavier than water itself. Ophelia, too, allows herself to be swept away by the current, singing, but she will inevitably die before the end of act four. Each human being has his own way of sleeping and dying, but the flood continues, time rains on us, drowns us. On the waxed surface of the floor raindrops collected and spread, having entered through the open window or spluttered from the sill. Some careless guests give no thought to humble labor, perhaps believing that the bees not only make the wax but also spread it on the floorboards and rub it and buff it until it shines, but it is maids, not insects, who do this work, and without them these shining floors would be drab and grimy. The manager will soon rebuke and punish them, because that is a manager's job, and we are in this hotel for the greater honor and glory of God, whose deputy is Salvador. Ricardo Reis rushed to close the window, with the newspapers mopped up most of the water, and having no other means to finish the job properly he rang the bell. That's the first time I've used it, he thought, like someone begging his own pardon.

He heard steps in the corridor, knuckles tapped discreetly on the door. Come in, words of entreaty rather than command. When the maid opened the door, he said, scarcely bothering to look at her, The window was open, the rain came in, there was water all over the floor. Then he fell silent, realizing that he had produced doggerel, he, Ricardo Reis, the author of Sapphic and Alcaic odes. He almost continued in stupid anapests, Could you do me a favor and clean up this mess. But the maid, without verses, understood what had to be done. She went out and returned with a mop and bucket, and down on her knees, her body wriggling, did her vigorous best to remove the offending moisture. Tomorrow she will give the floor another coat of wax. Can I do anything else for you, Doctor. No, much obliged. They looked straight into each other's eyes. Beating heavily on the windowpanes, the rain's rhythm accelerated, ruffling like a great drum, causing those who were asleep to wake up in alarm. What is your name. Lydia, sir, she replied, then added, At your service, Doctor. She could have expressed it more formally, saying, for example, in a louder voice, I was instructed to do my utmost to please the doctor, for the manager said, Look here, Lydia, take good care of the guest in room two hundred and one, Doctor Reis. The doctor made no reply, he appeared to be whispering the name Lydia in case he should need to call her again. There are people who repeat the words they hear, because we are all like parrots repeating one another, nor is there any other way of learning. This reflection is inappropriate, perhaps, since it was not made by Lydia, who is the other interlocutor and already has a name, so let us allow her to leave, taking her mop and bucket with her. Ricardo Reis remains there smiling ironically, moving his lips in a way that deceives no one. Lydia, he repeats, and smiles, and smiling goes to the drawer to look for his poems, his Sapphic odes, and reads the verses which catch his eye as he turns the pages. *And so, Lydia, sitting by the hearth, Lydia, let the image be thus, Let us show no desire, Lydia, at this hour, When our autumn comes, Lydia, Come sit with me, Lydia, on the riverbank, Lydia, the most abject existence is preferable to death.* There is no longer any trace of irony in his smile, if the word *smile* is an apt description for those parted lips exposing his teeth, the facial muscles fixed into a sneer or pained expression, with which one might say, This, too, shall pass. Like his face reflected in a tremulous mirror of water, Ricardo Reis leans over the page and recomposes old verses. Soon he will be able to recognize himself, It is I, without irony, without sorrow, content to feel not even contentment, as a man who desires nothing more or knows that he can possess nothing more. The shadows in the room thicken, some black nimbus must be passing in the sky, a cloud black as lead, like those summoned for the deluge. The furniture suddenly falls asleep. Ricardo Reis makes a gesture with his hands, groping the colorless air, then, barely able to distinguish the words he traces on the paper, writes, *All I ask of the gods is that I should ask nothing of them.* Having written this, he does not know how to continue. There are such moments. We believe in the importance of what we have just said or written, if for no other reason than that it is impossible to take back the sounds or erase the marks, but the temptation to be silent pervades our body, the fascination of silence, to be silent and immobile like the gods, watching and nothing more. He moves over to the sofa, leans back, closes his eyes, feels that he could sleep, is already half asleep. From the closet he takes a blanket, wraps himself in it, now he will sleep, and dream that it is a sunny morning and he is strolling along the Rua do Ouvidor in Rio de Janeiro, not exerting himself, for it is very hot. In the distance he hears shooting, bombs, but does not awaken. This is not the first time that he has had this dream, nor does he hear the knocking at the door and a voice, a woman's voice asking, Did you call, Doctor.

Let us say that it was because he slept so little the previous night that he slept so soundly now. Let us say that they are fallacies of doubtful depth, these interchanging moments of enchantment and temptation, of immobility and silence. Let us say that this is no story about deities and that we might have confidentially told Ricardo Reis, before he dozed off like any ordinary human being, What you are suffering from is a lack of sleep. There is, however, a sheet of paper on the table and on it is written, *All I ask of the gods is that I should ask nothing of them*. This page exists, the words occur twice, each word by itself and then together, and when they are read together they convey a meaning, no matter whether there are gods or not, or whether the person who wrote them has fallen asleep or not. Perhaps things are not as simple as we were inclined to show them at first. When Ricardo Reis awakens, the room is plunged in darkness, the last glimmer dispersed on the clouded windowpanes, in the mesh of the curtains. An enclosing heavy drape blocks one of the windows. There is not a sound to be heard in the hotel, now transformed into the palace of the Sleeping Beauty, where Beauty has withdrawn or never was. Everyone is asleep, Salvador, Pimenta, the Galician waiters, the guests, the Renaissance page, even the clock on the landing has stopped. Suddenly the distant sound of the buzzer at the entrance can be heard, no doubt the prince is coming to wake Beauty with a kiss, he is late, poor fellow, *I came feeling so merry and left in despair, the lady gave me her promise then sent me away*, it's a nursery rhyme rescued from the depths of memory. Children shrouded in mist are playing at the bottom of a wintry garden, singing with high, sad voices, they move forward and backward at a solemn pace, unknowingly rehearsing the pavane for the dead infants they will join upon growing up. Ricardo Reis pushes away the blanket, scolds himself for having fallen asleep without first undressing. He has always observed the code of civilized behavior, the discipline it requires, not even sixteen years in the languors of the Tropic of Capricorn succeeded in blunting the sharp edge of his dress and his verse, so that he can claim in all honesty that he has always tried to conduct himself as if he were being observed by the gods themselves. Getting up from the armchair, he goes to switch on the light, and, as if it were morning and he were awakening from some nocturnal dream, he looks at himself in the mirror and strokes his face. He should shave before dinner, at least change his clothes, he must not go to dinner with his clothes all crumpled. He needn't bother. He has not noticed how carelessly the other residents are dressed, their jackets like sacks, trousers bulging at the knees, ties with a permanent knot which are slipped on and off over the head, shirts badly cut, wrinkles, creases, the signs of age. And long, pointed shoes so that one has room to wiggle one's toes, although the result is otherwise, for in no other city in the world do calluses, corns, bunions, and growths, not to mention ingrown toenails, flourish in such abundance, an enigma for any podiatrist and one that requires closer study, which we leave to you. He decides not to shave after all, but puts on a clean shirt, chooses a tie to match his suit, combs his hair in the mirror, and parts it carefully. Although it is not yet time for dinner, he decides to go down, but before leaving, and without touching the sheet of paper, takes another look at what he wrote, looks with a certain impatience, as if finding a message left by one whom he dislikes or who once annoyed him beyond the bounds of tolerance and forgiveness. This Ricardo Reis is not the poet, but simply a hotel guest who, ready to leave his room, discovers a sheet of paper with one and a half stanzas written on it. Who could have left it here. Surely not the maid, not Lydia, this Lydia or any other, how aggravating. It never occurs to people that the one who finishes something is never the one who started it, even if both have the same name, for the name is the only thing that remains constant.

The manager Salvador was at his post, stationary, beaming his perennial smile. Ricardo Reis greeted him and walked on, but Salvador pursued him, wanting to know if the doctor would like to have a drink before dinner, an apéritif. No, thank you, this was another habit Ricardo Reis had not acquired, perhaps in years to come, first the taste, then the need, but not just yet. Salvador lingered for a moment in the doorway to see if the guest might change his mind or make some other request, but Ricardo Reis had already opened one of the newspapers. That entire day he had spent in ignorance of what was happening in the world. Not that he was an assiduous reader by nature, on the contrary, he found those large pages and verbose articles tiresome, but here, having nothing better to do and in order to avoid being fussed over by Salvador, he made the paper with all its news from abroad serve as a shield against this more immediate and encroaching world. The news of the distant world can be read as insignificant dispatches whose use and destination are questionable. The Spanish Government has resigned, the dissolution of Parliament has been decreed, says one headline. The Negus, in a telegram to the League of Nations, claims that the Italians are using asphyxiating gases. How typical of newspapers, all they can talk about is what has already happened and nearly always when it is much too late to rectify mistakes, prevent shortages, or avert disasters. A worthwhile paper should tell you, on the first day of January in the year nineteen fourteen, that war will break out on the twenty-fourth of July, then we would have almost seven months at our disposal to ward off the threat. Perhaps that would be enough time. Better still if a list were published of those about to die. The millions of men and women who, as they drink their morning coffee, come upon the announcement of their own deaths, their destinies sealed and shortly to be fulfilled, the day, hour, and place, their names printed in full. What would they have done, what would Fernando Pessoa have done if he had read two months beforehand, The author of *Mensagem* will die on the thirtieth of next November from hepatitis. Perhaps he would have consulted a doctor and stopped drinking, or else he would have started drinking twice as much in order to die sooner. Ricardo Reis lowers the newspaper to look at himself in the mirror, a reflection that is twice deceiving because it shows a deep space then shows that the space is a mere surface where nothing actually happens, only the illusion, external and silent, of persons and things, a tree overhanging a lake, a face seeking itself, a face undisturbed, unaltered, not even touched, by the images of tree and lake and face. The mirror, this one and all others, is independent of man. Before it we are like a conscript departing for the nineteen-fourteen war. Admiring his uniform in the mirror, he sees something more than himself, not knowing that he will never see himself again in this mirror. We are vanity and cannot endure, but the mirror endures, the same, because it rejects us. Ricardo Reis averts his eyes, changes position, leaves, he the one rejecting, turning his back on the mirror. Perhaps, then, he too is a mirror.

The clock on the landing struck eight, and the last echo had scarcely died away when an invisible gong rang out in muted tones. It can only be heard in the immediate vicinity, the guests on the upper floors certainly cannot hear it. But one must bear in mind the weight of tradition, it is not just a matter of pretending that wine bottles are encased in wickerwork when wicker is no longer available. Ricardo Reis folds the newspaper, goes to his room to wash his hands and tidy up. Returning immediately, he sits at the table where he has eaten from his very first day here and waits. Anyone watching him, following those rapid footsteps, would think that he must be either famished or in a great hurry, had an early lunch and eaten little or else bought a ticket for the theater. But we know otherwise, he didn't have an early lunch, we also know that he is not going to the theater or the cinema, and in weather such as this, becoming steadily worse, only a fool or an eccentric would dream of going for a walk. Why, then, the sudden haste, if people are only just arriving for dinner, the thin man in mourning, the placid fat man with the excellent digestion, those others whom I did not see last night. The mute children and their parents are missing, perhaps they were only passing through. As of tomorrow I shall not enter the dining room before half past eight. Here I am as ridiculous as any bumpkin newly arrived in the city and staying for the first time in a hotel. He ate his soup slowly, idly playing with his spoon, then toyed with the fish on his plate, pecked at it, not feeling the least bit hungry. As the waiter was serving the main course, the maître d' guided three men to the table where, the evening before, the girl with the paralyzed hand and her father had dined. So she won't be coming, they've left, he thought, or are dining out. Only then did he admit what he already knew but had pretended not to, that he had really come down early to see the girl whose left hand is paralyzed and who strokes it as if it were a little lap dog, even though it does nothing for her, or perhaps for that reason. Why. The question is a pretense, in the first place because certain questions are posed simply to call attention to the absence of any reply, in the second place because there is something both true and false about the possibility that his interest does not require any deeper explanation. He cut short his dinner and ordered coffee and a brandy. He would wait in the lounge, one way of killing time until he could ask the manager Salvador who those people were. That father and daughter, you know I believe I've seen them before, elsewhere, perhaps in Rio de Janeiro, certainly not in Portugal, that is obvious because sixteen years ago the girl would have been a mere child. Ricardo Reis spins and weaves this web of overtures, so much inquiring to discover so little. Meanwhile Salvador is attending to other guests, one who is leaving early tomorrow morning and wishes to settle his bill, another who complains that he cannot sleep when the window shade starts banging. Salvador attends to all the guests with tact and solicitude, with his discolored teeth and smooth mustache. The thin man dressed in mourning came into the lounge to consult a newspaper and left almost immediately. The fat man appeared at the door biting a toothpick, hesitated when confronted with a blank stare from Ricardo Reis, then quickly withdrew, his shoulders drooping from lack of courage. Some retreats are like this, moments of extreme moral weakness which are difficult to explain, especially to oneself.

Half an hour later the affable Salvador is able to inform him, No, you must have mistaken them for someone else, as far as I know they have never visited Brazil, they've been coming here for the last three years, we have often chatted and they would almost certainly have told me about such a voyage. Ah, so I was mistaken, but you say they have been coming here for the last three years. That's right, they are from Coimbra, they live there, the father is Doctor Sampaio, a lawyer. And the girl. She has an unusual name, she is called Marcenda, would you believe it, but they belong to an aristocratic family, the mother died some years ago. What is wrong with her hand. I believe her whole arm is paralyzed, that's why they come to stay here in the hotel for three days every month, so that she can be examined by a specialist. Ah, every month for three days. Yes, three days every month, Doctor Sampaio always warns me in advance so that I can keep the same two rooms free. Has there been any improvement during the last three years. If you want my frank opinion, Doctor, I don't think so. What a pity, the girl is so young. That's true, Doctor, perhaps you could offer them some advice next time, if you are still here. It's most likely I shall be here, but in any event I am not specialized in that field, I practice general medicine, I did some research into tropical diseases but nothing that would be helpful in a case like hers. Never mind, but it's very true that money doesn't bring happiness, the father so rich and the daughter a cripple, no one has ever seen her smile. You say she's called Marcenda. Yes, sir. A strange name, I've never come across it before. Nor I. Until tomorrow, Senhor Salvador, Until tomorrow, Doctor.

Upon entering his room, Ricardo Reis sees that the bed has been prepared, the bedspread and sheet neatly tucked back at an angle, discreetly, not that unsightly clutter of bedclothes tossed aside every which way. Here there is merely a suggestion, should he wish to lie down, his bed is ready. Not just yet, first he must read the one and a half stanzas he left on the sheet of paper, examine them critically, look for the door that this key, if key it is, can open, and imagine other doors beyond, doors locked and without a key. In the end, after much persistence he found something, it had been left there out of weariness, his or someone else's, but whose, and so the poem ended, *Neither tranquil nor troubled, I wish to lift my being high above this place where men know pleasure and pain*, the pause in the middle, the spondee, should be changed. Good fortune is a burden that oppresses the happy man, because it is no more than a particular state of mind. He then went to bed and fell asleep at once.

Ricardo Reis had told the manager, I would like breakfast brought up to my room at nine-thirty. Not that he intended to sleep so late, but he wished to avoid having to jump out of bed half-awake, struggling to slip his arms into the sleeves of his dressing gown, groping for his slippers, and feeling panic that he wasn't moving quickly enough to satisfy whoever was standing outside his door, arms laden with a huge tray bearing coffee and milk, toast, a sugar bowl, perhaps some cherry preserve or marmalade, a slice of dark grainy quince paste, a sponge cake, brioches with a fine crust, crunchy biscuits, or slices of French toast, those scrumptious luxuries served in hotels. We shall soon learn if the Bragança goes in for such extravagance, because Ricardo Reis is about to sample his first breakfast. It would be nine-thirty on the dot, Salvador promised him, and did not promise in vain, for here at nine-thirty on the dot Lydia is knocking on the door. The observant reader will say that this is impossible, she has both her arms occupied, but we would be in a sorry state if we had to hire only servants who possess three arms or more. This maid, without spilling a drop of milk, manages to knock gently with her knuckles, while the hand belonging to those knuckles continues to support the tray. One must see this to believe it, as she calls out, Your breakfast, Doctor, which is what she was instructed to say, and although a woman of humble origins, she has not forgotten her instructions. If Lydia were not a maid, there is every indication that she would make an excellent tightrope walker, juggler, or magician, for she has talent enough for any of those professions. What is incongruous about her is that, being a maid, she should be called Lydia and not Maria. Ricardo Reis is already dressed and presentable, he has shaved and his dressing gown is tied at the waist. He even left the window ajar to air the room, for he detests nocturnal odors, those exhalations of the body from which not even poets are exempt. The maid finally entered, Good morning, Doctor, and proceeded to put down the tray, less lavish in its offerings than he had imagined. Nevertheless, the Bragança deserves an honorable mention, and it is no wonder that some of its guests would never dream of staying at any other hotel when they visit Lisbon. Ricardo Reis returns the greeting, then dismisses her, No, many thanks, that will be all, the standard reply to the question every good maid asks, Can I get you anything else, sir. If the answer is no, she must withdraw politely, backing away if at all possible, for to turn your back would be to show disrespect to one who pays your wages and gives you a living. But Lydia, who has been instructed to be especially attentive to the doctor's needs, goes on to say, I don't know if you have noticed, Doctor, but the Cais do Sodré is under water. Trust a man not to notice, the water could be forcing its way under his door and he wouldn't see it, having slept soundly all night. He woke up as if he had only been dreaming about the rain. And even in a dream he would not dream that there has been so much rain that the Cais do Sodré is flooded. The water comes up to the knees of a man who finds himself obliged to cross from one side to the other, barefoot, his clothes hitched up, carrying an elderly woman on his back through the flood, she much lighter than the sack of beans carried from the cart to the warehouse. Here at the bottom of the Rua do Alecrim the old woman opens her purse and finds a coin, with which she pays Saint Christopher, who has already gone paddling back into the water, for on the other side there is already someone else making frantic gestures. The second person is young and sturdy enough to cross on his own, but, being smartly dressed, he has no desire to get his clothes dirty, for this water is more like mud than water. If only he could see how silly he looks riding piggyback with his clothes all crumpled, his shins exposed, revealing green garters over white long underwear. Some are laughing now at the spectacle, in the Hotel Bragança, on the second floor, a middle-aged guest is grinning, and behind him, unless our eyes are deceiving us, stands a woman also grinning, yes, a woman, without a shadow of doubt, but our eyes do not always see right, because this one appears to be a maid. It is hard to believe that that is really her station, unless there has been some dangerous subversion of social class and ranking, a thing greatly to be feared, we hasten to add, yet there are occasions, and if it is true that occasion can turn a man into a thief, it can also cause a revolution such as the one we are witnessing. Lydia, daring to look out of the window, stands behind Ricardo Reis and laughs, as if she were his equal, at a scene they both find amusing. These are fleeting moments of a golden age, born suddenly and dying at once, which explains why happiness soon grows weary. The moment has already passed, Ricardo Reis has closed the window, Lydia, once more simply a maid, backs toward the door. Everything must now be done in haste because the slices of toast are getting cold and no longer look quite so appetizing. I shall ring for you to come and remove the tray, Ricardo Reis tells her, and this happens about half an hour later. Lydia quietly enters and quietly withdraws, her burden not as heavy, while Ricardo Reis pretends to be absorbed as he sits in his room leafing through the pages of *The God of the Labyrinth* without actually reading.

Today is the last day of the year. Throughout the world where this calendar is observed, people amuse themselves by weighing the resolutions they intend to put into practice during the incoming year. They swear that they will be honest, just, and forbearing, that their reformed lips will utter no more words of abuse, deceit, or malice, however much their enemies may deserve them. Clearly we are speaking about the common people. The others, uncommon and superior, have their own good reasons for being and doing quite the opposite whenever it suits or profits them, they do not allow themselves to be deceived, and laugh at us and our so-called good intentions. In the end we learn from experience, no sooner is January upon us than we forget half of what we promised, and then there is little point in trying to carry out the rest. It is rather like a castle made of cards, better for the upper part to be missing than have the whole thing collapse and the four suits mixed up. This is why it is questionable whether Christ departed from life with the words we find in the Holy Scriptures, those of Matthew and Mark, My God, my God, why hast Thou forsaken me, or those of Luke, Father, into Thine hand I commit my spirit, or those of John, It is fulfilled. What Christ really said, word of honor, as any man on the street will tell you, was, Good-bye, world, you're going from bad to worse. But the gods of Ricardo Reis are silent entities who look upon us with indifference and for whom good and evil are less than words, because they never utter them, and why should they, if they cannot even tell them apart. They journey like us in the river of things, differing from us only because we call them gods and sometimes believe in them. We were taught this lesson lest we wear ourselves out making new and better resolutions for the incoming year. Nor do the gods judge, knowing everything, but this may be false. The ultimate truth, perhaps, is that they know nothing, their only task being precisely to forget at each moment the good as well as the evil. So let us not say, Tomorrow I shall do it, for it is almost certain that tomorrow we will feel tired. Let us say instead, The day after tomorrow, then we will always have a day in reserve to change our mind and make new resolutions. It would be even more prudent, however, to say, One day, when the day comes to say the day after tomorrow, I shall say it, but even that might not prove necessary, if definitive death comes first and releases me from the obligation, for obligation is the worst thing in the world, the freedom we deny ourselves.

It has stopped raining, the sky has cleared, and Ricardo Reis can take a stroll before lunch without any risk of getting soaked. He decides to avoid the lower part of the city because the flood has still not subsided completely in the Cais do Sodré, its paving stones covered with fetid mud which the current of the river has lifted from deep and viscous layers of silt. If this weather persists, the men from the cleaning department will come out with their hoses. The water has polluted, the water will clean, blessed be the water. Ricardo Reis walks up the Rua do Alecrim, and no sooner has he left the hotel than he is stopped in his tracks by a relic of another age, perhaps a Corinthian capital, a votive altar, or funereal headstone, what an idea. Such things, if they still exist in Lisbon, are hidden under the soil that was moved when the ground was leveled, or by other natural causes. This is only a rectangular slab of stone embedded in a low wall facing the Rua Nova do Carvalho and bearing the following inscription in ornamental lettering, *Eye Clinic and Surgery*, and somewhat more austerely, *Founded by A. Mascaró in 1870*. Stones have a long life. We do not witness their birth, nor will we see their death. So many years have passed over this stone, so many more have yet to pass, Mascaró died and his clinic was closed down, perhaps descendants of the founder can still be traced, they pursuing other professions, ignoring or unaware that their family emblem is on display in this public place. If only families were not so fickle, then this one would gather here to honor the memory of their ancestor, the healer of eyes and other disorders. Truly it is not enough to engrave a name on a stone. The stone remains, gentlemen, safe and sound, but the name, unless people come to read it every day, fades, is forgotten, ceases to exist. These contradictions walk through the mind of Ricardo Reis as he walks up the Rua do Alecrim, where tiny rivulets of water still course along the tram tracks. The world cannot be still, the wind is blowing, the clouds soaring, don't let us talk about the rain, there has been so much of it. Ricardo Reis stops before a statue of Eça de Queirós, or Queiroz, out of respect for the orthography used by the owner of that name, so many different styles of writing, and the name is the least of it, what is surprising is that these two, one called Reis, the other Eça, should speak the same language. Perhaps it is the language that chooses the writers it needs, making use of them so that each might express a tiny part of what it is. Once language has said all it has to say and falls silent, I wonder how we will go on living. Problems already begin to appear, perhaps they are not problems as yet, rather different layers of meaning, displaced sediments, new questioning formulations, take for example the phrase, *Over the great nakedness of truth, the diaphanous cloak of imagination*. It seems clear, compact, and conclusive, a child would be able to understand and repeat it in an examination without making any mistakes, but the same child might recite with equal conviction a

47

different phrase, *Over the great nakedness of imagination, the diaphanous cloak of truth*, which certainly gives one more to ponder, more to visualize with pleasure, the imagination solid and naked, the truth a gauzy covering. If our maxims are reversed and become laws, what world will be created by them. It is a miracle that men do not lose their sanity each time they open their mouths to speak. The stroll is instructive, a moment ago we were contemplating Eça, now we can observe Camões. They forgot to put any verses on his pedestal. Had they done so, what would they have put, *Here with deep sorrow, with mournful song*. Better to leave the poor, tormented creature and climb what remains of the street, the Rua da Misericórdia formerly the Rua do Mundo, unfortunately one cannot have it both ways, it has to be either Mundo or Misericórdia. Here is the old Largo de São Roque, and the church dedicated to that saint, whose festering wounds caused by plague were licked by a dog. The plague was almost certainly bubonic, the animal hardly of the same breed as the bitch Ugolina that knows only how to tear and devour. Inside this famous church you will find the chapel of São João Baptista, its decorations entrusted to Italian artists by Dom João V, king, mason, and architect par excellence, who won such renown during his reign. Take a look at the convent of Mafra and also the aqueduct of Águas Livres, of which the full history has yet to be written. Here too, on the diagonal of the two kiosks that sell tobacco, lottery tickets, and spirits, stands the monument in marble erected by the Italian colony to commemorate the marriage of King Dom Luís, the translator of Shakespeare, and Dona Maria Pia di Savóia, the daughter of Verdi, that is to say, of Vittorio Emmanuele, King of Italy, the only monument in the entire city of Lisbon which resembles a chastising rod or carpet beater with its five eyelets. At least that is what it suggests to the little girls from the orphanages, with their startled eyes, or if blind, they are so informed by their seeing companions, who from time to time pass this way dressed in little smocks and walking in formation, getting rid of the stench of the dormitory, their hands still smarting from the latest caning. This is a traditional neighborhood, exalted in name and location, but low in its way of life, for the laurel branches on the doors of the taverns alternate with women of easy virtue, although, because it is still morning and the roads have been washed by the recent rain, you can sense a freshness, an innocence in the air, an almost virginal breeze. Who would have thought this possible in such a disreputable place, but the canaries affirm it with their song, their cages hanging out on the balconies or at the entrances to the taverns, they warble as if demented. One has to take advantage of the fine weather, especially when it is not expected to last, for once the rain starts up again their singing will die away, their feathers will ruffle. One little bird, more prescient than the others, buries its head under its wing and pretends to be asleep, its mistress is coming to fetch it indoors, and now only rain can be heard, also the strumming of a guitar nearby, where it is coming from Ricardo Reis cannot tell. He has taken shelter in this doorway at the beginning of the Travessa da Água da Flor. It's often said that the sun is here then gone again, the clouds that let it through cover it quickly, but showers, too, come and go, the rain pours down, passes, the eaves and verandahs trickle water, the wash on the clotheslines is dripping, then a cloudburst so sudden there is no time for the women to do anything, to shout, as is their wont, It's raiiiiining, passing the word from one to another like soldiers in their sentry boxes at night. But the canary's mistress is on the alert and manages, in the nick of time, to retrieve it. Just as well that its frail little body has been protected, see how its heart is beating, Jesus, such violence, such speed. Was it the fright, no, it is always like this, a heart that lives for a short time beats fast, in compensation. Ricardo Reis crosses the park to take a look at the city, the castle with its walls in ruins, the terraced houses collapsing along the slopes, the whitish sun beating on the wet rooftops. Silence descends on the city, every sound is muffled, Lisbon seems made of absorbent cotton, soaked, dripping. Below, on a platform, are several busts of gallant patriots, some box shrubs, a few Roman heads out of place, so remote from the skies of Latium, as if one of Rafael Bordalo Pinheiro's native rustics had been set up to make a rude gesture to the Apollo Belvedere. The entire terrace is a belvedere as we contemplate Apollo, then a voice joins the guitar and they sing a fado. The rain appears to have finally disappeared.

When one idea is drawn from another, we say that there has

been an association. Some are even of the opinion that the whole human mental process derives from this succession of stimuli, sometimes unconscious, sometimes only pretending to be unconscious, which achieves original combinations, new relationships of thoughts interlinked by the species and together forming what might be called a commerce, an industry of ideas, because man, apart from all the other things he is, has been, or will be, performs an industrial and commercial function, first as producer, then as retailer, and finally as consumer, but even this order can be shuffled and rearranged. I am speaking only of ideas and nothing else. So, then, we can consider ideas as corporate entities, independent or in partnership, perhaps publicly held, but never with limited liability, never anonymous, for a name is something we all possess. The logical connection between this economic theory and the stroll Ricardo Reis is taking, which we already know to be instructive, will become apparent when he arrives at the entrance of the former convent of São Pedro de Alcântara, nowadays a refuge for little girls pedagogically chastised with the rod. In the vestibule he comes face to face with the tiled mural depicting Saint Francis of Assisi, *il poverello*, freely translated as poor devil, kneeling in ecstasy and receiving the stigmata, which in this symbolic representation reach him by means of five cords of blood that descend from on high, from Christ crucified, who hovers in the heavens like a star, or like a kite launched by urchins in the open countryside where there is no lack of space and where people still remember a time when men could be seen flying. With his hands and feet bleeding, his side a gaping wound, Saint Francis holds on to Christ's cross to prevent Him from disappearing into the cloistered heights. There the Father calls to His Son, Come, come, your time for being a man is at an end. That is why we see Saint Francis twitching in saintly fashion as he struggles to hold on, as he murmurs what some believe to be a prayer, I won't let you go, I won't let you go. From these events, which are only now being revealed, you can see just how urgent it is to dismiss orthodox theology and forge a new theology totally opposed to traditional beliefs. Here is an association of ideas for you, then, to illustrate, because first there were Roman heads on the terrace, which was a belvedere, then Ricardo Reis remembered the obscene gesture of the Portuguese rustic, and now, at the entrance to an old convent in Lisbon, not in Wittenberg, he discovers how and why the common people call that gesture the heraldic arms of Saint Francis, for it is the gesture the desperate saint makes to God when He tries to take away his star. There will be no lack of skeptics and conservatives who reject this hypothesis, but that need not surprise us, it is, after all, what always happens to new ideas, ideas born by association.

Ricardo Reis searches his memory for fragments of poems composed some twenty years ago, how time flies, *Unhappy God, essential to all, perhaps because He is unique. It is not you, Christ, whom I despise, but do not usurp what belongs to others. Through the gods we men stand united.* These are the words he mutters to himself as he walks along the Rua de Dom Pedro V as if looking for fossils or the ruins of an ancient civilization, and for a moment he wonders whether there is any meaning left in the odes from which he has taken these random lines, lines still coherent but weakened by the absence of what comes before and what follows, paradoxically assuming, by that absence, another meaning, one obscure and authoritative, like that of an epigraph to a book. He asks himself if it is possible to define a unity that joins, like a fastener or clip, two things opposed, divergent, such as that saint who went healthy to the mountain and returned oozing blood from five wounds. If only he had succeeded, at the end of the day, in winding up those cords and returning home, weary as any laborer after his toil, carrying under his arm the kite he was able to retrieve only by the skin of his teeth. It would rest by his pillow while he slept. Today he has won, but who can tell if he will win tomorrow. Trying to join these opposites is probably as absurd as trying to empty the sea with a bucket, not because that is so enormous a task, even if one has the time and energy, but because one would first have to find somewhere on land another great cavity for the sea, and this is impossible. There is so much sea, so little land.

Ricardo Reis is also absorbed by the question he posed himself upon arriving at the Praça do Rio de Janeiro, once known as the Praça do Príncipe Real and which one day may go back to that name, should anyone live to see it. When the weather becomes hot, one longs for the shade of these silver maples, elms, the Roman pine which looks like a refreshing pergola. Not that this poet and doctor is so well versed in botany, but someone must make up for the ignorance and lapses of memory of a man who for the last sixteen years has grown accustomed to the vastly different and more baroque flora and fauna of the tropics. This is not, however, the season for summer pursuits, for the delights of beach and spa, today's temperature must be around ten degrees Centigrade and the park benches are wet. Ricardo Reis pulls his raincoat snugly around his body, shivering, he goes back by other avenues, now descending the Rua do Século, unable to say what made him decide on this route, this street so deserted and melancholy. A few grand residences remain alongside the squat, narrow houses built for the poorer classes, at least the nobility in former days were not all that discriminating, they lived side by side with the common folk. God help us, the way things are going we will see the return of exclusive neighborhoods, nothing but private residences for the barons of industry and commerce, who very soon will swallow up whatever is left of the aristocracy, residences with private garages, gardens in proportion to the size of the property, dogs that bark ferociously. Even among the dogs one notices the difference. In the distant past they attacked both rich and poor.

Showing no haste, Ricardo Reis proceeds down the street, his umbrella serving as a walking stick. He taps the paving stones as he goes, beating time with every other step, the sound precise, distinct, sharp. There is no echo, yet the impact is almost liquid, if the term is not absurd, let us say that it is liquid, for so it seems as the tip of the umbrella strikes the limestone. He is absorbed by these puerile thoughts when suddenly he becomes aware of his own footsteps, almost as if, since leaving the hotel, he has not met a living soul. He would swear to that if called upon to testify, I saw no one on my walk. How is that possible, my good man, in a city one could scarcely regard as being small, where did all the people disappear to. He knows, of course, because common sense, the only repository of knowledge which common sense itself assures us is irrefutable, tells him so, that this cannot be true, he must have passed a number of people along the route, and now in this street, for all its tranquillity, there are groups of people, all walking downhill. They are poor people, some almost beggars, entire families with the elderly walking behind, dragging their feet, with sunken hearts, and the children are tugged along by their mothers, who shout, Hurry up, or everything will be gone. What has gone is peace and quiet, the street is no longer the same. As for the men, they try to adopt the severe expression one expects of the head of a family, they walk at their own pace, like someone who has another goal in sight. Together the families disappear. On the next street corner is a stately residence with palm trees in the courtyard, reminding one of *Arabia Felix*. Its medieval features have lost none of their charm, concealing surprises on the other side, not like these modern urban arteries designed in straight lines with everything in sight, as if sight can be so easily satisfied. Ricardo Reis is confronted by a dense multitude crowding the entire width of the road, patient and restless at the same time, heads bobbing like the playing of waves, like a cornfield ruffled by the breeze. Ricardo Reis draws close, asks to be allowed to pass. The person in front of him makes a gesture of refusal, turns to him and is on the point of saying, If you're in a hurry, you should have got here sooner, but comes face to face with a smart gentleman wearing neither beret nor cap, dressed in a light raincoat, white shirt and tie. That is all that is needed to persuade the man to step aside and, as if this were not enough, to tap the shoulder of the man in front, Let this gentleman pass. The other follows suit, which is why we can see the gray hat worn by Ricardo Reis advancing as smoothly amid this human mass as the swan of Lohengrin over the becalmed waters of the Black Sea. His crossing, however, takes time, for the crowd is vast. Besides, as one draws nearer the center, it becomes increasingly difficult to persuade people to let one through, not because of any sudden ill will but simply because no one can move in the crush. What is going on, Ricardo Reis asks himself, but does not dare ask the question aloud, reasoning that where so many have gathered for a purpose known to all, it would be wrong, improper, indelicate, to show one's ignorance. People might take offense, for how can we be certain of the feelings of others when we are often surprised by our own. Ricardo Reis is halfway down the street, standing before the entrance of the large building occupied by *O Século*, the country's leading newspaper. The crowd is less dense in the crescent fronting the building, and only now does Ricardo Reis become aware that he has been holding his breath to avoid the stench of overcooked onion, garlic, of sweat, of clothes that are scarcely ever changed, of bodies that are never washed unless they are going to be examined by a doctor. Olfactory organs in any way squeamish would find this journey a tribulation. Two policemen are posted at the entrance, close by are another two. Ricardo Reis is about to ask one of them, What is this gathering, officer, when the representative of law and order informs him respectfully, for one can tell at a glance that the gentleman making the inquiry is here by accident, It's the charity day organized by *O Século*. But there is such a crowd. Yes sir, they reckon that there are over a thousand here. Are all of them poor. All of them, sir, poor people from the back streets and slums. So many. Yes sir, and they are not all here. Of course, but all these people gathered to receive charity, it is a disturbing sight. It doesn't disturb me, sir, I'm used to it. And what are they given. Each pauper gets ten escudos. Ten escudos. That's right, ten escudos, and the children are given clothing, toys, and books. To help educate them. Yes sir, to help educate them. Ten escudos won't go very far. It's better than nothing, sir. Too true. Some of them spend the whole year just waiting for this distribution of charity, for this one and others, and there are even some who spend all their time running from charity event to charity event, grabbing what they can get, the trouble starts when they turn up in places where they are unknown, in other districts, other parishes, the poor who belong there chase them out, each pauper keeps a sharp eye on the other paupers. A sad business. It may be sad, sir, but otherwise there would be no controlling them. Thank you for the information, officer. At your service, sir, pass this way, sir. With these words the policeman took three steps forward, his arms outspread like someone shooing chickens toward the coop, All right now, move on quietly, unless you want to see me wielding my saber. With these persuasive remarks the crowd moves on, the women protesting as usual, the men acting as if they have heard nothing, the children thinking about the toys they will receive, perhaps a little car, perhaps a cycle, perhaps a celluloid doll, for these they would gladly exchange their sweaters and readers. Ricardo Reis climbed the slope of the Calçada dos Caetanos, from where he had a bird's-eye view and could estimate the size of the crowd. More than a thousand, the policeman was right, a country well endowed with paupers. Let us pray that charity will never dry up for this mob in shawls, kerchiefs, patched shirts, cheap cotton pants with the seats mended in a different material, some people in sandals, many barefoot. Despite the various colors, they form, massed together, a dark smudge, a black, fetid mud like that in the Cais do Sodré. They wait, and will continue to wait until their turn comes, hours and hours on their feet, some since dawn, mothers holding children in their arms, breast-feeding newborn infants, fathers conversing among themselves on topics that interest men, the aged taciturn and glum, shaky on their legs, drooling at the mouth. The day on which alms are distributed is the only day their families do not wish them dead, for that would mean fewer escudos. And there are plenty of people with fever, coughing their heads off, passing a few small bottles of liquor to help pass the time and ward off the cold. If the rain starts up again, they will get soaked, because there is no shelter here.

Ricardo Reis crossed the Bairro Alto, descending by the Rua do Norte, and when he reached the Rua de Camões he felt as if he were trapped in a labyrinth that always led him back to the same spot, to this bronze statue ennobled and armed with a sword, another D'Artagnan. Decorated with a crown of laurels for having rescued the queen's diamonds at the eleventh hour from the machinations of the cardinal, whom, however, with a change of times and politics he will end up serving, this musketeer standing here, who is dead and cannot reenlist, ought to be told that he is used, in turn or at random, by heads of state and even by cardinals, when it serves their interests. The hours have passed quickly during these explorations on foot, and it is time for lunch. This man appears to have nothing else to do, he sleeps, eats, strolls, and composes poetry line by line with much effort, agonizing over rhyme and meter. It is nothing compared to the endless dueling of the musketeer D'Artagnan, and the Lusiads run to more than eight thousand lines, yet

Ricardo Reis too is a poet, not that he boasts of that on the hotel register, but one day people will remember him not as a doctor, just as they do not think of Álvaro de Campos as a naval engineer, or of Fernando Pessoa as a foreign correspondent. Our profession may earn us our living but not fame, which is more likely to come from having once written *Nel mezzo del cammin di nostra vita* or *Menina e moça me levaram da casa de meus pais* or *En un lugar de la Mancha*, of which I do not wish to remember the name, so as not to fall once again into the temptation of saying, however appropriately, *As armas e os barões assinalados*, may we be forgiven these borrowings, *Arma virumque cano*. Man must always make an effort, so that he may deserve to be called man, but he is much less master of his own person and destiny than he imagines. Time, not his time, will make him prosper or decline, sometimes for different merits, or because they are judged differently. What will you be when you discover it is night and you find yourself at the end of the road.

It was almost nightfall before the Rua do Século was clear of paupers. Ricardo Reis had lunched in the meantime, browsed in two bookshops, lingered at the door of the Tivoli debating whether or not he wanted to see the film *I Love All Women* starring Jan Kiepura. In the end, he decided to see the film some other time and return to the hotel by taxi, because his legs were giving him trouble after all that walking. When it started raining, he retreated to a nearby café, read the evening newspapers, agreed to have his shoes shined, clearly a waste of polish on streets like these, where a shower can cause a flood without any warning, but the bootblack insisted that an ounce of prevention was better than a pound of cure, A shoe when it's polished keeps out the rain, sir, and the man was right, because when Ricardo Reis removed his shoes once back in his room, his feet were warm and dry. Just what one needs to keep healthy, warm feet and a cool head. Universities may not recognize this wisdom based on experience, but one has nothing to lose by observing the precept. The hotel is so peaceful, no banging doors, no sounds of voices, the buzzer silent. Salvador is not at the reception desk, most unusual, and Pimenta, who went to look for the key, moves as swiftly and ethereally as a sprite. Obviously he has not had to carry any luggage since early that morning, lucky for him. When Ricardo Reis went down to dinner, it was almost nine o'clock, the dining room, just as he had intended, was empty, the waiters chatting in a corner, but when Salvador appeared, the staff busied themselves, for that is what we must always do when our immediate superior suddenly enters. It is enough, for example, to shift our weight to the right leg if before it was resting on the left, that's all that's required, sometimes even less. Are you serving dinner, the guest asked hesitantly. But of course, that was what they were there for. Salvador told the good doctor that on New Year's Eve they generally had few customers, and the few they had generally dined out, the traditional *réveillon* or *révelion*, what was the word. Once, they used to celebrate the festivities in the hotel, but the owners found it a costly business, the practice was discontinued, such a lot of work involved, not to mention the damage caused by the boisterousness of the guests, you know how things happen, one drink follows another, people start quarreling, and then all the noise, bedlam, and the complaints of those in no mood for merrymaking, because there are always such people. We finally stopped having the *révelion*, but I must confess I'm sorry, it was such a jolly occasion and the hotel enjoyed the reputation of having class and moving with the times. Now, as you can see, it's completely deserted. Well, at least you can get to bed early, Ricardo Reis consoled him, but Salvador assured him that he always waited up to hear the bells ring in the New Year at midnight, a family tradition. They always ate twelve raisins, one for each chime, to bring luck during the next year, a popular custom widely observed abroad. You're talking about rich countries, but do you really believe such a custom will bring you good fortune. I do not know, but perhaps my year would have been even worse had I not eaten those raisins. It is with such arguments that the man who has no God seeks gods, while he who has abandoned his gods invents God. One day we shall rid ourselves of both God and gods.

Ricardo Reis dined with a single waiter in attendance, the maître d' decorously positioned at the end of the dining room, and Salvador installed himself behind the reception desk to while away the hours until it was time for his *révelion intime*. Nothing is known of Pimenta's whereabouts, and as for the chambermaids, either they have disappeared upstairs into the attics, if there are attics, where they will toast one another's health on the stroke of midnight with intoxicating homemade liquors served with biscuits, or else they have gone home, leaving an emergency staff, as in hospitals. The kitchen already looks like an abandoned fortress. But this is mere speculation, guests are generally not interested in knowing how a hotel functions behind the scenes, all they want is a comfortable room and meals at regular intervals. For dessert Ricardo Reis did not expect to be served a large slice of cake specially baked for the festivities of Epiphany or Dia de Reis. These are thoughtful little courtesies which make a friend of every customer. The waiter smiled and quipped, Dia de Reis, you pay, Doctor. Agreed, Ramón, for that was the waiter's name, I'll pay on the Dia dos Reis, but the pun was lost on Ramón. It is still not ten o'clock, time is dragging, the old year lingers on. Ricardo Reis looks at the table where two days before he watched Doctor Sampaio and his daughter Marcenda and felt himself being enshrouded by a gray cloud. If they were present now, they might converse together, the only guests on this night which marks an ending and a new beginning, what could be more appropriate. He visualizes again the girl's pitiful gesture as she took hold of her lifeless hand and placed it on the table, that tiny hand she so dearly cherished while the other, strong and healthy, helped its sister but had its own, independent existence. It could not always assist. For example, shaking the hand of others when formally introduced, Marcenda Sampaio, Ricardo Reis, the doctor's hand would grip that of the girl from Coimbra, right hand with right hand, but while his left hand, should it so desire, could hover close to witness the encounter, hers, dangling at her side, might just as well not be present. Ricardo Reis feels the tears come to his eyes. There are still some people who speak ill of doctors, convinced that because doctors are accustomed to illness and misfortune they have hearts of stone, but look at this doctor, he belies any such criticism, perhaps because he is also a poet, though somewhat skeptical in outlook, as we have seen. Ricardo Reis is engrossed in these thoughts, some of them perhaps too difficult to unravel for anyone who like ourselves is on the outside, but Ramón, who sees much, inquires, Do you wish anything else, Doctor, a tactful way of saying, though expecting the negative, that the doctor does. We are so apt at understanding that sometimes half a word suffices. Ricardo Reis rises to his feet, says Good-night to Ramón, wishes him a Happy New Year, and as he passes the reception desk slowly repeats the greeting and the wish to Salvador. The sentiment is the same, its expression more deliberate, after all Salvador is the manager. As Ricardo Reis goes slowly upstairs, he looks worn-out, like one of those caricatures or cartoons in a magazine of the period, the Old Year covered with white hair and wrinkles, his hourglass emptied, disappearing into the deep shadows of the past, while the New Year advances in a ray of light, as chubby as those infants nourished on powdered milk, reciting a nursery rhyme that invites us to the dance of the hours, I am the year nineteen thirty-six, come rejoice with me. Ricardo Reis enters his room and sits down. The bed has been prepared, fresh water stands in the carafe should he feel thirsty during the night, his slippers wait on the bedside mat. Someone is watching over me, a guardian angel, my heartfelt thanks. On the street there is the clatter of tin cans as revelers pass. Eleven o'clock has struck already, and at that moment Ricardo Reis jumps to his feet, almost in anger, What am I doing here, everyone else is out celebrating, having a good time with their families on the streets, in dance halls, theaters, cinemas, nightclubs, I should at least go to the Rossio to see the clock at Central Station, the eye of time, those Cyclopes who hurl not thunderbolts but minutes and seconds, every bit as cruel as thunderbolts and which we must all endure, until finally they shatter me along with the planks of the ship, but not like this, sitting here watching the clock, crouched in a chair. Having finished this soliloquy, he put on his raincoat and hat, grabbed his umbrella, suddenly eager, a man transformed by having made up his mind. Salvador had gone home to his family, so it was Pimenta who asked, You're going out, Doctor. Yes, I will take a little stroll, and he started downstairs. Pimenta pursued him to the landing, When you come back, Doctor, ring the bell twice, one short ring followed by a longer one, then I'll know it's you. Will you still be up. I'll turn in after midnight, but don't worry about me, sir, you come back whenever you like. Happy New Year, Pimenta. A very prosperous New Year, Doctor, the phrases one reads on greeting cards. They said nothing more, but when Ricardo Reis reached the bottom of the stairs he remembered that one normally tips the hotel staff at this time of the year, they rely on such tips. Forget it, I have been here only three days. The Italian page is asleep, his lamp extinguished.

The pavement was wet, slippery, the tram lines gleamed all the way up the Rua do Alecrim to the right. Who knows what star or kite holds them at that point, where, as the textbook informs us, parallel lines meet at infinity, an infinity that must be truly vast to accommodate so many things, dimensions, lines straight and curved and intersecting, the trams that go up these tracks and the passengers inside the trams, the light in the eyes of every passenger, the echo of words, the inaudible friction of thoughts. A whistling up at a window as if giving a signal, Well then, are you coming down or not. It's still early, a voice replies, whether of a man or woman it does not matter, we shall encounter it again at infinity. Ricardo Reis descended the Chiado and the Rua do Carmo, a huge crowd going with him, some in groups, entire families, although for the most part they were solitary men with no one waiting for them at home or who preferred to be outdoors to watch the passing of the old year. Perhaps it will truly pass, perhaps over their heads and ours will soar a line of light, a frontier, then we shall say that time and space are one and the same thing. There were also women who for an hour were interrupting their wretched prowling, calling a halt, wanting to be present should there be any proclamation of a new life, anxious to know what their share will be, whether it will be really new or the same as before. Around the Teatro Nacional the Rossio was crowded, there was a sudden downpour, umbrellas opened like the gleaming carapaces of insects or as if this were an army advancing under the protection of shields, about to assault an impassive citadel. Ricardo Reis mingled with the crowd, less dense than it had appeared from a distance, and pushed his way through. Meanwhile the shower has passed, the umbrellas close like a flock of birds shaking their wings as they settle down for the night. Everyone has his nose in the air, his eyes fixed on the yellow dial of the clock. From the Rua do Primeiro de Dezembro a group of boys come running, beating on the lids of pots and pans, tang, tang, while others keep up a shrill whistling. They march around the square in front of the station before settling under the portico of the theater, blowing their whistles all the while and banging on their tin lids, and this uproar combines with that of the wooden rattles resounding throughout the square, ra-ra-ra-ra, four minutes to go before midnight. Ah, the fickleness of mankind, so niggardly with the little time they have to live, always complaining that their lives are short, leaving behind only the hushed hiss of effervescence, yet they are impatient for these minutes to pass, such is the strength of hope. Already there are cries of anticipation, and the din reaches a crescendo as the deep voice of anchored ships can be heard from the direction of the river, dinosaurs bellowing with that prehistoric rumble that makes one's stomach churn. Sirens rend the air with piercing screams like those of animals being slaughtered, the frantic hooting of cars nearby is deafening, the little bells of the trams tinkle for all they are worth, which is not much, until finally the minute hand covers the hour hand, it is midnight, the happiness of freedom. For one brief moment time has released mankind, has allowed them to live their own lives, time stands aside and looks on, ironic, benevolent, as people embrace one another, friends and strangers, men and women kissing at random. These are the best kisses of all, kisses without any future. The clamor of the sirens now fills the air, the pigeons stir nervously on the pediment of the theater, some flutter in a daze, but in less than a minute the noise abates, a few last gasps, the ships on the river seem to be disappearing into the mist, out to sea. Speaking of this, there is Dom Sebastião in his niche on the façade, a little boy masked for some future carnival. Since he has not been placed elsewhere, but here, we shall have to reconsider the importance and paths of Sebastianism, with or without mist. It is clear that the Awaited One will arrive by train, subject to delays. There are still groups in the Rossio, but the excitement is over, people are clearing the pavements, they know what will happen next. From the upper stories rubbish comes hurtling down, it is the custom, not so noticeable here because few people inhabit these buildings, which are mainly offices. All the way down the Rua do Ouro the ground is strewn with litter. From windows people are still chucking out rags, empty boxes, cans, leftovers, fish bones wrapped in news-papers, it all scatters on the pavement. A chamberpot full of live embers bursts into sparks in every direction, and pedestrians seek protection under balconies, pressing themselves against the build-ings and shouting up at the windows. But their protests are not taken seriously, the custom is widely observed, so let each man protect himself as best he can, for this is a night for celebrating and for whatever amusements one can devise. All the junk, things no longer in use and not worth selling, is thrown out, having been stored for the occasion, these are amulets to ensure prosperity throughout the New Year. At least now there will be some empty space to receive any good that may come our way, so let us hope that we are not forgotten. A voice called from an upper story, Look out, something's coming, considerate of them to warn us, a large bundle came hurtling through the air, describing a curve, almost hitting the tram cables, how careless, it could have caused a serious accident. It was a tailor's dummy, the kind set on three legs and suitable for either a man's jacket or a woman's dress, the black padding ripped open, the frame worm-eaten. Lying there crushed by the impact, it no longer resembled a human body with the head missing and no legs. A passing youth pushed it into the gutter with his foot. Tomorrow the garbage truck will come and clear all this away, the scraps and peelings, the dirty rags, the pots of no use either to the tinker or the metal scavenger, a roasting pan without its bottom, a broken picture frame, felt flowers reduced to tatters. Soon the tramps will be rummaging through the debris and surely find something they can put to use. What has lost its value for one can profit another.

Ricardo Reis returns to the hotel. In many parts of the city the festivities go on, with fireworks, sparkling wine or genuine champagne, and wild abandon, as the newspapers never forget to say. Women of easy or not-so-easy virtue are also available, some quite open and direct, others observing certain rituals in the making of their advances. This man, however, is not adventuresome, he knows about such exploits only from the lips of others, and any experience he has had was a matter of walking in one door and out the other. A group of passing revelers call out in discordant chorus, Happy New Year old man, and he replies with a gesture, a raised hand. Why say anything, they are so much younger than I. He tramples through the rubbish on the street, avoiding the boxes. Broken glass crunches under his feet. They might as well have tossed out their old parents with the tailor's dummy, there is little difference, for after a certain age the head no longer governs the body and the legs do not know where they are taking us. In the end we are like small children, orphaned, because we cannot return to our dead mother, to the beginning, to the nothingness that was before the beginning. It is before death and not after that we enter nothingness, for from nothingness we came, emerging, and when dead we shall disperse, without consciousness yet still existing. All of us once possessed a father and mother, but we are the children of fortune and necessity, whatever that means. It is Ricardo Reis's thought, let him do the explaining.

Although it was already after twelve-thirty, Pimenta had still not gone to bed. He came downstairs to open the door and was surprised, So you came back early after all, you didn't do much celebrating. I was feeling tired, sleepy, and you know, this business of seeing in the New Year is no longer the same. That's true, the festivities are much livelier in Brazil. They made these polite exchanges as they went upstairs. On the landing Ricardo Reis wished him good-night, Until tomorrow, then tackled the second flight of stairs. In reply Pimenta said good-night, then switched off the lights on the landing, then the lights on all the other floors before finally turning in, confident of undisturbed sleep, because no new guests were likely to arrive at this hour. He could hear the footsteps of Ricardo Reis in the corridor. The place is so quiet, no lights from any of the bedrooms, either the occupants are asleep or the rooms are empty. At the end of the corridor the number plate two hundred and one glows dimly, and Ricardo Reis notices a ray of light coming from under the door. He must have forgotten to turn off the light, well, these things do happen. He inserted the key in the lock and opened the door, and there was a man sitting on the sofa. He recognized him at once, though they had not seen each other for many years. Nor did he think it strange that Fernando Pessoa should be sitting there waiting for him. He said Hello, not expecting a reply, absurdity does not always obey logic, but Pessoa did in fact reply, saying, Hello, and stretched out his hand, then they embraced. Well, how have you been, one of them asked, or both, not that it matters, the question is so meaningless. Ricardo Reis removed his raincoat, put down his hat, carefully rested his umbrella on the linoleum floor in the bathroom, taking the precaution of checking the damp silk, no longer really wet, because during the walk back to the hotel there had been no rain. He pulled up a chair, sat in front of his visitor, saw that Fernando Pessoa was casually dressed, which is the Portuguese way of saying that he was wearing neither overcoat nor raincoat nor any other form of protection against the inclement weather, not even a hat, all he wore was a black suit comprising a double-breasted jacket, vest, and trousers, a white shirt with black tie, and black shoes and socks, like someone attending a funeral, or an undertaker. They look at each other with affection, obviously happy to be reunited after years of separation, and it is Fernando Pessoa who speaks first, I believe you came to visit me, I wasn't there, but they told me when I got back. Ricardo Reis replied, I was sure I'd find you there, never imagining you could leave that place. Fernando Pessoa said, For the time being it's allowed, I have about eight months in which to wander around as I please. Why eight months, Ricardo Reis asked, and Fernando Pessoa explained, The usual period is nine months, the same length of time we spend in our mother's womb, I believe it's a question of symmetry, before we are born no one can see us yet they think about us every day, after we are dead they cannot see us any longer and every day they go on forgetting us a little more, and apart from exceptional cases it takes nine months to achieve total oblivion, now tell me, what brings you to Portugal. Ricardo Reis removed his wallet from his inside pocket and took out a folded piece of paper, which he offered to Fernando Pessoa, but the latter made a gesture of refusal, I can no longer read, you read it. Ricardo Reis obeyed, Fernando Pessoa has died Stop I am leaving for Glasgow Stop Álvaro de Campos. When I received this telegram, I decided to return, I felt it was almost an obligation. The tone of the communication is very interesting, unmistakably from Álvaro de Campos, even in those few words one detects a note of malign satisfaction, even amusement, Álvaro is like that. There was another reason, this one a matter of self-interest, in November a revolution erupted in Brazil, many died, many were arrested, and I feared that the situation might get worse, I couldn't make up my mind whether to leave or stay until this telegram arrived, that decided it. Reis, you seem destined to flee revolutions, in nineteen nineteen you went to Brazil because of a revolution that failed, now you are fleeing Brazil because of another that has probably failed as well. Strictly speaking, I did not flee Brazil, and perhaps I would be there still had you not died. I remember reading something about this revolution a few days before my death, I believe it was instigated by the Bolshevists. Yes, the Bolsheviks were responsible, a number of officers, some soldiers, those who weren't killed were arrested, and the whole thing blew over within two or three days. Were people frightened, They most certainly were, Here in Portugal, too, there have been several revolutions, I know, the news reached me in Brazil, Do you still believe in monarchism, I do, Without a king, One can be a monarchist without clamoring for a king, Is that how you feel, It is, A nice contradiction, No worse than some, To advocate by desire what you know you cannot advocate by reason, Exactly, you see I still remember you, Of course.

Fernando Pessoa rose from the sofa, paced a little, then paused in front of the bedroom mirror before returning to the sitting room. It gives me an odd feeling to look in the mirror and not see myself there, Don't you see yourself, No, I know that I am looking at myself, but I see nothing, Yet you cast a shadow, It's all I possess. He sat down again and crossed his legs, Will you now settle for good in Portugal or will you go back to Brazil. I still haven't made up my mind, I brought only the bare necessities, perhaps I'll stay, open an office, build up a clientele, I might also go back to Rio, I don't know, for the moment I'm staying, but the more I think about it, I believe I came back here only because you died, it's as if I alone can fill the void you left behind. No living person can substitute for a dead one. None of us is truly alive or truly dead. Well said, an aphorism suitable for one of your odes. They both smiled.

Ricardo Reis asked, Tell me, how did you know that I was staying at this hotel. When you are dead, replied Fernando Pessoa, you know everything, that's one of the advantages. And how did you get into my room, Just as anyone else gets in, Didn't you come through the air, didn't you pass through the walls, What a ridiculous idea, my good fellow, such things happen only in ghost stories, no, I came from the cemetery at Prazeres, and like any other mortal walked upstairs, opened that door, and sat on this sofa to await your arrival. And did no one express surprise upon seeing a stranger walk in, That is another privilege the dead enjoy, no one can see us unless we so desire, But I see you, Because I want you to see me, besides, if you think about it, who are you. The question was clearly rhetorical, expected no answer, and Ricardo Reis said nothing, had not even heard it. There was a long-drawn-out silence, opaque. The clock on the landing could be heard striking two, as if coming from another world. Pessoa rose to his feet, I must be getting back. So soon. My time is my own, I am free to come and go as I please, it's true that my grandmother is there but she no longer bothers me. Stay a little longer, No, it's getting late and you should rest, When will I see you again, Do you wish me to return, Very much, we could converse, renew our friendship, don't forget that after sixteen years I feel like a stranger here. Remember that we can be together only for eight months, then my time runs out, Eight months, at the beginning, seems a lifetime, Whenever possible, I will come to see you, Wouldn't you like to fix a day, an hour, a place, Impossible, Very well, see you soon, Fernando, it was good seeing you again, And you, Ricardo, Should I wish you a Happy New Year, Go ahead, go ahead, it can't do me any harm, they're only words, as you well know. Happy New Year, Fernando, Happy New Year, Ricardo.

Fernando Pessoa opened the bedroom door and went out into the corridor, his footsteps inaudible. Two minutes later, the time it took to descend that steep flight of stairs, the front door banged, the buzzer having droned briefly. Ricardo Reis went to the window. Fernando Pessoa was already disappearing down the Rua do Alecrim. The tram rails shone, still running parallel.

Whether because they themselves believe it or because someone took them in hand after they failed to respond to suggestions and hints, the newspapers inform us, as if it were a great prophecy, that over the ruins of the mighty states ours, the Portuguese state, will demonstrate its remarkable strength and the prudence and intelligence of the men who govern it. For fall those states shall, and their crash will be resounding. The proud nations who boast of their present supremacy are much deceived, because the day is fast approaching, the happiest day of all in the annals of this nation among nations, when the leaders of other states come to these Lusitanian shores to seek advice, assistance, wisdom, benevolence, oil for their lamp from our great Portuguese statesmen. Who are these rulers, starting with the next cabinet, which is already being formed. In supreme command is Oliveira Salazar, President of the Council and Minister of Finance, then, at a respectful distance and in the order in which the newspapers publish their photographs, Monteiro of Foreign Affairs, Pereira of Commerce, Machado of Colonies, Abranches of Public Works, Bettencourt of the Navy, Pacheco of Education, Rodrigues of Justice, Sousa of War, Sousa of the Interior, the former is Passos de Sousa and the latter Paes de Sousa, write their names out in full so that petitions will reach them without delay. And we must not forget to mention Duque of Agriculture, without whose opinion not a grain of wheat would be produced in Europe or elsewhere. For the posts that remain, In

Parentheses Lumbrales of Finance and Andrade of Corporations, because this new state of ours, although in its infancy, is corporate, which explains why an undersecretary is quite sufficient. The newspapers here also say that most of the country has reaped the abundant fruits of an exemplary administration keen on maintaining public order, and if such a statement smacks of self-praise, read that paper from Geneva, Switzerland, which at length and with greater authority, because it is in French, describes the abovementioned dictator of Portugal, calling us most fortunate to be led by this wise leader, and the author of the article is absolutely right, and we thank him with all our hearts. But please bear in mind that Pacheco is no less wise if tomorrow he should say, as say he will, that elementary education must be given its due and no more, because knowledge, if imparted too soon, serves no real purpose, and also that an education based on materialism and paganism, which stifle noble impulses, is much worse than the darkness of illiteracy, therefore Pacheco concludes that Salazar is the greatest educator of our century, if that is not too bold an assertion when we are only one-third of the way through it.

Do not think that these items all appeared on the same page of the same newspaper, for then they would be seen as linked, they would be given the mutually complementary and consequential meaning they appear to have. These are the reports, rather, of the last few weeks, juxtaposed here like dominoes, each half set against its equal unless it happens to be double, in which case it is placed crosswise. These are current events seen from a distance. Ricardo Reis reads the morning newspapers as he savors his coffee with milk and eats the delicious toast served at the Bragança Hotel, greasy and crisp, clearly a contradiction, the pleasure of an age long forgotten, which explains why combining the two adjectives might strike you as inappropriate. We already know the maid who brings in his breakfast, it is Lydia, who also makes the bed and cleans and tidies up the room. When speaking to Ricardo Reis, she addresses him always as doctor, whereas he calls her simply Lydia, nothing else, but being an educated man he never uses the familiar form when he requests of her, Do this, Bring me that. Unaccustomed to such politeness, she is flattered, because as a rule the guests treat her with the familiarity shown servants, believing that money bestows every right, although to be fair, there is another guest who treats her with the same consideration, that is Senhorita Marcenda, the daughter of Doctor Sampaio. Lydia must be about thirty years of age, a mature and well-developed young woman, dark-haired and unmistakably Portuguese, short rather than tall, if there is any point in mentioning the physical traits of an ordinary maid who so far has done nothing but scrub floors, serve breakfast, and on one occasion laugh as she watched a man on another man's back while this guest stood there smiling. Such a nice person, yet sad, he cannot be happy, although there are moments when his face lights up just like this gloomy room when the clouds allow the sun to come through. It is more moonlight than the light of day, a shadow of light. Because it caught Lydia's head at a favorable angle, Ricardo Reis noticed the birthmark at the side of one nostril. It becomes her, he thought, although later he could not say if he was referring to the birthmark or to her white apron, or to the starched cap on her head, or to the embroidered collar she wore around her neck. Yes, you may remove the tray.

Three days went by and Fernando Pessoa did not reappear. Ricardo Reis did not ask himself the obvious question, Could it have been a dream, he knew that Fernando Pessoa, with enough flesh and bone to embrace and be embraced, had been in this very room on New Year's Eve and had promised to return. He believed him, but was beginning to lose patience at the delay. His life now seemed suspended, expectant, problematic. Meticulously he scanned the newspapers for signs, threads, outlines of a whole, the features of a Portuguese face, not simply to evoke an image of the country but to clothe his own portrait with a new substance, to be able to raise his hands to his face and recognize himself, to be able to place one hand upon another and clasp them together, It is I and I am here. On the last page he came across a large advertisement, two columns wide. In the top right-hand corner was depicted Freire the Engraver, in monocle and cravat, an old-fashioned sketch. Underneath, down to the bottom of the page, a cascade of other drawings advertised his workshops, the only ones that could justly claim to offer a comprehensive range of goods, with explanatory and superfluous captions, as if proving that a picture is as good or better than any description in words, except that no picture can show the excellent quality of the products of a firm established fifty-two years ago by a master engraver, a man of unblemished character and reputation, who studied in the major capitals of Europe and whose children after him have learned the skills and techniques of his trade. Unique in Portugal, he has been awarded three gold medals, has installed in his factory sixteen machines worked by electricity, one worth sixty contos, and these machines can do almost everything except speak, good Lord. A whole world is portrayed here, and since we were not born in time to see the fields of Troy or the shield of Achilles that reflected all heaven and earth, let us admire this Portuguese shield here in Lisbon, depicting the nation's latest wonders, number plates for buildings and hotels, for rooms, cupboards, and umbrella stands, strops for razor blades, whetstones for knives, scissors, pens with gold nibs, presses and scales, glass plates with chains in polished brass, machines for punching checks, seals made of metal and rubber, enameled letters, stamps for labeling clothing, sealing wax, numbered disks for lines at banks, business firms, and cafés, irons with which to brand cattle and wooden boxes, penknives, municipal registration plates for automobiles and bicycles, rings, medals for every type of sport, badges for the caps worn by the employees in milk bars, cafés, and casinos. Look at this one for the Leitaria Nívea, not for the Leitaria Alentejana, since the employees of the latter do not wear caps with badges. And lockers, and those pennants in enameled metal that are placed above the doors of institutes and foundations, and soldering irons, electric lanterns, knives with four blades as well as other types, emblems, puncheons, printing frames, molds for biscuits, toilet soaps, rubber soles, monograms and coats of arms in gold, metal for every imaginable purpose, cigarette lighters, rollers for inking type, stone and ink for taking fingerprints, escutcheons for Portuguese and foreign consulates, yet more plaques for doctors, for lawyers, for registry offices where births and deaths are recorded for the parish council, Midwife, Notary Public, those that say No Entry, and rings for pigeons, and padlocks, etc., etc., etc., and another three etc.'s, to abridge and treat the rest as having been said. Let us not forget that these are the only workshops offering a comprehensive inventory, you can even have made to order ornamental iron gates for family tombs, but enough, period. Compared with this, what are the achievements of the divine blacksmith Hephaestus, he who chiseled and embossed the entire universe on the shield of Achilles but forgot to save a little space on which to engrave the heel of the illustrious warrior pierced by the quivering arrow of Paris. Even the gods forget about death, but no wonder, if they are immortal. Or was this an act of charity on the part of Hephaestus, a cloud cast over the transitory eyes of men, for whom it is enough, in order to be happy, to know neither where nor when nor how. Freire, however, is the more rigorous god and engraver, specifying everything, his advertisement is a labyrinth, a skein, a web. Studying it, Ricardo Reis allowed his coffee with milk to get cold, the butter to congeal on his toast. Please note, esteemed clients, our establishment has no branches anywhere, beware of those who call themselves agents and representatives, they are out to deceive the public with counterfeit tags for marking barrels and counterfeit branding irons for cattle. When Lydia arrived to collect the tray, she was worried, You haven't eaten anything, Doctor, didn't you like it. He protested that he had, but reading the newspaper he became distracted. Should I order some fresh toast, reheat your coffee. There's no need, I'm fine, besides he did not feel hungry, and saying this he got to his feet and placed a reassuring hand on her arm. He could feel the silky texture of her sleeve, the warmth of her skin. Lydia lowered her eyes, moved sideways, but his hand accompanied her and they remained like this for a few seconds. Finally Ricardo Reis released her arm and she gathered up the tray. The crockery shook as if the epicenter of an earthquake were located in room two hundred and one or, to be more precise, in the heart of this maid. Now she departs, she will not regain her composure in a hurry, she will go into the pantry and deposit the tray, her hand resting where that other hand rested, a delicate gesture unlikely in someone of so lowly a profession. That is what those who allow themselves to be guided by preconceived ideas must be thinking, perhaps even Ricardo Reis, who at this moment is bitterly upbraiding himself for having given in to foolish weakness, What an incredible thing I've done, and with a maid. It is his good fortune that he does not have to carry a tray laden with crockery, otherwise he would learn that even the hands of a hotel guest can tremble. Labyrinths are like this, streets, crossroads, and blind alleys. There are those who claim that the surest way of getting out of them is always to make the same turn, but that, as we know, is contrary to human nature.

Ricardo Reis invariably sets out from this street, the Rua do Alecrim, then takes any other, up, down, left, right, Ferragial, Remolares, Arsenal, Vinte e Quatro de Julho. These are the first unwindings of the skein, of the web, Boavista, Crucifixo. After a while his legs begin to tire, a man cannot wander about forever. It is not only the blind who need a walking stick to probe one step ahead or a dog to sniff out danger, even a man with the sight of two eyes needs a light he can follow, one in which he believes or hopes to believe, his very doubts serving in the absence of anything better. Now Ricardo Reis is watching the spectacle of the world, a wise man if one can call this wisdom, aloof, indifferent by upbringing and temperament, but quaking because a simple cloud has passed. One can easily understand the Greeks' and Romans' belief that they moved among gods, under the gaze of the gods at all times and in all places, whether in the shade of a tree, beside a fountain, in the dense, resounding depths of a forest, on the seashore, or on the waves, even in bed with one's beloved, be she woman or goddess, if she agrees. What Ricardo Reis requires is a guide dog, a walking stick, a light before him, because this world, and Lisbon too, is a dark mist in which north, south, east, and west all merge, and where the only open road slopes downward. If a man isn't careful, he will fall headlong to the bottom, a tailor's dummy without legs or head. It isn't true that Ricardo Reis returned from Rio de Janeiro out of cowardice or, to phrase it better, out of fear, it isn't true that he returned because Fernando Pessoa died, because one cannot put a thing back in the space and time from which it was removed, whether it be Fernando or Alberto. Each of us is unique and irreplaceable, which is the greatest of platitudes and may not be entirely true. Even if he appears before me at this very moment, as I make my way down the Avenida da Liberdade,

Fernando Pessoa is no longer Fernando Pessoa, and not only because he is dead. The important and decisive thing is that he is no longer able to add to what he was and what he achieved, to what he experienced and what he wrote. He can no longer even read, poor fellow. It will be up to Ricardo Reis to read him this other article published in a magazine with the poet's portrait in an oval frame. A few days ago death robbed us of Fernando Pessoa, the distinguished poet who spent his short life virtually ignored by the masses, one could say that because he knew the value of his work, he jealously hoarded it like a miser lest it be taken from him, some day full justice will be rendered to his dazzling talent, as has been rendered to other great geniuses in the past, dot dot dot. The bastards. The worst thing about journalists is that they believe they are authorized to put into the readily accepting heads of others ideas such as this one, that Fernando Pessoa hoarded his poems in the fear that others might steal them. How can they print such rubbish. Ricardo Reis impatiently tapped the pavement with the tip of his umbrella, which he could use as a walking stick but only so long as it didn't rain. A man can go astray even when he follows a straight line. He entered the Rossio and might just as well have been at a crossroads formed by four or eight choices which, if taken and retraced, would all end, as everyone knows, at the same point in infinity. There is little to be gained, therefore, in taking any of them. When the time comes, we will leave this matter to chance, which does not choose but simply drives and is driven in turn by forces about which we know nothing, and even if we knew, what would we know. Much better to rely on these nameplates probably manufactured in the fully equipped workshops of Freire the Engraver, which bear the names of doctors, lawyers, notaries, people to whom we have recourse in time of need and who have learned how to use a compass. Their compasses may not coincide, but this matters little, it is enough for the city to know that directions exist. You are not obliged to leave, because this is not the place where streets branch out, nor is it that magnificent point where they converge, rather, it is here that they change their sense, north becoming south, and south north. The sun has stopped between east and west, the city is a scar that has been burned, beset by earthquake, a teardrop that will not dry and has no finger to remove it. I must open an office, don a white coat, receive patients, even if only to allow them to die, Ricardo Reis muses. At least they will keep me company while they are alive, their last good deed being to play the ailing doctor of the ailing doctor. We are not saying that these are the thoughts of all doctors, but of this one certainly, for reasons of his own, reasons as yet barely glimpsed. What kind of practice shall I set up, where, and for whom. If you think that such questions require nothing but answers, you are deceived. We reply with actions, just as with actions we ask questions.

Ricardo Reis is about to descend the Rua dos Sapateiros when he sees Fernando Pessoa standing on the corner of the Rua de Santa Justa. Fernando Pessoa looks as if he has been kept waiting yet shows no sign of impatience, he wears the same black suit, his head uncovered, and, a detail previously unobserved by Ricardo Reis, he is without spectacles. Ricardo Reis thinks he knows why, it would be absurd and in thoroughly bad taste to bury a man in his spectacles, but that is not the reason, they had simply failed to hand them to him in time as he was dying. Give me my spectacles, he had asked, and was left lying there unable to see, for we are not always in time to satisfy the last wishes of the dying. Fernando Pessoa smiles and wishes him good afternoon, Ricardo Reis returns the greeting, and they walk together in the direction of the Terreiro do Paço. A little farther the rain starts up again. One umbrella shelters both of them, and although Fernando Pessoa has nothing to fear from this water, his huddling gesture was that of one who has still not completely forgotten life. Or it could have been the comforting thought of sharing the same roof and so close, Get underneath, there is room for two. No one will turn down such an offer by replying, There's no need, I don't mind the rain. Ricardo Reis is curious, If someone is watching us, whom does he see, you or me. He sees you, or rather he sees a shadowy form that is neither you nor I. The sum of both of us divided by two. No, I would say it is the result of multiplying the one by the other. Does this arithmetic exist. Two, whatever they may be, are not added up, they multiply. Be fruitful and multiply, says the commandment. Not in that restricted biological sense, dear fellow, take me, for example, I've left no children behind. I'm fairly certain that I, too, shall leave no children behind, nevertheless we are multiple, I wrote an ode in which I say that innumerable people exist within us. I don't recall it. Because I wrote it about two months ago. As you can see, each of us says the same thing. Then there was no point in our multiplying. If we had not multiplied, multiplying would not have been possible. Such a precious conversation, with its Paulist and intersectionist theories, as they walk along the Rua dos Sapateiros down as far as the Rua da Conceição, where they turn left into the Rua Augusta, then straight once more. Stopping, Ricardo Reis suggested, Let's go into the Café Martinho, and Fernando Pessoa replied brusquely, That would be unwise, the walls have ears and a good memory, we can go another day when there is no danger of anyone recognizing me, it's a question of time. As they lingered there under the arcade, Ricardo Reis closed his umbrella and said, apropos of nothing, I am thinking of settling here, of establishing a practice, So you have no intention of ever going back to Brazil, why, It's difficult to explain, I'm not even sure that I could give an explanation, let's say that I'm like the insomniac who finally finds a comfortable position on the pillow and can get some sleep. If it's sleep you're after, you've come to the right country. If I accept sleep, it's to be able to dream, To dream is to be absent, to be on the other side, But life has two sides, Pessoa, at least two, we can only reach the other side through dreams, you say this to a dead man, who can tell you from his own experience that on the other side of life there is only death. Well I don't know what death is, but I am not convinced that it is this other side of life we are discussing, because death, in my opinion, limits itself to being. Death is, it does not exist, it is. Are being and existing not the same thing then, No, my dear Reis, being and existing are not the same thing, and not simply because we have these two different words at our disposal, on the contrary it is because they are not the same thing that we have these two words and make use of them. They stood there arguing under the arcade while the rain formed tiny lakes in the square which gathered into larger lakes which became muddy seas. Not even on this occasion would Ricardo Reis go as far as the wharf to see the waves breaking. He was about to say this, to recall that he had been here before, when looking around he saw that Fernando Pessoa was walking away. Only now did he notice that the poet's trousers were too short, making him look as if he were walking on stilts. At last he heard his voice, nearby although Fernando Pessoa was already some distance away, We will continue this conversation another time, I must go now, over there. In the rain he waved his hand but did not say good-bye or I shall return.

The year has started in such a way that deaths are becoming an everyday occurrence. True, every age sweeps away what it can, sometimes with greater ease, when there are wars and epidemics, sometimes at a steady pace, one death after another, but it is most unusual to find so many famous people dying, both at home and abroad, within such a short space of time. We are not referring to Fernando Pessoa, who departed this world a while ago, no one is to know that he comes back from time to time, but to Leonardo Coimbra, who invented creationism, to Valle-Inclán, the author of *Romance de Lobos*, to John Gilbert, who starred in *The Big Parade*, to Rudyard Kipling, the poet who wrote If, and last but not least to the King of England, George V, the only monarch with his succession guaranteed. There have certainly been other misfortunes although much less important, such as the poor old man who was buried by a mud slide or those twenty-three people who came from Alentejo and were attacked by a cat with rabies. They disembarked, as black as a flock of ravens with lacerated wings, old folk, women, children being photographed for the first time in their lives, not knowing where they were supposed to look, their eyes gazing up at the sky, flustered and desperate, poor people, but that isn't all. What you don't know, Doctor, is that last November in the main towns of the region two thousand four hundred and ninety-two individuals died, one of them being Senhor Fernando Pessoa. It is not a large or small number, it is what has to be, but the saddest thing is that seven hundred and thirty-four were children under the age of five. If this is the situation in the main towns, thirty percent, imagine what it must be like in the villages, where even the cats have rabies. But we can always console ourselves with the thought that the majority of the little angels in heaven are Portuguese.

Furthermore, words can be most effective. When a government takes office, people go in droves to pay their respects to the honorable minister, everyone goes, teachers, civil servants, representatives of the three armed forces, leaders and members of the National Alliance, unions, guilds, farmers, judges, policemen, republican guards, excise men, and members of the general public. The minister thanks each of them with a little speech couched in the patriotism of the school primer and adapted to the ears of his audience. Those who are present arrange themselves so that they can all get into the photograph, the ones in the back rows craning their necks and standing on tiptoe to peek over the shoulder of their taller neighbors, That's me there, they will proudly tell their dear wife when they get home. The ones in front are puffed up with conceit, they have not been bitten by the cat with rabies but they have the same foolish expression, startled by the flashbulb. In the confusion some words were lost but can be deduced from the tone set by the Minister of the Interior at Montemor-o-Velho when he inaugurated the installation of electricity, a great improvement, I shall tell them in Lisbon that the leading citizens of Montemor know how to be loyal to Salazar. We can easily visualize the scene, Paes de Sousa explaining to the wise dictator the name he was given by the *Tribune des Nations* and that the good people from the land of Fernão Mendes Pinto are all loyal to your Excellency. With such a medieval regime, it's well known that peasants and laborers are often excluded from that goodness, people who have not inherited possessions, therefore they are not good men, perhaps neither good nor men but creatures no different from these insects that bite or gnaw or infest. You must have had occasion to observe what kind of people inhabit this country, Doctor, bearing in mind that this is the capital of the empire, when you passed the entrance to *O Século* the other day and saw the mob waiting for alms. If you wish to see real poverty, go into those districts, parishes, neighborhoods, and see for yourself the soup kitchens, the campaign for helping the poor during the winter months, an admirable enterprise, as the President of the Municipal Council of Oporto said in a telegram, God bless his soul. Don't you think it would have been better to let them die, then we would have spared ourselves the shameful spectacle of life in Portugal, beggars sitting on the curb eating a crust of bread and scraping the bottom of their bowls. They don't even deserve electric lights, all they need to know is the road from their plate to their mouth and that can be found in the dark.

Inside the body, too, there is profound darkness, yet the blood reaches the heart, the brain is sightless yet can see, it is deaf yet hears, it has no hands yet reaches out. Clearly man is trapped in his own labyrinth. The next two mornings, Ricardo Reis went downstairs to the dining room to have breakfast, a man frightened, alarmed at the possible consequences of a gesture as simple as that of placing his hand on Lydia's arm. He was not afraid that she had complained, after all it was just a gesture, nevertheless he felt some anxiety when he spoke for the first time after the incident with the manager Salvador. Needless anxiety, because the man could scarcely have been more respectful, affable. On the third day, Ricardo Reis decided that he was being foolish and did not go down to breakfast, he pretended to have forgotten breakfast and hoped they would do the same. He did not know Salvador. At the last minute there was a knock, Lydia entered carrying a tray, laid it down on the table and said, Good morning, Doctor, her natural self. It is nearly always like this, a man torments himself, frets, thinks the worst, believes that the world is about to demand a full explanation, when in fact the world has moved on, thinking about other things. It is not certain, however, that upon returning to his room to collect the tray, Lydia is still part of this world moved on, she seems to be waiting behind with an air of uncertainty. She goes through the usual motions, is about to lift the tray, has already gripped it, holds it level, hoists it into the air in a semicircle, and heads for the door. Oh my God, will he speak, not speak, perhaps he won't say anything, perhaps simply touch me on the arm like the other day, and if he does, what shall I do, it won't be the first time a guest has taken liberties, twice I gave into them, why, because this life is so sad. Lydia, Ricardo Reis spoke her name. She put down the tray, raised her eyes filled with terror, tried to say Doctor, but her voice stuck in her throat. He did not have the courage, repeated, Lydia, then said almost in a whisper, horribly banal, the ridiculous seducer,

I find you very pretty. He stood there staring at her for a second, he couldn't bear it for more than a second, and turned away. There are moments when it would be preferable to die, I who have made a fool of myself with hotel maids, you too, Álvaro de Campos, all of us. The door closed slowly, and only later could Lydia's footsteps be heard retreating.

Ricardo Reis spent the whole day out of doors brooding over his shame, all the more so because he had been unmanned not by an adversary but by his own fear. He decided that the following day he would change his hotel or rent part of a house, or return to Brazil on the first available ship. These may seem dramatic effects for such a tiny cause, but each person knows how much it hurts and where. Ridicule is like heartburn, an acidity continuously revived by memory, an incurable wound. He returned to the hotel, dined, and went out again, to see a film at the Politeama, *The Crusades*. Such faith, such ardent battles, such saints and heroes and splendid white horses. The film ended and an aura of religious fervor pervaded the Rua de Eugénio dos Santos, each spectator appearing to have a halo over his head, and yet there are people who remain unconvinced that art can improve mankind. Over and done with, the morning's episode assumed the right proportions, How foolish of me to get into such a state. Pimenta opened the door for him, the building was incredibly peaceful, obviously the hotel staff did not live in. He entered his room and immediately, almost by instinct, looked at the bed. The covers had not been folded back at an angle, as usual, but both sheet and eiderdown had been turned down straight from side to side, and instead of one pillow there were two, the message could not have been clearer. It remained to be seen how it would become explicit, unless it was not Lydia who made the bed but another maid, who thought the room was occupied by a couple. Yes, let us assume that the maids change floors every so often, perhaps so that they have equal opportunities for receiving tips, or to discourage them from becoming too set in their ways, or, and here Ricardo Reis smiled, to prevent them from becoming too friendly with the guests. Well, tomorrow we shall see. If Lydia appears with breakfast, then she must have prepared the bed. And then what. He lay down, switched off the light without bothering to remove the second pillow, closed his eyes firmly. Come, sleep, come, but sleep did not obey. A tram passed in the street, perhaps the last one. Who is that in me who doesn't wish to sleep, whose restless body possesses mine, or is it some intangible force that grows restless in all of me, or at least in this part of me that grows. Good Lord, the things that can happen to a man. He got up angrily and fumbling his way by the pale light that filtered through the windows went to release the latch on the door, then left the door slightly ajar, one only had to push it ever so gently. He returned to his bed. This is childish, if a man wants something, he does not leave it to chance but sets out to achieve it, consider what the Crusaders achieved in their time, swords against scimitars, prepared to die if necessary, and those castles and coats of armor. No longer knowing whether he is awake or finally asleep, he thinks about medieval chastity belts, the keys carried off by the knights, poor deluded creatures. The door of his room opens in silence, now it is closed, a shadowy figure crosses the room, groping toward the edge of the bed. The hand of Ricardo Reis reaches out and meets a frozen hand, draws it to him, Lydia trembles, all she can say is, I am cold. He remains silent, debating whether he should kiss her on the lips, such a depressing thought.

Doctor Sampaio and his daughter are due to arrive today, Salvador announced, as euphoric as if the good news would bring a reward. The lookout from the reception desk sees the train from Coimbra advancing from a distance through the afternoon haze, chug-chug, chug-chug. Quite paradoxical, because the ship that is anchored in port and gathering slime by the quay is the Hotel Bragança and it is the land that is coming here, sending smoke up the funnel. When the train arrives at Campolide, it goes underground before emerging from a black tunnel as it belches steam. There is still time to call Lydia and say, Go and make sure that everything is in order. The rooms of Doctor Sampaio and Senhorita Marcenda, as she is aware, are two hundred and four and two hundred and five. Lydia appeared not to notice that Doctor Ricardo Reis was standing there as she went bustling up to the second floor. How long are they staying, the doctor inquired. They usually stay for three days, tomorrow evening they will go to the theater, I have already reserved their seats. To the theater, which one. The Teatro Dona Maria. Ah. This interjection is not one of surprise, it has been inserted here to terminate a dialogue which we are unable or unwilling to continue. In fact, most people from the provinces, when they visit Lisbon, may Coimbra forgive me for putting it in the provinces, take the opportunity of going to the theater, perhaps a revue at the Parque Mayer or a film at the Apolo or the Avenida, while those with more refined tastes invariably go to the Teatro Dona Maria, also known as the Teatro Nacional. Ricardo Reis moved into the lounge, leafed through a newspaper, looked up the entertainment page, the theater guide, and saw advertised *Mar* by Alfredo Cortez. He decided then and there that he too would go to the theater. As a good Portuguese citizen he should support Portuguese artists. He almost asked Salvador to reserve him a seat by telephone, but changed his mind, deciding to tend to the matter himself next day.

There are still two hours to go before dinner. In the meantime the guests from Coimbra will arrive, unless their train is delayed. But why should I be interested, Ricardo Reis asks himself as he goes upstairs to his room. He tells himself that it is always agreeable to meet people from other parts, civilized people, besides there is the interesting clinical case presented by Marcenda. An unusual name, a name unknown to him, it resembles a murmuring, an echo, the bowing of a cello, *les sanglots longs de l'automne*, alabasters, balustrades, this morbid twilight poetry exasperates him, the things a name can provoke, Marcenda. He passes room two hundred and four, the door is open and inside Lydia is running a feather duster over the furniture. They look furtively at each other, she smiles, he does not. Shortly afterward he is back in his room and hears a gentle knocking on the door, it is Lydia, who steals in quietly and asks him, Are you annoyed with me. He barely replies, tight-lipped. Here in the light of day he does not know how to behave. She is only a chambermaid and he could lecherously stroke her hips now, but he feels much too awkward to make such a gesture. Earlier perhaps, but not after they have already been together, have lain in the same bed, a kind of consecration, mine, ours. If I can, I'll join you tonight, Lydia said, and he made no reply. That she should warn him beforehand seemed inopportune, with the girl with the paralyzed hand so near, sleeping and unaware of the nocturnal secrets of this corridor and of the room at the far end. But he was incapable of saying, Don't come. Lydia left, and he stretched out on the sofa to rest. Three nights of sexual activity after a long period of abstinence, and at his age, no wonder he can scarcely keep his eyes open. He knits his brow, asks himself, without finding the answer, whether he should pay Lydia, give her some little present, a pair of stockings, a cheap ring, something suitable for someone of her class. He must resolve this uncertainty, weighing the motives and reasons for and against. This is not like that business of whether or not to kiss her on the lips, circumstances made that decision for him, the so-called flame of passion, he himself did not know how it had happened, his kissing her as if she were the most beautiful woman in the world. Perhaps this will turn out to be just as easy, as they lie in each other's arms he will say, I'd like to give you a little memento, and she will find it quite natural. She is probably wondering even now why it has taken him so long.

Voices, footsteps can be heard in the corridor, Pimenta saying, Many thanks, sir, then two doors being closed. The travelers have arrived. He was almost asleep, now he stares up at the ceiling, examining the cracks in the plaster meticulously, as if tracing them with his fingertips. He imagines that he has the palm of God's hand overhead and is reading there the lines of life, of a life that narrows, is interrupted and revived, becomes more and more tenuous, a besieged heart solitary behind those walls. The right hand of Ricardo Reis, resting on the sofa, opens upward and reveals its own lines. Those two spots on the ceiling are like eyes. Who can tell who is reading us as we sit reading, oblivious of ourselves. Day turned to night some time ago, perhaps it is already time for dinner, but Ricardo Reis does not wish to be the first to go down. If I didn't hear them leaving their rooms, he thinks to himself, perhaps I slept without knowing it, and woke without realizing that I slept, I thought I was only dozing and I slept for a century. He sits up, uneasy, looks at his watch, it is already after eight-thirty, and at this very moment a man's voice can be heard in the corridor saying, Marcenda, I'm waiting for you. A door opens and there are vague sounds, footsteps moving away, then silence. Ricardo Reis rises, goes to the washbasin to freshen up, to comb his hair. The hair at his temples looks even whiter today, he ought to use one of those lotions or dyes that progressively restore the natural color to one's hair, Nhympha do Mondego, for example, a popular and reliable preparation that can be used to achieve the original tone without going any further, or it may be applied until the hair becomes as black as a raven's wing, if so desired. He is discouraged, however, by the idea of having to examine his hair each day, to check whether it is time to apply more lotion, mix more dye in a bowl, *Crown me with roses, I ask no more*. He changes his trousers and jacket, he must remember to tell Lydia they need pressing, and leaves his room with the incongruous and disagreeable presentiment that he will give this order without the neutrality of tone that an order should have when it is given by someone who naturally commands to someone who must naturally obey, if obeying and commanding are indeed natural. To put it more clearly, what Lydia will she be now, the one who heats the iron, folding the trousers on the ironing board to get a crease, inserting her left hand into the sleeve of the jacket near the shoulder so as to follow the line with the hot iron and restore its shape, no doubt remembering the body that wears these garments. If I can, I'll join you tonight, she said, and now brings down the iron nervously, alone in the laundry room. This is the suit Doctor Ricardo Reis will wear to the theater, if only I could accompany him. What a ninny, what's got into you, she dries two tears that will inevitably appear, they are tomorrow's tears. Ricardo Reis is still here, making his way down to the dining room, he has not told Lydia yet that he needs the suit she has just pressed, and she still does not know that she will weep.

Nearly all the tables are occupied. Ricardo Reis pauses at the entrance. The maître d' comes to guide him to his table, there's really no need, it's where he always sits, but what would life be like without these and other rituals, kneel when you pray, uncover your head when the flag is carried past, sit down, unfold your napkin on your knees, if you look around to see who is sitting near you, do it discreetly, nod to anyone you know. Which Ricardo Reis does. That couple, this guest sitting on his own, these people here. He also knows Doctor Sampaio and his daughter Marcenda, but they do not recognize him, the lawyer looks at him with a vacant expression, perhaps he is searching his memory, but he does not lean toward his daughter and whisper in her ear, Aren't you going to greet Doctor Ricardo Reis who has just arrived. It is she who glances at him a little later, looking over the waiter's sleeve as he serves her, the faintest tremor on her pale face, the faintest blush, an indication of recognition. She remembers, Ricardo Reis thought to himself, and in an excessively loud voice asked Ramón what there was for dinner. This might explain why Doctor Sampaio looked at him, but no, two seconds earlier Marcenda said to her father, That gentleman over there, he was staying in the hotel the last time we were here. As they rose from the table, Doctor Sampaio gave him a little nod, and Marcenda at her father's side not even that, restrained and discreet as befits a dutiful daughter. Ricardo Reis rose ever so slightly from his chair in acknowledgment, one has to be endowed with a sixth sense to measure these subtle gestures and greetings, and their reciprocation must be carefully balanced. Everything has been so perfect on this occasion that it augurs well for a blossoming friendship. Father and daughter have already withdrawn, no doubt they are making their way into the lounge, but no, they retire to their rooms. Later Doctor Sampaio will probably take a stroll despite the rainy weather, because Marcenda goes to bed early, she finds these train journeys exhausting. When Ricardo Reis enters the lounge, all he will see are a few taciturn guests, some reading newspapers, others yawning, while the radio quietly grinds out Portuguese songs from popular revues, strident and grating even though barely audible. In this light, or because of these somber faces, the mirror resembles an aquarium, and when Ricardo Reis crosses the lounge on the far side and comes back by the same route in order not to turn around and make a beeline for the doorway, he sees himself in the greenish abyss as if he were walking on the ocean floor amid wreckage and drowned corpses. He must leave this place at once, reach the surface, breathe again. He goes up to his chilly room. Why should these minor irritations depress him so, if that is what is troubling him, after all they are simply two people who live in Coimbra and come to Lisbon once a month. This doctor is not looking for patients, this poet has plenty of muses to inspire him, this man is not seeking a wife, he did not return to Portugal with that intention, and consider the difference in their ages. It is not Ricardo Reis who thinks these thoughts, nor one of those innumerable beings who exist within him, it is perhaps thought thinking itself while he looks on in amazement as a thread unwinds, leading him down unknown paths and corridors, at the end of which there waits a girl dressed in white, who cannot even hold a bouquet of flowers, because her right arm will be in his as they return from the altar treading the solemn red carpet to the strains of the wedding march. Ricardo Reis, as you can see, has already taken up the reins of thought, already controls and guides it, makes use of it to mock himself. The orchestra and red carpet are flights of fancy, and now, so that this poet's tale may have a happy ending, he accomplishes the clinical miracle of placing a bouquet of flowers in Marcenda's left arm and having it remain there without any assistance. The altar and priest can now disappear, the music cease, the wedding guests vanish in smoke and dust. The bridegroom withdraws, his services no longer required, the doctor has cured the patient, the rest must have been the work of the poet. These romantic episodes cannot be fitted into an Alcaic ode, which goes to prove, if any proof is needed, that what is written is often confused with what, having been experienced, gave birth to it, therefore one does not ask the poet what he thought or felt. It is precisely to avoid having to reveal these things that he composes verses.

The night passed and Lydia did not descend from the attic, Doctor Sampaio came back late, Fernando Pessoa is God knows where, then it was day, Lydia took away the suit for pressing, and Marcenda left with her father to keep their appointment with the specialist. She's gone for physiotherapy, says Salvador, who like most people cannot pronounce the word properly. For the first time Ricardo Reis finds it odd that a disabled girl should come to Lisbon when she lives in Coimbra, a city with such a wide range of specialists, for a course of treatment that can be administered just as easily there as here. Ultraviolet rays for example, unless applied with a certain frequency, provide little benefit. Ricardo Reis turns these doubts over in his mind as he goes down the Chiado on his way to the box office at the Teatro Nacional, but he was distracted at the sight of so many people wearing signs of mourning, a number of women in veils and the men even more conspicuous in their black suits and grave expressions, some even with mourning bands on their hats. George V of England, our oldest ally, was being buried. Despite the official mourning, there is a performance this evening, no disrespect intended, life must go on. The man in the box office sold him a seat in the stalls, and informed him, The fishermen will be in the audience tonight. What fishermen, asked Ricardo Reis before realizing that he had committed an unforgivable blunder. The box-office attendant frowned and altered his tone of voice, snapped, The fishermen from Nazaré, obviously. What others did he expect, there would be little sense in bringing fishermen from Caparica or from Póvoa. The journey and lodgings of the fishermen from Nazaré had been paid so that they might participate in this cultural event. Because they had inspired the play, it was only right that they should be represented, both the men and the women. Let's go to Lisbon, let's go and see the sea there, what gimmicks will be used to produce waves breaking over the stage, and what will Dona Palmira Bastos be like in the role of Ti Gertrudes, and Dona Amélia as Maria Bem, and Dona Lalande as Rosa, and Amarante in the role of Lavagante, how well will they imitate our lives. And since we are going, let's take this opportunity to ask the government, for the sake of the suffering souls in Purgatory, to build us the little port of refuge we have been in such need of since the first boat was launched from our shore, whenever that was. Ricardo Reis whiled away the afternoon in cafés, went to inspect the work being carried out on the Teatro Eden. Any day now they will remove the hoardings, the Chave de Ouro is almost ready to be inaugurated, and both natives and foreigners can see that Lisbon is progressing so rapidly that it will soon be able to compete with the great cities of Europe, and rightly so as the capital of a great empire. He did not dine in the hotel, only went back to change his clothes. His jacket, trousers, waistcoat too had been put neatly on a hanger, beautifully pressed, the work of loving hands, pardon the hyperbole, for how can there be love in the nocturnal coupling of a hotel guest and a chambermaid, he a poet, she by chance named Lydia, a different Lydia, although still fortunate, because the Lydia in his poems never heard his moans and sighs, she only sat on a riverbank listening to someone confide, *I suffer, Lydia, from the fear of destiny*. He ate a steak at the Restaurante Martinho, the one in the Rossio, and watched a keenly contested game of billiards, the chipped ball of Indian ivory rolling smoothly over the green baize. Since it was almost time for the performance to begin, he left, making a discreet approach and entering the theater, flanked by two large family groups. He had no wish to be seen until he himself chose the moment, heaven knows what emotional strategy he was pursuing, and crossed the foyer without pausing, one day it will be called a hallway or vestibule, unless some other term is borrowed from some other foreign language to say the same thing. At the entrance to the auditorium he was met by an usher, who led him down the left-hand aisle to the seventh row, It's that seat there, beside the lady. Don't let your imagination run riot, the man said lady, not girl, an usher in the Teatro Nacional can be relied upon to speak with decorum and the utmost clarity, his masters are the great dramatists of the classical and modern repertoire. Marcenda is sitting three rows ahead and to the right, too far to be near, and not even aware of my presence, she is sitting on her father's right, and just as well, for when she speaks to him and turns her head a little, Ricardo Reis can see her in profile. Is it because she is wearing her hair down that her face seems longer. She raises her right hand to the level of her chin, to clarify some word she has uttered or is about to utter, perhaps she is discussing the specialist who is treating her, perhaps the play they are about to see. Who is this Alfredo Cortez, her father cannot tell her much, he saw *The Gladiators* on his own two years ago and was not impressed, but this play caught his attention because of its traditional theme. It won't be long now before we discover what the play is like. This conversation, assuming it ever took place, was interrupted by the dragging of chairs overhead, by a loud whispering that made all the heads turn around and look upward. The fishermen from Nazaré have arrived and are getting into their seats in the boxes on the upper tier. They sit tall in order to see and be seen, both the men and the women are dressed in their own fashion, they are probably barefoot, one cannot see from down here. Some people in the audience applaud, others condescendingly join in. Irritated, Ricardo Reis clenches his fists, snobbish affectation in one who does not have blue blood, we might say, but this is not the case, it is simply a question of decorum, Ricardo Reis finds the outburst of applause vulgar, to say the very least.

The lights dim, the auditorium is in darkness, the loud knocks ascribed to Molière can be heard onstage, what terror they must strike in the hearts of the fishermen and their wives, perhaps they imagine them to be the last-minute hammerings of carpenters on the set. The curtain opens, a woman is lighting a fire, it is still night, from behind the scenery a man's voice can be heard, calling Mané Zé, Ah, Mané Zé, the play has started. The audience sighs, wavers, sometimes smiles, becomes excited as the first act ends with that great stampede of women, and when the lights go up, faces are animated, a good sign. There is shouting overhead, people calling from box to box, one could mistake those fishermen for the actors themselves, their way of speaking almost the same, whether better or worse depending on the measure of comparison. Reflecting on this, Ricardo Reis decides that the purpose of art is not imitation, that the author has made a serious error of judgment by writing the play in the dialect of Nazaré, or in what he supposed was the dialect of Nazaré, because reality does not tolerate its reflection, rather, it rejects it. Only a different reality, whatever it is, may be substituted for the reality one wishes to convey. The difference between them mutually demonstrates, explains, and measures them, reality as the invention it was, invention as the reality it will be. Ricardo Reis thinks these things with even greater confusion, it is difficult, after all, to think and clap one's hands at the same time. The audience applauds, and he joins in out of sympathy, for despite the use of dialect, grotesque as spoken by the actors, he is enjoying the play. Marcenda is not clapping, she cannot, but she is smiling. Most of the women remain seated, it's the men who need to stretch and exercise their legs, to pay a visit to the gents', to smoke a cigarette or cigar, exchange views with their friends, greet acquaintances, to see and be seen in the foyer. If they remain in their seats, it is generally for reasons of love and courtship. As they stand up, their eyes rove like those of hawks, they are the protagonists of their own drama, actors who perform during the intermission while the real actors back in their dressing rooms discard roles they will shortly resume. As he gets up, Ricardo Reis looks between the heads and sees that Doctor Sampaio is also getting up. Refusing with a nod, Marcenda remains seated. Her father, already on his feet, places his hand affectionately on her shoulder, then moves toward the aisle. Hurrying, Ricardo Reis reaches the foyer first. Shortly they will meet face to face, amid all these people who are walking up and down and conversing in an atmosphere soon thick with tobacco smoke. There are voices and commentaries, Palmira is splendid, In my opinion they've put far too many fishing nets on the stage, What a bunch of harpies, grappling with each other, you'd think they were in earnest, That's because you've never seen them, dear fellow, as I've seen them in Nazaré, there they fight like the Furies, At times it is difficult to make out what they're saying, Well that's how they talk there. Ricardo Reis moved among the groups, as attentive to their words as if he himself were the author of the play, while watching the movements of Doctor Sampaio from a distance, anxious that they should bump into each other as if by chance. Then he realized that Doctor Sampaio had spotted him, was heading his way, and was the first to speak, Good evening, how are you enjoying the play then. Ricardo Reis felt no need to say, What a surprise, what a coincidence, he immediately reciprocated the greeting, assured him that he was enjoying the play, and added, We are staying at the same hotel. Even so he ought to introduce himself, My name is Ricardo Reis. He hesitated, wondering whether he should add, I'm a doctor of medicine, I was living in Rio de Janeiro, I've been back in Lisbon less than a month. Doctor Sampaio barely listened, smiling, as if to say, If you knew Salvador as long as I have, you would realize that he has told me everything about you, and knowing him as well as I do, I guess he has told you about me and my daughter. Doctor Sampaio is undoubtedly shrewd, many years of experience as a notary bring certain advantages, We need hardly introduce ourselves, said Ricardo Reis. That's right. They went on almost immediately to discuss the play and the actors, treating each other with the utmost respect, Doctor Reis, Doctor Sampaio. A pleasant sense of equality is conferred upon them by their titles, and so they remained until the warning bell rang, when they returned to the auditorium together, and said, See you soon. Each went to his seat, Ricardo Reis, the first to sit down, kept watching, saw him speak to his daughter. She looked back, gave him a smile, he returned her smile, the second act was about to begin.

All three of them met during the next intermission. Even

though they knew all about each other, they still had to be introduced, Ricardo Reis, Marcenda Sampaio. It was inevitable, the moment they both awaited, they shook hands, right hand with right hand, her left hand hanging limp, trying to fade from sight, shy, as if nonexistent. Marcenda's eyes shone brightly, she was clearly moved by the sufferings of Maria Bem, perhaps there was a deep reason in her personal life for accompanying, word for word, that final speech made by the wife of Lavagante, If there is a hell, it can be no worse than this, Virgin Mother of the Seven Sorrows. Marcenda would have made this speech in the dialect of Coimbra, but speaking in a different dialect in no way changes these feelings which cannot be explained in words, I fully understand why you do not touch this arm, you who share the same hotel corridor, man of my curiosity, I am she who hailed you with a lifeless hand, don't ask me why, I haven't even asked myself that question, I simply hailed you, one day I will learn what prompted that gesture, or perhaps not, now you will withdraw rather than give me the impression that you are being indiscreet, inquisitive, taking advantage, as one would say, go, I will know where to find you, or you me, for you have not come here by chance. Ricardo Reis did not remain in the foyer but wandered in the aisles behind the boxes on the grand tier and peered up at the boxes overhead to get a closer look at the fishermen. But the warning bell started ringing, this second intermission was shorter, and when he reached the auditorium the lights were already beginning to dim. During the whole of the third act he divided his attention between the stage and Marcenda, who never once looked behind her. But she had slightly altered the position of her body so that he could see a little more of her face, a mere glimpse, and from time to time she drew back her hair on the left side with her right hand, very slowly, as if on purpose. What does this girl want, who is she, because people are not always what they seem. He saw her dry her cheeks as Lianor confesses that she stole the key of the life jacket so that Lavagante would die, and again when Maria Bem and Rosa, the one beginning, the other concluding, declare that this was an act of love and that love, being a noble sentiment, turns to torment when it is frustrated, and finally in the brief closing scene when Lavagante and Maria Bem are about to be united in the flesh. Suddenly the lights went up, the curtain fell to wild applause, and Marcenda was still drying her tears, now with a handkerchief. She was not alone, weeping women could be seen everywhere in the auditorium. Nervously smiling, the actors, such sensitive souls, acknowledged the ovation, made gestures as if returning it to the upper boxes occupied by the real heroes of these tales of love and adventure at sea. All inhibitions forgotten, the audience looked up in their direction, this is the communion of art, and applauded the intrepid fishermen and their courageous womenfolk. Even Ricardo Reis is clapping. Here in this theater one sees how easily understanding can be created between different classes and professions, between the rich, the poor, and those in-between, let us savor this rare spectacle of fraternity. The fishermen are now being coaxed to join the actors on the stage, the dragging of chairs can be heard once more. The performance is not over yet, the audience sits down. Now comes the climax, such merriment, such animation, such rejoicing, as the fishing community of Nazaré comes down the center aisle and climbs onto the stage. There they dance and sing the traditional airs of their region along with the actors, a night to be recorded forever in the annals of the Casa de Garrett. The leader of the group embraces the actor Robles Monteiro, the oldest of the fishwives receives a kiss from the actress Palmira Bastos, they all talk at once, utter bedlam, each speaking in his own dialect but managing to understand the others nonetheless, then there is more singing and dancing. The younger actresses demonstrate the traditional folk dance of Minho until the ushers finally start pushing us gently toward the exits. A dinner is to be served on stage, a communal love festival for the actors and their muses, corks will pop from the bottles of that sparkling wine which stings one's nostrils, the good women of Nazaré will be in fits of laughter once their heads start spinning, unaccustomed as they are to sparkling wine. Tomorrow, when the bus departs in the presence of journalists, photographers, and leaders of the corporations, the fishermen will give loud cheers for the New State and the Fatherland. One cannot be certain if they were paid to do so, but let us assume it is a spontaneous expression of gratitude at having been promised that port they so earnestly desire. If Paris was worth a mass, perhaps a few cheers will gain them salvation.

Ricardo Reis made no attempt to avert a second meeting as he left the theater. On the sidewalk he asked Marcenda if she had enjoyed the play. She confided that the third act had moved her deeply and brought tears to her eyes. Yes, I saw you weeping, he told her, and there the conversation ended. Having hailed a taxi, Doctor Sampaio suggested that Ricardo Reis might care to join them if he intended going straight back to the hotel. Thanking them, he declined. Until tomorrow then, Good-night, Pleased to meet you. The taxi drove off. He would have liked to accompany them, but realized it would be awkward, they would all feel ill at ease, be silent, finding another topic of conversation would not be easy, not to mention the delicate question of the seating arrangement, since there would not be room enough for three on the back seat, and Doctor Sampaio would not wish to travel in front leaving his daughter alone with a stranger. Yes, a stranger, and in propitious darkness, for even if there was not the slightest physical contact between them, the darkness would draw them together with hands of velvet, and they would be drawn together even more closely by their thoughts, which gradually would become secrets difficult to conceal. Nor would it be right to have Ricardo Reis sit beside the driver, you cannot offer someone a lift and then ask him to sit in front, facing the meter. Also, at the end of the ride it is inevitable that the person beside the driver will feel obliged to pay. The host, sitting in the back, cannot find his wallet but insists he will pay, saying, Leave this to me, telling the driver not to accept any money from the man in front, I'm paying the fare. The taxi driver patiently waits for them to make up their mind, this is an argument he has heard a thousand times, taxi drivers have to put up with such absurdities. With no other pleasures or obligations in store, Ricardo Reis walks back to his hotel. The night is cold and damp, but it is not raining. Now he feels like going for a stroll, he descends the entire Rua Augusta, crosses the Terreiro do Paço to take those steps leading down to the quayside where the dark polluted waters turn to spray only to fall back into the river from whence they came. There is no one else at the quayside, yet other men are watching the night, the flickering lights on the opposite embankment, the mooring lamps of the anchored ships. This one man, physically present, is watching today, but there are in addition the innumerable beings he claims to be, the others he has been each time he came here and who remember having been here, even though he does not remember. Eyes accustomed to the dark see much farther. In the distance are gray outlines of ships belonging to the squadron which has left the safety of the harbor. Although still rough, the weather is no longer too rough for the ships, a sailor's life is one of sacrifice. Seen from this distance, a number of ships appear to have the same dimensions, these must be the torpedo boats named after rivers. Ricardo Reis does not recall all of the luggage porter's litany, there was the *Tagus*, now sailing the Tagus, and the *Vouga*, and the *Dão*, which is nearest of all, as the man told him. Here then is the Tagus, here are the rivers that flow through my village, all flowing to the sea which receives water from all the rivers and then restores it. If only this regression were eternal, but alas, it will last only as long as the sun, mortal like all of us. Glorious is the death of those men who died with the setting sun, they did not see the first day but they will see the last.

This cold weather is not good for philosophical musings. His feet are freezing. A policeman paused warily to keep an eye on him. The man contemplating the water didn't strike him as a scoundrel or tramp but might be thinking of throwing himself into the river. At the thought of all the trouble this would cause, having to raise the alarm, fishing out the corpse, writing up a formal report of the incident, the policeman decided to approach him, not quite knowing what to say but hoping that his presence would be sufficient to discourage the would-be suicide, to persuade him to postpone this act of madness. Ricardo Reis heard footsteps, felt the coldness of the flagstones penetrate his feet. He must buy boots with thick soles. It was time to get back to the hotel before he caught a chill. He said, Good evening, officer. The policeman, reassured, asked, Is there anything wrong. No, nothing, it is the most natural thing in the world for a man to stroll along the quay, even at night, to watch the river and the ships. This is the Tagus which does not flow through my village, because the Tagus that flows through my village is called the Douro, but the fact that it does not have the same name does not mean that the river that flows through my village is any less beautiful. The policeman went off in the direction of the Rua da Alfândega, reflecting on the madness of certain people who appeared in the middle of the night. Whatever possessed this man to think he could enjoy a view of the river in such weather, if he were obliged like me to patrol the docks night after night he would soon find it tiresome. Ricardo Reis continued along the Rua do Arsenal and within ten minutes arrived at the hotel. Pimenta appeared on the landing with a bunch of keys, looked down, and withdrew, not waiting, as he usually did, for the guest to come upstairs, why should this be. Asking himself this natural question, Ricardo Reis began to worry. Perhaps he already knows about Lydia, he is bound to find out sooner or later, a hotel is like a glass house. Pimenta, who never leaves the place and knows every nook and cranny, must suspect something. Good evening, Pimenta, he said with exaggerated warmth, and the other replied with no apparent reserve, no trace of hostility. Perhaps I'm mistaken, Ricardo Reis thought, and when Pimenta handed him his key, he was about to continue on but turned back and opened his wallet, This is for you, Pimenta, and handed him a twenty-escudo note. He gave no explanation and Pimenta asked no questions.

No light came from any of the rooms. Ricardo Reis went quietly down the corridor for fear of disturbing the sleeping guests. For three seconds he paused outside the door of Marcenda's room. In his room the air was cold and damp, not much better than out by the river. He shivered, as if still gazing at those livid ships and listening to the policeman's footsteps. What would have happened had he replied, Yes, there is something wrong, although he would not have been able to elaborate. Approaching the bed, he noticed a bulge in the eiderdown, something had been placed between the sheets, a hot-water bottle, he was sure, but to make certain he put his hand on top. It was warm. She was a good sort, Lydia, just like her to remember to warm his bed, these were little comforts for the chosen few. She probably won't come tonight. He lay down, opened the book at his bedside, the one about Herbert Quain, glanced at a couple of pages without taking in the sense. Three motives had been suggested for the crime, each in itself sufficient to incriminate the suspect, on whom all three converged, but the aforesaid suspect, availing himself of the law, argued that the real motive, were it to be proven that he was in fact the criminal, might be a fourth or fifth or sixth motive, each motive equally feasible, and so the full explanation of the crime could be reached only in the interrelation between all these motives, in the effect of each on each in every combination until finally the effects all canceled out, the result being death. Moreover, one had to consider to what extent the victim himself was responsible, which possibility could provide, both morally and legally, a seventh and even definitive motive. Ricardo Reis felt restored, the hot-water bottle was warming his feet, his brain worked without any interference from the outside world, the tediousness of the book made his eyelids heavy. He shut his eyes for a moment, and when he opened them, Fernando Pessoa was sitting at the foot of the bed as if he had come to visit the sick. That same estranged look had been captured for posterity in several portraits, the hands crossed over the right thigh, the head slightly forward, deathly pale. Ricardo Reis put his book aside between the two pillows. I didn't expect you at this late hour, he said, and smiled amiably lest his visitor catch the note of impatience in his voice, the ambiguity of his words which amounted to saying, I could have done without your visit today. And he had good reason, two to be precise, the first being that he felt like talking, but not to Fernando Pessoa, about his evening at the theater, the second being that Lydia might enter the room at any moment. Not that there was any danger of her crying out, Help, a ghost, but Fernando Pessoa, though it was not in his nature, might wish to stay and witness these intimacies of flesh and spirit, the possibility could not be ruled out. God, who is God, frequently does this, nor can He avoid it, since He is everywhere, but that is something we accept. Ricardo Reis appealed to masculine complicity, We cannot chat for long, I am expecting a visitor, you must agree that it could be embarrassing. You don't waste time, you've been here less than three weeks and already you're involved in amorous intrigues, at least I presume they are amorous. It depends what you mean by amorous, she's a chambermaid in the hotel. My dear Reis, you, an aesthete, intimate with all the goddesses of Olympus, sharing your bed with a chambermaid, with a servant, and I used to listen to you speak incessantly and with the utmost constancy of your Lydia, Neaera, and Chloe, and now you tell me you are infatuated with a chambermaid, you deeply disappoint me. The chambermaid's name is Lydia and I am not infatuated, I am not one for infatuation. Ah, so this much-praised poetic justice exists after all, what an amusing situation, you clamored for Lydia at such length that Lydia finally came, you have been more fortunate than Camões who, in order to win his Natércia, was obliged to invent the name but got no further, so the name Lydia came but not the woman, don't be ungrateful, how do you know what the Lydia of your odes is like, supposing such a phenomenon exists, an intolerable embodiment of passivity, thoughtful silence, and pure spirit, indeed, it is doubtful, as doubtful in fact as the existence of the poet who wrote your odes. But I did write them. Allow me to be skeptical, my dear Reis, I see you there reading a detective story with a hot-water bottle at your feet and waiting for a chambermaid to come and warm the rest of you, if you'll pardon the expression, and you expect me to believe that you are the same man who wrote, *Serene and watching life from a distance*, I must ask you where you were when you watched life from a distance. You yourself wrote that a poet is someone who pretends. We utter such intuitions without knowing how we arrive at them, unfortunately I died without discovering whether it is the poet who pretends to be a man or the man who pretends to be a poet. To pretend and to deceive oneself are not the same thing. Is that a statement or a question. It is a question. Of course they're not the same, I only invented, but you invented yourself, if you want to see the difference, read my poems and go back and read your own. This conversation is certain to keep me up all night. Perhaps your Lydia will come and cradle you in her arms, from what they tell me chambermaids who worship their masters can be extremely affectionate. You sound vexed. Perhaps I am. Tell me something, is my pretense that of a poet or a man. Your situation, Reis my friend, is hopeless, you have invented yourself, you are your own invention, and this has nothing to do with either man or poet. Hopeless. Is that another question, It is, Yes, hopeless, first of all because you do not know who you are, And what about you, did you ever discover who you were, I no longer count, I'm dead, but don't worry, there will be lots of people ready to explain everything about me. Perhaps I came back to Portugal to learn who I am. Nonsense, my dear fellow, childish nonsense, revelations of this kind are only to be found in works of mysticism and on roads leading to Damascus, don't forget that we're in Lisbon and no roads lead from here. I can scarcely keep my eyes open. I'll leave you now to get some sleep, sleep is really the only thing I envy you, only fools believe that sleep is the cousin of death, cousin or brother, I can't remember, I think it's cousin, after so few words of sympathy, do you really want me to return. Please do, I don't have many people to confide in. That is certainly a valid reason. Listen, do me a favor, leave the door ajar, it will save me getting out of bed and catching cold. Are you still expecting company. One never knows, Fernando, one never knows.

Half an hour later, the door was pushed open. Lydia, shivering after a lengthy crossing of stairs and corridors, slipped into his bed, curled up beside him, and asked, Was the theater nice, and he told her the truth, Yes, very nice.

Marcenda and her father did not appear for lunch. To discover why did not require any great tactical subtlety on the part of Ricardo Reis, or any of the dialectical cunning of a detective carrying out an investigation, he simply gave Salvador and himself a little time, chatting idly, his elbows resting on the reception desk with the self-assured air of a friendly guest, and in passing, as a parenthesis or fleeting rhetorical digression, a melody that unexpectedly surfaces during the development of another, he informed Salvador that he had met and made the acquaintance of Doctor Sampaio and his daughter, the most agreeable and refined of people. The smile on Salvador's face became slightly contorted, after all he had spoken to the two guests when they left and they had not mentioned the encounter with Doctor Reis in the theater. Now he knew, true, but not until almost two in the afternoon. How could such a thing happen. Of course he did not expect a written note upon their return telling him, We came across Doctor Reis, I met Doctor Sampaio and his daughter, nevertheless he felt it was a great injustice to have kept him in the dark for so many hours. A hotel manager who is on such friendly terms with the guests should not be treated in this way, what an ungrateful world. For a smile to become contorted, since we are on the subject, only a moment is needed, and it may last only a moment, but to explain the contortion may require a little longer. The fact is that the human mind has such deep recesses that if we venture therein with the intention of examining everything, there is a good chance that we will not emerge quickly. Not that Ricardo Reis made any close examination, all he perceived was that a sudden thought had troubled Salvador, and so it had. Yet even had he tried to figure out what that thought was, he never would have succeeded, which goes to show how little we know each other and how soon our patience runs out when from time to time, though not frequently, we try to find motives, to explain impulses, unless we are dealing with a genuine criminal investigation as in *The God of the Labyrinth*. Salvador overcame his annoyance before one could count to ten, as the saying goes, and allowing himself to be guided solely by his good nature he expressed his delight, praising Doctor Sampaio and his daughter, he a thorough gentleman, she a most refined young lady so carefully brought up, what a pity her life was so sad, with that disability or illness. Between ourselves, Doctor Reis, I don't believe there is a cure. Ricardo Reis had not started the conversation to become involved in a medical debate for which he had already declared himself unqualified, therefore he turned the discussion to what mattered, or mattered to him, without knowing to what extent it mattered, the fact that Doctor Sampaio and Marcenda had not come down for lunch. Suddenly aware of the possibility, he asked, Have they already gone back to Coimbra. Salvador, who could at least claim to know everything in this regard, replied, No, not until tomorrow, today they lunch in the Baixa because Senhorita Marcenda has an appointment with the specialist and then they will take a look around and purchase a few items they need. But will they be dining here this evening. Most certainly. Ricardo Reis moved away from the reception desk, took two paces, changed his mind, and announced, I think I'll take a stroll, the weather looks settled. Salvador, with the tone of one who is merely passing on useless information, said, Senhorita Marcenda said she intended to return to the hotel after lunch and that she would not be accompanying her father on some business matters. Now Ricardo Reis went into the lounge, looked out the window with a weather eye, and returned to the reception desk. On second thought, I'll stay here and read the papers, it isn't raining but it must be cold. Salvador, wholeheartedly endorsing this new proposal, said, I'll have a paraffin heater put in the lounge right away. He rang the hand bell twice. A chambermaid appeared, but it wasn't Lydia. Ah, Carlota, light a heater and put it in the lounge. Whether such details are indispensable or not for a clear understanding of this narrative is something each of us must judge for himself, and the judgment will vary according to our attention, mood, and temperament. There are those who value broad ideas above all, who prefer panoramas and historical frescoes, whereas others appreciate the affinities and contrasts between small brush strokes. We are well aware that it is impossible to please everyone, but here it was simply a question of allowing enough time for the feelings, whatever they might be, to develop between and within the protagonists while Carlota goes back and forth, while Salvador struggles with some difficult calculations, while Ricardo Reis asks himself if he has aroused suspicions by suddenly changing his mind.

Two o'clock came, then two-thirty, the Lisbon newspapers with their faint print were read and reread, the headlines on the front page. Edward VIII to be crowned King of England, the Minister of the Interior congratulated by historian Costa Brochado, wolves are prowling urban areas, the Anschluss plan, which, for those who may not know, proposes the annexation of Austria to Germany, has been repudiated by the Austrian Patriotic Front. The French government has tendered its resignation, and the rift between Gil Robles and Calvo Sotelo could endanger the electoral bloc of the Spanish right-wing parties. Then the advertisements. Pargil is the best elixir for oral hygiene, tomorrow evening the famous ballerina Marujita Fontan will make her debut at the Arcádia, we present the latest automobiles manufactured by Studebaker, the President, the Dictator, if the advertisement of Freire the Engraver offered the universe, this one epitomizes the world in which we live today, an automobile called the Dictator, a clear sign of the times and of contemporary taste. From time to time the buzzer sounds, people leaving, people arriving, a guest checking in, a sharp ping on the bell from Salvador, Pimenta carrying up the luggage, then silence, prolonged and oppressive. The afternoon turns gloomy, it is after three-thirty. Ricardo Reis gets up from the sofa, drags himself to the reception desk, Salvador looks at him with sympathy, even compassion, So you've finished reading all the newspapers. Everything now happens so quickly that Ricardo Reis is given no time to reply. The sound of the buzzer, a voice at the bottom of the stairs, I say Pimenta, could I ask you to help me carry these parcels upstairs. Pimenta goes down, comes up again, Marcenda with him, and Ricardo Reis does not know what to do, should he remain where he is, go back and sit down and pretend that he is reading or dozing in the gentle warmth. If he does so, what will that cunning spy Salvador think. He is undecided between these two courses of action as Marcenda arrives at the desk and says, Good afternoon, and is taken by surprise, Why it's you, Doctor. I was reading the papers, he replies, but hastens to add, I've just this minute finished. These are disastrous sentences, much too peremptory, if I'm reading the papers I'm not interested in conversation, and if I've just finished reading them then I'm on my way out. Feeling utterly ridiculous, he goes on to say, It's quite warm in here. Appalled at the banality of this statement, he still cannot make up his mind, he cannot go back and sit down again, not just yet, if he does she will think he wishes to be alone, and if he waits until she goes up to her room she will think that he is going out. Any move on his part must be carefully timed so that she will think that he has been waiting for her. All of which proved unnecessary, because Marcenda simply said, I am going up to put these things in my room and will come right down for a little chat, if you have the patience to bear with me and don't have more important things to do. We should not be surprised that Salvador is smiling, he likes to see his clients strike up friendships, it is good for the hotel's image, creates a pleasant atmosphere, and even if we were surprised, it does not help the story to speak at length of a thing that no sooner does it surface than it disappears. Ricardo Reis also smiled, and speaking slowly, assured her, I would be delighted, or words to that effect, for there are many other expressions equally commonplace, although to our shame we never stop to analyze them. We should remember them, empty and colorless as they are, as they were spoken and heard for the first time, It will be a pleasure, I am entirely at your service, little declarations of such daring that they cause the person making them to hesitate, and cause the person to whom they are addressed to tremble, because that was a time when words were pristine and feelings came to life.

Marcenda lost no time in coming down. She had tidied her hair, freshened her lipstick, some consider such things automatic, responses in the mirror, while others believe that a woman is conscious of her appearance in all circumstances, and of her moods and the least flirtatious gesture. Ricardo Reis rose to greet her and led her to the sofa which stood at a right angle to his own, reluctant to suggest that they should move to another, more spacious sofa where they might sit side by side. Marcenda sat down, resting her left hand on her lap, and smiled in a strange remote way, as if to say, Take a good look, my hand is quite helpless. Ricardo Reis was about to ask, Are you tired, when Salvador appeared and asked if he could bring them anything, some coffee or tea. They accepted, a coffee would be most welcome in this cold weather. But first Salvador checked the heater, which filled the room with a smell of paraffin that made one feel slightly giddy, while the flame, subdivided into a thousand tiny blue tongues, whispered incessantly. Marcenda asked Ricardo Reis if he enjoyed the play. He said he did, although he found the naturalism of the performance somewhat artificial. He tried to explain more clearly, In my opinion, a stage performance should never be natural, what is presented on stage is theater, not life, life cannot be reproduced, even the most faithful of reflections, that of a mirror, transforms right into left and left into right. But did you enjoy it or not, Marcenda insisted. Yes, he said, and after all one word sufficed. At this moment Lydia entered, put the coffee tray down on the table, asked if they wished anything else. Marcenda said, No, many thanks, but Lydia was looking at Ricardo Reis, who had not raised his eyes and who was carefully taking his cup and asking Marcenda, How many spoons. Two, she replied. Lydia's presence was clearly no longer required, so she withdrew, much too hastily to Salvador's mind, and he reprimanded her from his throne, Be careful with that door.

Putting her cup down on the tray, Marcenda placed her right hand over her left. Both were cold, yet between the two was the difference between the quick and the dead, between what can still be salvaged and what is forever lost. My father would not be pleased if he knew that I am about to take advantage of our acquaintance by asking your medical opinion. Do you want my opinion about your infirmity. Yes, about this arm which cannot move, this wretched hand of mine. I hope you will understand my reluctance to offer any advice, first because I am not a specialist, second because I know nothing of your clinical history, third because professional etiquette forbids my interfering in a case being handled by a colleague. I know all that, but no one can prevent an invalid from having a doctor as a friend and consulting him about her personal problems. Of course not. Then answer my question as a friend. I am happy to be your friend, to use your own words, after all we have known each other for a month. Then you will give me your opinion. I will try, but first must ask you one or two questions. Ask me anything you like, this is another of those phrases we could add to the long list of expressions that meant a great deal once, when words were still in their infancy, At your service, Happy to oblige, It will give me great pleasure, Whatever you wish. Lydia came back into the lounge and saw at a glance that Marcenda was blushing, saw the tears in her eyes, saw Ricardo Reis resting his left cheek on his clenched fist. Both were silent, as if they had come to the end of an important conversation or were preparing for one, what could it have been, what will it be. Lydia took the tray. We all know how coffee cups shake if not placed firmly on their respective saucers, something we must always check when we are not altogether certain that our hands are steady and if we do not want to hear Salvador warn, Careful with that crockery.

Ricardo Reis seemed to reflect. Then, leaning forward, he extended his hands to Marcenda and asked, May I. She also leaned forward slightly, and with her right hand put her left into his hands as if it were an injured bird, its wing broken, a lead pellet embedded in its breast. Slowly, gently but firmly applying pressure, he ran his fingers over the hand, up to the wrist, for the first time in his life knowing what is meant by total surrender, the absence of any reaction, be it voluntary or instinctive, of any resistance, worse, it seemed an alien body, not of this world. Marcenda stared fixedly at her hand, that paralyzed mechanism. Other doctors have probed those lifeless muscles, those useless nerves, those bones that protect nothing, now they are being touched by this man to whom she has entrusted them, if Doctor Sampaio were to walk in this moment, he would not believe his eyes. But no one came into the lounge, usually the scene of so much traffic. Today it is a place for quiet intimacy. Slowly withdrawing his hand, Ricardo Reis looked at his own fingers without knowing why, then asked, How long has it been like this. Four years last December, Did it come about gradually or all of a sudden, Would you call a month gradually or all of a sudden, Are you telling me that within a month you completely lost the power in your arm, I am. Was there any prior sign that something might be wrong, No, No injury, heavy fall or blow, None, What did the doctor say, That it is the consequence of my heart disease, You didn't tell me that you suffer from heart disease, I thought you were interested only in my arm, What else did the doctor say, In Coimbra they told me there is no cure, here, the same thing, but the latest specialist, who has been treating me for almost two years now, says that I can get better. What treatment is he giving you, Massage, sunlamp treatment, electric shock, With what results, None, Your arm does not respond to electric shock, It responds, it jumps, trembles, then is still again. Ricardo Reis fell silent, perceiving a sudden note of hostility and resentment, as if Marcenda were telling him to stop asking so many questions, or to ask her other, different ones, this question for example, Can you remember if something important happened at that time, or, more to the point, have you experienced some misfortune. Marcenda's face showed that she was close to tears. Apart from this problem with your hand, are you troubled by some unhappiness, Ricardo Reis asked her. She nodded, began to gesture but could not finish, convulsed by a deep sob as if her heart had been wrenched, and tears ran uncontrollably down her cheeks. Alarmed, Salvador appeared in the doorway, but Ricardo Reis dismissed him brusquely. Salvador withdrew, lingering just outside the door. Marcenda pulled herself together, only her tears continued to flow, but quietly, and when she spoke, the note of hostility, if that was what it had been, was gone from her voice. After my mother died I found I could no longer use my arm. But you told me only a moment ago that the doctors said the paralysis was the result of heart disease. That is what they said, And do you believe them, I do, Then why do you think that there is a connection between your mother's death and the paralysis in your arm, I am certain of it, but cannot explain it. She paused, summoned what remained of her animosity, and snapped, I am not looking for a healer of souls. Nor am I a healer of souls, just an ordinary doctor in general practice. It was now Ricardo Reis who was irritated. Marcenda raised her hand to her eyes and said, Forgive me, I am annoying you. You are not annoying me, I would gladly help you in whatever way I can. Probably no one can, I had to confide in someone, that was all. So you are truly convinced that this connection exists, As truly as we're sitting here together, And are you not able to move your arm just by knowing that the paralysis came about only because your mother died. Is that all it is, Yes, that's all, which is saying a great deal, because for you, given your deep conviction, there was no other cause, the time has come to ask yourself a straightforward question, is your arm immobile because you cannot move it or because you do not wish to. These words were uttered in a whisper, sensed rather than heard, and Marcenda would not have sensed them had she not been expecting them. Salvador strained to hear, but Pimenta's footsteps could be heard on the landing, he came to ask if there were any documents to be taken to the police. This question, too, was asked in a low voice, and for the same reason, so that the reply would not be heard. Sometimes a reply is not even spoken, trapped between one's teeth, one's lips, and if spoken, it remains inaudible, a tenuous yes or no that dissolves in the shadows of a hotel lounge like a drop of blood in a transparent sea, present but invisible. Marcenda did not say, Because I cannot, she did not say, Because I do not wish to, instead she looked at Ricardo Reis and asked, Have you any advice to offer, something that might lead to a cure, some treatment. I already told you that I'm not a specialist, but as far as I can judge, Marcenda, if you are suffering from heart disease, you are also suffering from yourself. That's the first time anyone ever told me that. We are all ill, with one malaise or another, a deep-rooted malaise that is inseparable from what we are and that somehow makes us what we are, you might even say that each one of us is his own illness, we are so little because of it, and yet we succeed in being so much because of it. But my arm doesn't move, my hand is completely useless. Perhaps it does not move because it does not choose to. This conversation, forgive me, has got us nowhere. You said you feel no improvement, I do not, Then why do you keep coming to Lisbon, It is not my doing, my father insists, and he has his own reasons, What reasons, I am twenty-three years of age, unmarried, brought up never to discuss certain things even though I might think them, for thinking is something one cannot avoid. Can't you be more explicit, Is that necessary. *Lisbon, despite being Lisbon and having ships at sea*, What's that, A line of verse, I don't remember who wrote it, Now it's my turn not to understand. Although Lisbon has so much, it doesn't have every-thing, yet there are some who think that here they will find their heart's desire. If in this roundabout way you are asking me whether my father has a mistress in Lisbon, the answer is yes. Surely your father doesn't need to justify his visits to Lisbon when he has a daughter in need of medical advice, besides he is still a young man, widowed, and therefore free. As I said before, I was brought up not to mention certain things, yet I go on mentioning them slyly, I am like my father, given the position he holds and the kind of education he received, I believe that the more secretive the better. A good thing I didn't have children. Why. There is no mercy in the eyes of one's children. I love my father. I believe you, but love is not enough. Obliged to remain behind the desk, Salvador has no idea what he is missing, revelations, confidences freely exchanged between two people who barely know each other, but to hear he would have to be seated here, on this third sofa, leaning forward, reading on their lips the words they scarcely utter. It would almost be easier to understand the murmuring of the paraffin heater than these subdued voices, they come as if from the confessional, may we be forgiven all our sins.

Marcenda placed her left hand in the palm of her right. Untrue, she did not, the sentence suggests that her left hand was capable of obeying such a command transmitted by the brain. One would need to be present to see how this was done. First the right hand slipped underneath the left, then held the wrist with the little finger and fourth finger, and now both came toward Ricardo Reis, each hand offering the other, or pleading for help, or simply resigned to the inevitable. Tell me, do you think I will ever be cured. I cannot say, you have been like this for four years without any improvement, your own doctor has all the details of your medical history, which I don't, besides, as I've already explained, I have no competence in this field. Should I stop coming to Lisbon, tell my father that I accept the situation, that he shouldn't waste any more money trying to find a cure. Your father has two reasons for coming to Lisbon, if you take away one of them he may or may not find the courage to continue coming on his own, but he will have lost the alibi your illness provided, at present he sees himself only as the father who wishes his daughter cured. What should I do then. We two scarcely know each other, I have no right to give you advice, Please, I am asking it, Don't give up, keep coming to Lisbon for your father's sake, even if you no longer believe there is a cure, I have almost stopped believing in a cure, Cling to whatever belief you have left, believing will be your alibi, Alibi for what, To hope, Hope in what, Hope, just hope, one reaches a point where there is nothing but hope, and that is when we discover that hope is everything. Marcenda leaned back on the sofa, slowly stroking her left hand, her back to the window, her face scarcely visible. Normally Salvador would appear now to turn on the chandelier, the pride and joy of the Hotel Bragança, but on this occasion he does not, as if to show his displeasure at being excluded from a conversation which he, after all, made possible. This is how they repay him, sitting there rapt in conversation, whispering almost in darkness. No sooner did he think this than the chandelier went on, Ricardo Reis had taken the initiative, because anyone walking into the lounge would have been suspicious to find a man and a woman together in the shadows, even if the man was a doctor and the woman a cripple. Much worse, this, than the backseat of a taxi. As was to be expected, Salvador appeared, I was coming this very moment to switch on the light, Doctor. He smiled, and they smiled too, gestures and postures according to the rules of civilized behavior, part hypocrisy, part necessity, to disguise our anguish. After Salvador withdrew, there was a long silence, it seemed less easy to speak with all this light, then Marcenda said, Without wishing to pry into your affairs, can I ask you why you have been living for a whole month in this hotel. I still haven't decided whether or not to look for a place, I may return to Rio de Janeiro. Salvador tells me that you lived there for sixteen years, what made you decide to come back. I felt homesick. You've got over it quickly, if already you're talking about leaving. It isn't exactly that, when I embarked for Lisbon, I felt I could put it off no longer, there were important matters to be dealt with here. And now. And now, he broke off, staring into the mirror ahead, now I am like an elephant that senses its approaching end and begins heading for the place where it must die. If you return to Brazil for good, then that will be the place where the elephant goes to die. When a man emigrates, he thinks of the country where he might die as the country where he will spend the rest of his life, and that is the difference. Perhaps, when I return to Lisbon next month, you will no longer be here. By then I might have found a place to live, opened a practice, settled into a routine. Or you might have returned to Rio de Janeiro. You will be informed, our friend Salvador will pass on all the news. I will come in order not to lose hope, And I will be here, if I have not lost hope.

Marcenda is twenty-three. We don't know for certain what kind of education she has received, but being the daughter of a notary, and from Coimbra no less, she almost certainly attended grammar school. Had it not been for her illness, no doubt she would have enrolled in some faculty, perhaps law or arts, preferably arts, because apart from the fact that we already have a lawyer in the family, the tedious study of codes and regulations is not suitable for women. If only she had been born a boy, to continue the Sampaio dynasty and legal practice. But this isn't the problem, the problem here is to find a young woman at this time in Portugal capable of sustaining such a lengthy and elevated conversation, we mean elevated when compared with the standards of the day. She did not make a single frivolous remark, showed no pretentiousness, did not affect wisdom or try to compete with the male, if you'll pardon the expression, she spoke naturally, was obviously intelligent, perhaps in compensation for her disability, something which can happen with women as well as with men. She rises from the sofa, holds her left hand up to her breast and smiles, I am deeply grateful for the patience you have shown me. No need to thank me, I enjoyed our conversation. Are you dining here this evening, Yes, I am, Then we shall see each other soon, good-bye for now. Ricardo Reis watched her leave, she was not as tall as he remembered her, but slender, that was why his memory had deceived him. He heard her say to Salvador, Tell Lydia to come to my room as soon as she is free. Ricardo Reis alone will find this request startling, because certain shameful acts of promiscuity between social classes are weighing on his conscience. What could be more natural than a maid's being summoned to a guest's bedroom, especially if the guest in question needs help to change her dress, for example, because her arm is paralyzed. Ricardo Reis stays a little longer, switches on the radio just as they are broadcasting the music from *The Sleeping Beauty*, one of those coincidences which only a novelist would exploit to draw parallels between a silent lake and a young virgin. Although this has not been mentioned and she herself does not declare it, Marcenda is a virgin, a wholly private matter, even a fiancé, should she ever have one, will not dare to ask, Are you a virgin. For the time being and in this social ambiance one assumes that she is. Later, at the opportune moment, we may discover with some indignation that she wasn't after all. The music came to an end, was followed by a Neapolitan song, a serenata or something of the kind, *amore mio, cuore ingrato, con te, la vita insieme, per sempre*, the tenor was singing these heartfelt protestations when into the lounge came two guests sporting diamond tiepins in their cravats, their double chins concealing the knots. They sat down, lit their cigars, were about to discuss a business deal involving cork or canned fish, we would know for certain except that Ricardo Reis is now leaving, so engrossed that he even forgets to greet Salvador. Something strange is going on in this hotel.

Later that evening Doctor Sampaio arrives. Ricardo Reis and Marcenda have not left their rooms. Lydia has been seen from time to time on the stairs or in the halls, but only where she has been summoned. She was rude to Pimenta, and he gave her as good as he got, the incident occurring out of everyone's hearing, and just as well, because Salvador would certainly have demanded an explanation from Pimenta, who was muttering insinuations about certain people who walked in their sleep and could be found wandering down corridors in the middle of the night. It was eight o'clock when Doctor Sampaio knocked on the door. He would not bother coming in, thank you all the same, he had only called to invite Ricardo Reis to join them for dinner, Marcenda had told him about their little chat, I am greatly indebted to you, Doctor. Ricardo Reis insisted that he come in and sit down for a moment. I didn't do anything, simply listened and gave the only advice that could be given by someone without any special knowledge of the case, to persevere with the treatment, not to become disheartened. That's what I'm always telling her, but she no longer pays attention, you know what children are, yes Papa, but she comes to Lisbon without any real interest, and yet she must come so that the specialist can follow the progression of her illness, though of course the treatment itself is administered in Coimbra. But surely there are specialists in Coimbra. Very few, and those we consulted, without wishing to give offense, did not inspire much confidence, whereas the specialist in Lisbon is a man of considerable skill and experience. These absences from Coimbra must interfere with your work. Sometimes, but no father worthy of the name would refuse to sacrifice some time for his children. In this vein they exchanged a few more phrases matched in subtlety of intent, concealing as much as they revealed, as tends to happen in conversations in general and in this one in particular, for the reasons known to us, until Doctor Sampaio finally decided it was time to withdraw. Well then, we will knock on your door at nine, No, I will come by, I don't see why you should go to any trouble. And so at the appointed hour Ricardo Reis knocked on the door of room two hundred and five. It would have been most indelicate to have knocked on Marcenda's door first, another of those subtle formalities.

Their entrance into the dining room was unanimously greeted with smiles and little deferential nods. Salvador, his annoyance forgotten or diplomatically suppressed, threw open the glass-paneled doors, and Ricardo Reis and Marcenda walked in front as etiquette demanded, he is their guest. From where we are standing we can scarcely hear the radio, there would be much food for thought if it should happen to be the wedding march from *Lohengrin* or the one by Mendelssohn or, less well known, perhaps because it is played as the prelude to disaster, the one in *Lucia di Lammermoor* by Donizetti. Needless to say, the table where they will sit is that of Doctor Sampaio, which is invariably waited upon by Felipe, but Ramón does not abdicate his prerogative, he will assist his colleague and compatriot. Both of them were born in Villagarcia de Arosa, it is the destiny of humans to follow their own distinct paths in life. Some have followed theirs from Galicia to Lisbon, while this man Reis was born in Oporto, for a time lived in the capital, then emigrated to Brazil, and the two people with him have been shuttling back and forth between Coimbra and Lisbon for the last three years. Each is searching, for a cure, for money, for peace of mind, for pleasure, each has his own goal, which explains why it is so difficult to satisfy all who are in need. The dinner passes tranquilly. Marcenda is seated on her father's right, her left hand reclining as usual at the side of her plate, but curiously enough it is not hiding, on the contrary, it almost appears to glory in being seen, and if you think that word excessive, then you certainly haven't heard how ordinary people speak. Let us not forget, either, that this hand has rested in the hands of Ricardo Reis, and how should it feel if not glorious. Marcenda's disability is not discussed, the noose has been mentioned far too often already in the house of this woman condemned to the gallows. Doctor Sampaio is speaking of the wonders of the Athens of Portugal, There I was born into the world, there I was reared, there I graduated, there I exercise my profession, I swear the city is incomparable. His style is vigorous, but there is no danger of entering into an argument at the table about the merits of Coimbra compared with other cities, whether Oporto or Villagarcia de Arosa. Ricardo Reis does not care where one was born, and Felipe and Ramón would never dare to join in the conversation. They know their place, which is not the place of their birth. It was inevitable that Doctor Sampaio should learn that Ricardo Reis had gone to Brazil for political reasons, although it is hard to say how he learned it. Salvador did not tell him, because he does not know either, nor did Ricardo Reis confide it, but certain things are gleaned from broken words, moments of silence, a glance. He only had to say, I left for Brazil in nineteen nineteen, the year in which the monarchy was restored in the north, he only had to use a certain tone of voice, and the notary's sharp ear, accustomed to listening to falsehoods, oaths, confessions, was not deceived. It was inevitable, then, that the conversation should turn to politics. By indirect routes, testing the ground, trying to detect hidden mines or snares, but feeling incapable of changing the topic, Ricardo Reis allowed himself to be carried along, and before the dessert he had already stated that he had no faith in democracies and heartily despised socialism. You're among friends, Doctor Sampaio assured him with a smile. Marcenda showed little interest in their conversation, for some reason she placed her left hand on her lap. If there had been glorying, it was now burned out. What we need, my dear Reis, in this corner of Europe, is a man of vision and firm resolve to head our government and run the country. These were the words spoken by Doctor Sampaio, who continued, There is no possible comparison between the Portugal you knew when you left for Rio de Janeiro and the Portugal you have come back to find, I know that you have only recently returned, but if you have been around and kept your eyes open, you must have noticed enormous changes, greater prosperity, public order, a coherent plan to encourage patriotism, the respect of other nations for the achievements of our fatherland, for its secular history and empire. I haven't seen much, Ricardo Reis confessed, but I'm up to date on what is reported in the newspapers. The newspapers must be read, of course, but that is not enough, you must see with your own eyes the roads, the ports, the schools, the public works everywhere, and the atmosphere of discipline, my dear fellow, the calm on the streets and in people's hearts, an entire nation dedicated to honest labor under the leadership of a great statesman, truly an iron hand in a velvet glove, precisely what we needed. A splendid metaphor, that. Yes, I'm sorry not to have invented it myself, it stuck in my mind, how true it is that a single image can be worth a hundred speeches, it appeared two or three years ago on the front page of *Sempre Fixe*, or was it *Os Ridículos*, an iron hand in a velvet glove, and the drawing was so excellent that both the velvet and the iron were conveyed. In a satirical magazine. Truth, dear Doctor Reis, does not always choose the place. It remains to be seen if the place always chooses the truth. Doctor Sampaio frowned a little, the contradiction disturbing him somewhat, but he treated the remark as if it were too profound to be discussed then and there among the wines from Colares and the cheeses. Self-absorbed, Marcenda nibbled little bits of rind, she raised her voice to say that she did not want any dessert or coffee, then began a sentence which might have diverted the conversation to *Tá Mar*, but her father went on, It's not a literary masterpiece but it's certainly a useful book, easy to read, and should open many people's eyes. What is the book. The title is *Conspiracy*, written by a patriotic journalist, a nationalist, a certain Tomé Vieira, I don't know whether you've heard of him. No, I haven't, living so far away. The book was published only a few days ago, you really must read it and give me your opinion. I'll certainly read it if you recommend it with such enthusiasm. Ricardo Reis was beginning to regret that he had declared himself anti-socialist, anti-democratic, and also anti-Bolshevik, not because he was not all these things but because he was growing tired of such unrelieved nationalism, perhaps even more tired at not having been able to speak to Marcenda. As it so often happens, the thing left undone tires you most of all, you only feel rested when it has been accomplished.

The dinner at an end, Ricardo Reis drew back Marcenda's chair and allowed her to walk ahead with her father. Once outside, all three hesitated, wondering whether they should pass into the lounge, but Marcenda finally decided to retire to her room, complaining of a headache. Tomorrow we probably will not see each other, we are leaving early, she told him. Ricardo Reis wished them a good journey, Perhaps I will still be here when you return next month. Should you be gone, do leave us your new address, Doctor Sampaio urged him. Now there is nothing more to be said, Marcenda will go to her room, she has or claims to have a headache, Ricardo Reis does not know what he wants to do, Doctor Sampaio will be going out again later this evening.

Ricardo Reis also went out. He wandered, went into various cinemas to look at the posters, watched a game of chess, white won, and it was raining when he left the café, so he took a taxi back to the hotel. Entering his room, he noticed that the covers had not been turned back and that the second pillow had not been removed from the closet. *Vague, foolish sorrow stops at the door of my soul, stares at me awhile, and moves on*, he murmured, smiling to himself.

A man must read widely, a little of everything or whatever he can, but given the shortness of life and the verbosity of the world, not too much should be demanded of him. Let him begin with those titles no one should omit, commonly referred to as books for learning, as if not all books were for learning, and this list will vary according to the fount of knowledge one drinks from and the authority that monitors its flow. In the case of Ricardo Reis, educated by Jesuits, we can form some idea despite the considerable difference between the teachers of yesterday and those of today. Then come the inclinations of youth, those favorite authors, those passing infatuations, those readings of Werther spurring one to suicide or self-preservation, then on to the serious reading of adulthood. Once we reach a certain stage in life we all read the same things more or less, although the starting point always makes a difference, and the living have the distinct advantage of being able to read what others, because they are dead, will never know. To give but one example, here is Alberto Caeiro, who, having died in nineteen fifteen, poor fellow, did not read *Nome de Guerra*, he has no idea what he missed, and Fernando Pessoa, and Ricardo Reis too, will depart this world before Almada Negreiros publishes his novel. This is almost a repetition of the amusing tale about the gentleman from La Palice, who a quarter of an hour before dying was still alive and kicking, as those wits would say. Not for a moment did he contemplate the sorrow of no longer being alive and kicking a quarter of an hour hence. Let us move on. A man, then, will sample everything, even *Conspiracy*, and it will do him no harm whatsoever to come down every now and then from the clouds where he is in the habit of taking refuge, in order to see how commonplace thoughts are forged, because it is these that help people exist from day to day, not those of Cicero or Spinoza. All the more so, when the recommendation, a nagging exhortation, comes from Coimbra, Read *Conspiracy*, my friend, there you will find some sound opinions, any weaknesses of form or plot are compensated for by the worthiness of the message. Coimbra, most learned of cities, teeming with scholars, knows what it is talking about. The very next day Ricardo Reis went out and bought the slim volume, took it up to his room, unwrapped it furtively, for not all acts carried out behind closed doors are what they appear, sometimes they are nothing other than a person's shame at his own private habits, secret pleasures, picking his nose, scratching his scalp. Perhaps this cover, which shows a woman in a raincoat and cap walking down a street by a prison, the barred window and sentry box eliminating any doubt about the fate of conspirators, is no less embarrassing. Ricardo Reis, then, is in his room, comfortably settled on the sofa. It is raining wherever one looks, as if the sky were a suspended sea draining interminably through countless leaks. Everywhere there is flood and famine, but this little book will tell how a woman's soul launched itself into the noble crusade of restoring to reason and to the nationalist spirit a man whose mind became confused by dangerous ideas. Women are extremely able in such matters, perhaps to atone for those wiles more akin to their nature, by which they have perturbed and brought about the downfall of men since Adam. Ricardo Reis has now read the first seven chapters, namely, On the eve of the election, A bloodless coup, The fable of love, The feast of the Holy Queen, A university strike, Conspiracy, and The senator's daughter. The plot is as follows, a university student, a farmer's son, gets into some mischief, is arrested, locked up in the prison of Aljube, and it is the daughter of the aforementioned senator who with patriotic fervor and missionary zeal will move heaven and earth to secure his release, which is not all that difficult in the end, because to the astonishment of the man who brought her into the world, this senator who belonged to the democratic party but is now an un-masked conspirator, she is much esteemed in the upper spheres of government, a father can never tell how his own daughter will turn out. Though there are of course certain differences, she speaks like Joan of Arc. Papa was on the point of being arrested several days ago, I gave my word of honor that Papa would not evade his responsibilities, I also guaranteed that Papa would stop his plotting. Such filial devotion, so touching, Papa invoked three times in one sentence, the bonds of affection reach such extremes in life. The devoted girl continues, You may attend your meeting arranged for tomorrow, nothing will happen to you, I promise, because I know and the police also know that the conspirators are meeting again, but they have decided to turn a blind eye, such a benevolent, kind-hearted police force here in Portugal, and little wonder, since they have an informer in the enemy camp, none other, would you believe it, than the daughter of a former senator and opponent of this regime. Family traditions have been betrayed, but all will end happily for the parties in question if we take the author of the work seriously. Let us now hear what he has to say, The situation in our country has been discussed with enthusiasm in the foreign press, our economic strategy has been upheld as a model, there are constant admiring references to our monetary policies, throughout the land industrial projects continue to provide employment for thousands of workers, every day the newspapers outline governmental steps to overcome the crisis which, on account of world events, has also affected us, but when compared with that of other countries the state of our economy is most encouraging, the Portuguese nation and the states-men who guide her are quoted worldwide, the political doctrine we pursue here is being studied abroad, and one can confidently say that other nations regard us with envy and respect, the world's leading newspapers send their most experienced journalists to dis-cover the secret of our success, the head of our government is finally coaxed out of his persistent humility, out of his stubborn aversion to publicity, and is featured in newspaper columns throughout the world, his image is given maximum exposure and his political pronouncements are transformed into an evangelical mission. In the face of all this, which is only a pale shadow of what could be said, you must agree, Carlos, that it was utter madness to become involved in university strikes which have never achieved anything worthwhile, are you even aware of the trouble I'm going through to get you out of here. You are right, Marília, but the police have no proof that I did anything wrong, all they know for certain is that it was I who waved the red flag, which wasn't a flag at all or anything remotely like a flag, it was only a handkerchief that cost twenty-five cents, a prank. This conversation takes place in the prison, in the visitors' room, but in a village, also as it happens in the district of Coimbra, another farmer, the father of the sweet girl whom this Carlos will marry toward the end of the story, explains to a gathering of subordinates that there is nothing worse than being a Communist, the Communists want neither bosses nor workers, they don't accept laws or religion, they don't believe anyone should be baptized or get married, for them love does not exist, woman is a fickle creature, all men are entitled to use her, children are not answerable to their parents, and everyone is free to behave as he likes. In another four chapters and in the epilogue, the gentle but Valkyrian Marília rescues the student from prison and the political scourge, rehabilitates her father who abandons his subversive activities once and for all, and declares that within the new corporative plan the problem is being resolved without hypocrisy, conflict, or insurrection. The class struggle is over and has been replaced with a system of good values, capital, and labor. To conclude, the nation must be run like a family with lots of children, where the father imposes order to safeguard their education, because unless children are taught to respect their father everything falls apart and the household is doomed. Bearing these irrefutable facts in mind, the two landowners, the fathers of the bride and groom, after settling some minor disagreements, even help to resolve certain little conflicts between the workers, God need not have bothered expelling us from His paradise, seeing as we have succeeded in regaining it so soon. Ricardo Reis closed the book, it hadn't taken him long to read it. These are the best lessons of all, concise, brief, almost instantaneous, Such stupidity, with this outburst he repays the absent Doctor Sampaio and for a moment loathes the entire world, the incessant rain, the hotel, the book tossed on the ground, Marcenda. But then he decides, without quite knowing why, to exempt Marcenda, perhaps simply for the pleasure of saving something, just as we pick up a piece of wood or stone from a pile of rubble. The shape caught our eye, and without the courage to throw it away we end up putting it in our pocket, for no good reason.

As for us, we are doing fine, as fine as those wonders described above. In the land of *nuestros hermanos*, on the other hand, things are going from bad to worse, the family is sadly divided, Gil Robles may win the election, or Largo Caballero, and the Falange has made it clear that it will confront the Red dictatorship on the streets. In our oasis of peace we watch with regret the spectacle of a chaotic and quarrelsome Europe locked in endless debates, in political squabbles which according to Marília never achieved anything worthwhile. In France, Sarraut has now formed a Coalition Republican government and the right-wing parties have lost no time in pouncing on him, launching a hail of criticisms, accusations, and insults couched in the foul language one associates more with rowdy hooligans than with the citizens of a country that is a model of propriety and the beacon of Western culture. Thank heaven there are still voices in this continent, and powerful voices at that, who are prepared to speak out in the name of peace and harmony, we are referring to Hitler, the proclamation he made in the presence of the Brownshirts, all that Germany wants is to work in a climate of peace, let us banish once and for all mistrust and skepticism, and he dared to go further, Let the world know that Germany will pursue and cherish peace as no other nation has ever cherished it before. Indeed, two hundred and fifty thousand German soldiers are ready to occupy the Rhineland, and within the last few days a German military force invaded Czechoslovakian territory. If it is true that Juno sometimes appears in the form of a cloud, then all clouds are Juno. The life of nations, after all, consists of much barking and little biting, and you will see, God permitting, that all will end in perfect harmony. What we cannot accept is that Lloyd George should assert that Portugal has far too many colonies in comparison with Germany and Italy, when only the other day we observed public mourning to mark the death of their King George V, men in black ties and bands, women in crepe. How dare he complain that we have too many colonies, when in fact we have too few, take a look at the Pink Map of the Portuguese territories in Africa. Had that outrage been avenged as justice demanded, no one would be competing with us now, from Angola to Mozambique there would be no obstacle in our way and everything would be under the Portuguese flag, but the English, true to character, stalked us, the perfidious Albion, one doubts whether they are even capable of behaving otherwise, it is a national vice, and there is not a single nation that does not have reason to complain of them. When Fernando Pessoa turns up, Ricardo Reis must not forget to raise the interesting question as to whether colonies are a good or bad thing, not from the point of view of Lloyd George, whose sole concern is to appease Germany by handing over what other nations have acquired with considerable effort, but from his own point of view, the view of Pessoa, who revived Padre Vieira's dream by prophesying the advent of the Fifth Empire. He must also ask him, on the one hand, how he would resolve the contradiction of his own making, that Portugal has no need of colonies in order to fulfill her imperial destiny yet without them is diminished at home and abroad in material and moral terms, and, on the other hand, what he thinks of the prospect of our colonies being handed over to Germany and Italy, as Lloyd George is about to propose. What Fifth Empire will that be, when we are despoiled and betrayed, stripped like Christ on His way to Calvary, a people condemned to suffering, hands outstretched, the bonds loosely tied, for real imprisonment is the acceptance of imprisonment, hands humbly reaching to receive the alms distributed by *O Século*. Perhaps Fernando Pessoa will reply, as he has on other occasions, As you well know, I have no strong principles, today I argue for one thing, tomorrow for another, I may not believe in what I defend today or have any real faith in what I defend tomorrow. He might even add, by way of justification, For me there is no longer any today or tomorrow, how can I be expected to go on believing or expect it of others, and even if they believe, do they really know what they believe in. My vision of a Fifth Empire was vague and fanciful, why should it become a reality for you, people were too quick to believe in what I said, yet I never attempted to conceal my doubt, I would have done better to remain silent, simply looking on. As I myself have always done, Ricardo Reis will reply, and Fernando Pessoa will tell him, Only when we are dead do we become spectators, nor can we even be sure of that. I am dead and wander about, I pause on street corners, if there are people capable of seeing me, and they are rare, they will think that all I am doing is watching others pass, they do not know that if anyone falls I cannot pick him up, and yet I do not feel that I am simply looking on, all my actions, all my words continue to live, they advance beyond the street corner where I am resting, I watch them go and can do nothing to amend them, even when they are the result of an error. I cannot explain or sum up myself in a single action or word, even if only to replace doubt with negation, shadows with darkness, a yes with a no, both having the same meaning, but worse than that, perhaps they are not even the words I spoke or the actions I performed, worse because irremediable, perhaps they are the things I never did, the words I never uttered, the one word or gesture which would have given meaning to what I was. If a dead man can get so upset, death clearly does not bring peace. The only difference between life and death is that the living still have time, but the time to say that one word, to make that one gesture, is running out for them. What gesture, what word, I don't know, a man dies from not having said it, from not having made it, that is what he dies of, not from sickness, and that is why, when dead, he finds it so difficult to accept death. My dear Fernando Pessoa, you're reading things upside down. My dear Ricardo Reis, I can no longer read. Improbable on two counts, this conversation is reported as if it actually took place. There was no other way of making it sound plausible.

Since Ricardo Reis had given her no cause for jealousy other than to have conversed in public with Marcenda, albeit in a low voice, Lydia's anger could not be expected to last. First they had told her clearly that they wished nothing more, then they had waited in silence while she removed the coffee cups. This was enough to make her hands tremble. For four nights she wept into her pillow before falling asleep, not so much at the humiliation of being ignored, after all what right had she to indulge in such tantrums, but because the doctor stopped having his breakfast in his room, he was punishing her, Why, upon my soul, when I have done nothing wrong. But on the fifth morning Ricardo Reis did not come down to breakfast, and Salvador said, Ah Lydia, take some coffee up to two hundred and one, and when she entered the room, she shook with nerves, poor girl, she could not help it. He looked at her soberly, placed his hand on her arm, and asked, Are you angry with me. She replied, No, Doctor. But you haven't been back. Lydia did not know what to say, she shrugged her shoulders, wretched, and he drew her toward him. That same night she descended to his room, but neither mentioned the reason for their separation, unthinkable that she should dare, I was jealous, or that he should condescend, My darling, what on earth possessed you, no, it could never be a conversation between equals, everybody knows that there is nothing more difficult to achieve in this world.

Nations struggle against each other on behalf of interests that are not those of Jack or Pierre or Hans or Manolo or Giuseppe, all masculine names to simplify matters, yet these and other men innocently consider those interests to be theirs, or which will be theirs at considerable cost, when the moment arrives to settle accounts. The rule is that some eat figs while others watch. People struggle for what they believe to be their values but what may be merely emotions momentarily aroused. Such is the case of Lydia, our chambermaid, and Ricardo Reis, known to everyone as a doctor of medicine, should he finally resume his practice, and to some as a poet, should he ever allow anyone to read what he painstakingly composes. But people also struggle for other reasons, for the same reasons, power, prestige, hatred, love, envy, jealousy, sheer malice, hunting grounds marked out and trespassed on, competition and rivalry, even loot, as occurred recently in the neighborhood of Mouraria. Ricardo Reis had not seen it reported, but Salvador was devouring the details avidly, his elbows resting on the opened newspaper, the pages carefully smoothed out, A dreadful business, Doctor, they're a violent lot, those people in Mouraria, they've no respect for human life, the slightest excuse and they're ready to stab each other without compassion or pity, even the police are frightened, they go in there only when it's all over, to pick up the pieces, listen to this, it says here that a certain José Reis, nicknamed José Rola, fired five shots at the head of one António Mesquita, known as O Mouraria, and killed him, needless to say, no, it had nothing to do with women, the newspaper says it was a case of a quarrel over stolen goods, the one cheated the other, it happens all the time. Five shots, Ricardo Reis repeated, not to appear unconcerned, and grew pensive. He could visualize the scene, the gun firing five shots at the same target, the head receiving the first bullet while still erect, then the body on the ground spurting blood, rapidly growing weaker, and the other four bullets, superfluous yet somehow necessary, two, three, four, five, a whole barrelful of hatred in every shot, the head jerking on the pavement each time, terror and dismay on all sides, then uproar, women screaming out of the windows. It's doubtful that anyone would have had the courage to grab José Rola by the arm, most likely the bullets in the magazine were used up, or his finger suddenly froze on the trigger, or his hatred was satisfied. The assassin will escape, but he will not get far, for no one gets away with anything in Mouraria. The funeral is tomorrow, Salvador informs him, were I not on duty I would be there. Do you like funerals, Ricardo Reis asks him. It's not exactly a question of liking them, but a funeral such as this one is worth seeing, especially when there has been a crime. Ramón lives in the Rua dos Cavaleiros and he has heard rumors which he passes on to Ricardo Reis at dinnertime. The whole neighborhood is expected to turn up, Doctor, and it is even said that the cronies of José Rola are threatening to smash open the coffin, if they carry out their threat there will be merry hell, I swear by Jesus. But if O Mouraria is dead, what more can they do to him, a man like that is not likely to come back from the other world to finish what he began in this one. With people of that sort you can never tell, deep hatred doesn't end with death. I'm almost tempted to attend this funeral myself. Go, then, but don't get too close, and if there is trouble, take shelter under a staircase and let them fight it out among themselves.

Things did not come to that pass, perhaps because the threat had been nothing but bravado, perhaps because two armed policemen were patrolling the neighborhood, a symbol of protection which would have proved ineffectual if the troublemakers had gone ahead with their gruesome plan, but when all is said and done, the presence of the law commands some respect. Ricardo Reis appeared discreetly before the funeral cortege was due to set off, he watched from a distance as he had been advised, having no desire to find himself in the midst of a sudden riot, and was amazed at the hundreds of people cramming into the street in front of the morgue, just like the charity day organized by *O Século*, were it not for all those women dressed in garish red, their skirts, blouses, shawls, and their youths in suits of the same color, a most unusual expression of mourning if these are friends of the deceased, and a blatant provocation if they are his enemies. This looks more like a carnival parade. Now the bier comes into sight, drapes flapping as it heads for the cemetery, drawn by two mares with plumes and trappings, and two policemen march, one on either side of the coffin, a guard of honor for O Mouraria, these are the ironies of fate, who would have imagined it. There go the military policemen with their swords knocking against their legs and their holsters unbuttoned, and the mourners wail and sob, those dressed in red making as much noise as those in black, the latter for the dead man being carried to his grave, the former for his assassin locked up in jail. Lots of people barefoot and covered with rags. Some women, dressed in all their finery and wearing gold bracelets, walk arm in arm with their menfolk, the latter have black sideburns and clean-shaven faces still blue from the razor, they look around them with suspicion, other women shout insults, their bodies sway at the hips, but however sincere or false their sentiments all the people show a kind of ferocious gaiety which has brought friends and enemies together. This tribe of criminals, pimps, whores, pickpockets, and burglars fences the black horde that marches across the city. Windows open to watch them file past. The courtyard of the miracles, reminiscent of Victor Hugo's *Notre Dame de Paris*, has emptied, and the residents tremble with fear, because the thief who will enter their house tomorrow might be out there. Look, Mummy, the children shout, but for children everything is one big celebration. Ricardo Reis accompanied the funeral cortege as far as the Paço da Rainha. Women began to cast furtive glances at the well-dressed gentleman,

Who can he be, this is feminine curiosity, natural in those who spend their life sizing up men. The cortege disappeared around a corner, almost certainly heading toward the Alto de São João, unless it took another turn farther on, to the left, in the direction of Benfica, it was definitely not heading toward the Cemetery of Prazeres, and what a pity, for we are losing an edifying example of the equality bestowed by death, O Mouraria lying side by side with Fernando Pessoa. What conversations would those two have under the shade of the cypress trees as they watched the ships enter the harbor on sultry afternoons, the one explaining to the other how words must be juggled in order to pull off a confidence game or pull off a poem. That same evening, as he served the soup, Ramón explained to Doctor Ricardo Reis that the red garments indicated neither mourning nor disrespect, rather it was a custom peculiar to the neighborhood, whose inhabitants donned red for all special occasions. The tradition existed before he arrived from Galicia, and he learned about it from others. Did you catch sight of a very striking woman at the funeral, tall, dark eyes, dressed in fine clothes, wearing a stole made of soft merino wool. My dear fellow, there were so many women in the crowd, hundreds of them, who was she. The lover of O Mouraria, a singer. No, I didn't notice her. Such a beauty and what a voice, it will be interesting to see who grabs her now. It's not likely to be me, Ramón, and I don't think it will be you either. That I should be so lucky, Doctor, that I should be so lucky, but that kind of woman costs money. This is just talk, wishful thinking, a fellow has to say something, does he not, but as for the red garments, I believe the custom goes back to the time of the Moors, the devil's weeds, nothing to do with Christianity. When Ramón came back later to remove his plate, he asked Ricardo Reis what he thought about the news arriving from Spain as the elections drew near, and who in his opinion would win, The outcome won't affect me, I am doing all right here, but I'm thinking about my father back in Galicia, where I still have some relatives, although most of them have emigrated. To Portugal. All over the world, in a manner of speaking, between brothers, nephews, and cousins my family is scattered throughout Cuba, Brazil, and Argentina, I even have a godson in Chile. Ricardo Reis told him what he knew from press reports, the right-wing parties were expected to win, and Gil Robles had said, You know who Gil Robles is, I've heard the name, Well, he said that when he comes to power he will abolish Marxism and the class struggle and establish social justice. Do you know what Marxism is, Ramón, No I don't, Doctor, And the class struggle, No, And social justice, I've never had any dealings with the law, thanks be to God. Well, within the next few days we will know who has won, probably nothing will change, Better the devil you know, as my grandfather used to say, Your grandfather was right, Ramón, your grandfather was a clever man.

Whether he was or not, the left won. The following morning the newspapers reported that at first it looked as if the right had won in seventeen provinces, but when all the votes were counted, it became apparent that the left had elected more deputies than the center and right put together. Rumors were already circulating that a military coup was being planned with the connivance of Generals Goded and Franco, but these were being denied. President Alcalá Zamora entrusted Azaña with the task of forming a government. Let's see what this will bring, Ramón, whether it will be good or bad for Galicia. Here, walking in these streets, one sees grim faces, but a few dissimulate, if that gleam in their eye is not one of satisfaction, you could have fooled me. *Here* in the last sentence does not mean all of Lisbon let alone all Portugal, who knows what is happening in the rest of the country, *Here* means only the thirty streets located between the Cais do Sodré and São Pedro de Alcântara and between the Rossio and Calhariz, like an inner city surrounded by invisible walls that protect it from an invisible siege. The besieged and besiegers coexist, each side refers to the other as They, because the two are different, mutually foreign, they eye each other with suspicion, one side craves more power, the other side finds its strength insufficient. The wind blowing from Spain, what will it bring us, what nuptials. Fernando Pessoa replied, Communism, it won't be long in coming. Ironically he added, Hard luck, my dear Reis, you fled from Brazil in order to live the rest of your days in peace, and the next thing you know our neighbor, Spain, is in turmoil, soon they will invade us. How often do I have to tell you that if I came back, it was because of you. You still haven't convinced me. I'm not trying to convince you, all I ask is that you spare me your views on this matter. Don't be angry with me. I lived in Brazil, now I'm here in Portugal, I have to live somewhere, when you were alive you were sufficiently intelligent to understand this and more. This is the drama, my dear Reis, one has to live somewhere, for there is nowhere that is not somewhere and life cannot be other than life, at long last I am becoming aware of this, the greatest evil of all is that a man can never reach the horizon before his eyes, and the ship in which we do not sail, we would have that be the ship of our voyage, *Ah, the entire quay, a memory carved in stone.* And now that we have yielded to sentiment and started quoting verses, here is a line by Álvaro de Campos, who someday will achieve the recognition he deserves, *Console yourself in the arms of Lydia, if your love endures,* and remember that that too was denied me. Good-night, Fernando, Good-night, Ricardo. Carnival will soon be here, enjoy yourself but don't expect to see me for the next few days. They had met in a local café, half a dozen tables, no one there knew them. Fernando Pessoa came back and sat down again, I've just had an idea, why don't you dress up as a horse trainer, high boots and riding breeches, a red jacket with braiding, Red, Yes, red is just the color, and I will dress as death, in black mesh with bones painted on it, you cracking your whip and I scaring the old women, I'll carry you off, I'll carry you off, and fondling the young girls as we go, at a masked ball we would easily win first prize. I've never been one for dancing, There's no need, the crowd would only have ears for your whip and eyes for my bones, Don't you think we're both a little old for such games, Speak for yourself, I've stopped being any age. With these words Fernando Pessoa got to his feet and departed. It was raining outside and the waiter behind the bar said, Without a raincoat or umbrella that friend of yours is going to get a soaking. He doesn't mind, he's accustomed to it.

When Ricardo Reis returned to the hotel, he felt something stirring in the air, a restless buzz, as if all the bees in a hive had suddenly gone crazy. The weight on his conscience, of which we are well aware, made him immediately think, They've discovered everything. A romantic, he is convinced that the day his little adventure with Lydia comes to light the Bragança will crumble under the scandal, he lives with the constant fear or perhaps the morbid desire that this should happen, an unexpected paradox in a man who claims to be so detached from the world yet who after all wants the world to trample on him. Little does he suspect that the story is already circulating, whispered amid furtive smiles. This was the work of Pimenta, not the type of person to mince words. The guilty walk in innocence, but Salvador has not yet been informed, what verdict will he deliver when at last some envious informant, man or woman, says to him, Senhor Salvador, this affair between Lydia and Doctor Reis is scandalous. He would do well to repeat nobly the words of the Bible, *He that is without sin among you, let him cast the first stone.* Ricardo Reis walked up to the reception desk feeling apprehensive. Salvador was on the telephone, speaking in a loud voice, there was a bad connection, Your voice sounds as if it were coming from the other side of the world, hello, can you hear me, yes, Doctor Sampaio, I must know when you are coming, hello, hello, yes now I can hear you, the problem is that I have scarcely any rooms left, why, because of all the Spaniards, yes, from Spain, they arrived today, on the twenty-sixth then, after Carnival, very well, the two rooms are reserved, no, Doctor, not at all, our special guests come first, three years are not three days, my regards to Senhorita Marcenda, by the way, sir, Doctor Reis is standing right beside me and sends his regards. It was true, Ricardo Reis, by means of signs and mouthed words, was sending his greetings, for two reasons. First, to feel himself close to Marcenda, even through a third party, and second, to become friendly with Salvador, thus removing the man's authority over him, which may seem a blatant contradiction but is not. Relations between two people cannot be explained simply by adding and subtracting arithmetically. How often we think we are adding, only to end up with a remainder, and how often, on the other hand, we think we are subtracting, and it turns out to be not even the straightforward opposite, addition, but multiplication. Salvador put down the receiver, triumphant, having succeeded in a coherent and conclusive telephone conversation with the city of Coimbra, and now he was answering Ricardo Reis, who had asked how things were going. I've just signed in three Spanish families who turned up without any warning, two from Madrid and one from Cáceres, refugees. Refugees. Yes, because the Communists have won the election. It wasn't the Communists, it was the left-wing parties. It comes to the same thing. But are they really refugees. Even the newspapers are carrying the story. I missed that. Well, from now on he would no longer be able to say so, he could hear Spanish being spoken on the other side of the doors, not that he was listening, but the sonorous language of Cervantes penetrates everywhere. There was even a time when it was spoken throughout the universe, we Portuguese never achieved as much. That these were wealthy Spaniards became apparent at dinner, judging from their clothes, their jewels, both the men and women bedecked with rings, cuff links, tiepins, clasps, bangles, bracelets, chains, earrings, necklaces, strands, cords, chokers of gold studded with diamonds and an occasional ruby, emerald, sapphire, or turquoise. They spoke in high-pitched voices from table to table, flaunting their triumph in misfortune, if one may be permitted this contradiction in terms. Ricardo Reis could find no other expression which reconciled their imperious tone with their bitter lamentations. When they spoke of the Reds, they twisted their lips with contempt. The dining room in the hotel Bragança is transformed into a stage set, Calderón's droll *gracioso*. Clarín is likely to appear at any minute and tell us, *Here concealed, I watch the festivities*, that is to say, the Spanish festivities as seen from Portugal, *for death will not find me now, I don't give a damn for death*. The waiters Felipe and Ramón, and there is a third waiter, but he is a Portuguese from Guarda, are rushed off their feet and irritable. This is not the first time they have waited on their countrymen, but never so many at a time and in circumstances such as these. They who have seen so much of life are unaware or have not yet had time to notice that these families from Cáceres and Madrid do not address them as fond compatriots whom misfortune has reunited. Anyone standing on the side can hear the tone of voice, it is the same when they address the Galicians as when they refer to the Reds, substituting scorn for hatred, but now Ramón is seething with resentment, offended by their surly looks and haughty language, and when he comes over to serve Ricardo Reis he can contain himself no longer,

They needn't have troubled coming in here decked up in all that jewelry, nobody will steal it from their rooms, this is a respectable hotel. A good thing that Ramón says so, it will obviously take more than Lydia's visits to a guest's room to make him change his mind. Moral attitudes vary, as do other attitudes, sometimes for the slightest thing, more often than not because of knocks to one's self-esteem, now it is Ramón's that is bruised, hence his need to un-burden himself to Ricardo Reis. Let's be fair, however, at least as fair as possible, these people here in the dining room have been driven to Portugal by fear, they have brought their jewels, their money, in the circumstances of their hasty flight what else could they have brought to live on. It is doubtful that Ramón will give or lend them a cent, and why should he, charity is not one of God's commandments, and if the second commandment, *Love thy neighbor as thyself*, has any validity, it would still take another two thousand years, more, before these neighbors from Madrid and Cáceres would come to love Ramón. But the author of *Conspiracy* says we are on the right road, thanks be to God, capital, and labor, and it is probably in order to decide who will pave that road that our procurators and deputies have assembled for a confraternity dinner at the spa of Estoril.

Because of this wretched weather, day and night, which shows no sign of clearing and gives no respite to farmers and agriculturists, with flooding that is reckoned to be the worst in the last forty years, a fact confirmed by the records and testimonies of the elderly, Carnival will be memorable this year, memorable in itself but es-pecially with these dreadful floods that have nothing to do with it but will be talked about for years to come. As we have already stated, Spanish refugees are pouring into Portugal. If they can raise their spirits, they will find plenty of diversions here which are sadly lacking in their own country, now more than ever before. Here we have every reason to feel self-satisfied. Consider the government's decision to go ahead with the plan to build a bridge over the Tagus, or the decree that will limit the use of state automobiles to official functions and services, or the aid given to the workers in the Douro with the distribution of five kilos of rice, five kilos of dried cod, and ten escudos per worker, and no one need be surprised at such lavish generosity, because cod is the cheapest commodity available. And within the next few days a government minister will make a speech announcing the establishment of a soup kitchen for the poor in each parish, and the same minister, returning from Beja, will assure journalists as follows, I have witnessed in Alentejo the importance of organizing private charities in order to combat the labor crisis, which translated into everyday Portuguese reads, Some alms, kind sir, for the sake of your dear ones in Purgatory. Best of all, however, because it emanated from a supreme authority subordinate only to that of Almighty God, was the speech by Cardinal Pacelli in which he praised Mussolini as the mighty defender of Rome's cultural heritage. Clearly this cardinal, so wise and likely to become even wiser, deserves to be Pope, may the Holy Spirit and the conclave not forget him when that blissful day comes. Even now, the Italian troops are on their way to bombard Ethiopia, and God's humble servant is already prophesying empire and emperor, Hail Caesar, Hail Mary.

But how different Carnival is here in Portugal. Yonder, in that land across the ocean discovered by Cabral, where the thrush sings and the Southern Cross shines, beneath that glorious sky, and where even when the sky is overcast there is plenty of heat, at Carnival schools parade, dancing sambas down the city's main boulevard, bedecked with glass beads that look like diamonds, sequins that glitter like precious stones, clothes that may not be made from silk or satin but cover bodies as if they were plumes and feathers, with parrots, birds of paradise, and peacocks swaying on their heads, and the samba, the samba, that tremor in one's soul. Even Ricardo Reis, serious by nature, often felt a repressed Dionysian turmoil stirring within. Only the fear of his own body prevented him from throwing himself into that wild frenzy, we never know how such things will end. In Lisbon there are no such risks, the sky remains as before, drizzling, but cheer up, not so wet as to spoil the parade which is about to descend the Avenida da Liberdade, flanked on either side by the familiar hordes of poor families from the nearby neighborhoods. True, chairs can be rented by those who can afford them, but there will be few customers. Daubed with multicolored figures, the floats creak, sway above people laughing and making faces. Masqueraders both ugly and pretty throw streamers into the crowd, and little bags of corn and beans, which can maim when they hit their target, and the crowd retaliates with diminished enthusiasm. Some open carriages go past, carrying a supply of umbrellas. Young ladies and their beaux wave from their carriages and throw confetti at each other. Merry pranks such as these are also played among the spectators, for example take this girl watching the procession and this youth creeping up behind her with a handful of confetti. He presses it to her lips, rubs vigorously, then takes advantage of her surprise to fondle her as best he can, the poor girl coughs and sputters while he goes off laughing, these are flirtations in the Portuguese tradition, some marriages even begin like this and turn out to be happy. Atomizers are used to squirt water at people's necks or in their faces. They are still called perfume sprayers, the name remaining from the days when one used them to inflict gentle violence in drawing rooms, later they descended to the streets, and you are fortunate if the water is not from some sewer, as has been known to happen. Though soon bored with this tawdry procession, Ricardo Reis stayed, he had nothing more important to do. Twice there was a drizzle and once a downpour, yet there are those who continue to sing the praises of the Portuguese climate, I'm not saying the climate isn't good, but it's not good for carnival parades. By late afternoon, the procession over, the sky cleared, but too late. The floats and carriages went on to their destination, there they will remain to dry out until Tuesday, their faded paint will be touched up, their festoons hung to dry, but the masqueraders, although drenched from head to foot, continue their merrymaking in the streets and squares, alleyways and crossroads. What cannot be committed out in the open they pursue under some staircase, where things can be done more quickly and cheaply. The flesh is weak, the wine helps, the day of ashes and oblivion doesn't come till Wednesday. Ricardo Reis feels slightly feverish, perhaps he has caught a cold watching the procession go past, perhaps melancholy can bring on a fever, nausea, delirium, but he is not that far gone yet. A hopelessly drunk old man in a mask came up to him, armed with a large wooden cutlass and club, striking the one against the other, making an uproar and ambiguously pleading,

Punch me in the belly. He hurled himself on the poet, his bulging stomach padded with a cushion or a roll of cloth, and the crowd hooted with laughter at the sight of the gentleman in a hat and raincoat dodging an old clown dressed in a two-cornered hat, a silk jacket, breeches, and hose, Punch me in the belly. What the man really wanted was money for wine. When Ricardo Reis gave him some coins, the old drunk broke into a grotesque little dance, striking his cutlass against his club, before reeling off, followed by a trail of urchins, the acolytes of this expedition. In a little carriage resembling a pram sat an enormous man with his legs sticking out, his face painted, a baby's bonnet stuck on his head, a bib around his neck. He pretended to sob, or else was genuinely sobbing, until the ugly brute who was playing nanny pushed a feeding bottle filled with red wine into his mouth. This he sucked avidly, to the amusement and delight of the assembled crowd, from which a youth suddenly came running, quick as a flash, fondled the nanny's enormous false breasts, then scampered off, while the nanny yelled after him in a hoarse voice, unmistakably male, Come back here you son of a bitch, come and fondle this, and as he shouted he exposed something that caused all the women to avert their eyes once they had taken a good look. At what, Well, nothing too obscene, the nanny was wearing a dress that came down below the knee, and what protruded from under the dress he grabbed with both hands. Innocent horseplay, this is Carnival in Portugal. A man walks past in an overcoat. Unknown to him he has a sign stuck to his back, a paper dangling from a safety pin, Beast of burden for sale, no one has asked the price so far, even though they taunt him as they pass, Are you such a beast that you don't feel your burden. They amuse themselves teasing. Finally suspicious, he puts his hand behind his back, pulls away the sign, and tears it up in a rage. These same pranks are played on us year after year, and we always react as if it were something new. Ricardo Reis feels safe, knowing how difficult it is to stick a pin into a raincoat, but threats come from all sides. A broom attached to a cord suddenly descends from an upper story, knocking his hat to the ground, and he can hear the two girls who live above shrieking with laughter, Carnival time is fun time, they cry in unison, and the argument is so overwhelming that Ricardo Reis simply retrieves his hat, now covered with mud, and goes silently on his way. It is time he was getting back to the hotel. Fortunately there are the children, they walk about holding on to their mother, aunt, or grandmother, they show off their masks, enjoy being admired, for them there is no greater happiness than going around in disguise. They attend the matinées, fill the parquets and galleries of a bizarre world, utter bedlam, they trip in their long balloon-shaped skirts, their feet hurt, they twist their mouths and milk teeth to grip their pipe, their mustache and sideburns smear, there is surely nothing nicer in this world than children. There they go, the little innocents, carrying their gauze satchels filled with paper streamers, their cheeks painted red or white, wearing pirate eye patches, we do not know if they are dressed as they wish or are simply playing a role devised by the adults who selected and paid for these rented costumes, these Dutch boys, rustics, washerwomen, mariners, fado singers, grand dames, serving maids, soldiers, fairies, army officers, flamenco dancers, poultry vendors, pierrots, train engineers, girls from Ovar in traditional costume, pages, scholars in cap and gown, peasant girls from Aveiro, policemen, harlequins, carpenters, pirates, cowboys, lion tamers, Cossack riders, florists, bears, Gypsies, sailors, shepherds, nurses, later they will be photographed and appear in tomorrow's newspapers. Some of the little masqueraders who visited the newspaper office obliged the photographer by removing the domino they wore over their costume, even the mysterious domino of Columbine, to show their faces so that their grandmothers might boast with ecstasy, That's my little granddaughter. With a pair of scissors she will lovingly cut out the photograph, it will go into her box of souvenirs, that green one there in the shape of a little trunk, which will break open when it falls onto the pebbles on the quayside. Today we laugh, but the time will come when we will want to weep. It is almost night, Ricardo Reis is dragging his feet, it could be weariness, melancholy, that fever he suspected. Feeling a sudden chill in his back, he is tempted to hail a taxi, but the hotel is now near, In ten minutes I'll be tucked in bed, I'll skip dinner, he murmured to himself, and at this very moment there appeared a group of pretend-mourners approaching from the Rua do Carmo, the men all dressed as women, with the exception of the four pallbearers, who bore on their shoulders the coffin, on top of which lay a man representing a corpse, jaw bound and hands clasped. Now that the rain had stopped, they were venturing out into the street with their mummery. Ah my beloved husband whom I shall see no more, one of the louts, swathed in crepe, cried out in falsetto. Several others played the part of little orphans, Ah dear Papa whom we so greatly miss. Their cronies circled them begging alms from the bystanders for the funeral expenses, The poor man died three days ago and the corpse is beginning to smell something awful. Which was true, someone must have cracked open a bottle of hydrogen sulfide, corpses do not normally smell like rotten eggs but this was the nearest thing they could find. Ricardo Reis gave them a few coins, just as well he was carrying small change, and was about to proceed up the Chiado when he was struck by a strange figure in the procession, despite its being the most logical of all, namely Death, for this was a funeral even if only a mock one. The man was clad in close-fitting black fabric, probably tricot, and over this material were traced out all his bones from head to foot. The craze for fancy costumes often reaches extremes. Ricardo Reis began to shiver again, but this time he knew why, Could it be Fernando Pessoa, that's absurd, he murmured, he would never do such a thing, and even if he were so inclined, he would never keep company with such rabble. Before a mirror, yes, he might stand, that is certainly possible, and dressed thus he might be able to see himself. Muttering this or merely thinking it, Ricardo Reis approached the man to take a closer look, he had the height, the build of Fernando Pessoa, and although he looked slimmer, it might have been because of the close-fitting costume he was wearing. The fellow gave him a quick glance and moved to the back of the procession. Ricardo Reis pursued him, saw him ascend the Calçada do Sacramento, a terrifying sight, nothing but bones in the fading light, as if the man had painted himself with phosphorescent paint, and as he rushed away he appeared to leave a luminous trail. He crossed the Largo do Carmo, turned and ran past the gloomy and deserted Rua da Oliveira, but Ricardo Reis could see him distinctly, neither near nor far, a walking skeleton, a skeleton like the one he had studied in the Faculty of Medicine, the heel bone, the tibia and fibula, femur, ilium, spinal column, rib cage, the shoulder blades like wings incapable of growing, the cervicals supporting the cranium, pallid and lunar. Those who encountered him called out, Hey, Death, hey scarecrow, but the masquerader neither replied nor looked back, he rushed straight on, at a rapid pace, climbed the Escadinhas do Duque two steps at a time, an agile fellow, surely not Fernando Pessoa, who despite his British upbringing was never one for physical exertion. Nor is Ricardo Reis, who could be excused as a product of Jesuit teaching. But the skeleton halted at the top of the stairs, looked down as if to give him time to catch up, then crossed the square to enter the Travessa da Queimada. Where is wretched Death leading me, and I, why am I following him. Then, for the first time, he wondered if the masquerader was in fact a man. It could be a woman, or neither woman nor man, simply Death. It's a man, he thought, on seeing the figure enter a tavern to be greeted with cheers and applause, Look at the masquerade, look at Death. Watching carefully, he saw the skeleton drinking a glass of wine at the bar, head thrown back. Its chest was flat, this was no woman. The masquerader came toward him, and Ricardo Reis had no time to retreat, he broke into a run but the other caught up with him on the corner. The teeth were real, the gums moist with saliva, but the voice was not that of a man, it was that of a woman, or something in between, Tell me, you gawping idiot, who do you think you're following, are you a queer by any chance, or just in a hurry to die. No sir, from a distance I thought I recognized you as a friend of mine, but from your voice I can see I'm mistaken. How do you know I'm not shamming, and the voice now sounded quite different. Please excuse me, said Ricardo Reis, and the masquerader replied in a voice now resembling that of Fernando Pessoa, Go to hell you shit, and he turned away and disappeared into the gathering night. As the little girls with the broom said, Carnival time is fun time. It was raining again.

He spent the night in a fever, slept badly. Before stretching out on the bed, exhausted, he took two aspirins and put the thermometer under his armpit. His temperature was over a hundred, it was to be expected, influenza, he thought to himself. He fell asleep, woke up, dreamed of vast plains bathed in sunlight, flowing rivers meandering among trees, ships that solemnly drifted with the current, remote, alien, himself sailing in all of them, multiplied, divided, waving to himself like someone saying farewell or eager for an encounter. The ships entered a lagoon or estuary, tranquil, still water, they did not stir, there could have been ten of them, or twenty, or more, without sail or oar, within calling distance, but the sailors were all speaking at the same time. Since they were saying the same words they could not hear one another, and finally the ships began to sink, the chorus of voices died away. Dreaming, Ricardo Reis tried to capture those final words, thought that he had succeeded, but as the last ship went to the bottom, the syllables, disconnected, gurgling in the water, came to the surface. Sonorous yet meaningless, the drowned words carried no farewell, pledge, or testament, and even if they had, there was no longer anyone to hear them. Asleep or awake, he debated, had the masquerader really been Fernando Pessoa. First he decided yes, then rejected what was obvious for the sake of what was profound. The next time they met, he would ask. But would he receive a truthful answer. Reis, surely you cannot be serious, can you imagine me going around disguised as Death the way they did in medieval times, a dead man does not cut capers, he is sober, prudent, aware of his condition, discreet, he loathes the absolute nakedness to which he is reduced as a skeleton, therefore when he appears, either he appears as I do now, wearing the smart suit he was dressed in for burial, or, when he wants to give someone a fright, he wraps himself in his shroud, which is a thing that I as a man of some breeding and refinement would never do, I trust you will agree. I needn't have bothered asking him, Ricardo Reis muttered. He switched on the light, opened *The God of the Labyrinth*, read a page and a half, saw that it dealt with two men playing chess but could not tell whether they were playing or conversing. The letters became blurred and he laid the book aside. He was back in his apartment in Rio de Janeiro, from his window he could see planes in the distance dropping bombs over Urca and Praia Vermelha, smoke rising in great black coils, but no sound could be heard, perhaps he had grown deaf or had never possessed any sense of hearing and was therefore unable to imagine, even with the aid of sight, the roar of grenades, the discordant chatter of gunfire, the cries of the wounded. He woke up bathed in sweat. The hotel was submerged in the deep silence of night, the guests all fast asleep, even the Spanish refugees, should anyone suddenly rouse them and ask, Where are you, they would reply, I'm in Madrid, I'm in Cáceres, deceived by the comfort of their beds. At the top of the building Lydia is probably asleep. Some nights she descends, others she does not, their meetings are now arranged beforehand, it is with the utmost circumspection that she comes to his room in the middle of the night. The excitement of the first weeks has waned, as is only natural, nothing fades more rapidly than passion, yes passion, even in these ill-matched liaisons passion has some role. It is wise to allay suspicions, if there are any, to stop harmful gossip, if any is circulating; to avoid public scandal at all costs, let us hope Pimenta went no further than malicious insinuations. True, there could be other reasons for the waning, biological for instance, such as Lydia menstruating, or as the English put it having her period, or to quote a popular saying, The Redcoats have reached the straits, that irrigation canal of the female body, its crimson discharge. He woke, then woke a second time. The light, ashen, cold, dull, as yet more night than day, filtered through the lowered blinds, the windowpanes, the curtains, it traced out the heavy drapes not properly closed, it covered the polished surfaces of the furniture with the most subtle opalescence. The frozen room dawned like a gray landscape, and the hibernating animals, cautious Sybarites, were pleased, for there has been no news of any having died in their sleep. Ricardo Reis took his temperature once more. Still feverish, he started coughing, I've caught a bad flu this time and no doubt about it. The day, so slow in coming, suddenly arrived like a door thrown open, the murmur of the hotel merging with that of the city. This was Monday, Carnival, another day, in what room or grave will the skeleton of Bairro Alto be waking up or still be sleeping, perhaps he has not even undressed but went to bed in his costume, he too sleeps alone, poor fellow. Any living woman would run screaming in terror if such a bony arm were to embrace her under the sheets, even if it were her lover's, *We count for nothing, we are less than futile.* As these lines came to mind, Ricardo Reis recited them in a murmur, then thought to himself, I must get up, a cold or flu only requires precaution, little if any medication. But he continued to doze. Opening his eyes, he repeated, I must get up. He had to wash, shave, he detested the white hairs on his face, but it was much later than he imagined, he had not looked at the clock. Someone was knocking at his door, it was Lydia bringing his breakfast. Pulling his dressing gown around his shoulders, his slippers coming off, still half asleep, he went to open the door. Seeing that he still hadn't washed, hadn't combed his hair, Lydia thought at first that he must have turned in late, perhaps he went to a dance hall chasing after women. Would you like me to come back later, she asked. As he staggered back to bed, seized by a sudden longing to be treated and nursed like a child, he replied, I am ill, which was not what she had asked. She put the tray on the table and approached the bed, and quite spontaneously put her hand on his forehead, You have a fever. Not a doctor for nothing, Ricardo Reis did not need to be told this, but hearing her say it made him feel sorry for himself. He placed a hand over Lydia's and closed his eyes, If there are only these two tears, I will be able to keep them back, he thought, holding Lydia's work-roughened, almost coarse hand, so different from the hands of Chloe, Neaera, and that other Lydia, and from the tapered fingers, manicured nails, and soft palms of Marcenda. From Marcenda's one living hand, I should say, because her left hand is anticipated death. It must be influenza, but I'm getting up, Oh no, you mustn't, you will end up with pneumonia, I'm the doctor here, Lydia, I know what I have to do, there is no need for me to stay in bed playing the invalid when all I need is someone who will go to the pharmacist to fetch two or three medicines. Don't you worry, I'll go, or send Pimenta, but you mustn't get out of bed, eat your breakfast before it gets cold, then I can tidy up and air your room. With these words she eased Ricardo Reis into a sitting position, adjusted his pillow, brought the tray, poured some milk into his coffee, added sugar, cut the slices of toast in half, handed him the marmalade, blushing with happiness, a woman can feel happy just watching the man she loves prostrate on a bed of suffering. She looks at him with such a gleam in her eyes, or could it be worry and concern, that she herself appears to be feverish, one more example of the common phenomenon whereby different causes can produce the same effect. Ricardo Reis allowed himself to be tucked in, pampered, stroked gently by Lydia's fingers as if she were anointing him, whether the first anointing or the last it is difficult to say. Finishing his coffee, he felt deliciously languid. Open the closet for me, there is a black suitcase at the back on the right, bring it here, many thanks. From the suitcase he extracted a prescription pad with a printed heading, Ricardo Reis, general practitioner, Rua do Ouvidor, Rio de Janeiro. When he first bought this pad, he could not have imagined that he would be using it so far away, such is life, without any stability, or with the kind of stability that always has some surprise in store. He scribbled a few lines and instructed, You mustn't go to the pharmacy unless you are asked, give this prescription to Senhor Salvador, any orders should come from him. Bearing the prescription and the tray, she left, but not before kissing him on the forehead, such impudence, a mere servant, a hotel chambermaid, would you believe it, but perhaps she has the natural right, although no other, which he won't deny her, because this is a situation *in extremis*. Ricardo Reis smiled, made a vague gesture, and turned to the wall.

He fell asleep at once, unconcerned about his gray scraggly hair, his sprouting beard, his skin damp and sallow after a night of fever. A man can be more ill than this and still enjoy his moment of happiness, whatever it may be, even just to imagine that he is a desert island over which a migrating bird now flies, brought and carried by the inconstant wind.

All that day and the following, Ricardo Reis did not leave his room. Salvador, who had been informed by Pimenta, paid him a visit, The entire staff wishes you a speedy recovery, Doctor. As if by some tacit agreement rather than following formal instructions, Lydia assumed all the functions of a nurse in attendance, with no qualifications other than those with which women have always been endowed, changing the bedclothes, folding the sheets back with extreme care, bringing cups of lemon tea, giving the patient his pill or a spoonful of cough syrup at the appointed hour, and the disturbing intimacies concealed from others, a back rub, mustard poultices on the patient's calves to draw the humors oppressing his head and chest to the lower extremities, and if this medication did not help, it nevertheless served an important purpose. No one was surprised that Lydia, entrusted with these duties, should spend all her time in room two hundred and one. Any inquiry as to her whereabouts received the reply, She is with the doctor. Malice did not bare its fangs, it reserved its sharpened claws for the right moment, yet there could have been nothing more innocent than Ricardo Reis reclining on the pillow, Lydia insisting he take one more spoonful of chicken broth, but he refuses, he has no appetite, he also wants to hear her plead with him, a game which would seem absurd to anyone in a blissful state of perfect health. To tell the truth, Ricardo Reis is not so ill that he is unable to feed himself, but that is not our affair. If by chance a closer form of contact occurs between them, such as his placing his hand on her bosom, they go no further, perhaps because there is a certain dignity in illness, something almost sacred, although in this religion heresies are not uncommon, outrages against dogma, excessive liberties, such as the one taken by him but denied by her, It could do you harm. Let us praise the nurse's scruples, the lover's restraint. These are details we could dispense with, but there are others of greater relevance, such as the rains and storms which have intensified during the last two days, wreaking havoc on the ragged Shrove Tuesday procession, but to speak of them is as tiring for the narrator as for the reader. And then there are all those outside episodes that have no bearing on our story, such as that of the man who was reported missing last December and whose corpse has been found in Sintra, identified as Luís Uceda Ureña, a mystery in the criminal files which so far remains unsolved, and it looks as if we shall have to wait for the Day of Judgment, because no witness came forward at the time, so we are left with these two, guest and maid, at least until he gets over his flu or cold. Then Ricardo Reis will return to the world, Lydia to her chores, and both to those nocturnal embraces, which are brief or prolonged according to their need and the necessity for discretion. Tomorrow, Wednesday, Marcenda arrives. Ricardo Reis has not forgotten, but he discovers, and if the discovery surprises him it is in the same distracted manner, that illness has dulled his imagination. After all, life is little more than lying in bed convalescing from an illness that is incurable and recurring, with moments of respite we call health, we have to call it something in order to distinguish between the two states. Her hand dangling by her side, Marcenda will come in search of an impossible cure, with her father, the notary Sampaio, who is more hopeful of finding a mistress than a cure for his daughter. Perhaps it is because he has lost hope in a cure that he comes to unburden himself on a bosom not all that different from this bosom Ricardo Reis has just embraced, and Lydia is less reluctant now, even she, who knows nothing about medicine, can see that the doctor is feeling better.

On Wednesday morning Ricardo Reis is served a writ. Given the significance of the document, it is delivered by none other than Salvador in his capacity as manager. It comes from the Police Department for State Security and Defense, an entity whose full name was not mentioned until now because there was no opportunity, but not speaking about certain things does not mean that they do not exist, and here we have a good example. On the eve of Marcenda's arrival there appeared to be nothing more important in this world than the fact that Ricardo Reis was ill and Lydia was nursing him, meanwhile, unsuspected, a clerk was preparing the writ, that's life, old man, no one knows what tomorrow brings. Salvador shows reserve, he is not exactly frowning, his expression is one of puzzlement, that of a man who upon checking his monthly balance finds the total to be much less than what he calculated in his head. This writ has been delivered, he declares, his eyes fixed on the object of the writ as if suspiciously examining a column of figures, Where is the error, twenty-seven and five come to thirty-one when we know that they should add up to thirty-two. A writ addressed to me. Ricardo Reis has every reason to be alarmed, his only crime, and one not usually punishable by the law, if indeed it is a crime, is having received a woman into his bed in the dead of night. He is less disturbed by the document, which he still has not taken into his hand, than by Salvador's face and the hand that is almost trembling. Where does this come from. Salvador makes no reply, certain words must not be said aloud, only whispered or conveyed by signs or read in silence as Ricardo Reis now does, Police Department for State Security and Defense. What am I supposed to do with this, he asks airily with a note of contempt, then adds appeasingly, There must be some mistake. He says this to allay Salvador's suspicions. I'll just sign here on this line acknowledging safe receipt, confirming that I will present myself on the second of March at ten o'clock in the morning, Rua António Maria Cardoso. It is not far from here, first you go up to the Rua do Alecrim as far as the church on the corner, then you turn right, then right again until you come to a cinema, the Chiado Terrasse, opposite the Teatro São Luís, named after the King of France, ideal places for enjoying the arts of stage and screen, and the police headquarters is just a little farther on, you cannot go astray. But perhaps it is because he has gone astray so often in the past that he has been summoned. Salvador solemnly withdraws, to hand over to the police envoy the formal guarantee that the writ has been served, while Ricardo Reis, already out of bed and reclining on the sofa, reads the instructions over and over again, You are summoned to appear for questioning. But why, ye gods, if I have committed no crime, I neither borrow nor steal, I do not conspire, more opposed than ever to any such thing after reading *Conspiracy*, a work recommended by Coimbra, I can hear the words of Marília, dear Papa may be arrested, and if that can happen to a father, what will happen to those who have no children. The entire hotel staff already knows that the guest in room two hundred and one, Doctor Reis, the gentleman who arrived from Brazil two months ago, has been summoned to appear at police headquarters. He must have been up to something in Brazil, or here, I shouldn't like to be in his shoes, It will be interesting to see if they release him, although if this were a case of imprisonment, the police would simply have showed up and arrested him. That same evening Ricardo Reis feels steady enough to go down early to dinner, he will see how the staff eyes him, but Lydia does not behave in this cold, distrusting manner. Salvador no sooner descends to the first floor than she bursts into the room, They tell me you've been summoned by the International Police. The poor girl is terrified. It's true, the writ is right here, but there is no need to panic, it must be something regarding my papers. I hope you're right, from what I hear you can expect nothing but trouble from that lot, my brother has told me things. I didn't know you had a brother. There was no reason to tell you, I never talk much about other people. You've never told me about yourself, You never asked, That's true, all I know about you is that you live here in the hotel, that you go out on your days off, that you are single and unattached as far as one can see, What could be better, Lydia retorted, and with these four words she wrung the heart of Ricardo Reis. It is banal to say so, but that is precisely how they affected him, they wrung his heart. She probably wasn't even aware of what she said, was only expressing her resentment, why resentment, well perhaps resentment's too strong a word, perhaps she simply wanted to state a fact, as if announcing, Oh look it's raining, but instead voiced that bitter irony found in novels, Sir, I am a simple chambermaid scarcely able to read and write, therefore if I have a life of my own, how could it possibly interest you. We could go on in this manner multiplying words, adding them to the four already spoken, What could be better. If this were a duel with swords, Ricardo Reis would already be losing blood. Lydia is about to leave, a clear indication of not having spoken at random. Certain phrases may seem spontaneous, a thing of the moment, but God alone knows what millstone ground them, what invisible sieve filtered them, so that when pronounced they ring like the judgments of Solomon. The best one could hope for now is silence, or that one of the two interlocutors should depart, but people usually go on talking and talking, until what was for a moment definitive and irrefutable is completely lost. What did your brother tell you and what does he do, Ricardo Reis asked. Lydia turned back and began to explain, her outburst forgotten, My brother is in the navy. Which navy, He's on a warship, the Afonso de Albuquerque, Is he older or younger than you, He is just twenty-three, his name is Daniel, I don't even know your last name, My family name is Martins, On your father's side or your mother's, On my mother's side, I don't know my father's name, I never knew him, But your brother, He's my half-brother, his father died, I see. Daniel is opposed to the regime, he's told me so, Say no more unless you're sure you can trust me, Doctor, why shouldn't I trust you. Here there are two possibilities, either Ricardo Reis is an inept fencer who leaves himself exposed, or this Lydia is an Amazon with bow and arrow and broadsword. Unless we wish to consider a third possibility, that heedless of their relative strengths and weaknesses the two of them are finally speaking frankly, he seated, so entitled because convalescent, she standing though his social inferior, both of them probably surprised at how much they have to say to each other, because this is a lengthy conversation when compared with the brevity of their dialogues in the night, which are little more than the simple, primitive murmuring of bodies. Ricardo Reis has discovered that the police headquarters where he is to present himself on Monday is a place of ill repute and that its operations are even worse than its reputation, God help anyone who falls into their clutches, that place means torture, interrogation at any hour of day or night. Not that Daniel has experienced it himself, he is only repeating what others have told him, but if one believes in the proverbs, Tomorrow is another day, There are more tides than sailors, No one knows what the future will bring, then God does not reveal His intentions lest we take precautions. Besides, He manages His own affairs badly, seeing as He wasn't even able to escape His own fate. So even in the navy there are some who are dissatisfied with the regime, Ricardo Reis concluded. Lydia merely shrugged. These subversive opinions were not hers but those of Daniel, sailor, younger brother, man, for such bold statements are generally made by men. When women come to learn something, it's because they have been told, Careful what you say now, don't go blabbing, too late, but she meant well.

Ricardo Reis went down to dinner before the clock struck the hour, not particularly hungry but suddenly curious as to whether any more Spaniards had checked in or if Marcenda and her father had arrived. He spoke Marcenda's name in a low voice, and observed himself carefully, like a chemist who has mixed an acid with a base and is shaking the test tube. There is not much to see without the help of one's imagination, the salt produced was as expected, for so many thousands of years have we been mixing sentiments, acids and bases, men and women. He recalled the youthful infatuation with which he had first looked upon her, then persuaded himself that he had been moved by pity, compassion for that embittering infirmity, the limp hand, the pale, sad face. Then followed a long dialogue before the mirror, the tree of knowledge of good and evil, no knowledge is needed, it is enough to look. What extraordinary words could these reflections exchange. But there is nothing but a repeated image, a repeated movement of lips. Perhaps a different language is spoken in the mirror, different words uttered behind this crystal surface, different meanings expressed, perhaps gestures only appear to repeat themselves like shadows in that inaccessible dimension, until finally what was spoken on this side also becomes inaccessible, lost, only a few fragments of it preserved by memory, which explains why yesterday's ideas are not today's, they were abandoned en route, in the broken mirror of memory. As he goes downstairs, Ricardo Reis feels a slight trembling in his legs. Little wonder, as influenza tends to have this effect, and we would show great ignorance of the subject if we were to suppose that such trembling could be provoked by his laborious thoughts. It is not easy to think when you are walking downstairs, try it yourself, but watch that fourth step.

At the reception desk Salvador was answering the telephone, taking notes with a pencil and saying, Very well, sir, at your service. He flashed a cold and mechanical smile, which was meant to look like preoccupation, or was the coldness instead in his unflinching stare, like that of Pimenta, who had already forgotten the generous, sometimes even excessive tips. So, you are feeling a little better, Doctor, but his gaze said, I rather fancied there was something shady in your life. Those eyes will go on saying this until Ricardo Reis has been to the police and comes back, if he ever does. Now the suspect has passed into the lounge, the conversations in Spanish are noisier than usual, it is like a hotel on Madrid's Gran Via. Any whispering to make itself heard during a pause is some modest conversation between Lusitanians, the voice of our small nation timid even on its own soil, rising to a falsetto in order to affirm timidly some familiarity, real or assumed, with the language across the border, *Usted, Entonces, Muchas gracias, Pero, Vaya, Desta suerte*, no one can claim to be truly Portuguese unless he speaks another language better than his own. Marcenda was not in the lounge, but Doctor Sampaio was present, engaged in conversation with two Spaniards who were explaining current political events in Spain with a graphic description of their odyssey after fleeing their homes, *Gracias a Dios que vivo a tus pies llego*. Joining them, Ricardo Reis sat down at one end of the larger sofa, some distance away from Doctor Sampaio. Just as well, he had no wish to enter into this Spanish cum Portuguese discussion, wanting only to know if Marcenda had arrived or had remained in Coimbra. Doctor Sampaio, showing no sign of having noticed his presence, nodded gravely as he listened to Don Alonso, redoubled his attention when Don Lorenzo came up with some forgotten detail, and never once looked over, even when Ricardo Reis, still suffering the aftereffects of influenza, had a violent fit of coughing that left him breathless and with eyes watering. Ricardo Reis then opened a newspaper and read that in Japan there had been an insurrection of army officers who were demanding that war be declared on Russia. He had first heard the news this morning, but now appraised it in greater depth. If she is here, Marcenda will be down shortly, and you will be obliged to speak to me, Doctor Sampaio, whether you wish to or not, I am anxious to see whether your eyes are as unfriendly as those of Pimenta, for no doubt Salvador has already informed you that the police wish to question me.

The clock struck eight, the superfluous gong sounded, several guests got up and left. The conversation subsided, the two Spaniards uncrossing their legs impatiently, but Doctor Sampaio detained them with the reassurance that they would be able to live tranquilly in Portugal for as long as they wished. Portugal is an oasis of peace, here politics is no pursuit for the lower orders, that makes for a peaceful existence, the calm you witness on the streets is the calm in the souls of our people. But this was not the first time the Spaniards had listened to words of welcome and goodwill, and an empty stomach cannot be nourished on words, so they took their leave, See you soon, their families were waiting to be summoned from their rooms. Doctor Sampaio, coming face to face with Ricardo Reis, exclaimed, You've been here all this time, I didn't see you, how are things, but Ricardo Reis was fully aware that he was being watched by Pimenta, or was it Salvador, one could scarcely tell the difference between manager, notary, and porter, all three suspicious. I saw you but didn't want to intrude, I hope you had a good journey, how is your daughter. No better and no worse, that is the cross we share. One of these days you will see your perseverance rewarded, these cures take time. After this brief exchange they both fell silent, Doctor Sampaio feeling ill at ease, Ricardo Reis being ironic. The latter benevolently tossed a piece of wood onto the dying embers. By the way, I've read the book you recommended, Which book, The one about conspiracy, don't you remember, Ah yes, I suspect it made little impression. On the contrary, I found much to admire in its endorsement of nationalism, its command of idiom, the strength of its arguments, the finesse and penetration of its psychology, but above all the tribute it pays to the generous nature of womanhood, one comes away from the book purified, I truly believe that for many people in Portugal *Conspiracy* will be like a second baptism, a new Jordan. Ricardo Reis completed this encomium by assuming the expression of someone inwardly transfigured, which left Doctor Sampaio disconcerted by the contradiction between these words and the writ Salvador had mentioned in confidence. Oh, was as much as he could say, resisting an impulse to revive their friendship. He decided to remain aloof, to sever relations at least until this business with the police was resolved, I must go and see if my daughter is ready to come down to dinner, and he departed in haste. Ricardo Reis smiled and returned to his newspaper, determined to be the last guest to enter the dining room. Presently he heard the voice of Marcenda, Are we dining with Doctor Reis, whereupon her father said, We made no arrangement. The rest of the conversation, if any took place on the other side of the glass doors, might have gone something like this, As you can see, he is not even here, besides certain matters have been brought to my attention, it's better that we should not be seen together in public. What matters, Father. He has been summoned by the Police Department for State Security and Defense, can you imagine, between ourselves this comes as no great surprise, I had a feeling there was something there not right. By the police, Yes, the police. She retorted, But he is a doctor who only recently arrived from Brazil. All we know is that he claims to be a doctor, but he could be on the run, Really, Father, You are young, you have no experience of life, look, let's sit over there beside that Spanish couple, they seem personable, I'd prefer to be alone with you, Father, All the tables are occupied, we must either join someone or wait, and I'd rather sit down now and hear the latest news from Spain, Very well, Father. Ricardo Reis changed his mind, decided to return to his room, requesting that dinner be sent up. I still feel a little weak, he explained, and Salvador assented with a mere nod, anxious to discourage any further intimacy. That same night, after dinner, Ricardo Reis wrote some verses, *Like the stones that border flowerbeds we are placed by fate, and there we remain, nothing more than stones*. Later he would see if he could expand this fragment into an ode, to continue giving that name to a form that no one knew how to sing, if it indeed was singable, and with what music, what must the Greek odes have sounded like in their time. Half an hour later, he added, *Let us accomplish what we are, we possess nothing more than that*, and put the sheet of paper aside, muttering, How many times have I written this with different words. He was sitting on the sofa, facing the door, silence weighing upon his shoulders like a wicked goblin, when he heard the soft shuffling of feet in the hall. It sounds like Lydia, so soon, but it was not Lydia. From under the door appeared a folded white note, advancing slowly, then brusquely pushed. Ricardo Reis realized that to attempt to open the door would be a mistake. He knew with such conviction who had written the note that he was in no hurry to get up, he sat there staring at it, already half open. It had been badly folded, doubled in haste, written with a nervous, edgy handwriting now seen for the first time. How does she manage to write, perhaps by resting a heavy object on the upper part of the sheet to keep it steady, or by using her left hand as a paperweight, both equally inert, or with the help of one of those springed clamps used in a notary's office to keep documents together. I was sorry not to see you, the note reads, but it was better so. My father is only interested in being with the Spaniards. When they informed him, the moment we arrived, about your trouble with the police, he decided to avoid being seen in your company. I am anxious to talk to you and I will never forget your help. Tomorrow between three and three-thirty I will take a stroll through the Alto de Santa Catarina, and if you wish we could meet and converse a little. A young woman from Coimbra in a furtive note agrees to meet a middle-aged doctor who has arrived from Brazil, he perhaps on the run and certainly suspect, what a tragic love affair is about to be enacted here.

The following day, Ricardo Reis lunched in the Baixa. For no particular reason he returned to the Irmãos Unidos, perhaps attracted by the name of the restaurant. He who has never had any brothers or sisters and finds himself with no friends is assailed by such longings, especially when he is feeling weak, it is not only his legs that tremble in the aftermath of influenza but also his soul, as we pointed out on another occasion. The day is overcast, a trifle chilly, Ricardo Reis slowly ascends the Rua do Carmo, gazing at the shopwindows, still too early for his meeting. He tries to remember if he was ever before in such a situation, a woman actually taking the initiative to arrange a meeting, Be in such a place at such a time, he cannot remember a similar experience, life is full of surprises. But the greatest surprise of all is that he does not feel the least bit nervous, though given all this circumspection and secrecy it would be only natural. He has the impression of being trapped in a cloud, of not being able to focus his thoughts, perhaps he does not really believe that Marcenda will show up. He entered the Café Brasileira to rest his legs, he drank a coffee, listened to a conversation of a group of men, obviously men of letters, they were heaping abuse on some man or beast, Such an idiot, and another, authoritative voice intervened to explain, I received it directly from Paris, No one is arguing with you, someone said. Ricardo Reis could not tell who the remark was addressed to or its meaning, or whether the person was an idiot or not. He left, it was a quarter to three, time to be getting on his way, he crossed the square past a statue of the poet, all roads in Portugal lead to Camões, ever-changing Camões according to the beholder, in life his arms prepared for battle and his mind fixed on the muses, his sword is now in its scabbard, his book is closed, and his eyes blind, both of them, wounded by the pigeons and the indifferent stares of passersby. It is not yet three when Ricardo Reis arrives at the Alto de Santa Catarina. The palm trees look as if they have been pierced by the breeze coming from the sea, yet their rigid blades barely stir. He simply cannot remember if these trees were here sixteen years ago when he left for Brazil. What most certainly was not here is this huge, roughly hewn block of stone, it looks like an outcrop but is really a monument. If the furious Adamastor is here, then the Cape of Good Hope cannot be far away. Below are frigates navigating the river, a tugboat with two barges in tow, warships moored to the buoys, their prows facing the channel, a clear sign that the tide is rising. Ricardo Reis tramples the damp gravel of the narrow pathways, soft mud underfoot, there is no one here in this belvedere except for two silent old men seated on the same bench. They have probably known each other so long that they no longer have anything to say, perhaps they are waiting to see who will die first. Feeling chilly, Ricardo Reis turns up the collar of his raincoat and approaches the railing that surrounds the first slope of the hill. To think that they set sail from this river, what ship, what armada, what fleet can find the route, which route and leading where, I ask myself. I say, Reis, are you waiting for someone. The voice, biting and sardonic, is that of Fernando Pessoa. Ricardo Reis turned to the man dressed in black standing beside him and gripping the railing with his white hands. This was not what I expected when I sailed back here over the ocean waves, but yes, I am waiting for someone. You don't look at all well. I've had a bout of the flu, it was bad but soon passed. This is not the best place for someone recovering from influenza, up here you're exposed to the wind from the open sea. It's only a breeze blowing from the river, it doesn't bother me. Are you expecting some woman. Yes, a woman. Bravo, you've obviously given up those spiritual abstractions of the ideal woman, exchanged your ethereal Lydia for a Lydia one can hold in one's arms, as I saw with my own eyes back in the hotel, and now here you are waiting for another woman, playing Don Juan at your age, two women in such a short time, congratulations, at this rate you'll soon arrive at one thousand and three. Many thanks, I'm beginning to realize that the dead are worse than the elderly, once they start talking they don't know when to stop. You're right, perhaps they regret everything left unsaid when there was still time. I stand warned. However much one speaks, however much we all speak, there's no advantage in being warned, there will always be some little word we leave out. I won't ask you what it is. Very wise, by refraining from questions we can go on deluding ourselves that one day we may know the answers. Look, Fernando, I'd rather you didn't see the person I'm waiting for. Don't fret, the worst that can happen is that she will see you from a distance talking to yourself, and who cares, everyone in love behaves like this. I am not in love. Well, I'm sorry to hear it, let me tell you that Don Juan was at least sincere, capricious but sincere, but you are like the desert, you don't even cast a shadow. It is you who cast no shadow. I beg your pardon, I can most certainly cast a shadow when I please, what I cannot do is look at myself in the mirror. Which reminds me, was that you masquerading as Death in the Carnival procession, Really, Reis, can you imagine me going around disguised as Death, like an allegory in the Middle Ages, a dead man does not cut capers, he abhors the absolute nakedness of his skeletal form, therefore when he appears, either he does as I do, putting on his best suit, the one in which he was buried, or he wraps himself up in his shroud if he's out to give someone a good fright, but as a man with a sense of decorum and who values his reputation I would never indulge in such low pranks, that much you must concede. I had a feeling that that would be your answer, and now I must ask you to leave, the person I've been waiting for is approaching. That girl there, Yes, She's quite attractive, a little too thin for my taste, This is the first time I've ever heard you pass a comment on a woman, *Thou furtive satyr, Thou cunning knave*. Goodbye, dear Reis, until we meet again, I leave you to woo your maiden, you've turned out to be a disappointment, seducing chambermaids, chasing after virgins, I thought rather better of you when you viewed life from a distance. Life, Fernando, is always at hand. Well, you're welcome to it if this is life. Marcenda came down between the flowerbeds bereft of flowers, and Ricardo Reis walked up to meet her. Were you talking to yourself, she asked. Yes, after a fashion, I was reciting some poetry written by a friend of mine who died a few months ago, perhaps you've heard of him. What was his name. Fernando Pessoa. The name sounds familiar but I don't remember having read his poetry. *Between what I live and life, between what I appear to be and am, I slumber on a slope, a slope I will not leave.* Was that what you were reciting, It was, It could have been written for me, if I've understood it properly, it is so simple. Yet it needed this man to write it, it's like all things, both good and bad, someone has to do them, take the *Lusíadas* for instance, do you realize that we'd never have had the *Lusíadas* were it not for Camões, have you thought what our Portugal would be without them. It sounds like a word game, a riddle. Nothing could be more serious if we take it seriously, but let's talk about you, how have you been, is your hand improving. No better, I have it here in my pocket like a dead bird. You mustn't lose hope. I feel I've given up, one of these days I may make a pilgrimage to Fátima to see if an act of faith will save me. You have faith, I'm a Catholic, Practicing, Yes, I attend Mass, and I go to confession, and I take Communion, I do everything good Catholics are supposed to do. You don't sound terribly devoted, Pay no heed to what I'm saying. Ricardo Reis made no attempt to reply. Words, once uttered, remain open like doors, we nearly always enter, but sometimes we wait outside, expecting some other door to open, some other words to be uttered, these for example are as good as any, I must ask you to excuse my father's behavior, the outcome of the elections in Spain has unsettled him, he spent all of yesterday conversing with the refugees. And to make matters worse, Salvador had to go and tell him that Doctor Reis had been served a writ by the police. We hardly know each other, your father has done nothing to require my forgiveness, I suspect it is some trifling matter, and on Monday I shall find out and answer any questions put to me, and that will be the end of it. I'm glad you're not letting it worry you. There is no reason, I have nothing to do with politics, I lived all those years in Brazil without anyone hounding me and there is even less cause for anyone to hound me here, to tell you the truth I no longer even think of myself as being Portuguese. God willing, everything will be all right. We say, God willing, but it is meaningless, because no one can read God's mind or guess His will, you must forgive my petulant mood, who am I to say such things, it's just that we are born into this world, we watch others live, then we start living too, imitating others, repeating set phrases like God willing without knowing why or to what purpose. What you say makes me feel very sad. Forgive me, I'm not being very helpful today, I've forgotten my obligations as a doctor, I should be thanking you for coming here to apologize for your father's behavior. I came because I wanted to see you and speak to you, tomorrow we go back to Coimbra, and I was afraid there might not be another opportunity. The wind has started to blow more fiercely, wrap up well. Don't worry about me, I'm afraid I chose the wrong spot for our meeting, I should have remembered that you are still convalescing. It was simply a bout of influenza, perhaps not even that, a mere chill. It will be another month before I come back to Lisbon, there will be no way of finding out what happens on Monday. I've already told you it's not important. Even so, I'd like to know, That will be difficult, Why don't you write to me, I'll leave you my address, no, better still, address your letter poste restante, my father might be at home when the mail is delivered. Is it worth the bother, mysterious letters posted from Lisbon under a cloak of secrecy. Don't make fun of me, I should find it very distressing to wait a whole month for any news, a word is all I ask. Agreed, if you receive no letter it will mean that I've been condemned to some dark dungeon or locked up in the highest tower in the realm, from which you must rescue me. God forbid, but now I must leave you, my father and I have an appointment to see the specialist. Using her right hand, Marcenda maneuvered her left hand out of her pocket, then stretched out both, for no good reason, the right one was all she needed to shake his hand, now both her hands are nestled in those of Ricardo Reis. The old men look on and fail to understand. I'll be in the dining room this evening, but I will only nod to your father from a distance rather than embarrass him in front of his newfound friends from Spain. I was just about to ask you this favor, That I shouldn't approach him, That you should dine downstairs, so I can see you, Marcenda, why do you want to see me, Why, I don't know. She moved off, walked up the slope, paused at the top of the hill to rest her left hand more comfortably in her pocket, then continued on her way without turning around. Ricardo Reis noticed a large steamer about to enter the channel, it was not *The Highland Brigade*, one ship he'd had time to get to know extremely well. The two old men were chatting. He could be her father, one of them said, They are definitely having an affair, the other replied, what I don't understand is why that fellow in black has been hanging around all this time, What fellow, That one leaning against the railing, I can't see anyone, You need glasses, And you're drunk. It was always the same with these two old men, they would start chatting, then argue, then move to separate benches, then forget their quarrel and sit together once more. Ricardo Reis moved away from the railing, skirted the flowerbeds, followed the same route by which he had come. Looking to the left, he happened to spot a house with inscriptions on the upper story. A gust of wind shook the palm trees. The old men got to their feet. Then there was no one left on the Alto de Santa Catarina.

Anyone who says that nature is indifferent to the cares and sufferings of mankind knows little about mankind or nature. A regret, however fleeting, a headache, however mild, immediately disrupts the orbit of the stars, alters the ebb and flow of the tides, interferes with the moon's ascent, and troubles the currents in the atmosphere and the undulating clouds. Let one cent be missing from the sum collected at the last minute to settle a bill, and the winds grow violent, the sky becomes heavy, all nature commiserates with the anguished debtor. Skeptics, who make it their business to disbelieve everything, with or without proof, will say that this theory is unfounded, that it is nonsense, but what other explanation could there be for the continuous bad weather that has lasted months, perhaps years, because there have always been gales here, storms, floods, and enough has been said about the people of our nation for us to find in their misfortune sufficient reason for these unruly elements. Need we remind you of the wrath of the inhabitants of Alentejo, the outbreak of smallpox in Lebução and Fatela, or typhoid in Valbom. And what about the two hundred people who live on three floors of a building at Miragaia in Oporto, without electricity, in primitive conditions, waking each morning to shouting and screaming, the women lining up to empty their chamber pots, the rest we leave to your imagination, which ought to be put to some use. Little wonder, then, that the weather has unleashed this hurricane, with trees uprooted, roofs blown off, and telegraph poles knocked to the ground. Ricardo Reis is on his way to police headquarters, filled with anxiety, holding on to his hat lest it be carried away. If the rain should start falling in proportion to the wind that is blowing, God help us. The wind is coming from the south and at our back as we ascend the Rua do Alecrim, a blessing preferable to that bestowed by the saints, who assist only during one's descent. We have the itinerary more or less worked out, turn here at the Igreja da Encarnação, sixty paces to the next corner, you cannot go wrong. More wind, a head wind this time, which could be why he slows down, unless it is his feet refusing to walk that road. But he has an appointment and this man is punctuality personified, it is not yet ten o'clock and already he is at the door. He shows the paper they sent him, You are asked to appear, and he has appeared, hat in hand, relieved, absurd as it may seem, to be out of the wind. They send him up to the second floor, and up he goes, holding the writ like a lamp before him, without it he would not know where to put his feet. This document is a sentence that cannot be read, and he is an illiterate sent to the executioner bearing the message, Chop off my head. The illiterate may go singing, because the day has dawned in glory. Nature, too, is unable to read. When the ax separates the head from his trunk the stars will fall, too late. Told to wait, Ricardo Reis sits on a long bench, bereft, because they have taken the writ from him. He sits with other people waiting. If this were a doctor's office, they would be chatting among themselves as they waited, Something's wrong with my lungs, My trouble is my liver or maybe it's my kidneys, but no one knows what is ailing these people, who sit in silence. Were they to speak, they would say, I suddenly feel much better, may I go now. A foolish question, for as we know the best remedy for a toothache is to walk through the door when the dentist calls. Half an hour passed, and Ricardo Reis was still waiting to be called. Doors opened and closed, telephones could be heard ringing, two men paused nearby, one of them gave a loud laugh, He doesn't know what's in store for him, he said, then they disappeared behind a curtain. Are they referring to me, Ricardo Reis asked himself with a tightening in his stomach. At least we shall find out what the charges are. He raised his hand to his waistcoat pocket to take out his watch, to see how long he had been waiting, but stopped himself halfway, he must not betray any impatience. At last a man drew back a curtain ever so slightly, beckoned him with a nod, and Ricardo Reis rushed forward, then stopped himself, held back out of an instinctive sense of dignity, if dignity has anything to do with instinct. Not rushing was the only form of refusal open to him, albeit only a pretense of refusal. He followed the man, who reeked of onion, through a long corridor with doors on either side, all firmly shut. Upon reaching the far end, his guide knocked gently on one of the doors and opened it. A man seated at a desk told the guide, Wait here, you might be needed, and turning to Ricardo Reis he pointed at a chair, Sit down. Ricardo Reis obeyed, now feeling irritated, extremely frustrated, They are doing this just to intimidate me, he thought to himself. The man behind the desk took the writ, read it slowly, as if he had never seen such a document before, then put it down carefully on the green blotting paper and looked hard at him, the look of someone making a final check to avoid any mistake. Your identification if you please, were his opening words, and those three words, If you please, made Ricardo Reis feel less nervous. It is certainly true that one can achieve a great deal simply by being polite. Ricardo Reis took his identity card from his wallet and raised himself slightly in his chair to hand it over, causing his hat to fall on the floor, which made him feel ridiculous, nervous again. The man read the card line by line, compared the photograph with the face of the man before him, took some notes, then placed the card, with the same scrupulous care, in the folder beside the writ. Maniac, thought Ricardo Reis, but said, I'm a doctor, I arrived here from Rio de Janeiro two months ago. You have been staying at the Hotel Bragança all this time, asked the man. Yes sir. On which ship did you travel. The *Highland Brigade*, which belongs to the Royal Mail Line, I disembarked in Lisbon on the twenty-ninth of December. Did you travel alone or accompanied, Alone, Are you married, No sir, I am not married, and I should like to know why I have been summoned here, why the police want to question me, this is the last thing I ever expected. How many years did you reside in Brazil. I went there in nineteen nineteen, why do you ask. Just answer my questions and leave the rest to me, that way we will get along fine. Very well sir. Was there some special reason for your emigrating to Brazil, I decided to emigrate, that's all, Doctors don't usually emigrate, I did, Why, couldn't you find patients here, I had any number of patients, but I wanted to see Brazil, to work there, that's all. And now you've come back, Yes, I've come back. To do what, if you haven't come back to practice medicine. How do you know I'm not practicing medicine. I know. For the moment I'm not practicing, but I'm thinking of opening an office, of putting down roots once more, after all, this is my native land. In other words, after being away for sixteen years, you suddenly felt homesick for your native land. That is so, but really I fail to see the purpose of this interrogation. It is not an interrogation, your statements, as you can see, are not even being recorded. Then why am I here. I was curious to meet this Portuguese doctor who was earning a good living in Brazil, who returned after sixteen years, who has been living in a hotel for two months and does not work. I told you I intend to resume my practice, Where, I haven't yet started to look for a location, it is an important decision. Tell me something else, did you get to know many people in Rio de Janeiro or elsewhere in Brazil. I didn't travel much, my friends all lived in Rio, What friends, My private life is my own affair, I am under no obligation to answer such questions, otherwise I must insist upon my lawyer being present. You have a lawyer, No, but there is nothing to prevent me from hiring one. Lawyers are not permitted to enter these premises, besides, Doctor, you haven't been charged with any crime, we are simply having a little chat. But not of my choosing, and the drift of the questions being put to me suggests that this is more than a friendly chat. To return to my question, who were these friends of yours. I refuse to answer. Doctor Reis, if I were in your position, I would be more cooperative, it's in your best interest to answer, so as to avoid unnecessary complications. Portuguese, Brazilians, people who came to consult me professionally and subsequently became my friends, there's no point in my naming people you do not know. That is where you are wrong, I know a great many names, I am giving no names, Very well then, I have other means of finding out, should it prove necessary, Suit yourself. Were there any military personnel or politicians among those friends of yours. I didn't move in such circles. No one attached to the armed forces or engaged in politics. I cannot guarantee that such people might not have consulted me in my capacity as a doctor. But you did not become friendly with any of them. As it happens, no, With none of them, That's right. You were living in Rio de Janeiro when the last revolution took place, I was. Don't you find it something of a coincidence that you should return to Portugal so soon after a revolutionary conspiracy was discovered. No more than to discover that the hotel where I am staying is full of Spanish refugees after the recent elections held in Spain. Ah, so you are telling me that you fled from Brazil, That was not what I said, You compared your own situation with that of the Spaniards who have arrived in Portugal, Only to make the point that coincidences mean nothing, as I've already told you, I longed to see my native land once more. You did not return because you were afraid. Afraid of what. Of being hounded by the authorities there, for example. No one hounded me either before or after the revolution. These things sometimes take time, we didn't summon you until two months after your arrival. I'd still like to know why. Tell me something else, if the rebels had succeeded, would you have remained in Brazil. I've already told you that the reason for my return had nothing to do with either politics or revolutions, besides this was not the only revolution in Brazil during my stay there. A shrewd reply, but there are revolutions and revolutions and not all for the same cause. I am a doctor, I neither know nor wish to know anything about revolutions, I am interested only in caring for the sick. Apparently not all that interested these days. I will soon be practicing medicine once more. While living in Brazil, were you in trouble with the authorities, I am a peaceful man. And here in Portugal, have you renewed any friendships since your return, Sixteen years is long enough to forget and be forgotten. You haven't answered my question, I have no friends here. Did you ever consider becoming a Brazilian citizen, Never. Do you find Portugal much changed since you left for Brazil, I cannot answer that, I haven't been outside Lisbon. What about Lisbon itself, do you find much difference, Sixteen years have brought many changes. Don't you find more calm on the streets, Yes, I've noticed. The National Dictatorship has set the country to work, I don't doubt it, There is patriotism, a willingness to strive for the common good, no sacrifice is too great in the national interest. The Portuguese are fortunate. You are fortunate, since you are one of us. I will not refuse what is due me when these benefits are made available, soup kitchens, I understand, are to be organized for the poor. You are surely not poor, Doctor, I may be one day, God forbid, Thank you for your concern, but when that happens, I'll go back to Brazil. Here in Portugal there is little likelihood of revolution, the last one occurred two years ago and ended disastrously for those involved. I don't know what you're talking about and have nothing to add to what I've told you already. I have no more questions. May I go now, You may, here is your identity card, oh, Victor, will you show the doctor to the door. Victor approached, said, Follow me, his breath reeking of onion. Incredible, Ricardo Reis thought to himself, so early in the day and this awful stink, the man must eat onions for breakfast. Once in the corridor, Victor told him, I could see you were out to provoke our deputy chief, just as well you found him in a good mood, Provoke him, what do you mean, You refused to answer his questions, you beat around the bush, a grave mistake, luckily our deputy chief has some respect for the medical profession. I still don't know why I was asked to come here. No need, just raise your hands to heaven and thank God it's over. Let's hope so, once and for all. That's something one never knows, but here we are, hey Antunes, the good doctor here has permission to leave the building, good-bye, Doctor, if you need anything, you know where to find me, the name is Victor. Ricardo Reis touched the guide's extended hand with the tips of his fingers, afraid that he himself would start smelling of onions, that he would be sick. But no, the wind hit him in the face, jolted him, dispelled the nausea, he found himself in the street, not sure how he got there, the door behind him closed. Before Ricardo Reis reaches the corner of the Rua da Encarnação there will be a mighty downpour. Tomorrow's newspapers will report heavy showers, an understatement for torrential and persistent rain. The pedestrians all take shelter in doorways, shaking themselves like drenched dogs. There is only one man on the sidewalk by the Teatro São Luís, obviously late for an appointment, he looks as worried as Ricardo Reis had been, which explains all this rain overhead. Nature might have shown her solidarity in some other fashion, for example by sending an earthquake capable of burying Victor and the deputy chief in rubble. Let them rot until the stink of onion evaporates, until they are reduced to clean bones.

When Ricardo Reis entered the hotel, water was dripping from his hat as from a gutter, his raincoat was soaking wet, he looked like a gargoyle, a grotesque figure without any of the dignity one expects in a doctor, and his dignity as a poet was lost on Salvador and Pimenta, because when the rain falls, heavenly justice, it falls on everyone. He went up to the reception desk to retrieve his key. Why, Doctor, you're drenched to the skin, the manager exclaimed, but his dubious tone betrayed his thoughts, What condition are you really in, how did the police deal with you. Or, more dramatically, I didn't expect to see you back so soon. If we address God with the familiar you, even if it is in capital letters, what is to prevent us from taking such a liberty with a hotel guest suspected of subversive activities, both past and future. Ricardo Reis simply muttered, What a deluge, and rushed upstairs, dripping water all over the stair carpet. Lydia will be able to follow his trail, footprint by footprint, a broken twig, trampled grass, but we are daydreaming, talking as if we were in some forest, when this is only a hotel corridor leading to room two hundred and one. So, how was it, she will ask, did they treat you badly. Certainly not, Ricardo Reis will reply, what an idea, there was no problem, the police are very civilized, very polite, they invite you to have a seat. But why did they make you go there. It is apparently the normal procedure when people return after a number of years abroad, a routine check, that's all, to make sure everything is in order, to see if a person needs any assistance. You're joking, that's not what my brother told me. Yes, I'm joking, but don't worry, there was no problem, they only wanted to know why I've returned from Brazil, what I was doing there, what I plan to do here. Have they the right to ask these things. My impression is that they can ask anything they like, now be off with you, I must change before lunch. In the dining room the maître d', Afonso, for Afonso is his name, showed him to his table, keeping a distance of half a pace more than custom or etiquette required, but Ramón, who in recent days had also kept his distance and hurried off to attend to less contagious guests, took his time ladling out the soup, The smell is so appetizing, Doctor, it could awaken the dead. And he was right, after that stink of onions everything smelled good. There should be a study, Ricardo Reis reflected, about what smell we give off at any given moment and for whom, Salvador finds my smell unpleasant, Ramón now finds it tolerable, as for Lydia, her poor sense of smell deludes her into thinking I'm anointed with roses. Entering the dining room, he exchanged greetings with Don Lorenzo and Don Alonso, and also with Don Camilo, who had arrived only three days ago, but Don Camilo remained politely aloof. Whatever Ricardo Reis learns about the situation in Spain he overhears as guests converse over dinner, or he reads in the newspapers. Hotbeds of dissent, the wave of propaganda launched by Communists, anarchists, and trade unionists, which is infiltrating the working classes and has even influenced members of the army and navy. We can now understand why Ricardo Reis was summoned by the Police Department for State Security and Defense. He tries to recall the features of the deputy chief who interrogated him, but all he can see is a ring with a black stone worn on the little finger of the left hand, and the vague image of a round, pale face, like a bun that was not properly baked in the oven. He cannot make out the eyes, perhaps the man had none, perhaps he had been speaking to a blind man. Salvador appears unobtrusively in the doorway, to make sure that all is in order, especially now that the hotel has become international, and during this rapid inspection his eyes meet those of Ricardo Reis. He smiles from afar, a diplomatic gesture, what he wants to know is what happened at the police station. Don Lorenzo reads aloud for Don Alonso from *Le Jour*, a French newspaper published in Paris, he reads an article in which Oliveira Salazar, the Head of the Portuguese Government, is described as an energetic and unassuming man whose vision and judgment have brought prosperity and a sense of national pride to his country. That's what we need in Spain, remarks Don Camilo, and raising his glass of red wine he nods in the direction of Ricardo Reis, who conveys his gratitude with a similar nod but restrained, mindful of the famous battle of Aljubarrota, when Portugal's tiny army routed the Spanish forces. Satisfied, his mind at rest, Salvador withdraws, later or perhaps tomorrow Doctor Ricardo Reis will tell him what happened in the Rua António Maria Cardoso, and should he refuse or give the impression of withholding certain facts, Salvador has other means of finding out, an acquaintance of his works there, a man called Victor. If the news is reassuring, if Ricardo Reis is above suspicion, happiness will be restored, Salvador will simply have to caution him, with tact and diplomacy, to apply the utmost discretion in his dealings with Lydia, For the sake of the hotel's reputation, Doctor, at least to protect our good name, that is what he will tell him. We would take an even more favorable view of Salvador's magnanimity if we considered how much more advantageous it would be to have room two hundred and one vacated, because it is large enough to accommodate an entire family from Seville, a Spanish nobleman, for example, the Duke of Alba, the very thought makes me tremble with excitement. Finishing his lunch, Ricardo Reis nodded to the immigrants still savoring cheeses from the Serra, waved to Salvador, leaving him racked with expectation, with the moist eye of a dog begging for a bone, and went up to his room. He was anxious to write a quick note to Marcenda, poste restante, Coimbra.

It is raining out there with such a deafening noise that it seems that the rain is falling throughout the world, that as the globe turns, its waters hum in space as if on a spinning top. *The dense roar of the rain fills my mind, my soul is an invisible curve drawn by the sound of the wind that blows relentless, an unbridled horse rejoicing in its freedom, hooves clattering through these doors and windows while the voile curtains, inside, sway ever so gently.* A man surrounded by tall pieces of furniture is writing a letter, composing his text so that the absurd appears logical and the incoherent clear, so that weakness becomes strength, mortification dignity, and fear boldness, because what we would like to have been is as valuable as what we have been. Ah if only we had shown courage when called to account. To know this is to be halfway there, knowing this we will find the courage at the right moment to travel the other half. Ricardo Reis vacillated, debated which form of address to use. A letter is a most hazardous business, the written word allows no indecision, either distance or familiarity will emphasize the tone the letter establishes, and you end up with a relationship that is a fiction. Many an ill-fated attachment has started precisely in this way. Ricardo Reis did not even consider the possibility of addressing Marcenda as Most excellent Lady or Esteemed Madam, his concern about propriety did not go that far, but once he ruled out these conventional and therefore impersonal forms of address, he was left with a vocabulary that verged on the intimate. My dear Marcenda, for example. Why his, why dear. True, he could write Senhorita Marcenda, but Senhorita was ridiculous. After tearing up several sheets of paper, he found himself addressing her simply by her name, the way we should address everyone, that is why we were given names. Marcenda, I am writing as promised to give you my news. He stopped to think, then continued, composing the phrases, drawing them together, filling in gaps, if he did not tell the truth, or not all of it, he told one truth, the important thing is that the letter make the writer and the one who receives it happy, that both discover in it an ideal image of themselves. There had been no formal interrogation at police headquarters, nothing that could be used against him in the courts, he had simply been summoned for a little chat, as the deputy chief had been kind enough to point out. It is true that Victor witnessed everything, but he no longer remembers the details and tomorrow will remember even less, Victor has other, more important, matters on his mind. And there are no other witnesses, there is only the letter written by Ricardo Reis, and it may soon go astray, that is altogether likely, because certain documents should not be kept. Other sources may come to light, but they will be suspect, apocryphal if feasible, and in the absence of any firm evidence we will find ourselves obliged to invent a truth, a dialogue, a Victor, a deputy chief, a wet, windy morning, a nature that sympathizes, all false and at the same time all true. Ricardo Reis finished his letter with respectful greetings, wished her good health, a forgivable commonplace, and after some hesitation told her, in a postscript, that she might not find him here on her next visit to Lisbon, because he was beginning to find life in the hotel irksome, monotonous. He must find a place of his own, open an office, The time has come to see how deep these new roots of mine can go, all of them. He was about to underline the last three words but decided to leave them as they stood, their ambiguity transparent. When I finally get around to leaving the hotel, I shall write to you at this same address in Coimbra. He reread the letter, folded the sheet of paper, sealed the envelope, then concealed it among his books. Tomorrow he will post it, today, blessed are those, with this storm, who have a roof over their heads, even if it is only that of the Hotel Bragança. Ricardo Reis went up to the window and drew back the curtains, but the rain was pouring down in one vast sheet of water and he could see little, then not even that, his breath clouded the window-pane. Under the protection of the shutters he opened the window. The Cais do Sodré was already flooding, the kiosk that sold tobacco and spirits was transformed into an island, the world had broken free of its wharf, had drifted away. Sheltered in the doorway of a tavern on the other side of the street, two men stood smoking. They had been drinking and now were rolling their cigarettes slowly, deliberately, while they discussed some metaphysical problem or other, perhaps even the rain that was keeping them from getting on with their lives. They soon disappeared into the darkness of the tavern, if they had to wait, they might as well use the opportunity and have another drink. A man dressed in black and bareheaded came to the door to contemplate the sky, then disappeared as well. Closing the window, Ricardo Reis switched off the light, stretched out wearily on the sofa, and spread a blanket over his knees. Like a silkworm in its cocoon he listened to the mournful noise of the rain. Unable to sleep, he lay with his eyes wide open, *You are alone, no one knows you, be silent and pretend*, he murmured, words written in other times, despising them because they did not express loneliness, merely voiced it. And silence and pretense, these words too were not what they spoke, to be alone, my friend, is much more than a word or a voice saying it.

Later that afternoon he went down to the first floor, to give Salvador the opportunity he so craved, sooner or later he would be forced to broach the subject, so better that he choose the time and place, No, Senhor Salvador, it went extremely well, they were most courteous. The question, when it came, was phrased with great delicacy, Now then, Doctor, tell me, how did you get on this morning, did they give you a difficult time. No, Senhor Salvador, it went extremely well, they were most courteous, all they wanted was some information regarding the Portuguese Consulate in Rio de Janeiro, where I should have been given a signed document, pure bureaucracy and nothing more. Salvador appeared to be satisfied, but he remained suspicious, as one might expect of a man who has seen so much of life, especially working in a hotel. Tomorrow he will get to the bottom of this matter, ask his acquaintance, Victor, I should know the people I have staying in my hotel, and Victor will warn him, Salvador, my friend, keep an eye on that fellow, right after the interrogation the deputy chief said, This Doctor Reis is not what he appears to be, he must be watched, no, we have no definite suspicions for the moment, only an impression, keep an eye on him, tell us if he receives any mail, So far, not a single letter, That too is strange, we must pay a visit to the post office, to see if anything is being held for him, and contacts, does he have any, Here in the hotel, none whatsoever, Well, if you see anything suspicious, just let me know. After this private conversation, the atmosphere in the hotel will once again grow tense, every member of the staff will adjust his or her sights to conform to the aim of Salvador's rifle, a constant vigilance that might well be called surveillance. Even the good-natured Ramón has become cool, Felipe mutters, there is of course one exception, as everybody knows, Lydia, poor thing. She goes around looking worried, and with good reason, today Pimenta burst out laughing, malicious fellow that he is, We haven't seen the end of this story yet. Tell me what is going on, please, she said, I won't breathe a word to a soul. There is nothing going on, Ricardo Reis told her, it is just a pile of nonsense invented by people who have nothing better to do than meddle in the affairs of others. It might be a pile of nonsense, but it can turn a person's life into a nightmare. Don't you worry, once I leave the hotel, the talk will stop. Are you going away, you didn't tell me. Sooner or later I will go, I never intended to spend the rest of my life here. Then I will never see you again, and Lydia, who was resting her head on his shoulder, shed a tear, which he felt. Now then, you mustn't cry, that's life, people meet, they part, one of these days you will marry. Bah, marry, I'm already too old, but what about you, where will you go. I will look for a place, I will find something suitable. If you want, If I want what, I could come and spend my days off with you, I have nothing else in life. Lydia, why do you like me. I don't know, perhaps because of what I said, that I have nothing else in life. You have your mother, your brother, you must have had affairs with men before this, and no doubt there will be others, you are pretty, you'll marry one day, start a family. Perhaps, but for now you are all I have. You are a likable girl, You haven't answered my question, What was that, Do you want me to come and spend my days with you when you have a place of your own, Would you like that, Of course I would, Then you must come until such time as. Until you find someone of your own station. That was not what I was going to say. When that happens, you need only say to me, Lydia, I don't want you to come anymore. Sometimes I feel I don't really know you. I'm a hotel chambermaid. But your name is Lydia, and you have a curious way of saying things. When people start talking their hearts, as I'm doing now with my head on your shoulder, the words aren't the same. I hope you find yourself a good husband someday. It would be nice, but when I listen to other women, those who say they have good husbands, it makes me wonder. You think they're not good husbands, Not for me, What is a good husband, in your opinion, I don't know, You're hard to please. Not really, lying here without any future, I'm happy with what I have now. I will always be your friend. We don't know what tomorrow brings. And you will always be my friend. Who, me, that's something else. Explain yourself, I can't, if I could, I would be able to explain everything, You explain more than you imagine, Don't be silly, I'm not educated, You can read and write, Not very well, I can barely read and can't write without making mistakes. Ricardo Reis drew her to him and she embraced him, the conversation had gradually brought them to an inexplicable emotion akin to pain, so that what they did next was done with extreme delicacy, and we all know what that was.

During the days that followed, Ricardo Reis set about looking for lodgings. He left early each morning and returned at night, having lunched and dined out. The classified section in the *Diário de Notícias* served as his vade mecum, but he did not travel far, residential areas on the outskirts suited neither his needs nor inclinations. He would have hated to live, for example, near the Rua dos Heróis de Quionga in Moraes Soares, where apartments had been built with five or six rooms and the rent was incredibly cheap, from a hundred and sixty-five to two hundred and forty escudos a month, but they were so remote from the Baixa and had no view of the river. He was looking for furnished quarters, otherwise he would need to select furniture, linen, dishes, and without a woman at his side to advise him, because no one could possibly imagine Lydia, poor girl, going in and out of department stores with Doctor Ricardo Reis, telling him what to buy. And as for Marcenda, even if she were here and her father permitted it, what would she know about such practical matters, the only house she had ever known was her own, and it wasn't really hers at all, because strictly speaking the word mine means something made by me and for me. And these are the only two women Ricardo Reis knows, there are no others. Fernando Pessoa was exaggerating when he dubbed him Don Juan. It is not so easy, after all, to leave the hotel. Each life creates its own ties, each its own inertia, incomprehensible to any external observer and no less incomprehensible to the person observed. In a word, let us content ourselves with the little we understand of others, they will be grateful and perhaps even thank us. But Salvador does not content himself. The prolonged absences of this hotel guest, so different from the regime he previously kept, make him nervous. Salvador even considered having a word with Victor, but a qualm made him change his mind at the last moment, what if he became involved in some situation which, if badly handled, might implicate him too, or worse. He grew exceedingly attentive to Ricardo Reis, an attitude which altogether disconcerted the hotel staff, no longer sure how they were expected to behave. Forgive these prosaic details, but they also have their importance.

Such are the contradictions of life. Just recently it was reported that Luís Carlos Prestes was arrested. Let us hope the police do not arrive to ask Ricardo Reis if he knew Prestes in Brazil or if Prestes had been one of his patients. Just recently, Germany denounced the Locarno Pact and after endless threats finally occupied the Rhineland. Just recently, a spring was inaugurated in Santa Clara amid wild excitement on the part of the inhabitants, who formerly had to get their water supply via fire pumps, and it was a lovely ceremony, two little innocents, a boy and a girl, filled two pitchers of water to much applause and cheering. Just recently, there appeared in Lisbon a famous Romanian called Manoilescu, who upon his arrival declared, The new doctrine currently spreading throughout Portugal lured me across these frontiers, I come as a respectful disciple, as a jubilant believer. Just recently, Churchill made a speech in which he said that Germany is the only nation in Europe today that does not fear war. Just recently, the Fascist party in Spain, the Falange, was banned, and its leader, José Antonio Primo de Rivera, imprisoned. Just recently, Kierkegaard's *Human Despair* was published. Just recently, at the Tivoli, the film *Bozambo* opened, it portrays the noble efforts of the whites to extinguish the fierce warring spirit of the primitive races. And Ricardo Reis has done nothing except look for lodgings, day after day. He is disheartened, near despair, as he leafs through the newspapers, which inform him about everything except what he wants to know, they tell him that Venizelos is dead, that Ortins de Bettencourt has said an internationalist cannot be a soldier much less a Portuguese, that it was raining yesterday, that the Reds are on the increase in Spain, that for seven and a half escudos he can buy *The Letters of a Portuguese Nun*, what they do not tell him is where he can find the accommodations he needs so badly. Notwithstanding Salvador's great solicitude, he is anxious to escape the stifling atmosphere of the Hotel Bragança, particularly now that he knows he will not lose Lydia by leaving. She has given her promise, has guaranteed the gratification of those desires with which we are all familiar. Ricardo Reis seems to have forgotten Fernando Pessoa, the poet's image has faded, like a photograph exposed to sunlight or a plastic funeral wreath that has lost its color. The poet himself warned him, Nine months, perhaps not even that, and he has not reappeared, perhaps he is in a bad mood or angry, or perhaps, being dead, he cannot escape the obligations of his condition. We can only speculate, we know nothing, after all, of life beyond the grave, and Ricardo Reis forgot to ask him when he had the opportunity, the living are so selfish and unfeeling. The days pass, monotonous, gray. There is news of more storms in Ribatejo, cattle swept away by floods, houses collapsing, sinking into the mud, cornfields submerged. All that is visible, on the surface of the vast lake covering the marshes by the river, are the rounded crests of weeping willows, the battered spurs of ash trees and poplars, their highest branches entwined with floating brushwood and vernal grass that was torn from its roots. When finally the waters subside, people will say, Look, the water came up to here, and no one will believe it. Ricardo Reis neither suffers nor witnesses these disasters, he reads the newspaper reports and studies the photographs. Scenes of tragedy, says the headline, and he muses on the persistent cruelty of fate, which can remove us from this world in so many ways yet takes perverse pleasure in choosing iron and fire and this endless deluge. We find Ricardo Reis reclining on a sofa in the hotel lounge, enjoying the warmth of the paraffin heater and the cozy atmosphere. Were we not endowed with the gift of reading the human heart, we would never know the sad thoughts that assail him, the misery of his neighbor some fifty, eighty kilometers away. Here I am, meditating on the cruelty of fate and the indifference of the gods, for they are the same thing, as I hear Salvador telling Pimenta to go to the kiosk to buy a Spanish newspaper, and the unmistakable footsteps of Lydia climbing the stairs to the second floor. Distracted, I pick up the classifieds again, my current obsession, rooms to rent, carefully I go down the list with my forefinger, nervous, not wanting Salvador to catch me. Suddenly I come to a halt, Furnished rooms to let, Rua de Santa Catarina, deposit required. I can see the building as clearly as the photographs of the flood, its upper story decorated with inscriptions, it's the one I noticed that afternoon when I met Marcenda, how could I have forgotten it, I'll go there right now, but I must be calm, betray no excitement, behave naturally. Done reading the *Diário de Notícias*, I now fold it carefully, leave it just as I found it, not like some people who scatter the pages everywhere. I get up, say to Salvador, I'm going for a stroll, the rain has stopped, what further explanation should I give if pressed. Ricardo Reis suddenly realizes that his relationship with the hotel, or with Salvador, is that of a dependent. He looks at himself in the mirror and once more sees a pupil of the Jesuits, a rebel against the code of discipline simply because it is a code of discipline. But this is worse, because he cannot even muster the courage to say, Salvador, I'm off to look at an apartment, and if I find it suitable, I will be leaving the hotel, I'm fed up with you and Pimenta, with all of you, except Lydia, of course, who deserves something better than this place. He does not say any of this, but only, See you in a while, almost as if he were asking to be excused. Cowardice is shown not only on the battlefield or when one is confronted with a knife pointed at one's entrails. There are people whose courage wobbles like jelly, but it's not their fault, that's how they were born.

Within a few minutes Ricardo Reis had reached the Alto de Santa Catarina. Seated on the same bench were the same two old men gazing at the river. They turned around when they heard footsteps, and one remarked to the other, That's the fellow who was here three weeks ago. You mean, the other said, the one with the girl, because although many other men and women had come here, strolling past or stopping to take in the view, the old men knew perfectly well which man. It is a mistake to think that one loses one's memory with old age, that the elderly preserve only remote memories which gradually surface like submerged foliage as the swollen waters recede. There is a dreadful memory that comes with old age, the memory of the final days, the final image of the world, of life, That was how I left it, who can tell if it will remain like that, they say when they reach the other side, and these two old men will say the same, but today's image is not their last. On the front door of the building Ricardo Reis found a pinned notice. It read, Prospective viewers should apply to the agent. The address given was in the Baixa, there was still time. He ran all the way to the Rua do Calhariz, hailed a taxi, and came back accompanied by a stout gentleman, Yes sir, I am the agent, he had brought the keys. They went up, here is the apartment, spacious, adequate for a large family, furniture made of dark mahogany, an enormous bed, a tall closet, a fully furnished dining room, a sideboard, a credenza for silver or china according to one's means, an extending table, and the study paneled with maple, the desk covered with green baize like a billiard table, threadbare in one corner, and a kitchen, and a bathroom rudimentary but adequate. Every item of furniture was bare, empty, not a single utensil, dish, or ornament, no sheets or towels, The last tenant was an old woman, a widow, who has gone to live with her children and taken all her belongings, the place is to be let with only the furniture you see here. Ricardo Reis went to one of the windows, there were no curtains, and he could see the palm trees in the square, the statue of Adamastor, the old men seated on the bench, and beyond, on the mud-polluted river, the warships with their prows turned landward. One cannot tell, watching them, if the tide is about to rise or fall. If we linger here a little longer, we will see. How much is the rent, what kind of deposit do you expect for the furniture, and within half an hour, if that, of discreet bargaining they reached an agreement. The agent was reassured that he was dealing with a gentleman of some distinction, Tomorrow, sir, if you would care to call at my office we can sign the contract, here is your key, Doctor, the apartment is yours. Ricardo Reis thanked him, insisted on leaving a deposit in excess of the usual percent. The agent wrote out a receipt then and there, he sat at the desk and took out a fountain pen overlaid with a filigree of stylized leaves and branches. In the silence of the apartment all that could be heard was the scraping of the nib on the paper and the agent breathing, wheezing a little, clearly asthmatic, Done, there you are, no, please don't disturb yourself, I can take a taxi, I assume you'll want to stay a while to get the feel of your new home, I fully understand, people become attached to their homes, the woman who lived here, poor old girl, how she wept the day she left, inconsolable, but we are often forced by circumstances, illness, widowhood, what must be, must be, we are powerless, well then, I'll expect you at my office tomorrow. Now alone, holding the key in his hand, Ricardo Reis went through the rooms again, thinking of nothing, merely looking, then went to the window. The prows of the ships pointed upstream, a sign that the tide was going out. The old men remained seated on the bench.

That same night Ricardo Reis told Lydia that he had rented an apartment. She wept a little, complained that she would no longer be able to look at him at every moment, an exaggeration on her part, words spoken in passion, because she could not look at him at every moment when they spent the night together with the light off in case anyone was spying, and during the day Lydia avoided him or addressed him with the utmost formality, a scene relished by malicious witnesses who were waiting for an opportunity to take their revenge. He comforted her, Don't cry, we will see each other on your days off, undisturbed by anyone, that's if you want to come, a question that required no answer. Of course I want to come, I already told you so, when are you thinking of moving to your apartment. The moment it's ready, there is some furniture, but no linen, no kitchen things, I don't need much to start, a few towels, sheets, blankets, then little by little I will get the rest. If the place has been closed up for some time, it will need cleaning, so I'll do it. What an idea, I can employ some woman in the neighborhood. I won't have it, you can rely on me, why go looking for someone else. You are a good girl, Pooh, I am who I am. This is one of those statements that brooks no reply. Each of us should know who he is, there has certainly been no lack of advice on that score since the time of the Greeks and Romans, Know thyself, hence our admiration for this Lydia, who does not appear to have the slightest doubt.

Next day, Ricardo Reis went out and bought two complete sets of bed linen and towels in various sizes. Fortunately the water, gas, and electricity had not been cut off by the respective companies and the accounts could remain in the name of the previous tenant, or so the agent suggested, and he agreed. He also bought some pots and pans, enamel and aluminum, a coffee pot, cups and saucers, napkins, coffee, tea, and sugar, all the things he would be likely to need for breakfast. Lunch and dinner he would have out. He enjoyed this little shopping expedition, it reminded him of his first days in Rio de Janeiro, where without any assistance he had done the same thing. Between trips to and from the shops, he wrote a short letter to Marcenda, communicating his new address, by extraordinary coincidence very near the spot where they had had their meeting. How typical of this vast world, where men, like animals, have their own territory, each his own yard or coop, his own spider's web, which is the best comparison of all. One spider spins a web as far as Oporto, another as far as Rio, but these are only supports, points of reference, mooring posts, it is in the center of the web that the spider and the fly play out their destiny. In the late afternoon Ricardo Reis took a taxi from shop to shop collecting his purchases, then bought a few pastries, some crystallized fruit, and a selection of biscuits, tea, digestive, and arrowroot. He returned to the Rua de Santa Catarina, arrived just as the two old men were descending to their homes somewhere in the neighborhood. While Ricardo Reis lifted his parcels from the taxi and carried them up, making three trips, the old men stopped and watched, and seeing the lights go on in the apartment on the third floor, they said, Look, someone is living in the apartment Dona Luísa used to occupy. They only moved away when the new tenant appeared at the window and saw them. They went off in a state of nervous excitement, which sometimes happens, and just as well, a welcome break in the monotony of existence. We think we have arrived at the end of the road, but it is only a bend opening onto a new horizon and new wonders. From his windows bare of drapes Ricardo Reis watched the river's expanse. To get a better view he switched off the light. Gray light fell like pollen from the skies, becoming darker as it settled. Ferry boats to and from Cacilhas, their lamps already lit, plied the dingy waters alongside the warships and anchored barges. One last frigate, almost concealed behind the outline of the rooftops, is about to dock. The scene reminds you of a child's drawing. The evening is so sad that a desire to weep surges from the depths of the soul. His head resting against the windowpane, shut off from the world by a cloud of condensation as he breathes on the smooth, cold surface, he watches the contorted, defiant figure of Adamastor gradually dissolve. It was already dark when Ricardo Reis went out. He dined in a restaurant in the Rua dos Correeiros, on a mezzanine floor with a low ceiling, solitary among solitary men. Who were they, what kind of existence did they lead, what brought them to this place, chewing cod, baked hake, steak and potatoes, nearly everyone drinking red wine. More formal in their appearance than in their table manners, they rap on their glasses with their knives to summon the waiter, they pick their teeth, tooth by tooth, with fierce satisfaction, extracting some stubborn fiber with thumb and forefinger used like pliers. They belch, loosen their belts, unbutton their vests, unshoulder their suspenders. Ricardo Reis thought to himself, This is what all my meals will be like from now on, this clatter of cutlery, the voices of the waiters shouting into the kitchen, One soup, the muffled sounds of those eating, the dismal light, the grease congealed on the cold plates, the adjacent table still not cleared, wine stains on the tablecloth, bread crumbs, a cigarette butt still burning. Ah how different life is in the Hotel Bragança, even if it is not first class. Ricardo Reis suddenly feels bereft of Ramón's presence, even though he will see him again tomorrow, today is only Thursday, he is leaving the hotel on Saturday. Yet he knows that such moments of nostalgia tend to be short-lived, it is all a question of habit, you lose one habit and gain another. He has been in Lisbon less than three months and already Rio de Janeiro is like a distant memory, perhaps of some other life, not his, one of those innumerable lives. Yes, at this very moment another Ricardo Reis may be dining in Oporto or lunching in Rio de Janeiro, if not farther afield. It has not rained all day and he has been able to do his shopping with the utmost tranquillity. He is now making his way back to the hotel, there he will inform Salvador that he is leaving

Saturday, just like that, I am leaving Saturday, but he feels like the adolescent who, having been refused a key to the house by his father, dares to take it without permission, trusting in the power of deeds once they have been carried out.

Salvador is still behind the reception desk but has told Pimenta that as soon as the last guest leaves the dining room he will go home, his wife is laid up with the flu. A seasonal fruit, Pimenta quips in a familiar tone, as they have known each other for many years. Salvador growls in reply, No chance of my being ill, a sibylline statement open to several interpretations. It could be the complaint of one who enjoys robust health or a warning to the powers of evil that it would be a great loss to this hotel if the manager were to fall ill. Ricardo Reis enters, wishes everyone a good evening, wonders for a second whether he should call Salvador to one side, then decides that such secrecy would be ridiculous, to murmur, for example, Look, Senhor Salvador, it wasn't really my intention, but you know how these things are, one's circumstances change, life goes on, the point is that I've decided to leave your admirable hotel, I've found a place of my own, please don't take offense, I hope we can go on being friends. Suddenly he finds himself sweating, as if he were once more a pupil of the Jesuits kneeling at the confessional, I lied, I was envious, I had impure thoughts, I played with myself. Salvador, at the reception desk, has reciprocated his greeting and turned away to take the key from the hook. Ricardo Reis must utter these liberating words at once, before Salvador can catch him off balance or trip him up. Senhor Salvador, could I ask you to prepare my bill, I will be checking out on Saturday. No sooner did he speak in this dry manner than he felt remorseful, because Salvador, standing there with the key in his hand, was the very image of wounded surprise, the victim of an act of betrayal. This is no way to treat a hotel manager who has shown himself to be such a staunch friend. What we should have done was call him to one side and say, Look Salvador, It wasn't really my intention, but no, guests can be so ungrateful and this guest is the most ungrateful of all, he came here for sanctuary, was well treated despite his affair with one of the chambermaids, any other manager would have sent both of them packing or complained to the police. I should have heeded Victor's warning but I let my heart rule my head, everyone takes advantage of my good nature, but I swear it's the last time. If all the seconds and minutes were exactly the same, as marked on the clock, we would not always have time to explain what takes place in them, the substance they contain, but fortunately for us the episodes of greatest significance tend to occur in seconds of long duration and minutes that are spun out, which makes it possible to discuss at length and in some detail without any serious violation of the most subtle of the three dramatic unities, which is time itself. With a halting gesture Salvador handed him the key, assumed a dignified expression, addressed him in a grave, paternal tone, I hope we have given every satisfaction during your stay here, Doctor. These modest words, so professionally phrased, with their underlying acerbic note of irony, could be misunderstood as alluding to Lydia, but no, for the moment Salvador is only trying to convey his disappointment and wounded feelings. Every possible satisfaction, Senhor Salvador, Ricardo Reis assured him warmly, it is simply that I've found an apartment, I have decided to settle in Lisbon once and for all, and a man needs a place he can call his own. Ah, well, perhaps I could ask Pimenta to help you transport your luggage, if the apartment is here in Lisbon, obviously. Yes, it's in Lisbon, but I can manage, thanks just the same, I'll hire a porter. Pimenta, prompted by the manager's generous offer of his services, curious as to where Doctor Reis was moving, and aware of his employer's interest, took it upon himself to insist, Why hire a porter, Doctor, when I can carry your suitcases. Thanks for offering, Pimenta, but I can easily get a porter, and to avoid any further insistence Ricardo Reis made his little farewell speech in advance, I can assure you, Senhor Salvador, that I shall take away the happiest memories of your hotel, where I have found the service excellent, where I felt completely at home and was treated with the utmost care and solicitude, I should like to express my deep gratitude to the entire staff, without exception, for the cordiality and affection they have shown me upon my return to my native Portugal, where I now intend to remain, to all of you my heartfelt thanks. Not all the staff were present, but that did not matter. Feeling very self-conscious, Ricardo Reis, as he spoke, found himself using words that were sure to spark sarcastic thoughts in those of his listeners who would think of Lydia at the mention of solicitude and affection. Why is it that words often make use of us, we see them approach menacingly, like an irresistible abyss, yet are unable to ward them off and end up saying precisely what we did not wish to say. Salvador replied with a few words, not that it was necessary, all he needed to say was how honored they had been to have Doctor Ricardo Reis as their guest, We were only doing our duty, and I speak for the entire staff when I say that we will miss you, Doctor, is that not so Pimenta. With this unexpected question the solemnity of the moment was dissolved, he appeared to be asking for his sentiment to be seconded, but the effect was quite the opposite, a wink, a glint of malice, If you understand what I mean, and Ricardo Reis understood, he wished them good-night and went up to his room, certain that they were discussing him behind his back, already uttering Lydia's name. What he did not suspect was that the conversation continued like this, You must find out the name of the porter he hires, I want to know where he's moving to.

The clock has certain hours which are so empty of significance, the hands appear to crawl toward infinity, the morning drags, the afternoon is neverending, the night seems eternal. This was how Ricardo Reis spent his last day in the hotel. Moved by some unconscious scruple, he decided that he should be visible all the time. Perhaps he did not want to appear ungrateful or indifferent. His departure was acknowledged by Ramón as he ladled the soup into his plate, So you are leaving us, Doctor, words which convey deep sadness when uttered as only humble servants know how to utter them. And Lydia's name was never off Salvador's lips, he summoned her for everything and for nothing, ordered her to do one thing then the opposite, he watched her every movement, expression, her eyes, seeking signs of unhappiness, tears, only natural in a woman who is about to be abandoned and knows it. Yet he had never seen her look so peaceful and composed, one would think she had no sins on her conscience, no weakness of the flesh or willful prostitution. Salvador reproached himself for not having punished such immoral conduct the moment he suspected it, or when it became public knowledge, starting with rumors in the kitchen and the storeroom. It is too late now, the guest is leaving, no point in raking up mud, especially when his conscience tells him that he himself is not entirely without blame, he knew what was going on and said nothing, he was an accomplice. I simply felt sorry for him, he arrived from Brazil, from the wilderness, without any family to receive him, so I treated him as if he were a relative. Three or four times Salvador consoled himself with this thought, then spoke aloud, When room two hundred and one is vacated, I want it cleaned from top to bottom, it has been reserved for a distinguished family from Granada. As Lydia walked away, having received these instructions, he stared at the curve of her hips. Until today he has been an exemplary manager, upright, never mixing business with pleasure, but now he has a score to settle, Either she consents or she'll be out on the street. We feel certain that this anger will go no further, most men lose their courage at the last moment.

After lunch on Saturday, Ricardo Reis went to the Chiado, where he contracted the services of two young porters, and in order not to have them trailing after him down the Rua do Alecrim like a guard of honor, he told them what time they should come to the hotel. He waited in his room with the same sense of veering off course he experienced when he saw the mooring cables drop from *The Highland Brigade* to the quay in Rio de Janeiro. He is alone, seated on the sofa, Lydia will not appear, that was what they have agreed. A clatter of heavy footsteps in the corridor announces the arrival of the porters, Pimenta with them. This time Pimenta does not have to exert himself, at most he will make the same gesture Ricardo Reis and Salvador made when he first carried up the large suitcase, a helping hand underneath, a note of caution on the stairs, a word of advice, unnecessary for those who have mastered all there is to know about lifting luggage. Ricardo Reis goes to say good-bye to Salvador and leaves a generous tip for the staff, Share it among yourselves as you see fit. The manager thanks him. Some guests who happen to be present smile approvingly on the nice friendships formed in this hotel, and the Spaniards are deeply moved at the sight of such goodwill. Little wonder that their own divided land comes to mind, these are peninsular contradictions. Below, on the street, Pimenta has already asked the porters where they are taking the luggage, but the gentleman has said nothing, one of them thinks it cannot be far away, the other is not so sure. But there is no need for concern, Pimenta knows the two men, one of them even worked for the hotel, and they can always be found hanging around the Chiado. When he wants to get to the bottom of the mystery, he will not have far to go. Ricardo Reis tells him, I've left you a little token of gratitude, and Pimenta replies, Many thanks, Doctor, whenever you need any help, you can rely on me. Empty words, hypocritical words, the Frenchman who said that man has been endowed with words to hide his thoughts spoke true, still we should not make hasty judgments, what is certain is that words are the best tools we can hope for in our attempt, always frustrated, to express what we call thought. The two porters now learn where they must take the suitcases, Ricardo Reis tells them as soon as Pimenta has withdrawn, and off they go, up the street. They use the sidewalk, which is less broken. This is not a heavy load for men accustomed to moving pianos and other monstrosities with levers and ropes. Ricardo Reis walks in front, far enough ahead to avoid giving the impression that he is leading this expedition but not so far ahead as to make the porters feel they are unaccompanied. Nothing could be more delicate than these contacts between different classes. Social harmony is a question of tact, finesse, and psychology, and whether these three qualities strictly coincide with one's feelings is a problem we have given up trying to solve. Halfway up the street the porters are obliged to move to one side, and they take this opportunity to rest their load and get their breath back, because a procession of trams crammed with people with blond hair and pink complexions is coming down the road, German tourists, workers belonging to the German Labor Front. Nearly all of them are in Bavarian costume, knee breeches, shirt and shoulder straps, little hats with narrow brims. Some of the trams are open, like wheeled cages into which the rain can fall at will, the striped canvas awning giving little protection. What must these Aryan workers be saying about our Portuguese civilization, what do these sons of so privileged a race think of the rustics who pause now to watch them pass. Look at that dark-haired gentleman in the light raincoat, and those two unshaven types dressed like tramps, hoisting the load back onto their shoulders and resuming their climb. The last of the trams go by, there were twenty-three trams altogether, if anyone had the patience to count them, heading for the Torre de Belém, the Mosteiro dos Jerónimos, and the other landmarks of Lisbon, such as Algés, Dafundo and Cruz Quebrada.

With lowered heads, because of their burden no doubt, the porters crossed the square where the statue of the epic poet stands. Ricardo Reis now followed, embarrassed at traveling so light, his hands in his pockets. He had not even brought a yellow parrot from Brazil, and perhaps just as well, for he would not have had the courage to go through these streets carrying the stupid creature on a perch, with people teasing it, Give me your claw, yellow parrot, perhaps referring, with typical Portuguese wit, to those blond Germans going past in trams. At the bottom of this road you can see the palms of the Alto de Santa Catarina between the mountains on the opposite coast. Heavy clouds appear like buxom women at their windows, a metaphor that would make Ricardo Reis, a poet for whom clouds barely exist, shrug with scorn. Fleecy clouds, racing clouds, so white and hackneyed, and if it is raining, that means Apollo has hidden his face. This is the entrance to my apartment, here is the key and there is the staircase, second landing, number two, this is where I will live. No windows opened when we arrived, no doors were ajar, it would appear that the least inquisitive inhabitants of Lisbon all live in this building, or else they are spying through peepholes, the pupils of their eyes flashing. Now in we go, the two small suitcases, the larger one, the money agreed upon is paid, the expected tip. There is a pungent odor of sweat. Whenever you need any help, boss, we're always available. They said always so earnestly that Ricardo Reis believed them, but he did not reply. A man, if he has studied, learns to be skeptical, especially since the gods are so inconstant. The only certainty, theirs from knowledge, ours from experience, is that everything comes to an end, and always soonest. As the porters left, Ricardo Reis closed the door to the landing. Then, without switching on the lights, he went through the entire apartment, his footsteps echoing on the bare floorboards. Furniture empty and smelling of old mothballs, frayed sheets of tissue paper still lining some of the drawers, fluff accumulating in corners, and near the kitchen and bathroom a strong smell from the drains, because the water was low in the cistern. Ricardo Reis opened the spigots and flushed the toilet several times. The apartment filled with noises, the running of water, the vibration of pipes, a tapping sound from the meter, then gradually silence was restored. At the rear of the building was a yard with washing hanging up to dry, small vegetable patches the color of ashes, troughs, vats made of cement, a dog kennel, rabbit hutches, and chicken coops. Looking at them, Ricardo Reis reflected on the linguistic conundrum whereby rabbits had hutches and chicken had coops, and not the other way around. He returned to the front of the apartment to look out the grimy bedroom window at the deserted street. There stood Adamastor, livid against the dull clouds, a giant raging in silence. Some people are watching the ships, they look up from time to time as if expecting rain, and seated on the same bench, the two old men lost in conversation. Ricardo Reis smiled, Well done, they are so absorbed they did not even notice the arrival of the suitcases. He had never been one for jokes but was amused, as if he had just played a harmless trick on both of them, a friendly game. Still wearing his raincoat, as if having just dropped by for a second, a doctor's visit, as the adage cynically puts it, to make a quick inspection of the place where he might take up residence someday, he finally said aloud, like a message he must not forget, I live here, this is where I live, this is my home, this, I have no other, and suddenly he felt fear, the terror of a man who finds himself in a deep cave and pushes open a door that leads into the darkness of an even deeper cave, or to a void, an absence, nothingness, the passage to nonbeing. Removing his raincoat and jacket, he realized the apartment was cold. As if going through motions already made in another life, he unpacked methodically, his clothes, shoes, papers, books, and all those small objects, essential or nonessential, we take with us from one abode to another, the crossed threads of a cocoon. He found his dressing gown, put it on. Now he is a man settled in his own home. He turned on the lamp that hung from the ceiling, it needed a shade, tulip-shaped, spherical, conical, any of these will do so long as they eliminate the glare which is hurting his eyes. Engrossed in putting away his things, he did not notice at first that it had started to rain, but a sharp gust of wind sent the water drumming against the panes. Such weather. He went to the window. The old men, like somber insects attracted by the light, were standing on the sidewalk opposite, one tall, the other short, each armed with an umbrella, their heads upturned like praying mantises. This time they were not intimidated by the face that appeared. Only when the rain became much heavier did they proceed down the street. When they get home their wives, if they have wives, will scold them, Soaked to the skin, just look at you, you could catch pneumonia, then I'll have all the trouble of nursing you, and the old men will tell them, Someone has moved into Dona Luísa's apartment, a man who seems to be by himself, not another living soul to be seen, Imagine, a big place like that for a bachelor, what a waste of good space. You might well ask how these good women know the apartment is large. Who can tell, perhaps in the time of Dona Luísa they did some charring there. Women of that class will turn their hand to anything that comes their way if their husbands earn low wages or pocket some of it to spend on booze and whores. The unfortunate wives are forced to scrub stairs and take in washing, some even specialize, doing nothing except scrubbing stairs or laundry, and so become mistresses of their craft. They have their own little ways, taking pride in the whiteness of their sheets, the cleanliness of their stairs scrubbed with carbolic soap, and their sheets could pass for altar cloths, you could eat spilled marmalade from their doorstep without any qualms. But where is this digression leading us. Now the sky is overcast and night will soon be here. When the old men were standing on the sidewalk looking up, they appeared to bask in the full light of day, but this was simply the effect of their white beards after eight days without shaving. Not even today, Sunday, did they sit in the barber's chair or use their own razor, but tomorrow, if the weather clears up, they will be cleanshaven, their skin lined with wrinkles and alum. When we say their hair is white, we mean only lower down, because on top they have nothing but a few sad wisps over their ears. But to return to where we left off. When they were standing there on the sidewalk, there was still daylight, although it was fast waning, so after watching the tenant on the third floor while the rain became heavier, they started walking downhill, walked on as it grew steadily darker, and by the time they reached the corner it was night. A good thing the street lamps were lit, casting pearls on the windowpanes. It must be said that these street lamps are nothing like those of the future, when the fairy Electricity with her magic wand will reach the Alto de Santa Catarina and environs and all the lamps will light up in glory at the same time. Today we have to wait until someone comes to light them, one by one. With the tip of his spill the lamplighter opens the door of the lantern, with the hook he turns the gas valve, then this son of Saint Elmo moves on, leaving signs of his passing throughout the city streets. A man bearing light, he is Halley's comet with a star-spangled trail, this is how the gods must have seen Prometheus when they looked down from on high. This particular firefly, however, is named António. Ricardo Reis feels a chill across his forehead, which was pressed against the windowpane as he watched the falling rain. The lamplighter appears, then each lamp is left with its glow and aura. A pale light covers the shoulders of Adamastor, the Herculean muscles of his back glisten, perhaps from the water descending from the sky, or perhaps it is the sweat of his agony as Thetis smiles derisively and mocks him, What nymph could offer enough love to satisfy the love of a giant. Now he knows what those promises of riches were worth. Lisbon is a great murmuring silence, nothing more.

Ricardo Reis returned to his domestic chores, put away his suits, shirts, handkerchiefs, socks, item by item, as if composing a Sapphic ode, laboriously working with an awkward rhyme scheme. The color of the tie he has just hung up requires a matching suit, which he must buy. Over the mattress that belonged to Dona Luísa, certainly not the one on which she lost her virginity many years ago but the mattress where she bled giving birth to her last child, and where her dear husband, a high court judge, suffered and died, over this mattress Ricardo Reis spread sheets still smelling of newness, two fleecy blankets, a pale bedspread. He slipped the pillow and woolen bolster into their cases, doing the best he could, clumsy as any male. Eventually Lydia will appear, perhaps tomorrow, with those magical hands of hers, magical because they are the hands of a woman, to tidy up this chaos, this resigned sorrow of things badly arranged. Ricardo Reis carried the suitcases into the kitchen, hung up the towels in the ice-cold bathroom, stored his toiletries in the little wall cabinet, which had a definite mildew smell. As we have already seen, he is a man fastidious about his appearance, it is a question of personal pride. All that remains to be done now is arrange his books on those warped black bookshelves in the study and put his papers in the drawers of the wobbly black bureau. Now he feels at home, he has found his bearings, the compass rose, north, south, east, west, unless some magnetic storm comes to send this compass into a frenzy.

At half past seven the rain has not stopped. Ricardo Reis sits on the edge of the high bed and examines the cheerless room. The window is bare of any curtains or netting. It occurs to him that the neighbors across the way might be spying, whispering among themselves, You can see everything that's going on in there. Eagerly they look forward to sights even more provocative than this one of a man sitting alone on the edge of an old-fashioned bed, his face hidden in a cloud. Ricardo Reis gets up and closes the inner shutters. Now the room is a cell, four blind walls, the door, should he open it, would lead to another door, or to a dark yawning cave, we have already used that image, it does not bear repeating. Shortly, in the Hotel Bragança, the maître d', Afonso, will strike the three blows of Vatel on that ludicrous gong, and the Portuguese and Spanish guests, *nuestros hermanos, los hermanos suyos*, will descend to the dining room. Salvador will smile at each in turn, Senhor Fonseca, Doctor Pascal, Madame, Don Camilo, Don Lorenzo, and the new arrival in room two hundred and one, surely the Duke of Alba or of Medinaceli, dragging his mighty sword, pressing a ducat into Lydia's outstretched hand. She curtsies, as befits a servant, and smilingly accepts a pinch in the flesh of her arm. Ramón will be bringing in the soup, today there is something special and he is not joking, from the deep tureen comes the fragrant smell of chicken, from the platters intoxicating aromas. We need not be surprised that Ricardo Reis feels his stomach rumble, it is, indeed, time for dinner. But even with the shutters closed you can hear the water from the eaves spattering on the sidewalk. Who would be so bold as to venture forth in weather like this, except for some pressing obligation, to save one's father from the gallows, for example, if one's father is still alive. The dining room of the Hotel Bragança is a lost paradise, and like any lost paradise it is sorely missed by Ricardo Reis, who would like to return but not to remain. He goes to get his parcels, the pastries and crystallized fruit, to satisfy his hunger. For drinking there is only tap water, which tastes of carbolic acid. Adam and Eve must have felt just as deprived that first night after their expulsion from the Garden of Eden, clearly it was raining buckets then too. As they stood in the doorway and Eve asked Adam, Would you like a biscuit, having only one, she broke it in half and gave him the larger piece. Adam munched slowly, watching Eve peck at her tiny portion, tilting her head like an inquisitive little bird. On the other side of the door now closed to them forever, without any evil intent or any prompting on the part of the serpent, she had offered him an apple. It is said that Adam only became aware of her nakedness when he bit into the apple, and that Eve, who did not have time to get dressed, remained like the lilies of the field who neither spin nor weave. Not far from the threshold of Eden they both spent the night comfortably, having eaten a biscuit for their supper, while on the other side God listened and felt sad, barred from a feast He had neither provided for nor foreseen. One day another maxim will be invented, Where man and woman join, God is, because paradise is not at all where it was said to be, it is here on earth and God will be obliged to come every time He wishes to enjoy it. But certainly not in this house. Ricardo Reis is alone. The cloying sweetness of a crystallized pear has made him feel sick, a pear, not an apple, it is indeed true that temptations are no longer what they were. He went into the bathroom to clean his sticky hands, his mouth, his teeth, he cannot bear this *dolceza*, a word that is neither Portuguese nor Spanish but an adaptation of the Italian, it is the only word that seems appropriate at the moment. Solitude weighs on him like night, and the night devours him like bait. Through the long narrow corridor under the greenish light that descends from the ceiling he is a marine animal with sluggish movements, a defenseless tortoise without its shell.

He rummages at the desk, through the manuscripts of his poems, he called them odes and so they have remained, because everything must have a name. He reads at random and asks himself if he is their author, for he does not recognize himself in what is written, in this detached, calm, resigned person, almost godlike, for that is how gods are, composed as they assist the dead. Vaguely he muses, he must organize his life, his time, decide how he will spend his mornings, afternoons, and evenings, get to bed early and rise early, find one or two restaurants that serve simple, wholesome meals, and he must reread and revise his poems for the anthology he plans to publish at some future date, and he must find suitable premises for his practice, get to know people, travel to other parts of the country, visit Oporto, Coimbra, call on Doctor Sampaio, run into Marcenda unexpectedly in the city's Poplar Grove. He no longer thinks about his plans and objectives, he feels compassion for the invalid, then for himself, and his compassion turns to self-pity. As he sits there, he begins a poem, then suddenly remembers that he once wrote, *I stand firmly upon the foundation of the poems I fashioned*. Anyone who has drawn up a testament such as this cannot now say the opposite.

It is not yet ten o'clock when Ricardo Reis goes to bed. The rain is still falling. He has brought a book to bed, he chose two but then decided against *The God of the Labyrinth*. After ten pages of the Sermon for the first Sunday in Lent his ungloved hands were freezing, those ardent words were not enough to warm them, *Search your house, look for the most worthless thing therein, and you will find that it is your own soul*. He put the book on the bedside table, huddled up with a sudden shiver, pulled the fold of the sheet up to his mouth, and closed his eyes. He knew he ought to switch off the light, but if he did that, he would feel obliged to fall asleep and he was not ready just yet. On cold nights like this Lydia would put a hot-water bottle between the sheets, will she be doing that now for the Duke of Medinaceli, calm yourself, jealous heart, the duke was accompanied by the duchess, the nobleman who pinched Lydia's arm in passing was the other duke, the Duke of Alba. The Duke of Medinaceli is old, sick, and impotent, he carries a tin sword, swears it is the mighty Colada that belonged to Cid Campeador and was passed from father to son in the Alba dynasty. Even a Spanish grandee is capable of telling lies. Ricardo Reis had fallen asleep, he realized it when he awoke, startled, to the sound of knocking at the door. Could it be Lydia, who has cunningly slipped out of the hotel and come in all this rain to spend the night with me, foolish girl. Then he thought, I've been dreaming. And so it appeared, for he heard nothing more in the seconds that followed, Perhaps there are ghosts in this apartment, perhaps that is why they couldn't rent it, so central, so spacious. But the knocking started up again, rat-tat-tat, discreetly, so as not to disturb the neighbors. Ricardo Reis got out of bed, pulled on his slippers, wrapped his dressing gown around him, shuffled across the room into the hall-way, shivering all the while, and looked at the door as if it were threatening him, Who is there. His voice sounded hoarse and fal-tering. Clearing his throat, he repeated the question. The reply came in a murmur, It's me. It was no ghost, it was Fernando Pessoa, trust him to choose an awkward moment. Ricardo Reis opened the door, and it was he all right, wearing his black suit, with neither coat nor hat, yet though he was coming in off the street there was not a drop of water on him. May I come in, he asked. You've never asked my permission before, why the sudden scruple. Things have changed, you're in your own home now and, to use an English expression which I learned as a schoolboy, a man's home is his castle. Come in, I was in bed, Were you asleep, I believe I dozed off, No need to stand on ceremony with me, get back into bed, I'm only dropping by for a few minutes. Ricardo Reis slipped nimbly between the sheets, his teeth chattering with cold but also from a residue of fear. He did not take off his dressing gown. Fernando Pessoa sat in a chair, crossed his legs, clasped his hands on his knee, and looked around with a critical eye, So, this is where you've taken up residence. It would seem. I find it rather dreary. Places that have been empty for some time always give that impression. Do you mean to live here on your own. Evidently not, I only moved in today and already have a visitor. I don't count, I'm scarcely company for anyone. You counted enough for me to have to get out of bed in this cold to open the door, soon I will be giving you a key. I wouldn't know what to do with it, if I could pass through walls I would spare you the trouble. Don't give it another thought, you mustn't take my words amiss, to be frank, I'm delighted to see you, this first night is not easy. Are you frightened. I felt a little nervous when I heard knocking, I forgot that it might be you, but it wasn't fear, only loneliness. Come now, you have a long way to go before you know what loneliness is. I've always lived alone. I too, but loneliness is not living alone, loneliness is the inability to keep someone or something within us company, it is not a tree that stands alone in the middle of a plain but the distance between the deep sap and the bark, between the leaves and the roots. You're talking nonsense, the things you mention are connected, there is no loneliness there. Let us forget the tree, look inside yourself. As that other poet said, *To walk alone among men.* It is even worse to be alone where we ourselves are not. You are in low spirits today. I have my days, but I was speaking not of this loneliness but of another, the one that travels with us, a bearable loneliness that keeps us company, Even that loneliness, you must agree, is some-times unbearable, we long for a presence, a voice. Sometimes that presence and that voice only serve to render it intolerable. Is this possible. It most certainly is, the other day when we met at the belvedere, do you remember, you were waiting for your mistress. I've already told you that she is not my mistress. All right then, no need to lose your temper, but she might become your mistress, you don't know what tomorrow has in store for you. I am old enough to be her father. So what. Let us change the subject, finish what you were telling me. It was apropos of your having had the flu, it reminded me of a little episode during my own illness, this recent, terminal illness. How repetitive, your sense of style has sadly deteriorated. Death too is repetitive, it is in fact the most repetitive thing of all. Go on. A doctor came to the house, I was lying in the bedroom when my sister opened the door. You mean your half-sister, life is full of half-brothers and half-sisters. What are you trying to suggest. Nothing in particular, go on. She said, Do come in Doctor, the faker is in here, the faker in question was I, as you can see, loneliness has no bounds, it is everywhere. Have you ever felt yourself to be truly useless. Difficult to say, I don't recall ever having felt myself to be truly useful. I believe that this is the first loneliness, to feel that we are useless. Fernando Pessoa got up, half-opened the shutters, and looked out. An unpardonable oversight, he said, not to have included Adamastor in my *Mensagem*, such a popular giant, whose symbolic meaning is clear. Can you see him from there. Yes, poor creature, Camões used him for declarations of love which were probably in his own soul, and for prophecies that were less than clear. To forecast shipwreck to those who sail the high seas no special gifts of divination are needed. Prophesying disaster was ever a sign of loneliness, had Thetis reciprocated the giant's love, his discourse would have been quite different. Fernando Pessoa was sitting once more, in exactly the same position. Do you intend staying long, Ricardo Reis asked him. Why. I am tired. Don't worry about me, sleep to your heart's content, unless you find my presence disturbing. What disturbs me is to see you sitting here in the cold. The cold doesn't bother me, I could sit here in my shirt sleeves, but you shouldn't be lying in bed wearing your dressing gown, I'll take it off now. Fernando Pessoa spread the dressing gown over the top cover, pulled up the blankets, straightened the fold of the sheet maternally, Now sleep. I say Fernando, do me a favor, switch off the light, I'm sure you don't mind sitting in the dark. When Fernando Pessoa found the switch, the room was plunged into darkness. Then, very slowly, the light from the street lamps insinuated itself through the chinks of the shutters, a luminous band, a tenuous, uncertain pollen gathered on the walls. Ricardo Reis closed his eyes, murmured, Goodnight Fernando, and it seemed to him that a long time passed before he heard him reply, Good-night Ricardo. When he thought he had counted up to a hundred, he opened his eyes with difficulty. Fernando Pessoa was sitting in the same chair, hands clasped on one knee, the image of ultimate loneliness. Perhaps because he is without his glasses, Ricardo Reis thought, and this struck him, in his confused state, as being the most terrible of misfortunes. He awoke in the middle of the night. The rain had stopped, the world was traveling through silent space. Fernando Pessoa had not altered his position, he looked in the direction of the bed, his face expressionless, like a statue with vacant eyes. Much later, Ricardo Reis awoke again as a door banged. Fernando Pessoa was no longer there, he had left with the first light of morning.

As one has already seen in other times and other places, life has its vexations. When Ricardo Reis awoke late next morning, he sensed a presence in the room. Perhaps not quite loneliness, but silence, its half-brother. For several minutes he watched his courage desert him, it was like watching sand run through an hourglass, an overworked metaphor which nevertheless keeps recurring. One day, when we live two hundred years and ourselves become the hourglass observing the sand inside it, we will not need the metaphor, but life is too short to indulge in such thoughts, we were speaking of vexations. When Ricardo Reis went into the kitchen to light the heater and the range, he found that he had forgotten to buy matches, and since one lapse of memory tends to accompany another, he realized that he also was without a coffee strainer. It is indeed true that a man on his own is useless. The easiest and most immediate solution would be to knock on a neighbor's door, Please excuse me, senhora, I am the new tenant on the third floor, I only moved in yesterday, I was hoping to make myself some coffee, have a wash, shave, and I find I have no matches, I also am without a coffee strainer, but that is not important, I have tea, that at least I remembered, the main problem is hot water for a bath, if you could lend me a match, I'd be most grateful, forgive me for disturbing you. Since all men are brothers, or half-brothers, nothing could be more natural, he should not even have to go out into the cold stairway, they should come and ask him, Do you need anything, I saw you moving in yesterday, everybody knows that moving is like this, if it is not the matches that are missing, the salt has been forgotten, if the soap turns up, the scrubbing brush has been lost, what are neighbors for. But Ricardo Reis did not go to seek help, and no one came to ask if he needed anything. He had no choice but to dress, put on his shoes, wrap a scarf around his neck to conceal the fact that he had not shaved, and pull his hat down over his eyes. He was irritated at his forgetfulness and even more so at having to go out in this sorry state looking for matches. First he went to the window to see what the weather was like. The sky was overcast, no sign of rain. Adamastor stands alone, it is still too early for the old men to come and watch the ships, at this hour they will be at home shaving with cold water, or perhaps their careworn wives are heating mugs of water, but only tepid, not hot, because the Portuguese male, second to none in virility, cannot bear to be pampered. Let us not forget that we are the direct descendants of those Lusitanian heroes who bathed in the frozen lakes of the Serra da Estrela, no sooner emerging than they were off to impregnate some Lusitanian maiden. From a coal merchant who runs a tavern in the lower part of the neighborhood Ricardo Reis bought matches, a half-dozen boxes lest the man find this early morning sale insufficient. In fact the coal merchant could not remember ever having made such a sale at one go, here it is still customary for people to ask their neighbors for a light. Invigorated by the cold air, comforted by his scarf and the absence of people on the street, Ricardo Reis walked up to get a view of the river and the mountains on the other side. From here the mountains looked squat, and the sun's reflection on the water appeared and disappeared as low clouds passed. He walked around the statue, trying to find the name of the sculptor. The date is engraved there, nineteen twenty-seven. Ricardo Reis has the kind of mind which is always searching for patterns of symmetry in the chaos, Eight years after my departure into exile, the statue of Adamastor was erected on this spot, and Adamastor had been standing here for eight years when I returned to the land of my ancestors, O fatherland, it was the voices of your illustrious past that summoned me. The old men appear on the sidewalk, their cleanshaven faces marked with wrinkles and alum, an umbrella over one arm. They have left their capes unbuttoned and wear no tie, but their shirts are buttoned to the neck, not because it is Sunday, a day of respect, but out of a sense of what is fitting and dignified, however shabby their attire. Suspicious of this loitering at the statue, the old men come face to face with Ricardo Reis, they are convinced that there is something odd about the fellow, Who is he, what is he doing, how does he earn his living. Before sitting down, they place a length of folded sackcloth on the damp bench, then with the measured gestures of those who refuse to be hurried they make themselves comfortable, clear their throats loudly. The fat one produces a newspaper from the inside pocket of his cape, *O Século*, the newspaper that organizes charity events. They always buy it on Sunday, the fat man one week, the thin man the next. Ricardo Reis circles the statue of Adamastor a second time, a third. The old men, he sees, are becoming impatient, his restless presence makes it difficult for them to digest the news, which the fat one reads aloud to assist his own understanding and for the benefit of the thin one, who can neither read nor write. He pauses over the difficult words, but there are not too many of them, because the journalists never forget that they are writing for the masses. Ricardo Reis went over to the railing, where he pretended to ignore the old men absorbed in their paper, their murmuring, the one reading, the other listening and commenting, In Luís Uceda's wallet there was found a colored portrait of Salazar. This country is plagued with unsolved crime. A man is found dead on the road to Sintra, they say he was strangled after being put to sleep with ether, that he had been abducted, kept without food, that the crime was vile, a word that immediately shows our disapproval of crime, and now we learn that the murdered man was carrying a portrait of the wise, all-paternal dictator, to quote that French writer, whose name, recorded for posterity, is Charles Oulmont. Later on the investigation will confirm that Luís Uceda was indeed a great admirer of the eminent statesman, and it will be revealed that embossed on the leather of the aforesaid wallet was further proof of Uceda's patriotism, namely the emblem of the Republic, the armillary sphere with its castles and heraldic shields and the following inscription, Buy Portuguese Products.

Ricardo Reis discreetly withdraws, leaving the old men in peace. They were so absorbed in the mystery that they did not even notice his departure.

Nothing of consequence occurred that morning. There was a little trouble with an awkward heater that had not been used for weeks, he wasted match after match before getting the flame to stay on. Nor need we dwell on his melancholy repast, a cup of tea and three small sponge cakes left over from the previous evening's supper. Nor his bath amid a cloud of steam in the deep tub which was somewhat stained. He meticulously shaved, once, twice, as if in preparation for a secret rendezvous with some woman, her identity concealed by a high collar and a veil. How he would love to inhale the scent of her soap, of her lingering eau de Cologne, until that fused with more pungent and natural smells, the compelling smell of human flesh, which quivering nostrils take in and which leaves the breast panting, as if after a vigorous chase. The minds of poets, too, rove in this earthly fashion, stroking the bodies of women, even distant women, what is written here is a thing of the moment and of the imagination only, that mistress of great power and generosity. Ricardo Reis is ready to leave. He has no one waiting for him, and he is not going to eleven o'clock Mass to offer holy water to the Eternal Incognita. The sensible thing would be to stay at home until lunchtime. He has papers to arrange, books waiting to be read, and decisions to make, what kind of future does he want, what kind of job, where can he find the motivation to live and work, the reason. He had not intended to go out this morning, but now he must, it would be absurd to get undressed again, to admit that he got dressed to go out without being aware of what he was doing. This often happens, we take the first two steps because we are daydreaming or distracted and then have no choice but to take the third step, even when we know that it is wrong or ridiculous. Man, in the final analysis, is an irrational creature. Ricardo Reis returned to his room, thought perhaps he should make the bed before going out, he must not allow himself to become lax in his habits, but it was hardly worth the effort, he was not expecting visitors, so he settled in the chair where Fernando Pessoa had spent the night, crossed his legs as he had seen him do, clasped his hands on his knee, and tried to imagine himself dead, to contemplate the empty bed with the lifeless eyes of a statue. But there was a vein throbbing in his left temple, and the left eyelid twitched. I am alive, he murmured, then in a loud, sonorous voice he repeated, I am alive, and since there was no one there to contradict him, he was convinced. He put on his hat and went out. The old men had been joined by children playing hopscotch, jumping from chalked square to chalked square, each with its own number. This game has been given so many names, some call it monkey, others airplane, heaven and hell, roulette, also glory, but the most apt name of all would be the game of man, because that is what it looks like, the straight body, the extended arms, the upper circle forming the head or brain. The man lies on the paving stones looking up at the clouds while the children hop over him unaware of their cruelty, they will learn what it means when their time comes. Also present are some soldiers, who have arrived too early, because it is in the midafternoon that the housemaids take a stroll here if the weather is fair, otherwise their mistresses will say, Look, Maria, it is raining cats and dogs, you'd better stay in today, do a little ironing, I'll give you an extra hour on your day off, which is a whole two weeks away, a detail worth adding for those who never experienced such privileges firsthand or know nothing about the past and its customs. Ricardo Reis leaned over the upper railing. The sky had cleared a little, toward the straits there was a great strip of blue. If any steamships are due today from Rio de Janeiro, they will enter port in ideal conditions. Trusting in the signs of better weather, he started walking along the Calhariz, and descended as far as Camões, where he felt a sudden longing to visit the Hotel Bragança, like those timid students who have graduated and are no longer obliged to attend a school which they detested on so many occasions but who continue paying visits to their former teachers and classmates, until everyone grows weary of this pilgrimage, as useless as all pilgrimages, and the institution itself begins to ignore them. What would he do at the hotel, greet Salvador and Pimenta, So you haven't forgotten us, Doctor, Have a word with Lydia. Poor girl, so nervous, deliberately summoned to the reception desk out of malice, Come here, Doctor Reis wants to have a word with you. There was no particular reason for paying you a visit, I simply wished to thank you all for treating me so well and for giving me such excellent instruction on both the primary and secondary levels, if I failed to learn more, only my stupidity is to blame. On the sidewalk in front of the Igreja dos Mártires Ricardo Reis can smell balsam in the air, the precious exhalation of the devout women praying within. The Mass has just begun for those chosen souls who belong to a superior world. Here you can recognize, if you have a good nose, souls of worth and distinction. From the pleasant aroma one knows that the canopy over the altars is decked with pompons and tassels covered with talcum powder and that the chandler has added to the lavish candles a generous amount of patchouli. Once heated, fused, and fired with the quantum satis of incense, this ingredient inebriates the soul beyond resistance, it enraptures the senses, then the body grows weak, the face blank, ecstasy at last, Ricardo Reis doesn't know what he's missing, believing, as he does, only in dead religions, the religions of ancient Greece and Rome, for he invokes both in his poems, asking that there be gods rather than one God. He descends to the heart of the city, a familiar itinerary, the place as tranquil as a Sunday in the provinces. Not until later, after lunch, will the people of the surrounding neighborhoods come to gaze in the shop windows. They go through the week waiting for this day, entire families, the children carried in arms or led by the hand, exhausted by evening, their heels blistered because of a tight shoe, then they ask for a rice cake, and if their father is in a good mood and wishes to make a public show of his prosperity, the whole family ends up at a milk bar, large drinks all around so they can economize on the dinner. The man who goes hungry on a full belly will come to no great harm, besides he can always eat tomorrow. When it is time, Ricardo Reis goes to lunch, on this occasion to the Chave de Ouro, for a steak, to get rid of the sickening taste of all that sugar, and with so many hours to go before nightfall he buys a ticket for a movie, he will see *The Volga Boatmen*, a French film with Pierre Blanchard, what Volga can they possibly have invented in France. Films, like poetry, are the art of illusion, by adjusting a mirror you can transform a bog into the ocean. As he left the theater, it looked like rain, so he decided to take a taxi, and a good thing, because no sooner did he enter the apartment and hang up his hat and coat than he heard two raps coming from the iron knocker on the front door. Strange, for Fernando Pessoa to appear in daytime making such a din, a neighbor might come to her window and ask, Who's there, then start screaming her head off, Help, a spirit from the other world. If she can identify them so readily, then she must be familiar with them. He opened the window and looked out. It was Lydia, on the point of opening her umbrella as the first drops fell, what brought her here. A moment earlier he had been thinking that there was nothing more wretched than a solitary life, and now he felt annoyed that this woman was disturbing him, even though he could, if he wished, take advantage of the situation, a little erotic combat might steady his nerves and calm his thoughts. Going to the staircase to pull the wire cord, he saw that Lydia was already coming up, eager and on her guard. If there is a contradiction between these two states of mind, she had resolved it. He drew back into the doorway, cool, reserved, to the degree that being taken unawares could justify. I wasn't expecting you, how are things, these were his words as she entered, the door closing behind her. It is amazing, to have such neighbors, now we know neither their name nor what they look like. Lydia stepped forward to receive his embrace, and he obliged, meaning only to oblige her, but the next moment he was pressing her to him, kissing her neck. He still finds it awkward to kiss her on the lips, as if she were his equal, unless they are in bed together, the supreme moment approaching and he forgets everything, but she does not as much as dare, she allows him to kiss her to his heart's content, and the rest. But not today. I only came to see if you have settled in, an expression she has picked up in the hotel trade, I only hope no one notices that I've slipped out, besides I wanted to see what the apartment looks like. He tried to lead her into the bedroom, but she broke free, I mustn't, I mustn't, her voice faltered, but her mind was made up. In other words she would have liked nothing better than to lie on that bed and receive this man, to feel his head on her shoulders, to stroke the hair on his head, but behind the reception desk at the Hotel Bragança Salvador is asking, Where the devil is Lydia. She hurries through the entire apartment as if she can hear his voice, her experienced eye sees what is needed, there are no scrubbing brushes, buckets, mops or dusters, no marbled soap, no household soap, bleach, pumice stones, no brooms or hard brushes, no toilet paper. Men are as careless as children, they sail across the world in search of a route to India, and then find they do not have, so help me, the most basic thing, what could that be, I don't know, perhaps the color of life itself. Here, all one sees is dust, fluff, threads, sometimes gray hairs, which generations go on shedding. As their sight fails, the old no longer notice. Even spiderwebs age, weighed down by dust. One day the spider dies, suspended in its aerial tomb, its body dries up, its claws shrivel, and the remains of the flies are reduced almost to nothing. No creature escapes its destiny, no creature endures to give seed, this is the solemn truth. Lydia tells him she will come to do some cleaning on Friday, she will bring what is needed, Friday is her free day. But won't you be visiting your mother. I'll send her a message, then see what can be done, I'll telephone a store nearby. You will need money to buy things. I'll use my own money and you can pay me back. What an idea, take this, it should be enough. Holy Jesus, a hundred escudos is a small fortune. I'll expect you on Friday, then, but I feel bad that you're coming to do the cleaning. You can't live in this place the way it is now. Later, I'll give you a little present, I don't want any presents, just treat me as if I were the charwoman. Everyone should be paid a fair wage, My wage is to be treated kindly. These words certainly deserve a kiss, and Ricardo Reis gives her one, this time on the lips. His hand is already on the doorknob, there appears to be nothing more to say, the contract has been signed and sealed, but without any warning Lydia blurts out, as if unable to contain herself, Senhorita Marcenda arrives tomorrow, they telephoned from Coimbra, would you like me to give her your new address. With equal haste Ricardo Reis replies, almost as if he has rehearsed this, No, please don't, pretend you don't know where I am living. Happy to be the only person entrusted with his secret, Lydia leaves, completely deceived. Descending the stairs quickly and noticing that a door on the second floor has been left ajar, because sooner or later the other tenants in the building will have to have their curiosity satisfied, she calls up for all to hear, See you on Friday,

Doctor, when I come to do the cleaning, as if saying to the neighbor, Listen carefully, dear, I'm the new tenant's charwoman, so don't you go imagining things, and she greets the woman most politely, Good evening, senhora. But the woman barely replies, gives her a mistrusting look. Charwomen are not usually so bright and breezy, they tend to be surly, dragging their leg, which has stiffened up with rheumatism or varicose veins. The neighbor watches Lydia with a sour, hostile expression, Who is this little madam, while on the landing above, Ricardo Reis has already closed the door, conscious of his duplicity and turning it over in his mind. Had he been a faithful and honest man, he would have said to Lydia, I already gave Marcenda my address in a letter I sent her poste restante lest her father become suspicious. And he would have added, baring his heart, From now on I will be staying indoors, leaving the apartment only to have my meals and then coming straight back, and I will watch the clock at all hours, for as long as Marcenda remains in Lisbon. Tomorrow, Monday, she will certainly not come, the train gets in too late, but she might come on Tuesday, Wednesday, Thursday, or Friday. Not Friday, Lydia will be here doing the cleaning. Well, but what does that matter, the chambermaid and the girl from a good family, each in her own place, there is no danger of getting them mixed up, besides Marcenda never stays long in Lisbon, she only comes to consult the specialist, of course there is also that business of her father. Fine, but what do you expect will happen if she comes to your apartment. I don't expect anything, I only wish that she would. Do you really believe that a young woman like Marcenda, with her strict upbringing and the rigorous moral code upheld by her father, a man of the legal profession, would visit a bachelor in his own home, unaccompanied, do you think such things happen in real life. One day I asked her why she wanted to see me, and she replied that she didn't know, I find that the most hopeful reply of all. The one doesn't know, the other pleads ignorance. So it would appear, it's like Adam and Eve in the garden of Eden, not that she is Eve or I Adam. As you know, Adam was only a little older than Eve, a difference of several hours or days, I don't remember precisely. Adam is all men, Eve is all women, equal, different, and essential, and each one of us is the first man and the first woman. Fortunately, though, if I am not mistaken, woman continues to be more Eve than man Adam. Do you base this on your own experience. No, I say this because for all of us it should be so. What you would have liked, Fernando, is to go back to the beginning. My name is not Fernando. Ah.

Ricardo Reis did not go out to dine. He had some tea and cakes on the large table in the living room surrounded by seven empty chairs. Under a chandelier with seven branches and two bulbs he ate three small sponge cakes, leaving one on his plate. He counted again and saw that the numbers four and six were missing. He soon found the four, the corners of the rectangular room, but for six he had to get up and look around, which resulted in eight, the empty chairs. Finally he decided that he himself would be six, he could be any number if he was truly innumerable. With a smile that expressed both irony and sorrow he shook his head and went into the bedroom muttering to himself, I believe I'm going mad. From the street below came the incessant murmur of rain running down the gutters to the low-lying neighborhoods of Boavista and Conde Barão. Searching among the pile of books that were waiting to be sorted, he fished out *The God of the Labyrinth*, sat in the chair where Fernando Pessoa had sat, took one of the blankets from the bed to cover his knees, and started afresh on the opening page. The body discovered by the first chess player occupied the squares of the King and Queen and their two followers, its arms outstretched in the direction of the enemy camp. He continued to read, but even before reaching the place where he had left off last time, he began to feel drowsy. He lay down, read two more pages with effort, fell asleep between the thirty-seventh and thirty-eighth move, just as the second chess player was pondering the fate of the Bishop. He didn't remember turning off the light, but it was off when he awoke in the middle of the night, he must have got up and turned it off after all. These are things we do automatically, our body, acting on its own, avoids inconvenience whenever possible, that is why we sleep on the eve of battle or execution, and why ultimately we die when we can no longer bear the harsh light of existence.

Since he had forgotten to close the shutters, the gray light of an overcast morning filled the room. He had a long day before him, a long week, more than anything he wanted to stay in bed, under these warm blankets, let his beard grow, turn into moss, until someone came and knocked at the door, Who's there, It's Marcenda, One moment, he would cry out in excitement, within seconds make himself presentable, shaved, his hair combed, fresh from his bath, smartly dressed in clean clothes, ready to receive the expected visitor, Do come in, what a pleasant surprise. Not once but twice they came to knock at his door, first the milkman, to find out if the gentleman wished milk to be delivered every morning, then the baker, to find out if he required bread every day. Yes, he replied to both of them. In that case, sir, put the milk jug out on the doormat each evening, In that case, sir, hang the bread bag from the doorknob the night before. But who told you I had moved in here, The woman on the second floor, I see, and how would you like to be paid, Either weekly or monthly, Shall we say weekly then, That will be fine, Doctor. Ricardo Reis did not ask how they knew he was a doctor, there was no point in asking, but we heard Lydia address him as doctor when she left, and the woman downstairs was there and heard it. Provided with milk, tea, and fresh bread, Ricardo Reis enjoyed a wholesome breakfast. He had no butter or marmalade, but such bread is best savored on its own. Had Queen Marie Antoinette been served bread like this, she would not have needed to subsist on brioches. Now all that's wanting is a newspaper, but even that will soon be delivered. In his bedroom Ricardo Reis hears the cry of the newsvendor, *O Século, O Notícias*. He rushes to open the window, and the newspaper comes flying through the air, folded like a secret missive, moist from the ink which the weather has not allowed to dry. Greasy black smudges stain his fingers. Now each morning this carrier pigeon will tap on the windowpanes until they are opened from within. The newsvendor's cry can be heard from the far end of the street, and if the window is slow in opening, which nearly always happens, the paper is thrown up into the air, revolving like a discus, it strikes once, comes back, is thrown a second time. Ricardo Reis has already opened the window wide and received into his arms this winged messenger that brings him the world's news. He leans over the sill to say, Many thanks, Senhor Manuel, and the newsvendor replies,

Until tomorrow, Doctor. But this comes later, when an arrangement is reached, the payment this time will be monthly, as usual when dealing with reliable customers, it saves a person the effort of collecting three cents every day, a paltry sum.

Now, it is a question of waiting. On this first day, he can pass the time reading the newspapers, the evening editions too, he can reread, analyze, ponder, then work on his odes, or resume his reading of the labyrinth and its god, contemplate the sky from his window, and listen to the woman who lives on the second floor gossiping on the stairs with the woman from the fourth floor. He realizes that he will be hearing those shrill voices a great deal. And he will sleep, dozing and waking up, and leave the apartment only to have lunch, a hasty lunch at a nearby eating house on the Rua do Calhariz, then return to the newspapers he has already read, to his lukewarm odes, to the six hypotheses about the outcome of the forty-ninth move, and pass before the mirror, turning back to see if the person who passed is still there. He will decide that this silence is unbearable without a note of music, that one of these days he must buy a gramophone. To see which model will suit him best he looks through the advertisements for specific makes, Belmont, Philips, RCA, Philco, Pilot, Stewart-Warner. He takes notes, writes superheterodyne, understanding only the super in it and not even that with any certainty. Poor solitary creature, he is flabbergasted when confronted with an advertisement that promises women the perfect bosom within three to five weeks using the Parisian method, Exuber, which combines those three fundamental desiderata, Bust Raffermer, Bust Developer, and Bust Reducer. This Franglais is translated into concrete results under the supervision of Madame Hélène Duroy of the Rue de Miromesnil, which is in Paris, of course, where ravishing women firm up, develop, and reduce their busts, successively or all at the same time. Ricardo Reis examines other startling advertisements, for the restorative tonic Banacao, a wine with nutritional ingredients, for the Jowett automobile, for Pargil mouthwash, for a soap called Silver Night, for Evel wine, for the works of Mercedes Blasco, for Selva, for Saltratos Rodel, for those everpresent *Letters of a Portuguese Nun*, for the books of Blasco Ibañez, for Tek toothbrushes, for the painkiller Veramon, for Noiva hair dye, for Desodorol, which is rubbed into the armpits, then he returns with a sigh to the news items he has already digested, Alexander Glazunov, the composer of *Stenka Razin*, has died, Salazar, the all-paternal dictator, has installed canteens in the National Foundation to keep the workers happy, Germany swears that she will not withdraw her troops from the Rhineland, recent storms caused havoc in the Ribatejo, a state of war has been declared in Brazil and hundreds of people have been arrested, a quote from Hitler, Either we triumph over our destiny or we perish, and military forces were dispatched to the province of Badajoz, where thousands of workers have invaded rural estates. In the House of Commons several speakers declare that the Reich must be granted equal rights, there are new and interesting developments in the Uceda case, they have started filming *The May Revolution*, which tells the story of a refugee who arrives in Portugal to foment revolt, not this one, another one, and he is won over to the Nationalist cause by the daughter of the landlady at the boardinghouse where he is staying incognito. This last item Ricardo Reis read once, twice, three times, in an effort to rid himself of a faint echo buzzing deep inside his memory, but all three times his memory failed him, and it was only when he moved on to another news story, the general strike in La Coruña, that this tenuous thought became clear and defined. It was nothing distant, it was *Conspiracy*, that book, that Marília, that story of another conversion to Nationalism and its ideals, apparently the tale has its most effective propagandists among the women, with such magnificent results that literature and the seventh art pay tribute to these angels of chastity and self-sacrifice who seek out the wayward if not lost souls of men. No one can resist them when they place a hand upon a shoulder or cast a chaste glance beneath a suspended tear. They don't need to issue writs, interrogate, become inscrutable like the deputy chief of police, or hover vigilantly like Victor. This feminine influence surpasses the abovementioned techniques of making firm, developing, and reducing, although it might be more correct to say that this influence initially derives from these three, as much in the literary sense as in the biological, for it includes impassioned outbursts, exaggerated metaphors, and wild associations of ideas. Holy women, angels of mercy, Portuguese nuns, daughters of Mary and pious sisters, be they in convents or in brothels, in palaces or in hovels, the daughters of some boardinghouse landlady or of a senator, what astral and telepathic messages must they exchange among themselves, so that from such varied circumstances and conditions there should result so concerted an effect, which is nothing more or less than the redemption of a man in danger of losing his soul. As the supreme reward, these women offer him sisterly friendship, or sometimes their love, even their bodies and all the other advantages a beloved spouse can provide, and this sustains a man's hope in the happiness that will come, if it comes at all, in the wake of the good angel descended from the altars on high, for ultimately, let us confess it, this is nothing other than a secondary manifestation of the Marian cult. Marília and the daughter of the landlady, both incarnations of the Most Holy Virgin, cast pitying glances and place their healing hands on physical and moral sores, working the miracle of health and political conversion. Humanity will take a great step forward when such women begin to rule. Ricardo Reis smiled as he thought these sad irreverences. There is something disagreeable about watching a man smile to himself, particularly if he is smiling into his mirror, a good thing there is a closed door between him and the rest of the world. Then he asked himself, And Marcenda, what kind of woman is Marcenda. The question is beside the point, a mere mental game for one who has no one to talk to. First he must see if she has the courage to visit him in his apartment, then she will have to explain, however reluctant, however inarticulate, why she came to this enclosed and lonely place like an enormous spiderweb at the center of which lurks a wounded tarantula.

Today is the last day of the fixed term no one has agreed upon. Ricardo Reis looks at the clock, it's just after four. The window is closed, the few clouds in the sky are high. If Marcenda fails to come, she will not have the simple excuse so common of late, I dearly wanted to come but the rain was so heavy, and although my father was out, no doubt on one of his amorous pursuits, the manager Salvador would almost certainly have asked me, Surely you are not going out, Senhorita Marcenda, in this weather. Ricardo Reis looks at his watch, it is half past four. Marcenda has not come and will not come. The light indoors is fast disappearing, the furniture hides behind quivering shadows, one can now understand the suffering of Adamastor. The suspense grows almost unbearable, when suddenly there are two raps from the front door knocker. The building seems to tremble from top to bottom as if an earthquake were rocking the foundations. Ricardo Reis does not rush to the window, so he has no idea who will appear when he goes out onto the landing to pull the wire cord. He hears the woman upstairs open her door and say, Oh, I'm sorry, I thought it was for me, a familiar phrase handed down through generations of nosy women. It is Marcenda. Leaning over the banister, Ricardo Reis sees her. Halfway up the first flight of stairs, she looks up, anxious to make sure that the person she seeks really lives here, and she is smiling, it is a smile that has a future, unlike those reflected in a mirror, that is the difference. Ricardo Reis backs toward the door, Marcenda is climbing the last flight of stairs, only now does he notice that the light in the stairwell is off, that he is about to receive her almost in darkness, and while he vacillates, on another level of thought he wonders with surprise, How is it possible for her smile to be so radiant. When she stands before me, what should I say, I cannot ask, How have you been, nor exclaim in an even more plebeian fashion, Fancy seeing you here, nor sigh romantically, I had almost given up hope, I felt so desperate, why did you take so long. She walks in, I close the door, neither of us has said a word. Ricardo Reis takes her right hand, only to guide her into the domestic labyrinth. Into his bedroom would be improper, into the dining room would be absurd, in which of the chairs around that long table would they sit, side by side or facing, and how many would be seated there, he being innumerable, and she is certainly more than one, so let it be the study, Marcenda on one sofa, I on another. They have entered now, the ceiling light is on, also the lamp on the desk. Marcenda looks around at the heavy furniture, the two bookcases with their handful of books, the green blotting paper, then Ricardo Reis tells her, I am going to kiss you. She is silent. Slowly she supports her left elbow with her right hand, is it a protest, a plea for mercy, a surrender. She places her arm across her body like a barrier. Ricardo Reis takes a step forward,

209

but she does not move. When he is almost touching, Marcenda releases her elbow, allows her right hand to drop, it hangs as dead as her other hand, whatever life is within her is divided between her throbbing heart and her trembling knees as she watches this man draw near. She feels a sob forming in her throat, their lips touch, Is this a kiss, she wonders. But it is only the beginning of a kiss. His mouth presses against hers, his lips open hers, this is the body's destiny, to be opened. The arms of Ricardo Reis now are around her waist and shoulders, and for the first time her bosom is in contact with a man's chest. The kiss, she realizes, is not over yet, it is inconceivable that it could ever end and the world return to its primeval innocence, she also realizes that she must do something other than stand there with her arms down. Her right hand moves up to the shoulders of Ricardo Reis, her left hand, dead or asleep, dreams, recalls the movements it once made, fingers entwining fingers, crossing behind the man's neck. She repays Ricardo Reis kiss for kiss, her hands in his hands, I knew it when I decided to come, I knew it when I left the hotel, I knew it when I climbed those stairs and saw him leaning over the banister, I knew that he would kiss me. Her right hand leaves his shoulder, slips down, weary, her left hand was never there. This is the moment when the body recoils, almost staggers, when the kiss has reached the point where it is no longer enough. Let us separate them before the rising force compels us to proceed to the next stage, a renewed explosion of kisses, precipitate, short-lived, eager, lips no longer satisfied with lips yet constantly returning to them. Anyone with any experience knows this sequence, but not Marcenda, who is being kissed and embraced by a man for the first time in her life and suddenly finds that the longer a kiss lasts, the greater the need to repeat it, a crescendo of need that seems to have no end. Her escape lies elsewhere, in this sob in the throat, which neither swells nor finds release, a faint voice that pleads, Let me go, then adds, moved by who knows what scruples, as if afraid of having given offense, Let me sit down. Ricardo Reis leads her to the sofa, does not know what to do next, what to say, whether he should make a declaration of love or simply ask her forgiveness, whether he should kneel at her feet or remain silent, waiting for her to speak.

All this strikes him as false, the only true thing was when he said, I'm going to kiss you, and did. Marcenda is seated, her left hand resting in her lap in full view, like a witness. Ricardo Reis is also seated, and they look at each other, conscious of their bodies, as if each were a great whispering shell. Marcenda tells him, Perhaps I shouldn't say this, but I knew you would kiss me. Ricardo Reis leans forward, raises her right hand to his lips, and finally speaks, I don't know whether I kissed you out of love or despair. She replies, No one has ever kissed me before, therefore I cannot tell the difference between love and despair. But at least you must know what you felt. I felt your kiss as the sea feels the wave, if these words have any meaning. I have been waiting for you all these days, asking myself what would happen if you came, I never thought that things would turn out like this, but when you walked in here, I realized that to kiss you was the only thing I could do, when I said a moment ago that I could not tell whether I had kissed you out of love or despair, if I knew then what I meant, I no longer do. So you feel no despair after all, and no love for me. Every man feels love for the woman he kisses, even if the kiss is one of despair. What reasons do you have for despair. Only one, this sense of emptiness. How can a man who has the use of both hands complain. I am not complaining, I am simply saying that a man has to experience despair before saying to a woman, as I've just said to you, I am going to kiss you. You might have said it out of love. Had it been love, I'd have kissed you without telling you beforehand. So you do not love me. I'm extremely fond of you. But that is not why we kissed each other, Well, no. What are we going to do now, after what has happened, here I am in the apartment of a man with whom I've conversed three times in my whole life, I came here to see you, to speak with you and be kissed, I don't want to think about the rest. Someday we may have to think about it, Someday perhaps, but not today. I'll get you a cup of tea, I have some cakes. Let me help you, but then I must go, my father might return to the hotel and ask where I am. Make yourself comfortable, why don't you take off your jacket. I'm fine like this.

After they drank their tea in the kitchen, Ricardo Reis showed her around the apartment, they took only a glimpse at the bedroom, then returned to the study, where Marcenda asked him, Have you started seeing patients. Not yet, I might try setting up a practice, even if only for a few hours a day, it's a question of readjusting myself. It will be a start. That's what we all need, a start. Have the police given you any more trouble, No, and now they do not even know where I am living, If they want to, they can find out. And what about your arm. You need only look at it, I no longer hope for a cure, my father, Your father, My father thinks I should go to Fátima, he says that if I have faith, there might be a miracle, as there have been for others. When one starts to believe in miracles, there is no longer hope. I suspect that his amorous pursuits are coming to an end, they've been going on for some time. Tell me, Marcenda, what do you believe in, At this very moment, Yes, At this very moment I believe only in the kiss you gave me. We could have another, No, Why not, Because I'm not sure that I would feel the same thing, and now I must be off, we leave early tomorrow morning. At the door, she stretched out her hand, Write to me and I'll write to you, Until next month, If my father still wishes to return, If you don't come, I'll go to Coimbra. Let me go, Ricardo, before I start asking you for another kiss. Marcenda, please stay, No. She descended the stairs rapidly without once looking up. The front door slammed. When Ricardo Reis went into the bedroom, he heard footsteps above him, then a window open. It is the neighbor on the fourth floor, she wants to see for herself what sort of woman has been visiting the new tenant, wants to see if she sways her hips, either I'm much mistaken or there is something fishy going on, and to think that this building was so peaceful and respectable.

Dialogue and passing judgment. Yesterday one came, today another one, comments the neighbor on the fourth floor. I didn't see the one yesterday, but the one who was here today is coming to clean his apartment, reports the neighbor from the second floor. She doesn't look like a charwoman to me, You're right there, I'd have taken her for a housemaid from some well-to-do family had she not come laden with packages, and carrying household soap too, I could tell by the smell, and brushes, I was here on the stair shaking my doormat when she arrived. The one who came yesterday was a youngish girl with one of those fetching hats that are all the fashion these days, but she didn't stay long. What do you make of it, Frankly, I don't know what to say, he moved in only a week ago and two women have been here already. This one came to do the cleaning, it's only natural, a man on his own needs someone to keep the place tidy. The other one could be a relative, he must have relatives. But I find it very odd, did you notice that all this week he never left the apartment except at lunchtime. Did you know he's a doctor, I knew that right away, the charwoman addressed him as doctor when she was here Sunday, Do you think he's a doctor of medicine or a lawyer, I couldn't tell you, but don't worry, when I go pay the rent, I'll ask, the agent is bound to know. It's always good to have a medical doctor in the building, you never know when we might need him. So long as he's reliable. I must see if I can catch this charwoman of his, to remind her to wash her flight of stairs once a week, these stairs have always been kept spotless, Yes, do tell her, don't let her think she can treat us like a couple of dogs. She'd better know who she's dealing with, said the neighbor from the fourth floor, thus concluding the judgment and the dialogue. The only thing left to mention is the silent scene of her slowly climbing back upstairs to her apartment, treading softly in her woven slippers. At the door of Ricardo Reis she listens carefully, putting her ear to the keyhole. She can hear the noise of running water, and the charwoman singing in a low voice.

It was a very busy day for Lydia. She put on the smock she had brought with her, tied up her hair and covered it with a kerchief, rolled up her sleeves, and set to work with enthusiasm, nimbly avoiding the playful teasing that Ricardo Reis felt was expected of him when their paths crossed, an error on his part, from a lack of experience and psychological insight, because this woman at the moment seeks no pleasure other than that of dusting, washing, and sweeping. She is so accustomed to these chores that there is really no effort involved, and so she sings, but softly lest the neighbors think that the charwoman is taking liberties on this her first day working for the doctor. When it was time for lunch, Ricardo Reis, who during the morning had been driven from the bedroom to the study, from the study to the dining room, from the dining room to the kitchen, from the kitchen to the bathroom, emerging from the bathroom only to begin all over again in reverse order, with brief respites in the two empty rooms, saw that Lydia was showing no signs of interrupting her work, so he said, with embarrassment, As you know, I have no food in the house. An awkward rendering of his thoughts. Without disguise the sentence would sound like this, I'm going out for lunch, but I can't take you with me to the restaurant, it wouldn't look right, what will you do. She would reply with exactly the same words she uses now, Lydia, at least, cannot be accused of being two-faced, Go and have your lunch, I brought a small bowl of soup from the hotel and some stewed meat, I'll heat them up and that'll do me fine, and take your time, too, then we won't be tripping over each other's feet. She laughed as she spoke, wiped the perspiration from her face with the back of her left hand while with the other she adjusted the kerchief, which was slipping down. Ricardo Reis touched her on the shoulder, said, Well, good-bye for now, and left. He was halfway down the stairs when he heard doors open on the second and fourth floors, these were the neighbors coming to warn Lydia in chorus, Now then, dear, don't forget to wash your master's stairs, but on seeing the doctor they scurried back inside. The moment Ricardo Reis steps onto the pavement, the woman on the fourth floor will go down to the woman on the second floor and the two of them will whisper, I got such a fright, Have you ever known a tenant to go out and leave the charwoman in the apartment on her own, Very trusting, I must say, perhaps she cleaned for him at his previous place, Perhaps, senhora, perhaps, I don't deny it, but they could also be having an affair, men are such rogues, they never miss an opportunity. Away with you, he is a doctor of medicine, A doctor could still be a rogue, men are a bad lot, Mine isn't so bad, Nor mine. Until later, senhora, and don't let that hussy give us the slip, Don't you worry, she won't get past my door without being given her orders. It proved unnecessary. In the middle of the afternoon Lydia went out onto the landing armed with a brush, mop, and bucket. The woman on the fourth floor quietly watched from above as the wooden steps resounded to the blows of the heavy brush. The dirty water was mopped up and squeezed into the bucket, the bucket water was emptied three times, and the entire building filled with the clean smell of strong soap. There's no denying it, this charwoman knows her job, the neighbor on the second floor can tell at once, and she goes out of her way to speak to her on the pretext of taking in her doormat just as Lydia reaches her landing, My word, girl, you've done a splendid job on those stairs, it's nice to know we have such a reliable tenant on the third floor. The doctor insists that everything be clean and tidy, he likes to see things done properly, it makes a pleasant sight. It most certainly does. These words were spoken not by Lydia but by the neighbor on the fourth floor, who was leaning over the banister. There is something voluptuous in the contemplation of newly washed stairs, in the smell of scrubbed wood, this is a fraternity of women who take pride in their domestic chores, it is a kind of mutual absolution, even if more fleeting than the rose. Lydia wished them a good afternoon, climbed back upstairs carrying her bucket and brush, her cloth and soap, shut the door firmly behind her, and muttered, Snooty old bitches, who do they think they're bossing around. She has finished, everything is spick-and-span, Ricardo Reis can now return, pass his finger over the surfaces of the furniture like those housewives always trying to find fault, inspect every nook and cranny. Suddenly Lydia is overcome by a great sadness, a sense of desolation, not because she is tired but because she realizes, though unable to express it in words, that she has served her purpose, all that remains to be done now is await her master's arrival, he will thank her, will wish to offer compensation for her industry and diligence, she will listen with an impassive smile, receive or not receive payment, and return to the hotel. Today she did not even visit her mother in order to find out if there was any news from her brother, not that she feels remorse, but it is as if she possesses nothing of her own. Now she changes back into her blouse and skirt, and as the perspiration cools on her body she sits on a bench in the kitchen, hands folded in her lap, waiting. She hears footsteps on the stairs, the key inserted into the lock, it is Ricardo Reis, he is in the passageway saying jocularly, This is like entering the abode of angels. Lydia gets to her feet, smiles at such flattery, suddenly feels contented, then deeply moved as he approaches with hands outstretched and open arms, Oh, don't touch me, I'm covered with sweat, I was just about to leave. Don't go yet, it's early, have a cup of coffee, I bought some cream cakes, why don't you have a bath first to freshen up. What an idea, me have a bath in your apartment, who ever heard of such a thing. It has never been heard of, but there is always a first time, do as I say. She objected no more, could not object, even if social convention decreed otherwise, because this was one of the happiest moments in her life, running the hot water, taking off her clothes, lowering herself slowly into the tub, feeling her weary limbs relax in the sensuous warmth of the water, using soap and sponge to lather her body, her legs, her thighs, her arms, her belly, her breasts, knowing that on the other side of the door a man is waiting for her. I can imagine what he is doing, what he is thinking, but if he should come in here, if he should see me, watch me sitting here naked, how shameful. Can it be shame that causes her heart to beat so fast, or is it fear. She steps from the bath. The human body always looks beautiful when it emerges glistening from water, Ricardo Reis thinks as he opens the door. Lydia, stark naked, covers her breasts and crotch with her hands, begs, Don't look at me. It is the first time she has faced him like this. Please go away, let me get dressed, she says in a low voice of embarrassment, but he smiles a smile of tenderness, desire, even mischief, and tells her, Don't put your clothes on, just dry yourself. He holds out a large towel, wraps it around her, then goes into the bedroom and removes his own clothes. The bed has just been made, the sheets smell new. Lydia enters, holding the towel tightly to conceal her body, she does not hold it like a transparent veil, but as she approaches the bed she drops it, finally courageous. This is no day for feeling cold, her body is burning inside and out, and now it is Ricardo Reis who is trembling, reaching out to her like a child. For the first time they are both naked, after waiting for so long. Spring was slow in coming but better late than never. On the floor below, perched on two high kitchen stools, one atop the other, at the risk of falling and dislocating her shoulder, the downstairs neighbor is trying to decipher the meaning of the sounds that now penetrate the ceiling. Her face is crimson with curiosity and excitement, her eyes shine with repressed depravity, this is how these women live and die, Would you believe what the doctor and that minx are up to. But who knows, perhaps they are only engaged in the honorable task of turning and beating the mattresses, though that takes some believing. When Lydia departed half an hour later, the neighbor on the second floor did not dare open her door, even daring has its limits, but contented herself with looking through the peephole with the eye of a hawk at an agile figure that swiftly passed, swathed in the odor of man as if it were armor. Ricardo Reis, in bed, closes his eyes. Now that his flesh has been gratified, he can begin to add the delicate and elusive pleasure of loneliness. He rolls over into the spot that Lydia occupied. Such a strange smell, the smell of a strange animal, but mutual, not of the one nor the other but of both. Enough, let us be silent, we do not belong here.

Day starts with morning, the week with Monday. At first light,

Ricardo Reis began a long letter to Marcenda, laboriously pondering. What do we write to a woman whom we have kissed without declaring our love. To ask her forgiveness would be offensive, especially since she returned the kiss with passion. If on the other hand we did not say, upon kissing her, I love you, why should we invent the words now, at the risk of not being believed. The Romans assure us in the Latin tongue that actions speak louder than words, let us therefore consider the actions as done and the words superfluous, words are the first layer of a cocoon, frayed, tenuous, delicate. We should use words that make no promise, that seek nothing, that do not even suggest, let them protect our rear as our cowardice retreats, just like these fragmented phrases, general, noncommittal, let us savor the moment, the fleeting joy, the green restored to the budding leaves. I feel that who I am and who I was are different dreams, the years are short, life is all too brief, better that it should be so if all we possess is memory, better to remember little than much, let us fulfill what we are, we have been given nothing else. This is how the letter ends. We thought it would be so difficult to write yet out it flowed, the essential thing is not to feel too deeply what one is saying and not to think too much about what one is writing, the rest depends upon the reply. In the afternoon, as he had promised, Ricardo Reis went in search of employment as a locum tenens, two hours a day three days a week, or even once a week, to keep his hand in, even if it meant working in an office with a window looking onto a backyard. Any small consulting room would do, with old-fashioned furniture, a simple couch behind a screen for routine examinations, an adjustable desk lamp to examine a patient's coloring more closely, a spittoon for those suffering from bronchitis, a couple of prints on the wall, a frame for his diploma, a calendar that tells us how many days we still have to live. He began his search some distance away, Alcântara, Pampulha, perhaps because he had passed through those parts when he entered the straits. He inquired if there were any vacancies, he spoke to doctors he did not know and who did not know him, feeling ridiculous when he addressed them as Dear Colleague and when they spoke to him in the same way, We have a vacancy here but it is temporary, a colleague who is on leave, we expect him back next week. He tried the neighborhood around Conde Barão, then the Rossio, but all the vacancies had been filled. A good thing, too, that there is no shortage of doctors, because in Portugal we have more than six hundred thousand cases of syphilis, and the infant mortality rate is even more alarming. For every thousand infants born a hundred and fifty die. Imagine, then, what a catastrophe it would be if we did not have such excellent medical practitioners at our disposal. It must have been the hand of fate, because after searching so hard and so far afield, Ricardo Reis finally discovered, on Wednesday, a haven virtually on his own doorstep, in the Praça Camões, and such was his good fortune that he found himself installed in an office with a window overlooking the square. True, he had only a rear view of D'Artagnan, but communication was ensured, the receipt of messages guaranteed, as became apparent when a pigeon flew from the balcony onto the poet's head. It probably whispered in his ear, with columbine malice, that he had a rival behind him, a spirit akin to his and devoted to the muses but whose hand was skilled only in the use of syringes. Ricardo Reis could have sworn he saw Camões shrug. The post is a temporary replacement for a colleague who specializes in diseases of the heart and lungs and whose own heart has let him down. The prognosis is not serious, but his convalescence could take three months. Ricardo Reis was no luminary in this field, we may recall that he said he was not qualified to voice any opinion about Marcenda's heart condition, but fate not only sets things in motion, it is capable of irony, and so our doctor found himself obliged to scour the bookshops in search of medical texts that might refresh his memory and bring him up to date with the latest techniques in therapeutic and preventive medicine. He called on the colleague who was convalescing, assured him that he would do everything in his power to uphold the standards of a man who was and would continue to be, for many years to come, the foremost specialist in that venerable field, and whom I shall unfailingly consult, taking advantage of your great knowledge and experience. The colleague did not find these eulogies in the least exaggerated and promised his full cooperation. They then proceeded to discuss the terms of this Aesculapian sublease, what percentage toward the administration of the clinic, the salary of the nurse under contract, the equipment and running costs, and a fixed sum for the convalescing heart specialist, whether he be ill or return to health. The remaining income is not likely to make Ricardo Reis a rich man, but he still has a fair amount of Brazilian currency in reserve. In the city there is now one more doctor practicing medicine, and since he has nothing better to do, he goes to the office on Mondays, Wednesdays, and Fridays, invariably punctual. First he waits for patients who do not appear, then, when they do appear, makes sure they do not escape, then the novelty loses its excitement and he settles into the routine of examining collapsed lungs and necrotic hearts, searching the textbooks for cures for the incurable. He scarcely ever telephones his colleague, despite his promise to visit regularly and consult with him. We all make the best of our life and prepare for death, and what a lot of work this gives us. Besides, how awkward it would be to ask, What is your opinion, colleague, I myself have the impression that the patient's heart is hanging by a thread, can you see any way out, colleague, apart from the obvious one that leads into the next world. It would be like mentioning rope in the house of a man condemned to be hanged.

No reply, so far, from Marcenda. Ricardo Reis has sent her another letter, telling her of his new life, that he is practicing medicine once more, under the borrowed credentials of a well-known specialist, I receive my patients in consulting rooms on the Praça de Luís de Camões, within a stone's throw of my apartment and close to your hotel. With its multicolored houses Lisbon is a very small city. Ricardo Reis feels as if he is writing to someone he has never seen, to someone who lives, if she exists at all, in an unknown place, and when he reflects that this place has a name, Coimbra, which is a city he once saw with his own eyes, the thought seems as absurd as the sun rising in the west, because no matter how hard we look in that direction, we shall see the sun only dying there. The person he kissed, the memory he still preserves of that kiss gradually fades behind the mist of time. In the bookshops he can find no text capable of refreshing his memory. He finds, instead, information on cardiac and pulmonary lesions, and even so, it is often said that there are no diseases, only persons diseased. Does this mean that there are no kisses, only persons kissed. It is true that Lydia nearly always comes when she has a free day, and judging from the external and internal evidence Lydia is a person, but enough has been said about the aversions and prejudices of Ricardo Reis. Lydia may be a person, but she is not that person.

The weather improves, the world, however, is getting worse. According to the calendar it is already spring, and new buds and leaves can be seen sprouting on the branches of the trees, but from time to time winter invades these parts. Torrential rains are unleashed, leaves and buds are swept away in the flood, until eventually the sun reappears, its presence helping us forget the misfortunes of the last harvest, the drowned ox that comes floating downstream, swollen and decaying, the shack whose walls caved in, the sudden inundation that pulls the corpses of two men into the murky sewers of the city among excrement and vermin. Death should be a simple act of withdrawal, like a supporting actor who makes a discreet exit. He is denied the privilege of a final speech when his presence is no longer required. But the world, being so vast, contains events more dramatic, it ignores these complaints we mutter with clenched teeth about the shortage of meat in Lisbon. This is not news one should broadcast or leak abroad, leave that to other nations who lack our Lusitanian sense of privacy. Consider the recent elections in Germany, at Brunswick, where the mobilized National-Socialist corps paraded through the streets with an ox carrying a placard that read, This ox casts no vote. Had this been in Portugal, we would have taken the ox to vote, then would have eaten it, fillet, loin, and belly, and used the tail to make soup. The German race is obviously very different from ours. Here, the masses clap their hands, rush to watch parades, salute in Roman style, dream of uniforms for civilians, yet they play a most humble role on the great stage of the world. All we can hope for is to be hired as extras. This explains why we never know where to put our feet or what to do with our hands when we line the streets to honor the youths that march past. An innocent babe in its mother's arms doesn't take our patriotic fervor seriously, pulling at our middle finger which is within reach. With a nation like ours it is impossible to be smug and solemn or to offer one's life on the altar of the fatherland, we should take lessons, watch how the abovementioned Germans acclaim Hitler in the Wilhelmsplatz, hear how they fervently plead, We want the Führer, we beseech you Führer, we want to see you Führer, shouting until they become hoarse, faces covered with sweat, little old women with white hair weeping tender tears, pregnant women throbbing with swollen wombs and heaving breasts, men endowed with strong muscles and wills, all shouting and applauding until the Führer comes to the window, then their hysteria knows no bounds, the multitude cries out with one voice, Heil. That's more like it. If only I had been born a German. But one need not be quite so ambitious. Without comparing them with the Germans, consider the Italians, who are already winning their war. Only a few days ago their planes flew all the way to the city of Harar and reduced everything to ashes. If a nation like Italy, known for its tarantellas and serenatas, can take such risks, why should we be hindered by the fado and the vira. Our misfortune is the lack of opportunities. We have an empire, one of the greatest, which could cover the whole of Europe and still have land left over, yet we are unable to conquer our immediate neighbors, we cannot even win back Olivença. But where would such a bold initiative lead us. Let us wait and see how things turn out over the border, and in the meantime let us continue to receive into our homes and hotels those affluent Spaniards who have escaped the turmoil, this is traditional Portuguese hospitality, and if someday they are declared Spain's enemies, we will hand them over to the authorities, who will deal with them as they see fit, the law was made to be enforced. Among the Portuguese there is a strong desire for martyrdom, an eagerness for sacrifice and self-denial, only the other day one of our leaders said, No mother who has ever begotten a son could guide him to a loftier and nobler destiny than that of giving his life in defense of the fatherland. The bastard. We can just see him visiting maternity wards, probing the bellies of pregnant women, asking when they expect to give birth, telling them that soldiers are needed in the trenches, which trenches, never mind, there will be trenches. As we can see from these omens, the world promises no great happiness. Now Alcalá Zamora has been removed from the presidency of the Republic and the rumor is spreading that there will be a military coup in Spain. If that happens, sad times lie ahead for many people. But this is not the reason people emigrate. The Portuguese do not care whether they live in the fatherland or the outside world, the important thing is to find a place where we can eat and save a little money, whether it be Brazil, to which six hundred and six Portuguese emigrated in March, or the United States of North America, to which fifty-nine emigrated, or Argentina, to which more than sixty-five emigrated, but to all the other countries put together only two went. France is no place for Portuguese bumpkins, there one finds another kind of civilization.

Now that Easter has arrived, the government is distributing alms and provisions throughout the land, thus uniting the Roman Catholic commemoration of the sufferings and triumphs of Our Lord Jesus Christ with the temporary appeasement of protesting stomachs. The poor, not always orderly, form lines at the doors of the parish councils and almshouses, and there are already rumors that at the end of May a splendid banquet will be held on the grounds of the Jockey Club for the benefit of those left homeless by the floods in Ribatejo, unfortunates who have been going around with the seat of their pants soaking wet for many months. The organizing committee has already enlisted some of the most prominent names in Portuguese high society, one more distinguished than the next in terms of both moral and material wealth, Mayer Ulrich, Perestrello, Lavradio, Estarreja, Daun e Lorena, Infante da Câmara, Alto Mearim, Mousinho de Albuquerque, Roque de Pinho, Costa Macedo, Pina, Pombal, Seabra e Cunha, the inhabitants of Ribatejo are extremely fortunate, provided they can put up with their hunger until May. In the meantime, governments, even if they are as supreme as ours, which is perfect in every respect, are showing symptoms of failing eyesight, perhaps because of too much bookwork or strain. The fact is that, situated as they are on high, they can see things clearly only at a distance, not noticing that salvation is often to be found, as it were, under one's nose, or in this case in a newspaper advertisement. There is no excuse for missing this one, because it even has a sketch of a recumbent lady in a nightgown that allows a glimpse of a magnificent bosom that probably owes something to the treatment provided by Madame Hélène Duroy. Yet the delicious creature looks a trifle pale, not so pale as to suggest that her illness might prove fatal, we have every confidence in the doctor who is seated at her bedside, bald-headed with mustache and goatee, saying to her in tones of mild reproach, If you had taken It, you would not be so pale. He is offering her salvation in the form of a jar of Bovril. If the government paid more attention to those newspapers it scrupulously censors morning, noon, and night, sifting proposals and opinions, it would discover how simple is the solution to the problem of famine. The solution is here, it is Bovril, a jar to every Portuguese citizen, for large families a five-liter flagon, a national diet, a universal nutrient, an all-purpose remedy. If we had drunk Bovril from the outset, Dona Clotilde, we would not now be skin and bones.

Ricardo Reis gathers information, takes note of these useful remedies. He is not like the government, which insists on ruining its eyes by reading between the lines, overlooking the facts to dwell on the theories. If it is a fine morning, he goes out, a little gloomy despite Lydia's solicitude and attentiveness, to read his newspapers sitting in the sun under the protective gaze of Adamastor. As we have already seen, Luís de Camões greatly exaggerated the scowl, the tangled beard, the sunken eyes. The giant's attitude is neither menacing nor evil, it is only the suffering of unrequited love, Adamastor could not care less whether the Portuguese ships succeed in rounding the Cape. Contemplating the luminous river, Ricardo Reis recalls two lines from an old ballad, *From the window of my room I watch the mullet leap*. All those glints in the waves are fish leaping, restless, inebriated by the light. How true, that all bodies are beautiful as they emerge, quickly or slowly, from the water, like Lydia the other day, dripping, within arm's reach, or these fish too far away for the eye to distinguish. Seated on another bench, the two old men converse, waiting for Ricardo Reis to finish his newspaper, because he usually leaves it on the bench. The old men come here every day in the hope that the gentleman will appear in the park. Life is an inexhaustible mine of surprises, we reach an age where we have nothing else to do but watch the ships below from the Alto de Santa Catarina and suddenly we are rewarded with a newspaper, sometimes for two days in succession, depending on the weather. Once Ricardo Reis actually saw one of the old men break into a nervous trot and hobble toward the bench where he had been sitting, so he did the charitable thing, offering it with his own hand and saying, The newspaper. They accepted, of course, but are resentful now that they owe him a favor. Reclining comfortably on the bench with his legs crossed, feeling the gentle warmth of the sun on his half-closed eyelids, Ricardo Reis receives news of the vast world. He learns that Mussolini has promised the imminent annihilation of the Ethiopian military forces, that Russian weapons have been sent to the Portuguese refugees in Spain, besides other funds and resources intended to establish a Union of Independent Ibero–Soviet Republics, that in the words of Lumbrales, Portugal is God's creation throughout successive generations of saints and heroes, that some four thousand five hundred workers are expected to take part in a parade organized by the Corporative Movement in northern Portugal, in their number are two thousand stevedores, one thousand six hundred and fifty coopers, two hundred bottlers, four hundred miners from São Pedro da Cova, four hundred workers from the canning factories at Matosinhos, and five hundred associate members from the union organizations in Lisbon, and he learns that the *Afonso de Albuquerque*, a luxury steamboat, will depart for Leixões in order to attend the workers' celebration to be held there, that the clocks will be set forward by one hour, that there is a general strike in Madrid, that the newspaper *O Crime* is on sale today, that there has been another sighting of the Loch Ness Monster, that members of the government presided over the distribution of food to three thousand two hundred paupers in Oporto, that Ottorino Respighi, composer of *The Fountains of Rome*, has died. Fortunately the world has something for everyone. Ricardo Reis does not relish everything he reads, but he cannot choose the news and must accept it, whatever it is. His situation is entirely different from that of a certain old American who each morning receives a copy of *The New York Times*, his favorite newspaper. It is a special edition, which guards the precarious health of this senile reader who has reached the ripe age of ninety-seven, because each day it is doctored from start to finish, with nothing but good news and articles brimming with optimism, so that the poor old man will not be troubled by the world's disasters, which are likely to grow more disastrous. His private copy of the newspaper explains and proves that the economic crisis is fast disappearing, that there is no more unemployment, and that Communism in Russia is tending toward Americanism, as the Bolshevists have been forced to recognize the virtues of the American way of life. Fair tidings, these, that are read out to John D. Rockefeller over breakfast, and after he has dismissed his secretary he will peruse with his own weary, myopic eyes the paragraphs that reassure and delight him. At long last there is peace on earth, war only when it is advantageous, dividends are stable, interest rates guaranteed. He does not have much time left to live, but when the hour comes, he will die happy, the sole inhabitant of a world privileged with a strictly individual and non-transferable happiness. The rest of mankind has to be satisfied with whatever remains. Fascinated by what he has just learned, Ricardo Reis rests this Portuguese newspaper on his lap and tries to picture old John D. opening the magic pages of printed happiness with tremulous, scrawny hands, unaware that they are telling him lies. Everyone else knows it, because the deception has been telegraphed by news agencies from continent to continent, that in the editorial offices of *The New York Times* orders have been issued to suppress all bad news in the special copy for John D., the household cuckold who won't even be the last to know. Such a wealthy and powerful man allowing himself to be fooled in this way. The two old men pretend to be lost in conversation, arguing at their leisure, but keep looking out of the corner of one eye, waiting for their version of *The New York Times*. Breakfast used to be only a crust of bread and a cup of barley coffee, but our bad news is assured now that we have a neighbor who is so rich that he can afford to leave newspapers on park benches. Ricardo Reis rises to his feet, gestures to the old men, who exclaim, Oh, thank you so much, kind sir. The fat one advances, smiling, lifts the folded paper as if from a silver tray, good as new, this is the advantage of having the skilled hands of a medical practitioner, hands as soft as those of any lady, and he returns to his bench, settling once more beside the thin man. Their reading does not begin on the first page, first we must check to see if there are reports concerning riots or outbreaks of violence, disasters, deaths, crimes, especially, oh, how it makes one shudder, the mysterious death of Luís Uceda, still unsolved, and that dreadful business about the martyred child in the Rua Escadinhas das Olarias, number eight, ground floor.

When Ricardo Reis returns to his apartment, he discovers an envelope on the doormat, pale violet in color, bearing no indication of the sender, nor is that necessary. With some effort the smudged postmark can be deciphered as Coimbra, but even if for some inexplicable reason the name stamped there were Viseu or Castelo Branco it would make no difference, the city whence this letter really comes is called Marcenda. Soon a month will have passed since she was here in his apartment, where, if we are to believe what she said, she was kissed for the first time in her life. Yet once she returned home, not even this shock, which must have been profound, which must have shaken her to her very roots, was enough to prompt her to write a few lines, cautiously disguising her feelings, betraying them perhaps in two words brought together when her trembling hand was incapable of keeping them apart. Now she has written, to say what. Ricardo Reis holds the unopened letter in his hand, places it on the bedside table, on top of *The God of the Labyrinth*, illuminated by the soft light of the lamp. He would love to leave it there, perhaps because he has just come back, exhausted after hours of listening to the rattling of broken bellows, the tubercular lungs of the Portuguese, weary, too, of trudging through the circumscribed area of the city he constantly travels like a blindfolded mule turning a waterwheel, feeling at certain moments the menacing vertigo of time, the stickiness of the ground, the softness of the gravel. But if he doesn't open the letter now, he will never open it, he will say, if anyone should ask him, that it must have gone astray in the long journey between Coimbra and Lisbon, perhaps it dropped out of the courier's satchel as he was crossing a windy plain on horseback, sounding his bugle. It was in a violet envelope, Marcenda will tell him, envelopes of that color are not common. Then perhaps it fell among the flowers and merged with them. But someone may discover the letter and send it on, you can still find honest people who are incapable of keeping what does not belong to them. Unless someone opened and read it even though it was not addressed to him. Perhaps the words written there said exactly what he longed to hear, perhaps that person carries the letter in his pocket wherever he goes and reads it from time to time for consolation. I should find that very surprising, Marcenda replies, because the letter does not touch on such matters. I thought as much, that is why I have taken so long to open it, says Ricardo Reis. He sat on the edge of the bed and began to read. Dear friend, I received your letters with great pleasure, especially the second one in which you tell me that you have started seeing patients again, I enjoyed your first letter too, but didn't quite understand everything you wrote, or perhaps I am a little afraid of understanding, believe me, I do not wish to sound ungrateful, for you have always treated me with respect and consideration, but I cannot help asking myself what is this, what future is there, I don't mean for us but for me, I know neither what you want nor what I want, if only one's whole life could consist of certain moments, not that I've had much experience, but now I've had this one, the experience of a moment, and how I wish it were my life, but my life is my left arm which is dead and will remain dead, my life is also the years that separate us, one of us born too late, the other much too soon, you needn't have bothered traveling all those kilometers from Brazil, the distance makes no difference, it is time that keeps us apart, but I do not want to lose your friendship, that in itself will be something to treasure, and besides there is little point in my asking for more. Ricardo Reis passed a hand across his eyes, then read on. One of these days I will come to Lisbon as usual, I will visit your office, where we can have a chat, I promise not to take up too much of your time, it is also possible that I won't come, my father has grown disheartened, he admits that there probably is no cure for me, and I believe he is telling the truth, after all, he doesn't need this excuse to visit Lisbon whenever he pleases, his latest suggestion is that we go on a pilgrimage to Fátima in May, he is the one who has faith, not I, but perhaps his faith will suffice in the eyes of God. The letter ended with words of friendship, Until we meet, dear friend, I will call you the moment I arrive. If the letter were lost among fields of flowers, if it were being blown by the wind like a huge violet petal, Ricardo Reis would now be free to rest his head on the pillow and let his imagination run, What does it say, what doesn't it say, he could imagine the nicest things possible, which is what people do when they feel the need. He closed his eyes, thought to himself, I want to sleep, insisted in a low voice, Sleep, as if hypnotizing himself, Come now, sleep, sleep, sleep, but he still held the letter with limp fingers. To give greater conviction to his pretended scorn he let it drop. Now he sleeps gently, a twitch wrinkles his forehead, a sign that he is not sleeping after all, his eyelids tremble, he is wasting his time, none of this is true. He retrieved the letter from the floor, put it in its envelope, concealed it between two books. But he must not forget to find a safer hiding place, one of these days Lydia will come to clean and discover the letter, and then what. Not that she has any rights, she has none whatsoever, if she comes here it is because she wants to, not because I ask her, but let's hope she does not stop coming. What more does Ricardo Reis want, the ungrateful man, a woman goes to bed with him willingly so he does not need to prowl abroad and risk catching a venereal disease. Some men are extremely fortunate, yet this one is still dissatisfied, because he has not received a love letter from Marcenda. All love letters are ridiculous, ridiculous to write one when death is already climbing the stairs, even more ridiculous, it suddenly becomes clear, never to have received one. Standing before the full-length closet mirror, Ricardo Reis says, You are right, I never received a love letter, a letter that spoke only of love, nor did I ever write one, these innumerable beings that exist in me watch me as I write, then my hand falls, inert, and in the end I give up writing. He took his black suitcase, the one with the medical instruments, and went to the desk, and for the next half hour wrote up the clinical histories of several new patients, then went to wash his hands. Studying himself in the mirror, he dried his hands slowly, as if he had just finished carrying out an examination, checking samples of phlegm. I look tired, he thought, and went back into the bedroom and half-opened the wooden shutters. Lydia said she would bring the curtains on her next visit, they are badly needed, the bedroom is so exposed. Darkness was closing in. A few minutes later, Ricardo Reis went out to dinner.

One day, some curious person may inquire how Ricardo Reis

conducted himself at the table, whether he slurped as he drank his soup, whether he changed hands when using knife and fork, whether he wiped his mouth before drinking or left smears on his glass, whether he made excessive use of toothpicks, whether he unbuttoned his vest at the end of a meal, and whether he checked the bill item by item. These Galician-Portuguese waiters will probably say that they never paid much attention. As you are well aware, sir, one meets all sorts, after a while we don't notice anymore, a man eats as he's been taught, but the impression made by the doctor was that of someone refined, he would come in, wish everyone good afternoon or good evening, would order immediately what he wanted, and then it was almost as if he wasn't there. Did he always eat alone, Always, but he did have one curious habit, What was that, Whenever we began to remove the setting at the opposite side of the table, he always asked us to leave it there, he said the table looked more attractive set for two, and on one occasion when I was serving him there was a strange little incident. What incident. When I poured his wine, I made the mistake of filling both glasses, his and that of the missing guest, if you see what I mean. Yes, I see, and then what happened. He said that was perfect, and from then on he always insisted that the other glass should be filled, and at the end of the meal he would drink it in one go, keeping his eyes closed as he drank. How odd. As you probably know, sir, we waiters see some curious sights. Did he do this in all the other restaurants he frequented, Ah, that I couldn't tell you, you would have to ask around. Can you recall if he ever met a friend or acquaintance, even if they did not sit at the same table. Never, he always gave the impression of someone who had just arrived from abroad, just like me when I first came here from Xunqueira de Ambia, if you get my meaning. I know exactly what you mean, we have all had that experience. Do you require anything more, sir, I must go and serve the customer over in the corner, By all means, carry on, and many thanks for the information. Ricardo Reis finished drinking the coffee he had allowed to go cold and asked for his bill. While waiting, he held the second glass, still almost full, between his two hands, raised it as if he were toasting someone sitting across from him, then, slowly, half-closing his eyes, he drank the wine. Without checking the bill, he paid, left a tip neither miserly nor excessive, the tip one might expect from a regular client, wished everyone good-evening and left. Did you see that, sir, that's how he behaves. Pausing at the edge of the sidewalk, Ricardo Reis seems undecided. The sky is overcast, the air humid, but the clouds, although lying quite low, do not appear to augur rain. There is that inevitable moment when he is assailed by memories of the Hotel Bragança. He has just finished eating his dinner, has said, Until tomorrow, Ramón, and has gone off to sit on a sofa in the lounge, his back to the mirror. Presently Salvador will come to ask if he would like more coffee, A brandy perhaps, or a liqueur, Doctor, the specialty of the hotel, and he will say no, he rarely drinks spirits. The buzzer at the bottom of the stairs has sounded, the page raises his lamp to see who is entering, it must be Marcenda, today the train from the north was very late in arriving. A tram approaches, on its illuminated destination panel it has Estrela written, and the stop, as it happens, is right here, the driver sees the gentleman standing at the edge of the sidewalk. True, the gentleman made no sign requesting the tram to stop, but an experienced driver can tell that he has been waiting. Ricardo Reis gets on. At this hour the tram is practically empty, ping-ping, the conductor rings the bell. The journey takes some time, the tram goes up the Avenida da Liberdade, along the Rua de Alexandre Herculano, across the Praça do Brasil, and up the Rua das Amoreiras. Once at the top, it goes along the Rua de Silva Carvalho, through the Campo de Ourique to the Rua de Ferreira Borges, and there at the intersection with the Rua de Domingos Sequeira, Ricardo Reis gets out. As it is already after ten, there are not many people around and few lights are to be seen in the tall façades of the buildings. This is to be expected, the residents tend to spend most of their time in the rear of the building, the women in the kitchen washing up the last of the dishes, the children already in bed, the men yawning in front of their newspaper or trying, despite the bad reception due to atmospheric disturbances, to tune in Radio Seville, for no particular reason, perhaps simply because they never had the opportunity of going there. Ricardo Reis proceeds along the Rua de Saraiva de Carvalho in the direction of the cemetery. As he gets closer, he meets fewer and fewer people, and with some way to go, the road is already deserted. He disappears into the dark stretch between two lampposts, emerges once more into the amber light. Ahead in the shadows he can hear the sound of the keys of the local night watchman, who is starting his rounds. Ricardo Reis crosses the square toward the main gate, which is locked. The watchman looks at him from afar, then continues walking, Someone, he thinks, about to unburden his sorrow by weeping in the night, perhaps he has lost a wife or child, poor man, or his mother, probably his mother, mothers are always dying, a frail little woman and exceedingly old, who closed her eyes without seeing her son, I wonder where he is, she mused, then passed away, that is how people part. Perhaps it is because he is responsible for the tranquillity of these streets that the night watchman is given to such tender thoughts. He has no memories of his own mother. How often this happens, that we feel sorry for others, never for ourselves. Ricardo Reis goes up to the grating, touches the bars with his hands. From within, almost inaudible, comes a whispering, the breeze circling the branches of the cypress trees, poor trees, stripped bare of leaves. But the senses are deceived, the noise we hear is only the snoring of those who are asleep in those tall buildings, and in those low houses beyond the walls, strains of music, the hum of words, the woman who murmurs, I feel so tired, I'm going to lie down. That is what Ricardo Reis is saying to himself, I feel so tired. He puts his hand through the grating, but no other hand comes to shake his. Reduced to corpses, these people cannot even lift an arm.

Fernando Pessoa appeared two nights later. Ricardo Reis was returning after dining on soup, a plate of fish, bread, fruit, coffee. There are two glasses on the table. He finishes every meal, as we know, with a glass of wine, yet there is not a single waiter who can say of this customer, He was in the habit of drinking too much, he would rise from the table, almost fall over. Language owes its fascination to contradictions such as these, no one can rise and fall at the same time, yet we have seen it happen often or possibly even experienced it ourselves. But whenever Fernando Pessoa has appeared, Ricardo Reis has always been clearheaded, and he is clearheaded now as he watches the poet, whose back is turned to him, seated on the bench closest to Adamastor. That long, slender neck is unmistakable, and the sparse hair on the crown of the head. Besides, there are not many people who go around without a hat or raincoat. The weather has certainly been milder, but it still turns chilly at night. Ricardo Reis sat down beside Fernando Pessoa. In the darkness the pallor of the poet's skin, the whiteness of his shirt, is accentuated, the rest is dim, his black suit barely distinguishable from the shadow thrown by the statue. There is no one else in the park. Over on the other bank of the river, a row of flickering lights can be seen on the water, but they look like stars, they sparkle, quiver as if about to go out, but persist. I thought you would never come back, said Ricardo Reis. I came a few days ago to visit you, but at your door I saw that you were occupied with Lydia, so I left, I was never fond of tableaux vivants, Fernando Pessoa replied, and one could make out his wan smile. His hands were clasped on his knee, his expression that of someone patiently awaiting his turn to be summoned or dismissed and who speaks in the meantime because silence would be more insufferable. I never expected that you would show such enterprise as a lover, that the fickle poet who sang the praises of the three muses, Neaera, Chloe, and Lydia, should settle for one of the three in the flesh is quite an achievement, tell me, have the other two never appeared. No, nor is that surprising, they are names one rarely hears nowadays. And what about that attractive girl, so refined, the one with the paralyzed arm, did you ever get around to telling me her name. Her name is Marcenda. A pretty name, tell me, have you seen her lately. I saw her the last time she was in Lisbon, about a month ago. Are you in love with her, I don't know, And what about Lydia, do you love her, That's different, But do you love her or not. She does not deny me her body. And what does that prove. Nothing, at least not as far as love is concerned, but do stop questioning me about my private affairs, I am much more interested in knowing why you didn't come back. To put it bluntly, because I was annoyed, With me, Yes, with you as well, not because you are what you are but because you are on that side, What side, The side of the living, it is difficult for one who is alive to understand the dead. I suspect that it is just as difficult for a dead man to understand the living. The dead man has the advantage of having been alive, he is familiar with the things of this world and of the other world, too, whereas the living are incapable of learning the one fundamental truth and profiting from it. What truth is that, That one must die. Those of us who are alive know that we will die. You don't know it, no one knows it, just as I didn't when I was alive, what we do know without a shadow of a doubt is that others die. As a philosophy, that strikes me as rather trivial. Of course it's trivial, you have no idea just how trivial everything becomes when seen from this side of death. But I am on the side of life. Then you ought to know what things on that side are significant, To be alive is significant. My dear Reis, choose your words carefully, your Lydia is alive, your Marcenda is alive, yet you know nothing about them, nor could you learn, even if they attempted to tell you, the wall that separates the living from one another is no less opaque than the wall that separates the living from the dead. For anyone who believes this, death must be a consolation after all. Not really, because death is a kind of conscience, a judge who passes judgment on everything, on both himself and life. My dear Fernando, choose your words carefully, you put yourself at great risk of being absurd. If we do not say all words, however absurd, we will never say the essential words. And you, do you now know them. I have only started to become absurd. Yet once you wrote, *Neophyte, there is no death*, I was mistaken, Are you saying that now because you are dead, No, I am saying it because I was once alive, but I am saying it, above all, because I will never be alive again, if you can imagine what that means, never to be alive again. It sounds like something Pero Grulho would say. We've never had a better philosopher.

Ricardo Reis looked across the river. Some lights had gone out, others, barely visible, grew even dimmer as a soft mist began to gather over the water. You said the reason you didn't come back was that you were annoyed, It's true, Annoyed with me, Not so much with you, what has annoyed me and left me feeling weary is all this going back and forth, this tug of war between memory that pulls and oblivion that pushes, a useless contest, for oblivion and forgetting always win in the end. I haven't forgotten you. Let me tell you something, on this scale you do not weigh much. Then what is this memory that continues to summon you, The memory I retain of the world, I thought you were summoned by the memory the world retains of you, What a foolish idea, my dear Reis, the world forgets, as I've already told you, the world forgets everything. Do you think you've been forgotten. The world is so forgetful that it even fails to notice the absence of what has been forgotten. There is much vanity in these words. Of course, no poet is vainer than a minor one. In that case, I must be vainer than you. Allow me to say, without wishing to flatter you, that you are not a bad poet, But not as good as you, I believe you are. After we are both dead, if by then we are still remembered, or for as long as we are still remembered, it will be interesting to see on whose side the pointer of the scale leans. We will not care in the least about weights and weighers then. Neophyte, does death exist, It does. Ricardo Reis drew his raincoat tightly around him, It's getting chilly, if you wish to accompany me home, we can converse a while longer. Aren't you expecting any visitors today. No, and you are welcome to stay, as you did the last time. Are you feeling lonely tonight. Not to the extent of being desperate for company, but only because it occurs to me that a dead man might occasionally like to sit on a chair, under a roof, in comfort. I don't remember your being so facetious, Ricardo. I'm not trying to be facetious. He got to his feet and asked, Well, are you coming. Fernando Pessoa followed him, caught up with him at the first lamppost. At the entrance they encountered a man with his nose in the air. From the way he tilted his body, as if he were about to lose his balance, he appeared to be examining the windows, he looked as if he had paused for a moment after a hard climb up that steep road. Anyone seeing him would have said to himself, Here is one of the many night birds you come across in this city of Lisbon, not everyone goes to bed with the lamb. But when Ricardo Reis drew closer, he was overcome by a strong whiff of onion. He recognized the police informer immediately. There are smells, each worth a hundred words, smells both good and bad, smells as revealing as full-length portraits, what brings this fellow prowling here. Perhaps because he did not wish to disgrace himself in the presence of Fernando Pessoa, he took the initiative and spoke first, What brings you here at this hour of night, Senhor Victor. The other replied as best he could, having no explanation prepared at this early stage of the surveillance, A coincidence, dear Doctor, a pure coincidence, I have just been visiting a relative who lives in the Rua do Conde Barão, poor woman, she has caught pneumonia. Victor did not entirely lose face, And so, Doctor, you are no longer staying at the hotel, with this clumsy question he showed his hand. After all, one can be a guest at the Hotel Bragança and take a stroll at night on the Alto de Santa Catarina. Ricardo Reis pretended not to notice, or he really did not notice, No, I am now living here, on the third floor. Oh. This cry of regret, although brief, polluted the atmosphere with an overpowering stench, a good thing that Ricardo Reis had the wind at his back, these are mercies granted by heaven. Victor said good-bye, releasing another whiff of foul breath, I wish you good luck, Doctor, should you need anything, remember, come and speak to Victor, only the other day our deputy chief remarked that if everybody was like Doctor Reis, so honest and polite, our job would be almost a pleasure, he will be delighted when I tell him we bumped into each other. Good-night, Senhor Victor, common courtesy demanded that he say something in reply, besides, he had his reputation to consider. As Ricardo Reis crossed the street followed by Fernando Pessoa, the police informer had the impression there were two shadows on the ground. These are the effects of reflected light, an illusion, after a certain age the eyes are not capable of distinguishing between the visible and the invisible. Victor continued to loiter on the sidewalk, waiting for the light to go on on the third floor, a routine, simple confirmation, he now knew that Ricardo Reis lived there. Not much walking or interrogating had been necessary, with the help of Salvador he had tracked down the porters and with the help of the porters had located the building, people are right when they say that anyone with a tongue in his head can travel to Rome, and from the Eternal City to the Alto de Santa Catarina the distance is not great.

Comfortably settled on the sofa in the study, Fernando Pessoa asked as he crossed his legs, Who was that friend of yours. He is not a friend. Thank goodness, he stank to high heaven, I've been wearing the same suit and shirt for the last five months, I haven't even changed my underwear, and I don't smell like that, but if he's not your friend, who is he then, and that deputy chief who seems to think so highly of you. They're both members of the police force, not long ago I was called in for questioning. I thought you were a law-abiding man, incapable of upsetting the authorities, I am a law-abiding man, You must have done something to be called in for questioning, I arrived here from Brazil, that is all. I'll bet Lydia was a virgin and she went, anguished and dishonored, to lodge a formal complaint. Even if Lydia had been a virgin and I had dishonored her, it would not be to the Department for State Security and Defense that she would have taken her complaint. Is that the department that called you in, Yes, And here I was thinking it was an offense against public morality, There is nothing wrong with my morals, they are certainly no worse than those I see around me. You never mentioned this brush with the police, There was no opportunity, you stopped coming to see me. Did they do you any harm, arrest you, charge you, No, I was only asked a few questions, who were my friends in Brazil, why did I come back here, what contacts I made in Portugal since my return. What a joke if you had told them about me. I can imagine the look on their faces if I told them that from time to time I met with the ghost of Fernando Pessoa. Excuse me, my dear Reis, but I am no ghost. What are you then, I can't tell you, a ghost comes from the other world, I simply come from the cemetery at Prazeres. Then is the dead Fernando Pessoa the same as the Fernando Pessoa who was once alive. In one sense, yes. Anyhow, it would be extremely difficult to explain these meetings of ours to the police. Did you know that I once wrote some verses attacking Salazar, Did he realize that he was the object of the satire, I don't believe he did, Tell me, Fernando, who is or what is this Salazar that fate has wished upon us. He is Portugal's dictator, protector, paternal guide, professor, gentle potentate, one quarter sacristan, one quarter seer, one quarter Sebastião, one quarter Sidónio, the best of all possible leaders, given our character and temperament. Many p's and s's. A coincidence, I was not trying for alliteration. There are certain people who have that mania, they go into rapture over repetitions, actually believing that this device brings order to the world's chaos. We must not laugh at them, they are fastidious people, like the fanatics of symmetry. The love of symmetry, my dear Fernando, comes from a vital need for balance, it keeps us from falling, Like the pole used by tightrope walkers, Precisely, but to get back to Salazar, he is much praised in the foreign press. Bah, those are articles commissioned and paid for by the contributors themselves, as I've heard people say, But the press here also waxes lyrical in singing his praises, you only need to pick up a newspaper in order to learn that our Portugal is the most prosperous and contented nation on earth, or will be very soon, and that if other nations follow our example they will prosper. That's the way the wind is blowing. I can see you don't have much faith in newspapers, I used to read them, You say that in a tone that suggests resignation, Exhaustion, rather, you know what I mean, after one makes a strenuous physical effort the muscles become slack, one feels like closing his eyes and sleeping. You are sleepy. I still feel the exhaustion I experienced in life. Death is a strange thing, Stranger still when you see it from the shore where I am standing and suddenly realize that no two deaths are alike, to be dead is not the same for everyone, in some cases a man takes with him all life's burdens. Fernando Pessoa closed his eyes and lay back on the sofa. Ricardo Reis thought he saw tears between his eyelashes, but they might have been like the two shadows seen by Victor, the effects of reflected light, for as everyone knows, the dead do not weep. That exposed face without glasses, and with a thin mustache, because the hair on one's face and body lives longer, expressed a deep sorrow, a sorrow without redress, like the hurts of childhood. Then Fernando Pessoa opened his eyes, smiled, I dreamed I was alive. An interesting illusion. What is interesting is not that a dead man should dream he is alive, after all he has known life, he has something to dream about, but rather that a man who is alive should dream that he is dead, because he has never known death. Soon you will be telling me that life and death are the same. Precisely, my dear Reis. In the space of one day you have stated three quite different things, that there is no death, that there is death, and now that life and death are the same. There was no other way of resolving the contradiction of the first two statements. And, as he said this, Fernando Pessoa gave a knowing smile.

Ricardo Reis got to his feet, I'm going to heat some coffee, I'll be right back. Listen Ricardo, since we've been discussing the press, I'd like to hear the latest news, it's one way of rounding off our evening. For the last five months you have not been in touch with the world, there are lots of things you will find difficult to understand. You, too, must have been puzzled by certain changes when you disembarked here after an absence of sixteen years, no doubt you had to connect the threads across time, finding certain threads without knots and certain knots without threads. The newspapers are in my bedroom, I'll go and fetch them, said Ricardo Reis. He went to the kitchen, returned with a small white-enamel coffeepot, a coffee cup, spoon, and sugar bowl, which he placed on the low table between the sofas, went out again, returned with the newspapers, poured the coffee into the cup, stirred in some sugar. Obviously you are no longer able to drink, If I had an hour of existence left, I would probably exchange it this very minute for a hot cup of coffee, You give more than England's King Henry, who exchanged only his kingdom for a horse, In order not to lose his kingdom, but forget the history of England and tell me what is happening in the world of the living. Ricardo Reis drank half a cup of coffee, then opened one of the newspapers and asked, Did you know it was Hitler's birthday, he is forty-seven. I don't consider that an important item of news. That's because you aren't German, if you were, you'd be less contemptuous. What else is there of interest. It says here that Hitler reviewed a parade of thirty-three thousand soldiers in an atmosphere of veneration that was almost sacred, the very words used here, and just to give you an idea, listen to this extract from the speech made by Goebbels to mark the occasion. Read it to me. When Hitler speaks, it is as if the vault of a temple were raised over the heads of the German people, How poetic, But that is nothing compared with the words of Baldur von Schirach. Who is this von Schirach, I don't recall the name, He is the leader of the Reich's Youth Movement, And what did he have to say. Hitler is God's gift to Germany, worship for our Führer transcends all differences of creed and allegiance. Satan himself couldn't have thought up that one, worship for a man uniting what worship for God has divided. And von Schirach goes further, he declares that if German youth pledges its love for Hitler, who is its god, if German youth strives to serve him loyally, it will be obeying the commandment received from the Eternal Father. Magnificent logic, here we have a god acting on behalf of another god for his own ends, the Son as arbiter and judge of the authority of the Father, which makes National Socialism a most holy enterprise. And here in Portugal we are not doing that badly when it comes to confusing the divine with the human, it looks almost as if we are turning back to the gods of antiquity. To those of your choice. I only borrowed the names. Go on. Well, according to a solemn declaration made by the Archbishop of Mitilene, Portugal is Christ and Christ is Portugal. Is that written there, Word for word, That Portugal is Christ and Christ is Portugal, Exactly. Fernando Pessoa reflected for a moment, then laughed, a dry chuckle like a cough, really rather unpleasant, Pity this land, pity this people. Pity this land, he repeated with real tears in his eyes, still chuckling, I thought I had gone too far when I called Portugal holy in *Mensagem*, it is written there, São Portugal, and here a prince of the Church comes and proclaims that Portugal is Christ. And that Christ is Portugal, don't forget. If that is the case, we had better find out, and soon, what virgin gave birth to us, what devil tempted us, what Judas betrayed us, what nails crucified us, what grave we lie in, what resurrection awaits us. You forgot the miracles. What greater miracle could you wish for than the simple truth that we exist, that we continue to exist, I'm not speaking about myself, obviously. The way we're going, I don't know how long we will continue to exist. But you have to admit that we are well ahead of Germany, here it is the Church itself that establishes our divinity, we could even do without this God-sent Salazar since we are Christ Himself. A pity that you died so young, my dear Fernando, because Portugal is now about to fulfill her destiny. Then let us and the world believe the words of the archbishop. No one can deny that we are doing our utmost to achieve happiness, would you now like to hear what Cardinal Cerejeira said to the seminarians. I'm not sure whether I could stand the shock. You are not a seminarian. All the more reason, but who am I to question the will of God, go ahead, read it to me. Be angelically pure, eucharistically fervent, and ardently patriotic. He said that, He did, It only remains for me to die, But you are already dead, Poor me, not even that is left. Ricardo Reis poured himself another cup of coffee. If you drink one coffee after another, you won't sleep, Fernando Pessoa warned him. Never mind, a sleepless night never did anyone harm, and sometimes it can be a help. Read me some more news. In a minute, first tell me, don't you find this latest novelty in Portugal and Germany disturbing, the political use of God. It may be disturbing but it is hardly a novelty, ever since the Hebrews promoted God to the rank of general others have followed suit, the Arabs invaded Europe to the cries of God wills it, the English enlisted God to guard their king, and the French swear that God is French. Our Gil Vicente swore that God is Portuguese. He must be right, if Christ is Portugal, but read me some more news before I take my leave. Aren't you staying, There are certain rules I must observe, last time I broke three in a row. Do the same tonight. No. Then listen carefully, I will now read without interruption, and if you have any comments to make, save them till the end, Pope Pius I condemns the immorality of certain films, Maximino Correia has declared that Angola is more Portuguese than Portugal, because since the time of Diogo Cão the only sovereignty Angola has recognized is that of the Portuguese, in Olhão bread has been distributed to the poor in the barracks square of the National Republican Guard, there are rumors that a secret faction has been formed by the military in Spain, at a reception held at the Geographical Society to celebrate Colonial Week women prominent in high society sat cheek by jowl with the lower orders, according to the newspaper *Pueblo Gallego* fifty thousand Spaniards have taken refuge in Portugal, in Tavares salmon is selling at thirty-six escudos per kilo, That's much too expensive, Do you like salmon, I used to loathe it. That's all, unless you want to hear about outbreaks of disorder and violence. What time is it, Almost midnight, How time passes, Are you going, I am, Would you like me to accompany you, For you it is still too early, Precisely, You misunderstand, what I meant is that it is too early for you to accompany me where I am going. I am only one year older than you, by the natural order of things. What is the natural order of things. That is how one usually expresses it, by the natural order of things I should have died first. As you can see, things have no natural order. Fernando Pessoa rose from the sofa, buttoned his jacket, and adjusted the knot in his tie, going by the natural order of things he would have done just the opposite, Well, I'm off now, I'll see you one of these days, and thanks for being so patient, the world is in even worse shape than when I left it, and Spain is almost certainly heading for civil war. Do you think so. If the best prophets are those who are already dead, then at least I have that advantage. Try not to make any noise when you go downstairs, on account of the neighbors. I shall descend like a feather. And don't bang the front door, Don't worry, the lid of the tomb makes no echo. Good night, Fernando, Sleep well, Ricardo.

Whether it was the effect of this somber conversation or because he had drunk too much coffee, Ricardo Reis did not sleep well. He woke up several times, and in his sleep imagined he could hear his own heart beating inside his pillow. When he awoke, he lay on his back to stop the noise, then he began to hear it again inside his chest, his rib cage, he remembered the autopsies he had witnessed and could see his living heart throbbing in anguish as if each contraction were its last. Difficult sleep returned, and finally settled into deep sleep as dawn began to break. When the paper boy arrived and threw the newspaper at his window, he made no attempt to get up. In such cases the boy climbs the stairs and leaves the paper on the doormat, the new one on top, because the others, delivered on previous days, are now used to clean the dirt off one's shoes, *Sic transit notitia mundi*, blessed be he who invented Latin. Standing in one corner of the doorway is the pitcher with the daily quart of milk, hanging from the doorknob is the bag of bread. Lydia will bring these things inside when she arrives after eleven o'clock, because this is her day off. She could not get away any earlier, at the last minute Salvador, as demanding and unreasonable as ever, ordered her to clean and prepare another three rooms. Nor can she stay long, she must go and visit her mother, who is all on her own, to find out if there is any news from her brother, who sailed to Oporto aboard the *Afonso de Albuquerque* and has returned. Hearing her come in, Ricardo Reis called out in a sleepy voice. She appeared in the doorway, still holding the key, the bread, the milk, and the newspaper in her arms, and said, Good morning, Doctor. He replied, Good morning, Lydia. This is how they greeted each other the first day they met and this is how they will go on greeting each other, she will never summon the courage to say, Good morning, Ricardo, even if he asks her to, which is not likely, he is being much too familiar as it is, receiving her in this state, unshaven, unwashed, hair uncombed, breath bad. Going to the kitchen to deposit the milk and bread, Lydia returned with the newspaper, then went off to prepare breakfast, while Ricardo Reis unfolded and opened the pages, holding them carefully by the margins so as not to dirty his fingers, lifting the paper high so as not to dirty the top fold of his sheet. These are the fussy little gestures, consciously cultivated, of a man who surrounds himself with boundaries. Opening the paper, he remembered doing the exact same thing several hours earlier, and once more felt that Fernando Pessoa had been there a very long time ago, as if a memory so recent were really a memory from the days when Fernando Pessoa, having broken his glasses, had asked him, I say, Reis, read me the news, the more important items. The reports on the war, No, they're not worth bothering with, I'll read them tomorrow, besides they never vary. This was in June in the year nineteen sixteen, and only a few days before that Ricardo Reis had written the most ambitious of his odes, the one that begins, *I have heard it said that in times gone by, when Persia.* From the kitchen comes the appetizing smell of toasted bread, the muffled sounds of crockery, then Lydia's footsteps in the hallway. Quite composed this time, she carries in the tray, goes through the same professional routine, except there is no need to knock, the door is open. Without fear of appearing to take liberties she can ask this long-standing guest, So you're still in bed this morning. I didn't have a very good night, it took me forever to get to sleep, Did you stay out late, I wish I had, as it happened I was in bed before midnight, I didn't even leave the apartment. Whether Lydia believes him or not, we know that he is telling the truth. The tray rests on the guest's lap in room two hundred and one, the maid pours his coffee and milk, arranges the toast and marmalade within his reach, adjusts the position of the napkin, then informs him, I can't stay today, I'll give the place a quick tidy-up and then I'm off, I want to visit my mother, she is starting to complain that she hardly ever sees me these days, I rush in and out, she even asked me if I found myself a man and was thinking of getting married. Ricardo Reis smiles, disconcerted, not knowing how to react. We certainly do not expect him to say, You already have a man, and as for marriage, it is just as well that you brought up the subject, it is time we discussed our future. No, he simply smiles, looks at her with an expression that has suddenly become paternal. Lydia retired to the kitchen, took with her no reply, if she ever expected one. She blurted out these words unintentionally, her mother has never once mentioned either men or marriage. Ricardo Reis finished eating, pushed the tray to the foot of the bed, leaned back to read the newspaper. The grand parade organized by the corporative organizations has shown that it is not impossible to reach a fair and reasonable agreement between employers and workers. He went on reading quietly, paying little attention to the argument, in his heart of hearts he could not decide whether he agreed or disagreed. Corporatism, the adjustment of each social class to the ambiance and setting best suited to it, provides the best way of transforming modern society. With this new prescription for a heaven on earth he concluded his reading of the lead article, then turned to the foreign news, In France the first ballot in the legislative elections will be held tomorrow, the troops under the command of Badoglio are preparing to resume their advance on Addis Ababa. At this moment Lydia appeared at the door of the bedroom with her sleeves rolled up, anxious to know, Did you see the airship yesterday, What airship, The Zeppelin, it passed right over the hotel, I didn't. But he was seeing it this very minute, on the open page of the newspaper, the gigantic, Adamastorlike dirigible bearing the name and title of the man who built her, Graf Zeppelin, German count, general, and aeronaut. There it goes flying over the city of Lisbon, over the river and the houses. People stop on the sidewalk, emerge from the shops, lean out of tram windows, appear on their balconies, they cry out to one another in order to share this wondrous sight, and a wit makes the inevitable quip, Look at the flying sausage. There's a picture here, Ricardo Reis said, and Lydia approached the bed, came so close that it seemed a shame not to embrace her hips with his free arm. She laughed, Behave, then said, It's huge, in the paper it looks even bigger than the real thing, and what about that cross stuck there at the back. They call it the gammadion or swastika. It's ugly. I can assure you there are many people who think it is the nicest cross of all, It reminds me of a spider, There were once religions in the Orient for which this cross represented happiness and salvation, Really, Yes, I'm not joking. Then why put the swastika on the tail of the Zeppelin. Because the airship is German and the swastika has now become the emblem of Germany, Of the Nazis, What do you know about the Nazis, Only what my brother has told me, Your brother who is in the Navy, Yes, Daniel, the only brother I have. Has he come back from Oporto, I haven't seen him yet, but he has, How do you know, His ship is anchored in front of the Terreiro do Paço, I would recognize it anywhere. Don't you want to come to bed, I promised my mother I would be there in time for lunch, Just for a little while, then you can go. Ricardo Reis lowered his hand to stroke the curve of her leg, lifted her skirt, reached above her garter, touched her bare skin. Lydia said, No, no, but started to weaken, her knees trembling. That was when Ricardo Reis found that his penis, for the first time in his life, was not reacting. In panic he withdrew his hand and muttered, Run the water for me, I want to take a bath. She did not understand, had started to unfasten the waistband of her skirt, to unbutton her blouse, when he repeated in a voice suddenly shrill, I must have a bath, run the water for me. He tossed the newspaper to the floor, brusquely slipped under the sheets and turned his face to the wall, almost overturning the breakfast tray. Lydia watched him in bewilderment, What have I done, she wondered. His hands, unseen by her, were trying to rouse his limp penis, they struggled in vain, one moment with violent rage, the next with despair. Sadly, Lydia withdrew, taking the tray with her, she went to wash the dishes until they sparkled like the morning sun, but first she lit the heater, started running water into the bathtub, checked the temperature as it poured from the spigot, passed wet fingers over her wet eyes. What could I have done to upset him when I was ready to get into bed with him. Misunderstandings of this nature are impossible to avoid, if only he had said to her, I cannot, I'm not in the mood, she would not have minded. Even if there was no question of coupling she would have joined him, she would have lain down beside him in silence, and comforted him until he overcame that moment of panic, perhaps she would have placed her hand on his penis, gently, without any design, simply to reassure him, Stop worrying, it's not the end of the world. They would both sleep peacefully, she having forgotten that her mother was expecting her with the lunch on the table, the mother finally saying to her sailor son, Let's have our lunch, you can no longer rely on your sister, she doesn't seem to be the same girl these days. Such are life's contradictions and injustices.

Lydia appeared at the door of the bedroom. I'll see you in a week, she said, and departed, miserable, leaving him no less miserable, she not knowing what evil she has done, he knowing full well what evil has befallen him. The sound of running water, the smell of steam pervades the apartment. Ricardo Reis remains in bed a few more minutes, he knows that the bathtub is immense, a Mediterranean sea when full, finally he gets up, throws his dressing gown over his shoulders, and shuffles on slippered feet to the bathroom. Fortunately he cannot see himself in the mirror clouded by steam, this must be the compassion shown by mirrors at certain critical moments. Then he thinks, It's not the end of the world, this can happen to anyone, my turn had to come sooner or later. What do you think, Doctor. Don't worry, I'll give you a prescription for some new pills that ought to remedy this little problem, the important thing is not to worry, to get out and distract yourself, go see a movie, if this is truly the first time it has happened, then you can consider yourself a lucky man. Removing his clothes, Ricardo Reis ran a little cold water into that great scalding lake and immersed himself little by little, as if he were abandoning the world of air. Relaxed, his limbs were pushed to the surface, to float between two bodies of water, even his withered penis stirred, caught like uprooted seaweed on the tide, beckoning. Ricardo Reis gloomily watched, as if the thing did not belong to him, Is it mine or do I belong to it, he sought no answer, the question alone causing as much anguish as he could bear.

Three days later, Marcenda appeared at the office. She told the receptionist that she wished to be seen last, that she was not there as a patient. Tell the doctor, when all the other patients have gone, that Marcenda Sampaio is here, and she slipped a twenty-escudo note into the receptionist's pocket. The message was delivered at the opportune moment, when Ricardo Reis had already removed his white coat, almost like a cassock and barely three-quarter length, which explains why he was not and never would be a high priest of this hygienic cult, but only the sacristan responsible for emptying and washing the altar cruets, for lighting and putting out the candles, for inscribing the certificates, needless to say, of death. At times he experienced the vague regret that he had not specialized in obstetrics, not because this dealt with women's most private and precious organs but because it meant bringing children into the world, other people's children, who serve as consolation when we have no children of our own, at least none we are aware of. As an obstetrician he would feel new hearts beating as they came into the world, on occasion hold in his own hands those skinny, sticky little creatures covered with blood and mucus, tears and sweat, and hear that first cry which has no meaning or a meaning beyond our understanding. He slipped back into his dressing gown, struggled to find the sleeves, which were suddenly twisted, and tried to decide whether he should receive Marcenda at the door or wait for her behind his desk with one hand placed professionally on his vade mecum, the font of all medical knowledge, the bible of sorrows. Approaching the window that looked onto the square, the elms, the linden trees in flower, the statue of the musketeer, he chose the square as the place to receive Marcenda, if he could say to her without sounding absurd, It is spring, look how delightful, that pigeon perched on the head of Camões, others perched on his shoulders. The only real justification for statues is to provide perches for pigeons. But social convention prevailed, Marcenda appeared at his door, Do go in, the receptionist was saying obsequiously, a woman of subtle perception, experienced in the art of discriminating between the different social classes. Ricardo Reis forgot the elms, the linden trees, and the pigeons took flight, something must have startled them. In the Praça de Luís de Camões shooting is prohibited throughout the year. If this woman were a pigeon, she would be unable to fly with that injured wing. How have you been, Marcenda, I'm delighted to see you, and your father, is he well. He's fine, thank you, Doctor, he was unable to come but sends his greetings. Obeying her instructions, the receptionist withdrew, closed the door behind her. Ricardo Reis continued to hold Marcenda's hand, and they remained thus, in silence, until he pointed to a chair. She sat, left hand still in her pocket. Even the receptionist, who misses nothing, would swear that the girl now in the consulting room shows no signs of any physical infirmity, in fact she is really quite attractive, a little on the thin side, perhaps, but she is so young, thinness suits her. Now then, how is your health these days, Ricardo Reis inquired. Marcenda replied, Much the same, I doubt that I will be going back to the specialist, at least not the one here in Lisbon. There are no signs of improvement, no indication of movement or that you are getting back some feeling. Nothing that encourages me. And what about your heart, That is functioning perfectly, do you wish to check it, I am not your doctor. But now that you are a heart specialist, you must have gained some knowledge, which means I can consult you. Sarcasm doesn't become you, I do my best, and that is precious little, I'm merely standing in for a colleague temporarily, as I explained in my letter. In one of your letters. Pretend you never received the other letter, that it went astray. Do you regret having written it. There is nothing more pointless in this world than regret, people who express it merely want to be forgiven, then they fall back into their weakness, for each of us, deep down, continues to take pride in his weakness. I did not regret that I went to your apartment, I do not regret it even now, and if it is a mistake to have allowed you to kiss me, to have kissed you, I still take pride in this mistake. Between us there was only a kiss, not a mortal sin. It was my first kiss, perhaps that is why I feel no remorse. No one ever kissed you before, That was my first kiss. It will soon be time to close the office, would you like to come back to the apartment, where we can talk in greater privacy. I'd rather not. We could enter the building separately, letting some time elapse in between, I won't expose you to shame. No, I'd prefer to stay here a little longer, if you can spare the time. Believe me, I wouldn't harm you, I'm really quite harmless. What does that smile mean. Nothing, only that I'm a gentle soul by nature, if you want me to spell it out, I would say that at this moment I'm at peace with the world, the waters are tranquil, that was all my smile was saying. I'd rather not go to your apartment, let's stay here and talk, pretend I am one of your patients. What's the problem, then. This smile is much better than the other one. Marcenda took her left hand from her pocket, settled it on her lap, covered it with the other hand, seemed about to say, as one confiding an ailment, Can you believe it, Doctor, fate saddled me with this arm after saddling me already with an errant heart, but instead she said, We live so far apart, there is such a difference in our ages, in our destinies. You repeat what you wrote in your letter. The truth is that I like you, Ricardo, only I cannot say to what extent. A man, when he reaches my age, looks foolish when he starts making declarations of love. But I enjoyed reading them, and now hearing them. I am making no declaration of love, But you are. We are exchanging greetings, sprigs of flowers, it is true that they are pretty, I mean the flowers, but they are cut, they will soon wilt, they are unaware of this and we pretend not to notice. My flowers I place in water, and will watch them until the colors fade. Then you will not watch them long. Now I am watching you. I am no flower. You are a man, I am capable of knowing the difference. A tranquil man, who sits on a riverbank watching what the current carries past, perhaps waiting for himself to be swept away. At this moment it is me that you are watching, your eyes tell me so, It is true, I see you being swept away like a branch in flower, a branch on which a bird sits warbling, Don't make me cry. Ricardo Reis went to the window, drew back the curtain. There were no pigeons perched on the statue, instead they were flying in rapid circles above the square, a swirling vortex. Marcenda approached him, On my way here I saw a pigeon perched on the statue's arm, close to its heart. That's quite common, they prefer a sheltered spot, You cannot see the statue from here, it faces the other way. The curtain was closed once more. They moved away from the window, and Marcenda said, I must go. Ricardo Reis held her left hand, brought it to his lips, then stroked it slowly, as if he were reviving a bird numb with cold. The next moment he was kissing Marcenda on the lips and she him, a second kiss, then Ricardo Reis can feel his blood descending, thundering like a mighty cascade, into deep caverns, a metaphorical allusion to the corpora cavernosa, in other words his penis stiffens, So it wasn't dead after all, he didn't believe me when I told him not to worry. Marcenda feels it and pulls away, then embraces him again to feel it. If questioned, she would swear that was not true, foolish virgin, but their lips have not separated. At last she moaned, I must go. Her strength drained, she broke free and collapsed into a chair. Marcenda, marry me, Ricardo Reis pleaded. She looked at him, pale, and said, No, said it very slowly, who would have believed that anyone could take so long to utter so short a word, it did not take her as long to say what followed, We would not be happy. For several minutes they remained silent. For the third time Marcenda said, I must go, but this time she got up and made for the door. He followed her, tried to detain her, but she was already in the hall, the receptionist appeared at the far end, whereupon Ricardo Reis said in a loud voice, I'll see you out, which he did. They said good-bye and shook hands. He said, Give my regards to your father. She began, One day, but did not finish, someone else will finish it, who knows when and for what reason, but for now there is only this, One day. The door is closed, the receptionist asks, Do you need me, Doctor. No. Well, if you will excuse me, I'll be off, everyone has gone now, the other doctors too. I'll stay a few more minutes, I must sort out some papers. Good evening, Doctor, Good evening, Carlota, because that was her name.

Ricardo Reis returned to his office, drew back the curtain. Marcenda still had not reached the bottom of the stairs. The shadows of twilight enshrouded the square. The pigeons were nestling on the uppermost branches of the elm trees, as silent as phantoms, or else it was the shadows of the pigeons that had perched on those very branches in years gone by, or perched on the ruins that once stood here, before the ground was leveled in order to build the square and erect the statue. Now, crossing the square in the direction of the Rua do Alecrim, Marcenda turns around to see if the pigeon is still perched on the arm of Camões, and between the flowering branches of the linden trees she catches a glimpse of a white face behind a windowpane. If anyone witnessed these movements he would not have understood their meaning, not even Carlota, who had concealed herself under the stairs to spy, suspecting that the visitor would return to the office to converse to her heart's content with the doctor. Not at all a bad idea, but it never even occurred to Marcenda, and Ricardo Reis never got around to asking himself if that was the reason he stayed behind.

A few days later a letter arrived, the same pale violet color, the same black postmark, the unmistakable handwriting, angular because the sheet of paper is not held in place by the other hand. There is the same long hesitation before Ricardo Reis finally opens the envelope, the same jaded face, and the same words, What a fool I was to visit you, it won't happen again, we will not see each other anymore, but believe me, I will never forget you as long as I live, if things had been different, if I had been older, if this incurable arm, yes, the specialist finally admitted that there is no cure, that the sun-lamp treatment, the electric shocks, and massage were a waste of time, I suspected as much, I did not even weep, it is not myself I pity but my arm, I nurse it as if it were a child that will never leave the cradle, I stroke it as if it were a small stray animal found abandoned on the street, my poor arm, what would become of it without me, and so farewell, dear friend, my father continues to insist that I go to Fátima and I have decided to go, just to please him, if this is what he needs to ease his conscience and convince him that it is the will of God, for we can do nothing contrary to the will of God and should not try, I am not asking you to forget me, my friend, on the contrary, I hope you will think of me every day, but do not write, I will make no more visits to the poste restante, now I must close, I have said all I had to say. Marcenda does not write in this manner, she observes all the rules of syntax and punctuation, it is Ricardo Reis who jumps from line to line in search of the essential, ignoring the texture of her phrasing. The exclamation marks are his, the sudden breaks that make for eloquence, but though he read the letter a second and third time, he learned no more, because he had read everything, just as Marcenda had said everything. A man receives a sealed letter as his ship leaves port, and opens it in midocean. There is nothing except sea and sky and the deck on which he is standing, and the letter says that from now on there will be no more ports of refuge for him, no more uncharted lands to discover, no destination, nothing left for him but to navigate like the Flying Dutchman, hoist and furl the sails, man the pump, mend and sew, scrape away the rust, and wait. Still holding the letter, he goes to the window and sees Adamastor, the two old men seated in the giant's shadow, and he asks himself if his disappointment is genuine, not playacting, if he truly believed he was in love with Marcenda, if in his heart of hearts he ever really wanted to marry her, or whether all this might not be the banal effect of loneliness, the simple need to believe that there are some good things in life, love, for example, that happiness which unhappy people are continually talking about, if happiness and love are possible for our Ricardo Reis, or for Fernando Pessoa, if he were not dead. There is no doubt that Marcenda exists, this letter was clearly written by her, but Marcenda, who is she, what is there in common between the girl seen for the first time in the dining room of the Hotel Bragança, when she was a stranger to him, and this Marcenda whose name and person now fill the thoughts and feelings and words of Ricardo Reis. Marcenda is a place of anchorage. What was she then, what is she now, a wake on the surface of the sea that disappears once the ship has passed, there is still some spray, the churning of the rudder, I have passed through the spray, what thing has passed through me. Ricardo Reis reads the letter one more time, the closing paragraph, where she writes, Do not write to me, and tells himself that of course he will write, to say who knows what, he will decide later, and if she keeps her promise, then let the letter sit at the poste restante, the important thing is to write. But then he remembers that Doctor Sampaio is well known in Coimbra, a notary is always a prominent figure in society, and post offices are staffed, as everyone knows, by many conscientious and loyal employees, so it is not at all impossible that the secret letter will find its way to his residence, or worse still, to his office, provoking outrage. He will not write. In this letter he would have put all the things he never got around to saying, not in the hope of changing the course of events but in order to make it clear that those events are so numerous that even saying everything about them will not change their course. Yet he would have liked at least to let Marcenda know that Doctor Reis, the man who kissed her and asked her to marry him, is a poet and not just an ordinary general practitioner acting as locum tenens for an indisposed specialist in diseases of the heart and lungs, and not a bad locum tenens either, despite his lack of scientific training, for there is no evidence that the mortality rate has risen since he came into the practice. Imagine Marcenda's surprise if he had said to her at the outset, Did you know, Marcenda, that I am a poet, in the casual tone of one who does not attach any great importance to his talent. Naturally she would realize that he was being modest, she would be flattered that he took her into his confidence, would look at him with romantic tenderness, How wonderful, how fortunate I am, I can now see what a difference it makes to be loved by a poet, I must ask him to read me his poems, I feel certain he will dedicate some to me, a common habit among poets, who are much given to dedications. Ricardo Reis, to avoid any eventual outbursts of jealousy, will explain that the women Marcenda finds mentioned in his poems are not real women, only lyrical abstractions, fictions, imaginary interlocutresses, if one can give the name of interlocutress to one who has no voice. A poet does not ask that his muses speak, only that they exist, Neaera, Lydia, Chloe. There's a coincidence for you, that after writing poems for so many years to an anonymous, ethereal Lydia I should come across a chambermaid with this name, only the name, in all other respects there is no resemblance whatsoever. Ricardo Reis explains, and then explains a second time, not because the matter is so very complicated but because he is apprehensive about the next step, which poem will he choose, what will Marcenda say when she hears it, what will be the expression on her face, she might ask to see with her own eyes what she has heard him read, then read the poem herself in a low voice, *In a changing, uncertain confluence, as the river is formed by its waves, so contemplate your days, and if you see yourself pass as another, be silent.* He reads it, reads it a second time, he sees from her face that she understands, perhaps some memory has helped her, the memory of those words he spoke in the consulting room the last time we were together, about a man who sits on a riverbank watching what the water carries past, waiting to see himself going past with the current. Clearly there is a difference between prose and poetry, that is why I understood it so well the first time and now find myself struggling to understand it. Ricardo Reis asks her, Do you like it, and she says, Oh, very much. There could scarcely be a more gratifying response, but poets are eternally dissatisfied, this one has been told everything a poet could wish to hear, God Himself would be delighted to hear such praise for the world He created, Ricardo Reis, however, looks gloomy and sad, an Adamastor who cannot wrench himself free of the marble in which he has been trapped by fraud and deception, his flesh and bones transformed into stone, his tongue likewise. Why have you become so quiet, Marcenda asks, but he does not answer.

If these are private sorrows, Portugal, taken as a whole, is not without its joys. Two anniversaries have just been celebrated, the first was Professor António de Oliveira Salazar's entrance into public life eight years ago, it seems like yesterday, how time flies, to save his country and ours from the abyss, to restore its fortunes, to provide a new political doctrine, to instill faith, enthusiasm, and confidence in the future, as the newspaper says. The other anniversary also concerns the esteemed professor, albeit the event is one of more personal joy, his and ours, namely his forty-seventh birthday, he was born the same year Hitler came into the world, only a few days separate them, there is a coincidence for you. And we are about to celebrate National Labor Day with a parade of thousands of workers in Barcelos all with their arms outstretched in Roman style, the gesture has survived from the time Braga was called Bracara Augusta, and a hundred decorated floats will depict scenes of country life, one representing the wine harvest, another the pressing of grapes, then hoeing, husking, threshing, then the kiln where they make clay cocks and fifes, then the embroideress with her lace bobbins, the fisherman with his net and oar, the miller with his donkey and sack of flour, the spinstress with her spindle and distaff, that makes ten floats and there are ninety more. Ah how the people of Portugal strive to be good and industrious, and as a reward they are well provided with entertainments, concerts given by their philharmonic band, light shows, dance exhibitions, fireworks, battles with flowers, banquets, one long continuous festival. Now, in the face of such high-spirited merrymaking we might remark, indeed it is our duty to do so, that May Day everywhere has lost its traditional meaning, if in the streets of Madrid they sing the *Internationale* and applaud the Revolution. It is not our fault, such excesses are not tolerated in our country. Thanks be to God, cry in chorus the fifty thousand Spaniards who have taken refuge in this oasis of peace. And now that the Left has won the elections in France and the Socialist leader Blum has declared himself ready to form a Popular Front government, we can expect another horde of refugees. Over the august forehead of Europe storm clouds gather, they are not content with riding on the haunches of the raging Spanish bull, Chanticleer now triumphs with his ardent crowing, but when all is said and done, the first corn may go to the sparrows but the pick of the harvest goes to the deserving. Let us listen attentively to Marshal Pétain who despite his eighty venerable winters does not mince words. In my experience, the old man says, everything that is international is pernicious, everything that is national is beneficial and productive. One who speaks in this vein will not die without leaving his mark.

And the war in Ethiopia has ended. Mussolini made the announcement from the palace balcony, I hereby declare to the Italian people and the world that the war has ended, and in response to this powerful voice the multitudes of Rome, Milan, Naples, and all Italy acclaimed him il Duce, farmers abandoned their fields, workers left their factories, dancing and singing through the streets with patriotic fervor. Benito was telling the truth when he said that Italy had an imperial soul. From historic tombs arose the majestic shadows of Augustus, Tiberius, Caligula, Nero, Vespasian, Nerva, Septimius Severus, Domitian, Caracalla, and *tutti quanti*, restored to their former glory after years of waiting and hoping, there they stand lined up, forming a guard of honor for the new heir, for the imposing presence of Victor Emmanuel III, proclaimed in every tongue Emperor of Italian East Africa, while Winston Churchill gives his blessing, In the present world situation, the maintenance or escalation of sanctions against Italy could result in a shameful war without bringing the slightest benefit to the Ethiopian people. So let us remain calm. Should it come, war will be war, since that is its name, but it will not be shameful, just as the war against the Abyssinians was not shameful.

Addis Ababa, such a poetic name, such a handsome race, it means New Flower. Addis Ababa is in flames, her streets covered with dead bodies, marauders are destroying homes, committing rape, looting and beheading women and children as Badoglio's troops approach. The Negus has fled to French Somalia, from where he will sail to Palestine aboard a British cruiser, and later, toward the end of the month, before a solemn gathering of the League of Nations in Geneva he will ask, What reply should I take back to my people. But after he speaks, no one replies, and before he got up to speak, he was jeered by the Italian journalists. Let us show tolerance, it is well known that nationalist fanaticism can easily dim one's intelligence, so he that is without sin, let him cast the first stone. Addis Ababa is in flames, her streets are covered with dead bodies, marauders are destroying homes, committing rape, looting and beheading women and children, as Badoglio's troops approach. Mussolini declared, This remarkable achievement has sealed the fate of Ethiopia, and the wise Marconi warned, Those who would seek to offer resistance to Italy are committing the most dangerous of follies, and Anthony Eden argued, Circumstances advise the lifting of sanctions, and *The Manchester Guardian*, speaking for the British Government, said, There are many reasons why colonies should be handed over to Germany, and Goebbels said, The League of Nations is a good thing but flying squadrons are better. Addis Ababa is in flames, her streets are covered with dead bodies, marauders are destroying homes, committing rape, looting, beheading women and children, as Badoglio's troops approach, Addis Ababa was in flames, homes burned, castles were sacked, bishops stripped, women raped by knights, their children pawns skewered with swords, and blood flowed in the streets. A shadow crosses the mind of Ricardo Reis. What is this, where do these words come from, the newspaper says only that Addis Ababa is in flames, that marauders are looting, committing rape, and beheading women and children as Badoglio's troops approach, the *Diário de Notícias* makes no mention of knights, bishops, and pawns, there is no reason to think that in Addis Ababa chess players were playing a game of chess. Ricardo Reis consulted *The God of the Labyrinth* on his bedside table. Here it is, on the opening page, The body discovered by the first chess player, its arms outstretched, occupies the squares of the King and Queen and their two pawns, its head is toward the enemy camp, its left hand in a white square, its right hand in a black square. In all the pages he has read there is only this one corpse, so it clearly was not along this route that the troops of Badoglio advanced. Ricardo Reis puts *The God of the Labyrinth* back in its place, he now knows what he is looking for. He opens a drawer of the desk that once belonged to an Appeals Court judge, in years gone by handwritten notes relating to the Civil Code were kept in it, he takes out a folder tied with a ribbon, it contains his odes, the secret poems he never discussed with Marcenda, and manuscript pages, all first drafts, jottings, Lydia will come across them one day, at a time of irreparable loneliness. *Master, placid are*, the first sheet reads, and other sheets read, *The gods are in exile, Crown me with roses while yet others tell, The god Pan is not dead, Apollo in his chariot has driven past, Once more, Lydia, come sit beside me on the riverbank, this is the ardent month of June, War comes, In the distance the mountains are covered with snow and sunlight, Nothing but flowers as far as the eye can see, The day's pallor is tinged with gold, Walk empty-handed, for wise is the man who contents himself with the spectacle of the world*. More and more sheets of paper pass, just as the days have passed, the sea stretches level, the winds wail in secret, each thing has its season, so let there be days for renewal, let us keep this moist finger on the page, here it is, *I heard how once upon a time when Persia*, this is the poem, no other, this the chessboard and we the players, I Ricardo Reis, you, my reader. They are burning homes, castles have been sacked and bishops stripped, but when the ivory King is in peril who cares about the flesh and bones of sisters and mothers and children, if my flesh and bones have been turned to stone, transformed into a player playing chess. Addis Ababa means New Flower, all the rest has been said. Ricardo Reis puts away his poems, locks the drawer. Cities have fallen and people are suffering, freedom and life are ending, but you and I, let us imitate the Persians of this tale. If we jeered at the Negus like good Italians in the League of Nations, let us now croon like good Portuguese to the gentle breeze as we leave our homes. The doctor is in good spirits, the neighbor on the fourth floor remarks. Are you surprised, the one thing there is never any shortage of is patients, the neighbor from the second floor retorts. Two opinions, as the doctor from the third floor leaves the building talking to himself.

Ricardo Reis is in bed, Lydia's head resting on his right arm, their perspiring bodies covered only by a sheet. He is naked, and her chemise is above her waist. Both have forgotten, or put from their minds, the morning he was impotent and she did not know what she had done to be rejected. The neighbors, on their balconies at the rear of the building, exchange words with broad hints, emphatic gestures, much nodding and winking. They're at it again, The world is depraved, Who would believe it, They've lost all shame. These sour and envious women are unable to recapture their youth, when as little girls in short dresses they danced and sang Ring-a-ring-o' roses in the garden, ah how pretty they were in those days. Lydia is happy. A woman who goes to bed so willingly with a man is deaf to gossip, let voices slander her in hallways and courtyards, they cannot harm her, nor can hostile eyes when she bumps into those virtuous hypocrites on the stairs. Soon she will have to get out of bed and wash the dirty dishes which have accumulated, and iron the bedsheets, the shirts worn by this man who is lying beside her. Who could have told me that I would be, how shall I describe myself, his mistress. Not mistress, for no one will say of this Lydia, Did you know that she is having an affair with Ricardo Reis, or, Do you know Lydia, that woman who is the mistress of Ricardo Reis. If anyone ever mentions her, he will say, Ricardo Reis has a really good maid, she does everything, he got a bargain there. Lydia stretches her legs, draws close to him, one last gesture of tranquil pleasure. It's hot, Ricardo Reis says, and she moves away a little, frees his arm, then sits up in bed and looks for her skirt, it is time to start doing some work. At that moment he tells her, Tomorrow I'm going to Fátima. She thought she had misunderstood, You're going where. To Fátima. I thought you didn't approve of such things. I'm going out of curiosity. I've never been there myself, my family doesn't go in much for religion. You surprise me. What Ricardo Reis meant was that it is usually people from the lower classes who believe in these devotions, but Lydia did not reply. Dressing in haste, she barely heard Ricardo Reis add, The trip will do me good, I've been cooped up here for so long, because she had other things on her mind now. Will you be away long, she asked, No, there and back, And where will you sleep, the place is so crowded, people have to sleep out in the open. I'll see when I get there, no one ever died from spending a night out of doors. Perhaps you'll bump into Senhorita Marcenda, Who, Senhorita Marcenda, she told me that she was hoping to go to Fátima sometime this month. Oh. She also said that she no longer visits the specialist in Lisbon, they've told her there is no cure, poor girl. You seem to know a great deal about Senhorita Marcenda. Very little, only that she is going to Fátima and that she won't be coming back to Lisbon anymore. Are you sorry. She was always very kind to me. I shouldn't think it likely that I will meet her among that multitude. Sometimes these things happen, look at me here in your apartment, who would ever have believed it, when you arrived from Brazil, after all, you might have gone to another hotel. Such are life's coincidences. It is fate. Do you believe in fate, There is nothing more certain than fate, Death is more certain, Death, too, is part of fate, but now I must iron your shirts and wash the dishes, and if there is still time I'll go and visit my mother, she's always complaining that she doesn't see much of me these days.

Lying back on the pillows, Ricardo Reis opened a book, not the one about Herbert Quain, which he had begun to wonder if he would ever finish, this was O Desaparecido by Carlos Queirós, a poet who might have been the nephew of Fernando Pessoa, had fate so ordained. A minute later he became aware that he was not reading, his eyes, rather, were fixed on the page, on a line whose meaning had suddenly become obscure. An extraordinary girl this Lydia, she says the simplest things, as if she were merely skimming the surface of more profound words which she cannot or will not utter. If I had not told her that I was going to Fátima, who knows whether she would have mentioned Marcenda, concealing her knowledge out of resentment and jealousy, emotions she betrayed back in the hotel. And these two women, the guest and the chambermaid, the rich girl and the poor servant, what did they have to discuss with each other. What if they should discuss me, neither suspecting the other, or just the reverse, playing Eve against Eve with much probing, scheming, parrying, subtle insinuations, clever silences. It is not inconceivable, on the other hand, that Marcenda simply said one day, Doctor Reis gave me a kiss, but we didn't go any further, and that Lydia simply replied, I sleep with him and I slept with him before he ever kissed me, that they then proceeded to discuss the significance of these differences. He only kisses me when we are in bed together before and during you-know-what, never afterward. To me he said, I'm going to kiss you, but as for you-know-what, what men do to women, I am ignorant of it, because they've never done it to me. Do not worry, Senhorita Marcenda, one day you'll get married and then you'll find out what it's all about. You've experienced it, tell me, is it good. When you like the other person, And do you like him, I do. So do I, but I shall never see him again. You could marry him. If we married, perhaps I wouldn't like him anymore. As for me, I think I will always like him. The conversation did not end there, but their voices lowered to a whisper, perhaps they are confiding their intimate feelings, the weakness of women, now the talk is truly between Eve and Eve. Begone, Adam, you are not wanted here. Ricardo Reis, reading, not reading, came across a fishwife on the page, capitalized, *O Fishwife, pass, I beseech you pass, flower of the race. Lord do not forgive them, for they know exactly what they are doing.* The poetic discussion between this uncle and nephew would be intense. You're incorrigible, Pessoa, and you too Queirós, I'm content with what the gods in their wisdom have given me, a lucid and solemn awareness of things and human beings. He got up, put on his dressing gown, and in his slippers went to look for Lydia. In the kitchen ironing, she had removed her blouse in order to feel a little cooler. Seeing her like this, her white skin flushed with exertion, Ricardo Reis thought he owed her a kiss. He gripped her gently by her bare shoulders, drew her toward him, and without any further thought kissed her slowly, giving time to time and space to their lips, their tongues, their teeth. Lydia was breathless, he had never kissed her like this before, now she will be able to tell Marcenda if she ever sees her again, He didn't say, I'm going to kiss you, he just kissed me.

Early next morning, so early that he thought it prudent to set his alarm clock, Ricardo Reis departed for Fátima. The train pulled out of the Rossio station at five-fifty-five, but half an hour before it even arrived, the platform was crammed with passengers, people of all ages carrying baskets, sacks, blankets, demijohns, all chatting in loud voices and calling out to each other. Ricardo Reis had taken the precaution of buying a first-class ticket, with a reserved seat, the guard obsequious with cap in hand. He had scarcely any luggage, a simple suitcase, ignoring Lydia's warning that in Fátima people slept out in the open, he would see when he arrived, there was bound to be accommodation for tourists and pilgrims of some social position. Seated comfortably by the window, Ricardo Reis contemplated the landscape, the mighty Tagus, the marshlands still flooded here and there, bulls grazing at random, frigates sailing upriver over resplendent water. After an absence of sixteen years, he had forgotten this view, and now fresh images imprinted themselves beside those restored by memory, as if it were only yesterday that he had made this journey. At the stations and signal stops en route, more and more people got on. The train is a real cattle train, there cannot have been a single empty seat in third class since it left the Rossio, and passengers are crammed into the gangways. No doubt second class has already been invaded, and soon they will start invading here, but there's no use complaining, anyone who wants peace and quiet should travel by car. After Santarém, on the long climb up to the Vale de Figueira, the train puffs along, sends up sudden gusts of steam, wheezes under its heavy load, and goes so slowly that one could easily step off, pick some flowers on the embankment, and with three strides jump back onto the running board. Listening, Ricardo Reis learns that among the passengers traveling in this compartment only two will not alight in Fátima. The pilgrims talk of their vows, debate who has made the greatest number of pilgrimages. One claims, perhaps truthfully, perhaps lying, that in the last five years he has not missed a single pilgrimage, another says that counting this one he has made eight. So far no one has boasted that he knows Sister Lúcia personally. Hearing these exchanges, Ricardo Reis is reminded of the talk in his waiting room, those depressing confidences about the orifices of the human body, where every pleasure is experienced and every misfortune can strike. At the station of Mato de Miranda, despite the fact that no passengers boarded the train, they were delayed. The noise of the engine could be heard in the distance, but here, on the bend, among the olive groves, reigned the most perfect calm. Ricardo Reis lowered his window to look outside. An elderly woman, barefoot and in dark clothes, was embracing a skinny little boy about thirteen years old and saying, My dear. Both were waiting for the train to move so they could cross the track. These two were not traveling to Fátima, the old woman had come to meet her grandson who lived in Lisbon. At last the station master blew his whistle, the locomotive hissed, went puff, puff, and slowly began to accelerate. Now the route is straight, and one could almost believe that this is a fast train. The morning air gives Ricardo Reis an appetite, and although it is much too early for lunch, people are starting to untie bundles of food. Eyes closed, he dozes, rocked by the swaying carriage, as if in a cradle. He has vivid dreams, yet when he awakes he cannot remember them. He remembers that he had no opportunity to tell Fernando Pessoa that he was going to Fátima. What will he think if he comes to the apartment and doesn't find me there, he may think I've gone back to Brazil without a word of farewell, my last farewell. Then he imagines a scene with Marcenda as the central figure, he sees her kneeling, the fingers of her right hand folded with those of her left, supporting in the air the dead weight of her withered arm. The effigy of Our Blessed Lady passes but no miracle takes place, not surprising, given Marcenda's lack of faith. She gets to her feet, resigned. Ricardo Reis sees himself approach, touch her, his middle and index finger together, on the breast, near her heart, no more is needed. Miracle, miracle, the pilgrims cry, their own woes suddenly forgotten, another's miracle is all they ask. Now they come flocking, swept along by the crowd or dragging themselves, the crippled, paralytic, consumptive, diseased, demented, blind, a multitude surrounds Ricardo Reis, beseeching another act of mercy. Behind this forest of wailing pilgrims Marcenda waves, both arms upraised, then disappears from sight. Ungrateful creature, she was healed and departed. Ricardo Reis opened his eyes, uncertain as to whether he had slept or not, and asked the passenger beside him, How much longer. We're almost there. So he had slept, and for a considerable time.

At the station in Fátima, the train emptied. Stirred by the odor of sanctity in the air, pilgrims jostled each other, there was alarm and confusion as families suddenly found themselves divided. The broad open space resembled a military encampment preparing for a battle. Most of the pilgrims will make the twenty-kilometer journey on foot to the Cova da Iria, but some rush to join the lines for buses, these are the pilgrims with weak legs and little stamina, who tire at the slightest exertion. The sky was clear, the sun bright and warm. Ricardo Reis went off in search of a place to eat. There were plenty of street vendors selling pancakes, cheesecakes, biscuits from Caldas, dried figs, pitchers of water, fruits in season, garlands of pine kernels, peanuts, and pips and lupine seeds, but not a single restaurant worthy of the name. The few eating houses were full, the taverns were packed to the door, he will need a lot of patience before he finds himself seated in front of a knife and fork and a plate of food. Yet he benefited from the Christian spirit that permeated this place, for when they saw him so smartly turned out in his city clothes, a number of customers in the line, like good provincials, allowed him to go before them, thus Ricardo Reis was able to have his lunch sooner than he had hoped, a little fried fish with boiled potatoes dressed with oil and vinegar, then a couple of scrambled eggs. He drank wine that tasted like altar wine, ate good country bread, moist and heavy, and having thanked his hosts he went to look for transportation. The square was less crowded, ready for another trainload from the south or north, but pilgrims steadily continued to arrive on foot from remote parts. A bus gave a raucous honk, touting for passengers to fill the few remaining empty seats. Ricardo Reis, breaking into a trot, stepping over baskets and bundles of mats and blankets, managed to obtain a seat, a major struggle for a man who is trying to digest his food and is exhausted by the heat. Rattling loudly, the bus pulled away, sending up clouds of dust from the poorly paved road, and the filthy windows barely allowed one to catch a glimpse of the rolling, arid land. The driver honked without respite, sending groups of pilgrims scattering into the ditches at the side of the road, steered sharply to avoid potholes, and every few minutes spat noisily out an open window. The road swarmed with an endless column of pilgrims on foot, but there were also wagons and ox-driven carts, each advancing at its own pace. From time to time an expensive limousine with a chauffeur in livery would pass, sounding its horn, carrying elderly women dressed in black or gray or midnight blue, and corpulent gentlemen in dark suits with the circumspect air of those who have just finished counting their money only to find that it has multiplied. The occupants could be seen when the limousine was forced to slow down because of some large procession of pilgrims led by their parish priest, the priest acts as both spiritual and tour guide, and deserves our praise for making the same sacrifices as his flock, on foot like them with his hooves in the dirt. The majority of the faithful walk barefoot. Some carry open umbrellas to protect themselves from the sun, these are people with delicate heads, not of the lower orders, and prone to fits of fainting and vertigo. The hymns they sing out of tune. The shrill voices of the women sound like an endless lamentation, a weeping as yet without tears, and the men, who nearly always forget the words, sing only the rhyming syllables by way of accompaniment, in a sort of basso continuo, no more is asked of them, only that they keep up the pretense. From time to time people can be seen sitting along hedgerows under the shade of trees, gathering strength for the final stretch of the journey, taking advantage of this pause to nibble a chunk of bread and sausage, a cod fritter, a sardine fried three days ago back in their obscure village. Then they get back on the road, feeling restored. Women carry baskets of food on their heads, some even suckle infants as they walk, and the dust descends on them all in clouds as yet another bus goes past, but they feel nothing, pay no attention, it shows what habit can do. Sweat trickles down the foreheads of monk and pilgrim, forms tiny channels in the dust, they wipe their faces with the back of their hands, worse than they thought, this is not just dirt but mud. The heat blackens their faces, yet the women do not remove the kerchiefs from their heads and the men keep on their jackets, they neither undo their shirts nor loosen their collars. This race preserves unawares the custom of the desert, which says that what protects from the cold protects also from the heat, therefore they wrap up as if to conceal themselves.

At a bend in the road a crowd has gathered under a tree, people are shouting, women are tearing their hair, and the body of a man is stretched out on the ground. The bus slows to allow the passengers to watch this spectacle, but Ricardo Reis says, or rather shouts to the driver, Stop here, let me see what has happened, I'm a doctor. Murmurs of protest can be heard, the passengers are in a hurry to reach the land of miracles, but they soon quiet down, anxious not to appear hard-hearted. Ricardo Reis got off, pushed his way through the crowd, knelt in the dust at the old man's side, and felt the artery in his neck. He is dead, he said. He need not have bothered interrupting his journey just to make this announcement. The news provoked a renewed outburst of tears, the dead man had numerous relatives, but his widow, a woman even older than the dead man, who now was no age, looked at the corpse with dry eyes, only her lips trembled as she stood there twining the fringes of her shawl. Two of the men in the crowd got on the bus, to report the death to the authorities in Fátima, who will make arrangements for the corpse to be taken away and buried in the nearest cemetery. Ricardo Reis has returned to his seat on the bus, now the object of everyone's curiosity, Fancy that, we have a doctor in our midst, who could ask for more reassuring company, even though he did nothing on this occasion but confirm a death. The two men inform those around them, He was already very sick when he got here, he should have stayed home, but he insisted on coming, he said he would hang himself from the rafters of the house if we left him behind, in the end he died far from home, no one escapes his destiny. Ricardo Reis nodded in agreement, not knowing that his head was moving. Yes sir, that's destiny, let's hope someone sticks a cross under that tree so future travelers can say a paternoster for the soul of one who died unconfessed and without receiving the last rites of the Church though he was already heading for heaven the moment he left his house. If this old man were called Lazarus and Jesus Christ appeared at the bend in the road on His way to the Cova da Iria to witness the miracles, He would understand at once what had happened, having experience in such things, and would elbow His way through all those gaping onlookers, and if anyone tried to stop Him, Jesus Christ would rebuke him, saying, Don't you know who you're talking to. Going up to the old woman who finds herself unable to weep, He would say, Leave this to me, and take two steps forward, make the sign of the Cross, remarkable prescience on His part, since we know that He has not been crucified yet, and He would cry out, Lazarus, arise and walk, whereupon Lazarus would get to his feet, another miracle. Lazarus would embrace his wife, who could now weep at last, and everything would be as before, and when the wagon came with the stretcher bearers and the authority to take away the body, someone would be sure to ask, Why are you looking for a dead man among the living, he is not here, he has been brought back to life. But in the Cova da Iria no such miracle, hard as people tried, was ever achieved.

This is the place. The bus comes to a halt with several final blasts of exhaust, its radiator is boiling like one of hell's cauldrons, and as the passengers step out, the driver goes to unscrew the cap, protecting his hands with old rags. Clouds of steam, the sweet-smelling incense of mechanics, rise into the air in this scorching heat, little wonder that we feel delirious. Ricardo Reis joins the stream of pilgrims. He tries to imagine what the spectacle must look like seen from heaven, a swarm of ants converging from every cardinal and collateral point like a huge star. This thought, or was it the noise of an engine, made him raise his eyes to lofty heights and ethereal visions. Overhead, tracing out an enormous circle, an airplane was dropping leaflets, perhaps prayers for intoning in unison, perhaps maps showing the way to the gates of paradise, or could they be messages from our Lord God, an apology for not being with us today, in His place He has sent His Divine Son, who already worked a miracle at the bend in the road, and a good miracle it was too. The leaflets descend slowly, there is not a breath of wind. Noses in the air, the pilgrims reach out eagerly to catch them, white, yellow, green, blue. Many who cannot read, and they form the majority in this spiritual gathering, hold the leaflets, not knowing what to do with them. A man dressed in peasant attire, after deciding that Ricardo Reis looks like someone who can read, asks, What is written here, sir. Ricardo Reis tells him, It's an advertisement for Bovril. The man looks at him suspiciously, debates whether to ask him to explain what Bovril is, then folds the paper in four and puts it into his jerkin pocket. Always hold on to what is useless, you will always find a use for it.

A sea of people. Around the great concave esplanade are pitched hundreds of canvas tents under which thousands are camping, there are frying pans on open fires, dogs guarding provisions, children crying, flies getting into everything. Ricardo Reis strolls between the tents, intrigued by this courtyard of miracles, it is as large as any city. This is a Gypsy encampment, complete with wagons and mules, and the donkeys, to the delight of the horseflies, are covered with sores. Carrying his suitcase, he does not know where he is heading, he has no shelter awaiting him, not so much as a tent, and has now satisfied himself that there are no lodging houses in the vicinity, let alone hotels. And if there should be, hidden somewhere, a hospice for pilgrims, it is unlikely that it will have any spare pallets left, they will have been reserved God knows how long in advance. May the will of God Himself be done. The sun is scorching, night is still a long way off, and there are no indications that it will become any cooler. When Ricardo Reis betook himself to Fátima it was not with physical comfort in mind, he came in the hope of seeing Marcenda. His suitcase is light, containing only his razor, soap, shaving brush, a change of underwear, socks, and a pair of sturdy shoes with reinforced soles which he must change into or he'll ruin the patent shoes he is wearing. If Marcenda is here, she will not be sitting in a tent, a notary's daughter from Coimbra deserves something better, but where will she find it. Ricardo Reis went to the hospital, a good place to start. Using his credentials as a doctor, he was allowed in, and forced his way through the rabble. Everywhere he looked, in complete confusion throughout the wards and corridors, the sick lay on stretchers and mattresses on the ground, but their relatives made far more noise than they did, keeping up an endless drone as they prayed, a drone interrupted from time to time by deep sighs, piercing cries, and pleas to the Virgin. In the infirmary there were not more than thirty beds and the sick numbered around three hundred. People lay wherever space could be found, one had to step over them, a good thing we no longer believe in the evil eye, You bewitched me, now break the spell, and the custom is to repeat the movement in reverse, if only all misfortunes could be made to disappear so easily. Marcenda is not here, nor is Ricardo Reis surprised, after all she is perfectly capable of walking on her own two feet, only her arm is crippled, and so long as she refrains from taking her hand out of her pocket, no one even notices. Outside, the heat is worse, but the sun, to his relief, does not give off a bad smell.

If such a thing is possible, the crowd is growing, as if reproducing itself by fission. Like a great black swarm of bees in pursuit of divine honey it buzzes, drones, crackles, moves in slow waves, lulled by its own size. Impossible to find anyone in this cauldron, which is not the cauldron of Pêro Botelho but burns all the same. Ricardo Reis is resigned, whether he finds or doesn't find Marcenda seems of no great importance now. If fate decrees that we meet, then we will meet, even if we attempt to hide from each other. How foolish he was, to express his thoughts with these words, Marcenda, if she is here, does not know that I am here so she will not attempt to hide, therefore the chance is greater that we will meet. The airplane continues to circle overhead, the colored leaflets dance through the air, but no one pays attention now, only the new arrivals seeing them for the first time. What a pity these leaflets do not carry the much more persuasive illustration from the newspaper advertisement, the one depicting the doctor with the goatee and the ailing damsel in the negligee, If only she had taken Bovril, she would not be in this condition. Here in Fátima there are many people in much worse condition, they would surely find that miraculous jar a godsend. His face flushed, Ricardo Reis has removed his jacket and rolled up his sleeves, and fans himself with his hat.

His legs suddenly heavy with exhaustion, he goes in search of shade. Some of his fellow pilgrims are having their siesta, worn out by the long journey and all those prayers en route, they are recovering their strength before the statue of the Virgin is brought out, before the procession of candles begins, and the long nocturnal vigil by the light of bonfires and oil lamps. He, too, dozed a little, his back against the trunk of an olive tree, the nape of his neck on soft moss. Opening his eyes, he saw patches of blue sky amid the branches and remembered the skinny boy at the train station, whose grandmother, she must have been his grandmother, called him My dear. What is the child doing at this very minute, almost certainly he has taken off his shoes, that is the first thing he does when he arrives at the village, the second is to go down to the river. His grandmother is probably cautioning him, Don't go yet, the sun is too hot, but he does not listen and she does not expect to be heard. Boys of his age want to be free, not clinging to their mother's skirts, they throw stones at the frogs and do not think they are causing any harm, but one day they will feel remorse. Too late, because for frogs and other tiny creatures there is no resurrection. Ricardo Reis finds this all absurd, the idea that he has traveled from Lisbon like someone pursuing a mirage, knowing all the while that it was a mirage and nothing more, his sitting in the shade of an olive tree among people he does not know, waiting for nothing whatsoever, and these thoughts about a boy whom he saw for only a moment in a remote provincial train station, this sudden desire to be like him, to wipe his nose with his right arm, play in puddles, pick flowers, admiring them and forgetting them, steal fruit from the orchards, scamper away weeping when pursued by dogs, or chase girls and lift up their skirts because they don't like it or do like it but pretend they don't, and because it gives him secret pleasure. Have I ever really experienced life, Ricardo Reis murmured to himself. The pilgrim lying beside him thought the murmur was some new prayer, a prayer yet to be put to the test.

The sun goes down but the heat does not abate. In the immense square there does not appear to be room for a pin, yet the crowd continues to mill around the periphery, there is a steady, constant stream of people, on this side they are still trying to get better vantage points, they must be doing the same over there. Ricardo Reis, strolling in the immediate vicinity, suddenly becomes aware of another pilgrimage, that of beggars. He sees true beggars and false beggars, and the difference is important, a true beggar is simply a poor man who begs, while your false beggar has turned begging into a profession, it is not unknown for people to become rich this way. Both use the same techniques, the whimpering, the pleading with outstretched hand, or sometimes two hands, a theatrical tour de force which is difficult to resist, Alms for the sake of the souls of your dear departed, God will reward you, Have pity on a poor blind man, have pity on a poor blind man, and some display an ulcerated leg, an amputated arm, but not what we are searching for. It is as if the gates of hell have been opened, for only from hell could such horrors have come. And now it is the turn of those selling lottery tickets, they make such an uproar as they call out winning numbers that prayers are arrested in midflight to heaven. A man interrupts his paternoster because he has a sudden hunch about the number three thousand six hundred and ninety-four. Clutching his rosary in a distracted hand, he fondles the ticket as if weighing its potential, then shakes from his handkerchief the necessary number of escudos and resumes his prayer where he broke off, *Give us this day our daily bread*, words now recited with greater hope. An attack is now launched by vendors of blankets, ties, handkerchiefs, and baskets, and by the unemployed, who wear armbands and sell holy pictures. They are not really selling, first they receive alms, then they hand over the picture, it is one way of maintaining their dignity. This poor wretch is neither a true beggar nor a false beggar, he asks for alms only because he is out of work. Now here is an excellent idea, let all the unemployed wear armbands, strips of black cloth bearing bold white letters for all the world to see, Unemployed, it would make the counting of them easier and ensure that we do not forget them. But worst of all, because they upset our spiritual peace and disturb the tranquillity of this holy place, are the hordes of hawkers. Let Ricardo Reis steer clear, otherwise they will pounce on him at once with that infernal shouting, Look, it's a bargain, Look, this has been blessed, the image of Our Blessed Lady painted on trays and statues, bunches of rosaries, crucifixes by the dozen, tiny medals, Sacred Hearts of Jesus and Ardent Hearts of Mary and three little shepherds with their hands joined in prayer and kneeling on the ground. One shepherd is a boy, but there is no evidence in either the hagiographical reports or the process of beatification that he ever lifted the skirts of little girls. The entire merchant confraternity cries out as if possessed, Woe to the trading Judas who tries with sly blandishments to steal a fellow trader's customer, whereupon the veil of the temple is torn and curses and insults rain down on the head of the treacherous rogue. Not even in Brazil can Ricardo Reis recall ever having heard such fiery rhetoric, clearly this branch of oratory has made considerable progress.

The precious gem of Catholicism sparkles with many facets, the facet of suffering for which there remains no hope other than that of returning each year, the facet of faith which in this holy place is sublime and fertile, the facet of common charity, the facet of Bovril, the facet of trading in scapulars and the like, the facet of trinkets and baubles, of printing and weaving, of eating and drinking, of lost and found, searching and finding. Ricardo Reis continues searching, but will he find. He has been to the hospital, he has explored the tents, he has gone through the open-air market in every direction, now he descends into the bustling esplanade, plunges into the dense multitude, sees their spiritual exercises, their acts of faith, their pitiful prayers, the vows they fulfill by crawling on all fours with bleeding knees, sees hands supporting a penitent woman under the armpits before she faints from pain and unbearable ecstasy, and the sick who have been brought from the hospital, their stretchers set out in rows. Between those rows the statue of Our Blessed Lady the Holy Virgin will be carried on a litter adorned with white flowers. Ricardo Reis lets his eyes wander from face to face, they search but do not find, as if he were in a dream that has no meaning, like the dream of a road that goes nowhere, of a shadow cast by no object, of a word which the air has uttered and then denied. The hymns are primitive, sol and do, sol and do, the choir is one of quavering shrill voices that constantly break off and start again. On the thirteenth of May in the Cova da Iria there is suddenly a great silence, the statue is about to make its exit from the Chapel of the Apparitions. A shudder goes through the crowd, the supernatural has come and blown over two hundred thousand heads, something is bound to happen. Gripped by mystical fervor, the sick hold out handkerchiefs, rosaries, medals, the priests take them, touch the statue with them, and return them to the supplicants, while the poor wretches implore, Our Lady of Fátima give me life, Our Lady of Fátima grant me the miracle of walking, Our Lady of Fátima help me to see, Our Lady of Fátima help me to hear, Our Lady of Fátima give me back my health, Our Lady of Fátima, Our Lady of Fátima, Our Lady of Fátima. The dumb do not plead, they simply look on, if they still have eyes to see with. However hard Ricardo Reis strains, he does not hear, Our Lady of Fátima look upon this left arm of mine and cure me if you can. Thou shalt not tempt the Lord Thy God or His Holy Mother, and if you think it over carefully you will realize that one should not ask for anything, instead one should resign oneself, that is what humility demands, because only God knows what is good for us.

The statue was brought out, carried around in procession, then it disappeared. The blind still could not see, the dumb still could not speak, the paralyzed still were paralyzed, missing limbs did not grow back, and the pains of the afflicted were not diminished. Weeping bitter tears, they accused and blamed themselves, My faith was lacking, *mea culpa, mea culpa, mea maxima culpa.* Prepared to concede a few miracles, the Virgin had left her chapel, but she found the faithful wavering, No burning bushes here, no everlasting oil lamps, this will not do, let them come back next year. The evening shadows lengthen as twilight approaches, it too at a processional pace. Little by little the sky loses the vivid blue of day, turns pearl, but over there the sun, hidden behind the trees on distant hills, explodes into crimson, orange, red, more volcano than sun, it seems incredible that this should happen in silence. Soon night will fall, campfires are lit, the vendors have stopped shouting, the beggars are counting their coins, beneath trees bodies are being nourished, knapsacks are opened, people munch stale bread, raise the cask or wineskin to their parched lips, all eat, but the food varies according to their means.

Ricardo Reis found shelter with a group of pilgrims sharing a tent. There was no discussion, they saw him standing there with a lost look on his face, a suitcase in his hand, a blanket he had bought rolled up under his arm. He in turn saw that the tent would do him nicely as long as the night did not become too cold. They told him, Make yourself comfortable. He started to say, No, thanks just the same, but they insisted, Look, our offer comes from the heart, and it was true, he realized, and joined the large group from Abrantes. This snuffling, which can be heard throughout the Cova da Iria, comes as much from chewing as from praying, because while some seek solace for their tormented souls, others satisfy the pangs of hunger, or alternate between the two. By the dying light of the campfires Ricardo Reis does not find Marcenda, nor will he see her later on during the procession of candles, nor in his sleep, when he is overcome with exhaustion, frustration, the desire to disappear from the face of the earth. He sees himself as two people, the dignified Ricardo Reis who each day washes and shaves, and this other Ricardo Reis, a vagrant with a stubble, crumpled clothes, creased shirt, hat stained with sweat, shoes covered with dust. The first asks the second to explain, please, why he has come to Fátima without any faith, with only a wild dream, And if you do see Marcenda, what will you say to her, can you imagine how absurd you would look if she appeared before you now at her father's side, or, worse still, alone, take a good look at yourself, do you really believe that a girl, even one with only one arm, would fall madly in love with a ridiculous middle-aged doctor. Ricardo Reis humbly accepts this criticism and, deeply ashamed that he is in such shabby and filthy condition, pulls the blanket over his head and goes back to sleep. Nearby, someone is snoring without a care in the world, and behind that sturdy olive tree there is murmuring that cannot be mistaken for prayers, chuckling that scarcely suggests a choir of angels, sighs that are not provoked by spiritual ecstasy. Dawn is breaking, some early risers stretch their arms and get up to poke the fire, a new day is beginning, posing fresh trials to those who seek the fruits of paradise.

Ricardo Reis decides to leave before noon, he does not wait for the farewell ceremony in honor of the Virgin, he has said his good-byes. The airplane passed over twice, meanwhile, and dropped more leaflets advertising Bovril. The bus back has few passengers, as expected, the great exodus will come later. At the bend in the road a wooden cross has been stuck into the ground. There was no miracle after all.

Trusting in God and Our Blessed Lady from the time of Afonso Henriques to the Great War. This is the phrase that has haunted Ricardo Reis since his return from Fátima. He cannot recall whether he read it in a newspaper or book, or whether he heard it in a sermon or speech, it may even have been in the advertisement for Bovril. The words fascinate him, the expression is eloquent and calculated to rouse passions and kindle hearts, for it proves that we are a chosen people. There have been other peoples in the past and there will be other peoples in the future, but there are none that have endured as long, eight hundred years of steadfast loyalty, of constant intimacy with the heavenly powers. It is true that we were slow in creating the fifth empire, that Mussolini forged ahead of us, but the sixth empire will not elude us, nor the seventh, all we need is patience, and patience is in our nature. We are already on the right road, according to a public statement made by His Excellency the President of the Republic, General António Oscar de Fragoso Carmona, in a speech that should serve as a model for all the supreme magistrates of the nation to come. In his words, Portugal is now respected throughout the world, and we should be proud to be Portuguese, a sentiment no less noble than the one that precedes it, both of them eminently quotable. We can take pride in this worldwide respect, we who navigated the high seas, even if it is only in the capacity of most loyal ally, it does not matter of whom, what matters is loyalty, without it how could we live. Ricardo Reis, who returned from Fátima tired and sunburnt, without seeing either a miracle or Marcenda, and who for three days after that did not leave his apartment, reentered the outside world through the great door of this patriotic speech by the Honorable President. Taking his newspaper with him, he went to sit in the shadow of Adamastor. The old men were there, watching and perplexed by the arrival of the ships that had come to visit this promised land so avidly discussed by other nations, numerous ships bedecked with flags, sounding their festive sirens, their crews lined up on deck saluting. Light finally dawned in the heads of these two sentinels when Ricardo Reis gave them the newspaper he had by now digested and practically memorized, Yes, it was worth waiting eight centuries to feel proud of being Portuguese. From the Alto de Santa Catarina eight centuries salute you, O mighty sea. The old men, the thin one and the fat one, wipe away a furtive tear, sorry that they cannot remain for all eternity on this belvedere to watch the ships arriving, such bliss is harder to bear than the shortness of their lives. From the bench where he is seated Ricardo Reis witnesses love play between a soldier and a housemaid, the soldier takes liberties, the housemaid wards him off with provocative little slaps. This is a day for singing alleluias, which are the evoes of those who are not Greek, the flower beds are in full bloom, all a man needs to be happy unless he is eaten by insatiable ambitions. Ricardo Reis takes stock of his own ambitions and concludes that he craves nothing, that he is content to watch the river and the passing ships, the mountains and the peace that reigns there, yet he feels no happiness inside him, only this dull insect-gnawing that never stops. It's the weather, he murmurs, then asks himself how he would be feeling now if he had met Marcenda in Fátima, if, as people often say, they had fallen into each other's arms, We shall nevermore be parted, only when I thought I had lost you did I realize just how much I love you. She would use similar words, and then they would not know what else to say, even if they were free to run behind an olive tree and repeat for themselves the whispers, laughter, and sighs of others. Once more Ricardo Reis doubts, once more he feels the insect-gnawing in his bones. One cannot resist time, we are within it and accompany it, nothing more.

Finished with the newspaper, the old men toss a coin to see who will take it home, even the one who cannot read covets this prize, as there is nothing better than newspaper for lining drawers.

When he arrived at his office that afternoon, the receptionist Carlota informed him, A letter has come for you, Doctor, I left it on your desk. Ricardo Reis felt as if a blow had been delivered to his heart or stomach. At such moments we lose all our self-possession, nor can we locate the blow, because the distance that separates the heart from the stomach is so small and there is also a diaphragm in the middle which is as much affected by the palpitations of the former as by the contractions of the latter. If God, who has learned so much over the years, were to create the human body today, He would make it much less complicated. The letter is from Marcenda, it must be, she has written to tell him that she could not travel to Fátima after all, or that she did go and saw him in the distance, even waved with her good arm, and felt despair, first because he did not see her and second because the Virgin did not heal her, Now, my love, I await you in the Quinta das Lágrimas, if you still love me. Obviously a letter from Marcenda, there it lies in the middle of the rectangular sheet of green blotting paper, the envelope pale violet. No, seen from the door it is white, an optical illusion, we are taught in school that blue and yellow make green, green and violet make white, and white and anxiety make us pale. The envelope is not violet, nor does it come from Coimbra. Ricardo Reis opened it carefully and found a small sheet of paper, on which was written, in the awful scrawl one expects from a doctor, Dear colleague, this is to let you know that I have made a good recovery and hope to resume my practice as of the beginning of next month, I wish to take this opportunity to express my deep gratitude for your willingness to stand in for me during my illness, I also wish you every success in soon finding a new appointment that will permit you to put your considerable skill and experience to good use. The letter continued for several more lines, the usual formalities observed by nearly everyone when he writes letters. Ricardo Reis, rereading these clichéd phrases, appreciated his colleague's finesse, which transformed the favor he had done for Ricardo Reis into the favor Ricardo Reis had done for him, thus allowing Ricardo Reis to leave with his head held high. And he would have a reference now to show when he went to look for work, not simply a letter of recommendation but written evidence of good and loyal service, just like the one the Hotel Bragança will give to Lydia if she ever decides to leave for another job or to marry. He put on his white coat and called in the first patient. In the waiting room there are five more patients to be examined, he will not have time now to cure them, happily their conditions are not so serious that they will die on his hands in the next twelve days, before the month expires, just as well.

No sign of Lydia. This is not her day off, true, but knowing that his trip to Fátima was simply a matter of going and coming straight back, and knowing that he could have met Marcenda there, she might at least have come to see if there was any news of her friend and confidante, to find out if Marcenda was well, if her arm had been cured. In half an hour Lydia could come to the Alto de Santa Catarina and go back, or she could call at his office, which is even closer and quicker. But she has not come, she has not asked. It was a mistake for him to have kissed her without taking her to bed, perhaps she thought that he was buying her with that kiss, if such thoughts occur to people of humble background. Alone in his apartment, Ricardo Reis leaves only to work and to dine, from his window he watches the river and the distant slopes of Montijo, the rock of Adamastor, the punctual old men, the palm trees. Occasionally he goes down to the park and reads a few pages of some book. He retires early, thinks about Fernando Pessoa, who is dead now, and about Alberto Caeiro, who disappeared in his prime and for whom there had been such high hopes, and about Álvaro de Campos, who went to Glasgow, at least that is what he said in his telegram, he will probably settle there, building ships to the end of his days or until he is pensioned off. Occasionally Ricardo Reis goes to the movies and sees *Our Daily Bread* directed by King Vidor, or *The Thirty-Nine Steps* with Robert Donat and Madeleine Carroll, and he could not resist going to the São Luís to see *Audioscopes*, a 3-D film. As a souvenir he brought home the celluloid spectacles one has to wear, green on one side, red on the other, these spectacles are a poetic instrument to see things for which normal vision is not enough.

They say time stops for no man, that time marches on, commonplaces that are still repeated, yet there are people who chafe at the slowness with which it passes. Twenty-four hours to make a day, and at the end of the day you discover that it was not worthwhile, and the following day is the same all over again, if only we could leap over all the futile weeks in order to live one hour of fulfillment, one moment of splendor, if splendor can last that long. Ricardo Reis starts toying with the idea of returning to Brazil. The death of Fernando Pessoa, apparently, was a valid reason for crossing the Atlantic after an absence of sixteen years, for staying in Portugal, resuming his practice, writing a poem now and then, growing old, taking the place, after a fashion, of the poet who died, even if no one noticed the substitution. But now he wonders. This is not his country, if, in fact, it is anyone's. Portugal belongs only to God and Our Blessed Lady, it is a dreary, two-dimensional sketch with no relief in sight, not even with the special spectacles of *Audioscopes*. Fernando Pessoa, whether shadow or ghost, appears from time to time in order to make some ironic comment, to smile benevolently, then disappear. Ricardo Reis need not have bothered returning because of him. And Marcenda has ceased to exist, she lives in Coimbra on an unknown street, her days pass, one by one, without a cure. She may have hidden his letters in some corner of the attic, in the padding of a chair, or in a secret drawer used by her mother before her, or, even more cleverly, in the trunk of a housemaid who cannot read and is trustworthy, perhaps Marcenda reads them over and over, like one who recites a dream lest he forgets it, in vain, because in the end our dreams and what we remember of them have nothing in common. Lydia will come tomorrow because she always comes on her day off, but Lydia is the nursemaid of Anna Karenina, she is useful for keeping the house clean and for certain other needs, she cannot fill, with the little she has to offer, the emptiness of Ricardo Reis, not even the universe would suffice, if we accept his image of himself. As of the first of June he will be unemployed, he will have to go forth once more in search of a vacancy, a locum tenens position to make the days pass more quickly. Fortunately he still has a large wad of English pound notes he has not touched, and there is the money still deposited in a Brazilian bank, these various sums would be more than enough to rent an office and build a general-medicine practice of his own, for general medicine is all most patients require. No need to dabble in diseases of the heart and lungs. He might even employ Lydia to attend the patients, intelligent and easygoing Lydia would soon learn how, with a little guidance she could improve her spelling and escape the drudgery of life as a chambermaid. But this is only the daydream of one who is passing the time in idle thought. Ricardo Reis will not seek work, no, the best thing for him to do is take *The Highland Brigade* back to Brazil when she makes her next voyage. He will discreetly return *The God of the Labyrinth* to its owner, and O'Brien will never discover how the missing book suddenly reappeared.

Lydia arrived, said good afternoon, but seemed a little cold, withdrawn, she asked no questions and he was forced to speak first, I went to Fátima. She asked, Oh, how did you like it. How should Ricardo Reis reply, as a nonbeliever he is not likely to have experienced spiritual ecstasy, on the other hand he did not go purely out of curiosity, therefore he confines himself to generalities, Lots of people, dust everywhere, I had to sleep in the open, as you warned me, fortunately the night was warm. Doctor, you are not the sort of person to be roughing it on pilgrimages. I went to see what it was like. Lydia stays in the kitchen, is now running the hot water to wash the dishes, without saying much she has made it clear that there will be no carnal pleasures today. Could the reason for this embargo be the familiar problem of menstruation, or is it some lingering resentment, or the combination of both blood and tears, two insurmountable rivers making an impassable, murky sea. He sat on a bench in the kitchen watching her as she worked, not something he was in the habit of doing, it was a gesture of goodwill, a white flag waving over the fortifications to test the mood of the enemy general. I didn't come across Doctor Sampaio and his daughter after all, which was only to be expected with such a crowd, these words are spoken casually, they hover in midair, waiting for someone to pay attention. But what kind of attention, he could be telling the truth, he could be telling a lie, such is the inadequacy, the built-in duplicity of words. A word lies, with the same word one can speak the truth, we are not what we say, we are true only if others believe us. Lydia's belief is unknown, for she simply asks, Were there any miracles. If there were, I didn't see them, and no miracles were reported in the newspapers. Poor Senhorita Marcenda, if she went there in the hope of being cured, how disappointed she must have been. She had little hope, How do you know. Lydia fixed her gaze on Ricardo Reis as quick as a startled bird. Trying to catch me, he thought to himself as he replied, When I was still staying at the hotel, Marcenda and her father were already planning a visit to Fátima. Oh, really. These are the little duels with which people wear themselves out and grow old. Better to change the subject, and this is where newspapers become useful, they store facts in one's memory and help keep conversations going, both for the old men on the Alto de Santa Catarina and for Ricardo Reis and Lydia, because some silences are not preferable to words. What news about your brother, this is just an opening. My brother is fine, why do you ask. I was reminded of him because of something I read in the paper, a speech by a certain engineer named Nobre Guedes, I still have the paper here. I've never heard of the gentleman. Given what he has to say about sailors, I doubt that your brother would call him a gentleman. What does he say. Wait, I'll get the paper. Ricardo Reis left the kitchen, went into the study, returned with *O Século*, the text of the speech took up almost an entire page, This is the speech Nobre Guedes made on the National Radio condemning Communism, and at one point he refers to sailors. Does he say anything about my brother. He doesn't mention your brother by name, but to give you an example, he had this to say, There is in circulation an execrable leaflet known as *The Red Sailor*. What does execrable mean. Execrable means that something is evil, wretched, very bad. It means you want to curse it. Exactly, to execrate is to curse. I've seen *The Red Sailor* and it didn't make me feel like cursing. Did your brother show it to you. Yes, it was Daniel. Then your brother is a Communist. I'm not sure about that, but he's certainly in favor of Communism. What's the difference. To me he doesn't look different from other people. Do you think that if he were a Communist he would look different. I don't know, I can't explain. Well, this engineer Guedes also says that the sailors of Portugal are not red or white or blue, they are Portuguese. What, he thinks Portuguese is a color. That's very witty, anyone looking at you would say you couldn't break a plate, yet every so often you pull down a whole cupboard of plates. My hand is steady, I'm not in the habit of breaking plates, take a look, here I am washing your dishes and nothing slips from my hands. You're an extraordinary girl. This extraordinary girl is only a hotel chambermaid, but tell me, did this fellow Guedes have anything else to say about the sailors. About the sailors, no. I now remember that Daniel did mention a sailor, also Guedes, but his first name was Manuel, Manuel Guedes, and he is waiting to be sentenced, there are forty men altogether who are facing trial. Many have the name Guedes. Well, this one is Manuel. The dishes are washed and left to drain, Lydia has other chores to do, she must change the sheets, make the bed, open the window to air the room, clean the bathroom, put out fresh towels. This done, she returns to the kitchen and is drying the dishes when suddenly Ricardo Reis steals up from behind and puts his arm around her waist. She tries to avoid him, but he kisses her on the neck, causing the plate to slip from her hands, and it breaks into pieces on the floor. So you've finally broken a plate, it had to happen sooner or later, no one escapes his fate, he laughed, turning her toward him and kissing her full on the lips. She no longer resisted, but simply said, We cannot today. Now we know that the problem is physiological, the other obstacles have been overcome. It doesn't matter, he replied, it can keep until next time, and went on kissing her. Later she will have to sweep up the bits of crockery that are scattered all over the kitchen floor.

Then it was Fernando Pessoa who visited Ricardo Reis. Several days later, he appeared just before midnight, when all the neighbors were in bed. He came upstairs on tiptoe, taking this precaution because he was never sure that he would be invisible. Sometimes people looked right through him, he could tell from their lack of expression, but on rare occasions they stared, as if there was something strange about him but they could not put their finger on it. If anyone were to tell them that this man dressed in black was a ghost, they would not believe it, we are so familiar with white sheets and tenuous ectoplasms, but a ghost, if he is not careful, can be the most solid thing in the world. So Fernando Pessoa climbed the stairs slowly and rapped on the door with the agreed signal, anxious not to cause a scene, the clatter of someone stumbling upstairs could bring a bleary-eyed neighbor out on the landing, and she would scream at the top of her voice, Help, a thief. Poor Fernando Pessoa a thief, he who has been robbed of everything, even life. In his study, trying to compose a poem, Ricardo Reis had just finished writing, *Not seeing the Fates that destroy us, we forget their existence*, when the silence that filled the building was broken by a gentle tap-tap. He knew immediately who it was and hastened to open the door, What a pleasant surprise, where on earth have you been. Words can be tricky, these used by Ricardo Reis suggest a note of black humor in the worst possible taste, when he knows as well as we do that Fernando Pessoa has come from in the earth and not on it, from the rustic graveyard at Prazeres, where he does not even rest in peace, because his ferocious grandmother Dionísia, also buried there, demands a detailed account of his comings and goings. I've been for a stroll, her grandson replies sourly, just as he is now replying to Ricardo Reis, but without the same irritation. The best words are those that reveal nothing. Fernando Pessoa sank to the sofa with a gesture of infinite weariness, raised his hand to his forehead as if trying to assuage a pain or drive away some cloud, then he ran his fingers down his face, uncertainly over his eyes, pressing the corners of his mouth, smoothing his mustache, stroking his pointed chin. The fingers seemed to want to remodel his features, to restore them to their original design, but the artist has picked up an eraser instead of a pencil, and it obliterates as it passes, one whole side of the face loses its outline, which is only to be expected, because almost six months have passed since Fernando Pessoa's death. I see less and less of you these days, Ricardo Reis complained. I warned you on the first day, I become more forgetful as time passes, even now, there on the Rua do Calhariz, I had to rack my brains to remember the way to your apartment. You only had to locate the statue of Adamastor. If I had thought of Adamastor I would have been even more confused, I would have started to believe myself back in Durban, eight years old again, and then I would have been twice lost, in time as well as space. Try coming here more often, that will be one way of refreshing your memory. Today I was guided by a lingering smell of onion, A smell of onion, That's right, onion, your friend, it would appear, has not given up spying on you. That is ridiculous, the police must have precious little to occupy them when they can afford to waste time with someone who is innocent of any crime and has no intention of committing one. You can never tell what is going on in the mind of a policeman, perhaps you made a good impression, perhaps Victor would like to win your friendship but realizes that you live in the world of the chosen, he in the world of the damned, and that is why he whiles away the night gazing up at your window, watching to see if there is any light, like a man madly in love. Go ahead, have your little joke at my expense. You cannot imagine how sad one has to be to joke like this. But this constant spying is totally unjustified. I wouldn't say totally unjustified, after all is it normal for someone to be visited by a person who comes from the beyond. But no one can see you. That depends, my dear Reis, that depends, sometimes a dead man does not have the patience to be invisible, or sometimes he lacks the energy, and this does not take into account the fact that certain people among the living have eyes that can see the invisible. Surely that isn't true of Victor. Perhaps, although you must agree that one could hardly imagine a more useful ability in a policeman, by comparison Argos of the thousand eyes would be a nearsighted wretch. Ricardo Reis lifted the sheet of paper on which he had been writing, I have some lines here, I don't know how they will turn out. Read them to me. They are just a beginning, and they might even begin in a different way. Read them. *Not seeing the Fates that destroy us, we forget that they exist.* I like it, but as I recall, you wrote much the same thing, a thousand times and in a thousand different ways, before you left for Brazil, the tropics don't appear to have enriched your poetic genius. I have nothing more to say, I'm not like you. You will become like me, don't worry. My inspiration is what one might call internal. Inspiration is only a word. I am an Argos with nine hundred and ninety-nine eyes and all blind. A nice metaphor, which also implies that you would not be much good as a policeman. By the way, Fernando, did you ever come across a certain António Ferro, Secretary for National Propaganda. Yes, we were friends, I owe it to him that I was awarded a prize of five thousand reis for *Mensagem*, why do you ask. You will see in a moment, I have a piece of news here, did you know that the literary prizes administered by that department were awarded several days ago. How could I have known. Forgive me, I keep forgetting that you can no longer read. Who won the prize this year, Carlos Queirós, Ah, Carlos, Did you know him, Carlos Queirós was the nephew of a woman named Ophelinha, spelled with a *ph* instead of an *f*, whom I loved for a time, we worked in the same office. I cannot imagine you falling in love. We all fall in love at least once in our lifetime, and that is what happened to me. I'm curious to know what kind of love letters you wrote. I remember them as being rather less banal than most love letters. When was this, The affair began as soon as you left for Brazil, And did it last long, Long enough for me to be able to say, like Cardinal Gonzaga, I, too, have known love. I find this hard to believe, Do you think I'm lying, Certainly not, how could you say such a thing, we have never lied to each other, when the need arose, we confined ourselves to using words that lied. What do you find so hard to believe, then. That you should have fallen in love, the fact is that as I see and know you, you are precisely the kind of person who is incapable of loving. Like Don Juan, Yes, like Don Juan, but for a different reason, Explain, In Don Juan there was an excess of lust, which had to be dispersed among the women of his desire, while your situation, as far as I can recall, was pretty much the opposite. And what about you. I am somewhere in the middle, I am ordinary, average, neither too much nor too little. In other words, the well-balanced lover, Not well balanced, it is not a question of geometry or mechanics. Are you telling me that your love life, too, is less than perfect, Love is complicated, my dear Fernando, You can't complain, you have your Lydia, Lydia is a chambermaid, And Ofélia was a typist. Instead of discussing women, we seem to be discussing their professions. And there is also that girl you met in the park, what was her name, Marcenda, That's it, Marcenda is nothing to me. You dismiss her so roughly, it sounds like resentment. My limited experience tells me that resentment is the common attitude of men toward women. My dear Ricardo, we should have spent more time together. The empire decreed otherwise.

Fernando Pessoa got to his feet, paced awhile up and down

the study, lifted the sheet of paper on which Ricardo Reis had written the lines he had read, How did you express it, *Not seeing the Fates who destroy us, we forget that they exist*, one would have to be blind indeed not to see how the fates destroy us day by day, as the proverb says, *There are none so blind as those who will not see*. Fernando Pessoa put down the sheet of paper, You were telling me about Ferro, let's get back to where we were. During the awards ceremony, António Ferro observed that writers who grumble under repressive regimes, even when the repression is purely intellectual, such as that which emanates from Salazar, forget that creative output has always increased during reigns of law and order. This idea of the benefit of intellectual repression, that the Portuguese have become more creative under the surveillance of Victor, is absurd. Then you don't agree. History itself disproves what Ferro claims, you need only think of your own youth, of *Orfeu*, tell me if that was a reign of law and order, although your odes, my dear Reis, if one looks at them closely, might be considered a paean to law and order. I never thought of them like that. But that is what they are, human unrest is futile, the gods are wise and indifferent, and above them is fate, the supreme order to which even gods are subject. And what of men, what is their function. To challenge order, to change fate. For the better. For better or for worse, it makes no difference, the point is to keep fate from being fate. You sound like Lydia, she is always talking about fate. Fortunately when it comes to fate, one can say whatever he likes. We were speaking of Ferro. Ferro is a fool, believing that Salazar is Portugal's fate. The Messiah. Rather the parish priest who baptizes, christens, and marries us, and commends our souls to God when we die. In the name of order. Exactly, in the name of order. As I recall, when you were alive you were much less subversive. When one dies, one sees things differently, and with this irrefutable sentence I take my leave, irrefutable because you, being alive, cannot possibly dispute it. Why are you reluctant to spend the night here. The dead should not fall into the habit of living with the living, just as the living should not keep the dead with them. Humanity consists of both the living and the dead. That is true, but not altogether true, otherwise you would not only have me here, you would have the Court of Appeals judge too and all the other deceased members of his family. How do you know a Court of Appeals judge lived here, I don't remember ever having told you. It was Victor. Which Victor, mine. No, a Victor who is dead but who also has a tendency to stick his nose into the affairs of others, not even death has cured him of this obsession. Does he stink of onion. He does, but it's bearable, the smell is gradually disappearing as time passes. Farewell, Fernando. Farewell, Ricardo.

There are signs that Salazar's intellectual repression is not spreading as effectively as intended by its prime mover. A recent episode right here on the banks of the Tagus showed its weakening influence, when the second-class dispatch boat *João de Lisboa* was launched with all due ceremony in the presence of our venerable Head of State. The boat is on the slipway, festooned, everything spick-and-span, the tracks greased, the wedges adjusted, the crew lined up on the quarterdeck, and His Excellency the President of the Republic, General António Oscar de Fragoso Carmona, the very same who declared that Portugal is now respected throughout the world and that we should be proud to be Portuguese, arrives with his entourage, civilian and military, the latter in dress uniform, the former in tails, top hat, and striped trousers. The President, proudly stroking his handsome white mustache, proceeds with caution, perhaps on his guard not to repeat on this occasion the phrase he always uses when he is invited to open an exhibition of paintings, Very chic, very chic, most enjoyable. They are now mounting the steps to the platform, the highest dignitaries in the land, without whose presence not a single vessel can be launched, there is also a representative from the Church, the Catholic Church of course, from which advantageous blessings are expected, may it please Almighty God that this ship kill many and lose few. All present are proud to be part of this splendid occasion with its gathering of notables, curious bystanders, shipyard workers, and photographers and reporters. The bottle of sparkling wine from Bairrada awaits its moment of explosive glory, when lo and behold, the *João de Lisboa* begins to slip down the slipway though no one has as much as touched it. There is confusion, the President's white mustache quivers, puzzled top hats wave, and there goes the ship. As she enters the water, the crew shout hip hip hurrah according to custom, the seagulls soar, startled by the sirens of the other ships and also by the loud guffaws that echo now throughout the Ribeira de Lisboa. The shipyard workers, a particularly nasty lot, are clearly responsible for this insult, and Victor is already investigating the incident. The tide recedes, the hatchways even now give off the toxic stench of onion, the President withdraws in a rage as his entourage disperses in shame and indignation, he demands to know im-me-diately the names of those responsible for this unpardonable outrage against the dignity of our sailors not to mention the Fatherland in the person of its highest magistrate. Yes, Mr. President of the Council, says Captain Agostinho Lourenço, Victor's boss. But they cannot shake off the public ridicule, such fun, the whole of Lisbon is talking about it, even the Spaniards at the Hotel Bragança, although somewhat nervously, *Cuídense ustedes, eso son artes del diablo rojo*, but since these are matters concerning Lusitanian politics, they make no further comment. The dukes of Alba and Medinaceli arrange a visit to the Coliseu, an outing for the men only, to watch the terrifying, amazing wrestling contests featuring their compatriot José Pons, Count Karol Nowina a Polish nobleman, the Jewish wrestler Ab-Kaplan, the White Russian Zikoff, the Czech Stresnack, the Italian Nerone, the Belgian De Ferm, the Fleming Rick de Groot, the Englishman Rex Gable, and a certain Strouck whose nationality remains obscure, all champions *extraordinaires* of this other human spectacle, who have mastered the graceful art of slams and kicks, head butts and scissor holds, full nelsons and bridges. If Goebbels had to enter this ring, he would play safe and send the *Luftwaffe* on ahead.

It is precisely about planes and aviation that discussions are taking place in the capital now. As for the serious breach of discipline committed by certain members of the navy, we should mention in passing, since we shall not touch on the subject again, that despite Victor's investigations the culprits were not found, for no one believed that the incident of the *João de Lisboa* could possibly have been the work of a simple caulker or riveter. Since it is evident to everyone that the clouds of war are gathering over the skies of Europe, the Portuguese government has decided, by way of example, which is the best lesson of all, to show its citizens what they must do to protect themselves in the event of an air raid. The name of the enemy is not mentioned, but everyone assumes that it is the traditional enemy, that is, Castilian, which is now Red. The range of modern planes is still very limited, so we are not likely to be attacked by the French, and even less by the English, who in addition happen to be our allies. As for the Italians and Germans, they have given so many proofs of friendship, our nations linked by a common ideal, that we are confident they will help us one day rather than attempt to exterminate us. Therefore the government has announced in the newspapers and over the radio that on the twenty-seventh of this month, the eve of the tenth anniversary of the National Revolution, Lisbon will witness a spectacle without precedent, namely a mock air raid somewhere in the Baixa, more technically it will be a demonstration of an attack by air with the purpose of destroying the Rossio railroad station and blocking all points of access to the aforementioned station by filling the area with tear gas. First a reconnaissance plane flies over the Rossio and marks the target with a smoke signal. Certain critics say that the attack would be far more effective if the planes dropped their bombs without giving any warning, what perverted disregard for the laws of chivalry. The moment the smoke rises in the air, the defense artillery fires a shot and the appropriate sirens sound, an alarm that no one could possibly fail to hear. The police, the National Republican Guard, the Red Cross, and the fire brigade go into action immediately, the population is evacuated from those streets at greatest risk, while emergency squads rush to offer assistance and fire engines, their hoses at the ready, head for the areas where fire is most likely to break out. Meanwhile the rescue teams have been assembled, and among them is the well-known actor of stage and screen, António Silva, who leads a group of volunteer firemen from Ajuda. The squadron of enemy bombers, a fleet of biplanes, can now finally advance, they are obliged to fly low because their open cockpits are exposed to the rain and wind, and then the defending machine guns and antiaircraft artillery go into action, but since this is only a mock air raid, no planes are shot down, they swoop and attack without fear of reprisal, they do not even have to make the pretense of dropping bombs, the bombs explode by themselves down here in the Praça dos Restauradores, whose patriotic name could not save it if this were a real air raid. Nor was there any salvation for an infantry division that was heading for the Rossio, it was wiped out to the last man, we cannot imagine what they hoped to accomplish at a location which the enemy had humanely warned us was to be heavily bombed. Let us hope that this lamentable episode, a shameful blot on our army's reputation, will not be hushed up and that the General Staff will be brought before the Council of War for collective and summary execution by firing squad. The emergency services are beginning to feel the strain, stretcher bearers, nurses, and doctors selflessly struggle in the line of fire, collecting corpses, saving the wounded, the latter daubed with Mercurochrome and tincture of iodine, swathed in bandages that later will be washed and reused when there are real wounds to deal with, even if it means waiting another thirty years. Despite this heroic defense, the enemy planes launch a fresh attack, incendiary bombs land on Rossio Station, which is now devoured by flames and reduced to a pile of rubble, but our hopes of a final victory have not been entirely dashed, because there on his pedestal, bareheaded, miraculously unharmed, the statue of the king, Dom Sebastião, remains standing. Elsewhere the bombardment has caused havoc, fresh ruins now cover the old ruins of the Convento do Carmo, columns of smoke emerge from the Teatro Nacional, the casualties increase, on all sides are houses in flame, mothers scream for their little ones, children cry for their mothers, and husbands and fathers are forgotten, war is hell. In the sky overhead, the pilots, satanic, drink to the success of their mission with glasses of Fundador brandy, which also restores warmth to their frozen limbs now that the heat of the battle is waning. They make notes, draw sketches, take photographs for their dispatches, then, dipping their wings in derision, off they fly in the direction of Badajoz. We were right when we surmised that they had come from across the river Caia. The city has been transformed into a sea of flame, thousands have lost their lives, another earthquake has befallen us. Then the antiaircraft artillery fires a final shot, the sirens sound once more, and the exercise is over. The people leave their shelters and return to their homes, there are no dead or wounded, the buildings are still standing, it was all one huge joke. This, at any rate, is the program for today's spectacle.

Ricardo Reis has seen the bombardment of Urca and Praia Vermelha, but at such a distance that they might well have been mistaken for training maneuvers similar to this one, except that the next day the newspapers reported real deaths. He decides to go and take a look at the scene and the actors from the Santa Justa footbridge, keeping far enough from the center of operations to preserve the illusion of reality. But others had thought of it before him, and when Ricardo Reis arrived, there was no room on the bridge, so he started to walk down the Calçada do Carmo and found himself taking part in a pilgrimage. Had the pavement been broken and dusty, he would have thought himself on the road to Fátima, for these are all things of the spirit, airplanes, airships, and visions. He was reminded, for some reason, of the flying machine, the giant bird of Padre Bartolomeu de Gusmão, perhaps by some association of ideas, going from today's mock exercise to the air raids on Praia Vermelha and Urca, and from them, since that was Brazil, to the flying priest and the Passarola that immortalized his name, even though Padre Bartolomeu himself never flew it, whatever people may have said or will say to the contrary. At the top of the steps that descend in two flights to the Rua do Primeiro de Dezembro, Ricardo Reis sees that a crowd has gathered in the Rossio. Surprised that the public is allowed to get so close to the bombs, he nevertheless allows himself to be swept along with the stream of avid spectators who press toward the theater of war. Entering the square, he finds that the crowd is much larger than it seemed before, and too packed for anyone to pass. But he has had time to master the wiles practiced in these parts, and says as he goes, Excuse me, please, I'm a doctor. Thanks to this strategy, a lie though it is the truth, he succeeds in reaching the front lines, where he can see everything. So far no airplanes have been sighted, but the police are nervous, in the cleared areas in front of the theater and the railroad station the commanding officers issue orders, an official State automobile passes, inside are the Minister of the Interior and members of his family, including women. Other members of the entourage follow in the car behind. They will watch the exercise from the windows of the Hotel Avenida Palace. Suddenly the warning shot is fired, the anguished sirens wail, the pigeons in the Rossio soar in a flock, flapping. Something has gone wrong with the plan, excessive haste, perhaps, on the part of novices, the enemy plane was supposed to drop a smoke signal first, then the sirens were to begin their mournful chorus and the antiaircraft guns their firing. What does it matter, the day will come when bombs fall ten thousand kilometers away and we know exactly what the future holds for us. Finally the plane appears, the multitude sways, they raise their arms, There she is, there she is. A cavernous roar, an explosion, and a dense cloud of smoke rises into the sky, there is great excitement, anxiety makes people's voices hoarse, the doctors put their stethoscopes to their ears, the nurses prepare their syringes, the stretcher bearers, in their impatience, drag the stretchers on the ground. In the distance now you can hear the hum of the engines of the flying fortresses. As the moment approaches, the more timid of the spectators begin to wonder if this is not in earnest after all, some hurriedly retreat and huddle in doorways to avoid being hit by shrapnel, but the majority stay put, and once it has been confirmed that the bombs are harmless, the crowd doubles. Shells explode, the soldiers slip on their gas masks, there are not enough masks for everyone, but the important thing is to give an impression of real warfare, we know immediately who will die and who will be saved from this attack with chemical weapons, because the time has not yet come for all to perish. There is smoke everywhere, the spectators cough and sneeze, behind the Teatro Nacional erupts a turbulent black volcano, the theater itself seems to be on fire. But it is difficult to take any of this seriously. The police drive back the people in front, they are in the way of the rescue teams, while the wounded, on stretchers, forget the dramatic role assigned them and giggle like idiots, perhaps the gas they inhaled was laughing gas. Even the stretcher bearers have to stop to wipe away tears of laughter. To cap it all, just as the imaginary peril reaches its climax, a municipal road sweeper arrives on the scene with his pushcart and broom and starts sweeping up the bits of paper strewn along the gutter. He lifts the litter with his shovel, empties it into his trash can, and moves on. Oblivious of the uproar, of the people running in every direction, he enters clouds of smoke and reemerges unscathed, he does not even look up to see the Spanish planes. Once is usually enough, twice is often too much, but history is indifferent to the fine points of literary composition, which explains why she now causes a postman to appear with his bag of mail, tranquilly crossing the square. How many people must be anxiously awaiting his arrival, a letter from Coimbra may come today, a message saying, Tomorrow I shall be in your arms. This postman, aware of his responsibilities, is not one to waste time on spectacles in the street. Ricardo Reis is the only man of learning in the crowd, the only one who can see a Lisbon road sweeper and a postman and think of that famous youth in Paris who sold his cakes in the street while the enraged mob stormed the Bastille. There is really no difference between us Portuguese and the civilized world, we too have our alienated heroes, self-absorbed poets, road sweepers who tirelessly sweep, and postmen who cross the square without remembering that the letter from Coimbra should be delivered to that gentleman over there. But there's no letter from Coimbra, he says as the road sweeper sweeps and the pastry seller cries out, Cheesecakes from Sintra.

A few days later, Ricardo Reis narrated what he had seen, described the airplanes, the smoke, the deafening noise of the anti-aircraft artillery, the volleys of the machine guns, and Lydia listened attentively, sorry to have missed the fun. She laughed, Oh how funny, the business with the road sweeper, when suddenly she remembered that she also had something to tell, Do you know who escaped. She did not wait for Ricardo Reis to answer but went on, Manuel Guedes, the sailor I mentioned the other day, do you remember. Yes, I remember, but where did he escape. As he was being taken before the tribunal, and Lydia laughed with gusto. Ricardo Reis simply smiled. This country is going to the dogs, ships that launch themselves prematurely, prisoners who escape, and road sweepers, but what can one expect from a road sweeper. But Lydia was very pleased that Manuel Guedes had managed to escape.

Invisible, the cicadas sing in the palm trees on the Alto de Santa Catarina. Adamastor is deafened by their strident chorus, which scarcely merits the sweet name of music, but the question of music depends a great deal on who is listening. The enamored giant would not have heard them as he paced the shore waiting for the procuress Dóris to arrive and arrange the much desired encounter, for the sea was singing then and the beloved voice of Thetis hovered over the waters, as is usually said of the spirit of God. But it is the male cicada that sings, rubbing his wings furiously to produce this obsessive, relentless sound, like a marble cutter's screech upon striking some harder vein inside the stone. It is stifling hot. In Fátima the sun had been a burning ember, but then for days the sky was overcast, it even drizzled. In the lowlands, the flood has finally subsided, all that remains of that vast inland sea are small pools of scummy water which the sun is gradually drying up. In the morning, when the air is still fresh, the old men bring their umbrellas, but the heat now has grown oppressive, so the umbrellas serve as parasols, which leads us to conclude that the usefulness of an object is more important than the names we give it, yet in the final analysis, like it or not, we always come back to words. The ships enter and leave with their flags, smokestacks, antlike sailors, deafening sirens. A sailor, after hearing that din so often during storms at sea, ends up learning to speak on equal terms with the deity of the deep. These two old men have never been to sea, but their blood does not chill when they hear that mighty roar, mighty though muffled by distance, it is deeper down that they quake, as if there were ships sailing through the channels of their veins, ships lost in the darkness of their bodies, amid the gigantic bones of the world. As the heat becomes sultry, the old men retrace their steps, it is time for lunch and those time-honored hours of siesta in the shade of their own homes. When the heat abates, they will return to the Alto to sit on the same bench, but with their umbrellas open, because the protection of the trees, as we know, is unreliable, the sun only has to descend a little and the shade of the palm trees is gone. These old men will die without learning that palm trees are not trees, incredible, that people can be so ignorant. But, as in the case of umbrella and parasol, it is of no importance that a palm tree is not a tree, what matters is the shade it gives, and if we were to ask that gentleman, the doctor who comes here every afternoon, whether a palm tree is a tree or not, he would have to go home to consult his encyclopedia of botany, unless he left it behind in Brazil. Most likely all he knows about the vegetable world is the skimp imagery with which he adorns his poems, flowers in general, a few laurels because they date from mythological times, some trees bearing no name but tree, vines and sunflowers, the rushes that tremble in the current, the ivy of oblivion, the lilies, and the roses, the roses. The old men converse freely with Ricardo Reis, but when he leaves his apartment it does not cross his mind to ask them, Did you know that a palm tree is not a tree. And because they are so sure of what they think they know, it will never occur to them to ask him, Doctor, is the palm tree a tree. One day they will go their separate ways and the fundamental question of whether the palm tree is a tree because it resembles a tree, or whether this passing shadow we cast on the ground is life because it resembles life, will remain unanswered.

Ricardo Reis has got into the habit of rising late. He has learned to suppress any desire to eat in the morning. The opulent trays Lydia used to bring to his room at the Hotel Bragança now seem to belong to someone else's past. He sleeps late, wakes up and goes back to sleep again, he studies his own sleeping, and after numerous attempts has succeeded in fixing his mind on a single dream, always the same dream, about one who dreams that he does not wish to conceal one dream with another, like erasing telltale footprints, It is simple, all you have to do is drag the branch of a tree behind you, leaving only scattered leaves and pieces of twig, which soon wither and merge with the dust. When he gets up, it is time for lunch. Washing, shaving, dressing are mechanical acts in which the mind barely participates. This face covered with lather is a mask that could fit any man's face, and when the razor little by little reveals what is underneath, Ricardo Reis is intrigued by what he sees, and disturbed, as if afraid that some evil might emerge. He examines himself carefully in the mirror, comparing this face with the different, unknown face he once had. He tells himself that as long as he shaves every day, sees every day these eyes, this mouth, this nose, this chin, these pale cheeks, these crumpled, absurd appendages called ears, that such a change is impossible, and yet he feels certain he spent years in some place without mirrors, because today he looks and does not recognize himself. Often, going out to lunch, he encounters the old men coming down the street, they greet him, Good afternoon, Doctor, and he replies, Good afternoon, though he does not know their names, they might as well be trees or palms. When he feels inclined, he goes to a movie, but usually he returns to his apartment after lunch. The park is deserted in the fierce glare of the sun, the river's shimmering gleam dazzles the eyes, and Adamastor, embedded in rock, is about to send forth a mighty cry, enraged at the face the sculptor gave him, aggrieved for reasons we have known ever since Camões's epic. Like the old men, Ricardo Reis takes refuge in the shade of his dwelling, where little by little the former mustiness has returned. Lydia opens all the windows when she comes, but it doesn't help, the smell seems to emanate from the furniture, from the very walls, the contest is definitely unequal, and Lydia comes less frequently these days. Toward evening, with the first breeze, Ricardo Reis goes and sits on a bench in the park, neither too close nor too far from the old men. Giving them his morning newspaper when he is done with it is his only act of charity. He does not offer them food, they have not asked for any, although they have not asked for these printed sheets of news either, you can decide which act of generosity would be the greater if both were made. If we asked Ricardo Reis what he does at home, alone all that time, he would simply shrug, perhaps he has forgotten that he did some reading, wrote a little poetry, wandered down corridors, spent some time at the rear of the building looking into the courtyard below, the clotheslines, white sheets, towels, and the hen coops, and the cats sleeping on the walls in the shade. There are no dogs, but, then, there are no possessions that need guarding. Then he went back to his reading, to his poetry, writing, rewriting, or tearing up when the poem was not worth keeping. Then he waited for the heat to abate, for the first breeze of the evening. As he was going downstairs, the neighbor on the second floor appeared on the landing. Time had softened the malicious gossip, there was no longer the same interest, the entire building had been restored to harmony and amiable coexistence. Well now, is your husband feeling better, he inquired, and the neighbor replied, Thanks to you, Doctor, your help was an act of providence, a miracle. That is what we are all seeking, acts of providence and miracles, and is it not a miracle to have a doctor living next door who can come to our assistance when we have a pain in the tummy. Has he emptied his bowels. He got rid of the whole load, thanks be to God, Doctor. Such is life, the hand that writes the prescription for the laxative also writes the sublime or at least acceptable line, *You have sun if there is sun, flowers if there are flowers, and good fortune if fortune smiles.*

The old men read the newspaper. We already know that one of them is illiterate, he is therefore more generous when it comes to making comments, his opinions are a way of balancing the scale. If one man knows, the other explains. I say, this story about Loon Six Hundred is really very funny, I've known him for years, I knew him when he drove a tram, he was always crashing into carts and wagons, he loved it, they put him in jail thirty-eight times and finally sacked him, he was incorrigible, but the cart drivers were partly to blame, they go at a snail's pace, never hurry, and there was Loon Six Hundred stamping on the bell with the heel of his boot, foaming at the mouth until he could stand it no longer, so he rammed them, bang, and there was a fight, and the police came and marched everybody off to jail, but now Loon Six Hundred drives a cart too and fights with the tram drivers, his former colleagues, because they treat him the way he used to treat the cart drivers, as the old saying goes, As ye sow. Thus concluded the old man who could not read, with an aphorism, which had a medicinal, binding effect on his speech. Ricardo Reis was seated on the same bench, a rare occurrence, but today all the others were occupied. Aware that the old man's monologue was for his benefit, he asked, This nickname Loon Six Hundred, how did he get it. Whereupon the illiterate replied, Six hundred was his number when he worked for the tram company and people called him Loon because of his behavior. I see. When the old men went back to their reading, Ricardo Reis allowed his thoughts to wander, What nickname would suit me, perhaps Doctor Bard, Back-from-Brazil, the Spiritualist, Jack the Ode Maker, Chess Player, Casanova of Chambermaids. Suddenly the old man who was reading said, Orphan of Fortune, the nickname of a petty thief, a pickpocket caught in the act. Why not Orphan of Fortune for Ricardo Reis and Ricardo Reis for the pickpocket, a criminal could have his name, names do not choose destinies. The old men love to read about the colorful dramas of everyday life, the cases of fraud, disorderly conduct, acts of violence or despair, dark deeds in the night, crimes of passion, an abandoned fetus, a car crash, a calf born with two heads, a bitch that suckles cats, at least this bitch is not like Ugolina who ate her young. Their conversation now turns to Micas Saloia whose real name is Maria Conceição and who has received one hundred and sixty prison sentences for theft besides being exiled to Africa several times. Then there was Judite Meleças the bogus countess from Castelo Melhor who cheated a lieutenant of the National Republican Guard out of two contos and fifty reis, a sum of money that will seem rather paltry fifty years from now but in these lean times it is almost a fortune, as the women of Benavente, who work from dawn to dusk for ten thousand reis, can testify. The rest is less interesting. As announced, a gala day was held at the Jockey Club with thousands of guests, we need not be surprised that so many attended, we know how the Portuguese love celebrations, particularly celebrations organized on behalf of the flood victims of Ribatejo, among whom is Micas da Borda d'Agua from Benavente, who will receive her share of the forty-five thousand seven hundred and fifty-three escudos and five and a half centavos collected, although some accounting still has to be done, because there are a few not inconsiderable invoices outstanding, and tax bills. But the high standard and elegant presentation of the events on the program made it all worthwhile, the band of the National Republican Guard gave a concert, two troops of horsemen from the same guard staged a carousel and charge, patrols from the Cavalry School of Torres Novas demonstrated various maneuvers, there was a display of cowboy skills, the rounding up and throwing of steers from Ribatejo, and *nuestros hermanos* were represented, cattle drovers from Seville and Badajoz come expressly to take part in the festivities. In order to have a chat with them and hear the latest from Spain, the dukes of Alba and Medinaceli, guests at the Hotel Bragança, descended into the arena, a fine example of peninsular solidarity on their part, there is nothing like being a Spanish grandee in Portugal.

News from the rest of the world has not changed a great deal, the strikes continue in France, where there are now about five hundred thousand workers on strike, the government headed by Albert Sarraut is expected to resign and be succeeded by a new ministry which Léon Blum will organize, and the impression will be created, at least temporarily, that the demonstrators are satisfied. As for Spain, the drovers from Seville and Badajoz converse with the dukes, Here we are respected more than grandees of Portugal, Then remain here with us and we shall drive cattle together. In Spain, as we were saying, the strikers are sprouting up like mushrooms and Largo Caballero warns that until the working classes are protected by the law, outbreaks of violence can be expected, and if he says that, a man who supports the working classes, it must be true, therefore we must prepare ourselves for the worst. Better late than never, on the other hand there's no point closing the stable door after the horse has bolted, look at the British, they abandoned the Ethiopians to their fate and now applaud their Emperor, if you ask me, my dear fellow, this is nothing but one great swindle. The old men on the Alto de Santa Catarina chat pleasantly on, though the doctor has returned to his apartment, they talk about animals, about the white wolf that appeared in Riodades, near São João da Pesqueira, and that the local inhabitants call Pombo, and about the lioness Nádia that mauled the fakir Blacaman's leg in the Teatro Coliseu in full view of the audience, thus proving that circus artists really do put their lives at risk. If Ricardo Reis had not left so soon he could have taken this opportunity to tell them the story of the bitch Ugolina, completing the triumvirate of wild beasts, the wolf still at large, the lioness whose dose of drugs will have to be increased, the bitch, who eats her children, Pombo, Nádia, Ugolina, animals have nicknames as well as men.

Early one morning, as Ricardo Reis lies dozing, very early indeed considering his indolence of late, he hears the warships on the Tagus firing salvos, twenty-one solemn booms at regular intervals, making the windowpanes rattle. He thought another war had broken out, then remembered what he had read the previous day, this is the tenth of June, Portugal's National Holiday commemorating our forefathers and affirming our dedication to the achievements of the future. Half-asleep, he wondered whether he had the energy to jump out of these grubby sheets and throw the windows wide open to let the heroically echoing salutes enter unimpeded and disperse the shadows from his apartment, the mildew, the insidious smell of must. But while he was turning this over in his mind and debating with himself, the last vibrations fell away. Once more a great silence descended upon the Alto de Santa Catarina, but Ricardo Reis did not notice, he had closed his eyes and gone back to sleep. Such is a life badly managed, we sleep when we should be on our guard, we depart when we should be arriving, we close the window when we should leave it open. In the afternoon, returning from lunch, he saw bunches of flowers at the foot of the statue of Camões, homage from the Federation of Patriots to the epic poet, the great bard of the nation's valor, that all may know that we have shaken off the enfeebling and degrading melancholy we suffered in the sixteenth century. Today, believe me, we are a very happy people. As soon as darkness falls we will switch on floodlights here in the square and Senhor Camões will be lit up, what am I saying, he will be completely transformed by the dazzling splendor. True, he is blind in the right eye, but he can still see with his left, and if he finds the light too strong let him speak up, we can easily dim the intensity to twilight, to the original gloom that we have by now grown so accustomed to. Had Ricardo Reis gone out this evening, he would have met Fernando Pessoa in the Praça de Luís de Camões, seated on one of those benches as if enjoying the breeze. Both families and solitary souls have come in search of the same refreshment, and there is so much light, it is almost like day, faces glow as if touched by ecstasy, one can understand why this day is called the Feast of the Nation. To mark the occasion, Fernando Pessoa tries to recite, in his mind, the poem from *Mensagem* that is dedicated to Camões, and it takes him some time to realize that there is no such poem. Can this be possible. Only by looking it up can he be certain. From Ulysses to Dom Sebastião not a single hero escaped him, not even the prophets Bandarra and Vieira, yet apparently he failed even to mention the One-Eyed Bard. This omission causes Fernando Pessoa's hands to tremble, his conscious asks, Why, his unconscious can provide no explanation, then Luís de Camões smiles, his bronzed mouth has the knowing expression of one who died long ago, It was envy, my dear Pessoa, but forget it, don't torment yourself so, here nothing has importance, the day will come when they disown you a hundred times, another day will come when you wish to be disowned a hundred times. At this very moment, in his third-floor apartment on the Rua de Santa Catarina, Ricardo Reis is trying to write a poem to Marcenda so that posterity will not say she passed in vain, *Already impatient for the summer, I also weep for its flowers, knowing they must fade.* This will be the first part of the ode, so far no one would guess that he speaks of Marcenda, but poets often begin at the horizon, for that is the shortest path to the heart. Half an hour later, or an hour later, or more, because when it comes to writing poetry time either drags or races, the middle part has taken form, it is not the lament it first seemed, rather the acceptance of that which has no remedy, *Having crossed the inevitable threshold of each year, I begin to see before me the flowerless valley, the rumbling abyss.* It is dawn, the entire city sleeps, and the floodlights on the statue of Camões, because with no onlookers they now serve no purpose, have gone out. Fernando Pessoa returns home, says, I'm back,

Grandmother, and at that precise moment the poem completes itself, with difficulty, a semicolon was reluctantly inserted, Ricardo Reis long resisted it, did not want it, but it won, *And I pick the rose because fortune picks Marcenda, and cherish it, let it wither on my breast and not on the vast diurnal curving bosom of the globe.* Ricardo Reis lay fully dressed on the bed, his left hand resting on the sheet of paper, if he should pass now from sleep to death, people will mistake it for his will, a letter of farewell, they will not know what to make of it even after they read it, for whoever heard of a woman called Marcenda. Such a name comes from another planet, Blimunda too is an example, a mysterious name waiting to be used by an unknown woman. At least a woman named Marcenda has been found, but she lives far away.

Here beside him on this same bed was Lydia, when they felt the earth move. The tremor was brief but shook the building from top to bottom before it passed, sending the neighbors onto the stairs in hysterics and causing the chandelier to swing like a pendulum. Gripped by terror, those voices sounded obscene. The entire city, perhaps with the terrible memory of other earthquakes still embedded in its stones, waited in suspense, in the unbearable silence that follows the tremor, when one cannot think but asks himself, Will the tremor return, Will I die. Ricardo Reis and Lydia stayed in bed. They were naked, lying on their backs like statues without even a sheet covering them. Death, had it come, would have found them submissive, satisfied, still breathing heavily, wet with sweat and intimate secretions, their hearts pounding, because their bodies had separated only a few minutes ago, as full of life as possible. Suddenly the bed shudders, the furniture rocks, the floor and ceiling creak, this is not the vertiginous final moment of orgasm, it is the earth roaring from its depths. We are going to die, Lydia said, yet she did not clutch the man beside her as one might have expected. Women as a rule are like this, it is the men who say in terror, It's nothing, stay calm, it has passed, words spoken to reassure themselves, not others. Trembling with fear, Ricardo Reis said this too, and he was right, the tremor passed, the neighbors shouting on the stairs gradually calmed, but the discussion continued, one of them went down to the street, another went to her window, both watching the general uproar. As peace is gradually restored, Lydia turns to Ricardo Reis and he to her, the arm of each over the body of each, and he repeats, It was nothing, and she smiles, but her smile has a different meaning, she is clearly not thinking about the tremor. They lie looking at each other yet so distant from each other, so apart in their thoughts, as we now see when suddenly she confides, I think I'm pregnant, I'm ten days late. The student of medicine has been taught the mysteries of the human body, he knows therefore how the spermatozoa swim upstream inside the woman until they reach the source of life, from books he learns these things and sees them confirmed in practice, yet look how stunned he is, as stunned as an ignorant Adam who cannot fathom how this could have happened however much Eve explains. He tries to gain time, What did you say. I'm ten days late, I think I'm pregnant. Once again, of the two she is the more composed. For the past week, every day, every second, she has thought of nothing else, perhaps she thought of this even a moment ago when she said, We are going to die. One wonders whether Ricardo Reis was included in that plural. He expects her to ask a question, for example, What should I do, but she remains silent, concealing her pubis with a slight bending of the knees. There is no visible sign of pregnancy, unless we can decipher what her eyes are saying, fixed on some personal horizon, if eyes possess such a thing. Ricardo Reis searches for the right words but all he finds within himself is indifference, as if, though aware that he is obliged to help solve the problem, he does not feel implicated in its cause. Rather, he sees himself in the role of the doctor to whom a patient has blurted out her guilty secret, Ah, Doctor, what is to become of me, I am pregnant and this could not have happened at a worse moment. The doctor does not tell her, Have an abortion, don't be a fool. On the contrary, he puts on a grave air, If you and your husband have taken no precautions, in all probability you are pregnant, but let's wait a few more days, you could simply be late, sometimes that happens. But Ricardo Reis cannot speak with such neutrality, he is the father, for there is no evidence that in the last few months Lydia has slept with any man but him, still the father is at a loss for words. Finally, feeling his way with the utmost caution, weighing every phrase, he distributes the blame, We were careless, this had to happen sooner or later. But Lydia does not ask, What care should I have taken. He never withdrew at the critical moment, never used those rubber caps, but this does not worry her, she simply says, I'm pregnant. After all, it happens to nearly every woman, becoming pregnant is no earthquake. Ricardo Reis makes a decision, he must know her intentions, there is no point in evading the issue any longer, Are you thinking of having the child. Just as well that there is no one eavesdropping, otherwise Ricardo Reis would find himself accused of suggesting an abortion, but before the witnesses have been heard and the judge passes sentence, Lydia steps forward and declares, I am going to have the baby. For the first time, Ricardo Reis feels a finger touch his heart. It is not pain he experiences, or a twitch or chill, but a sensation like no other, like the first hand-shake of men from two different planets, both human beings yet completely alien to each other. What is an embryo of ten days, Ricardo Reis asks himself, and can find no answer. In his years as a doctor he has seen cells multiply through a microscope, he has seen detailed illustrations in books, but now he sees nothing but this silent, somber, unmarried woman, a hotel chambermaid by profession, Lydia, her breasts and belly exposed, only her pubis shyly hidden as if keeping a secret. He pulled her to him, and she yielded like someone finally taking refuge from the world, suddenly blushing and overjoyed and pleading like a timid bride, You aren't angry with me. What an idea, why should I be angry. These words are not sincere, because a great anger now surges inside Ricardo Reis, I've got myself into a fine mess, he is thinking, if she doesn't have an abortion, I'll end up with a child on my hands, I'll have to acknowledge it as mine, I am morally obliged, what a mess, I never thought anything like this would happen to me. Snuggling up closer, Lydia wanted him to hold her tight, because it felt good, and casually she uttered these incredible words, If you don't want to acknowledge the child, I don't mind, the child can be illegitimate, like me. Ricardo Reis felt his eyes fill with tears, some tears of shame, some of pity, if anyone can tell the difference, and in a sudden impulse, sincere at last, he embraced and kissed her. Imagine, he kissed her long and on the lips, relieved of this tremendous burden. There are such moments in life, we think we are experiencing passion and it is merely a rush of gratitude. But sensuality pays little attention to these subtleties, within seconds Lydia and Ricardo Reis are copulating, moaning and sighing, they need not worry now, the child has already been conceived.

These are days of bliss. On vacation from her job at the hotel, Lydia spends nearly all her time with Ricardo Reis and goes home only to sleep at her mother's house, out of propriety, to avoid gossip among the neighbors, who notwithstanding the good relations established ever since the doctor offered some medical advice, continue to comment slyly on these disgraceful associations between master and servant, all too common in this Lisbon of ours no matter how carefully disguised. Someone of greater moral fastidiousness might insinuate that people can also do during the day what they normally do at night, but another could reply that during the day there is no time, because of the great spring cleaning done in houses every Easter after the long winter, which explains why the doctor's charwoman comes early each morning and leaves almost at dusk, and work she does, for all to see and hear, with feather duster and cloth, scrub brush and broom. Sometimes the windows are closed and there is a sudden silence, but is it not natural for a person to rest between one chore and another, to untie the kerchief on her head, to loosen her clothes, to groan from a new and sweet exertion. The apartment is celebrating Resurrection Saturday and Easter Sunday by the grace and labor of this humble servant who passes her hands over things and leaves them spotless and gleaming, not even in the days of Dona Luísa and the Appeals Court Judge, with a regiment of maids to do the shopping and the cooking, did these walls and furniture shine with such luster, blessed be Lydia among women. Marcenda, were she living here as the legitimate mistress of the household, could not compete, not even with two good hands. A few days ago the place smelled of mildew, dust, must, blocked drains, and now light penetrates the most remote corners, makes all the glass look like crystal, polishes every surface, the ceiling itself becomes starlit with reflections when the sun enters the windows, a celestial abode, a diamond within a diamond, and it was through menial housework that this sublime transformation was achieved. Perhaps also the abode is celestial because of the frequency with which Lydia and Ricardo Reis make love, such is their pleasure in giving and taking, I cannot think what has come over these two that they are suddenly so demanding and so generous with their favors. Could it be the summer that is heating their blood, could it be the presence of that tiny ferment in her womb, the ferment is nothing in this world as yet, yet already it has some influence in governing it.

But now Lydia's vacation is over and everything returns to normal, she will come, as before, once a week on her day off. Now, even when the sun finds an open window, the light is different, weaker, and the sieve of time has started once more to sift the impalpable dust that makes outlines fade and blurs features. When Ricardo Reis turns down the bedcover at night, he barely sees the pillow where he will rest his head, and in the morning he cannot rise without first identifying himself with his own hands, line by line, what he can still find of himself, like a fingerprint partially obliterated by a large scar. One night Fernando Pessoa, who does not always appear when he is needed, knocked on his door. I was beginning to think I'd never see you again, Ricardo Reis told him. I haven't been out much of late, I get lost so easily, like a forgetful old woman, the only thing that saves me is the mental picture I still have of the statue of Camões, working from there, I can usually get my bearings. Let's hope they don't remove him, given this latest mania of removing things, you should see what's happening on the Avenida da Liberdade, they have stripped it bare. I haven't been back there, I know nothing about it. They have removed or are about to remove the statue of Pinheiro Chagas, and that of a certain José Luís Monteiro, whom I've never heard of. Nor I, but as for Pinheiro Chagas, they have done the right thing. Be quiet, you don't know what awaits you. They will never erect a statue to commemorate me, only if they have no shame, I'm not one for statues. I couldn't agree more, there can be nothing more depressing than having a statue as part of one's destiny, let them raise statues to military leaders and politicians, who like that sort of thing, we are men of words only and words cannot be set in bronze and stone, they are words, nothing more, look at Camões, where are his words. That is why they made him a fop at court. A D'Artagnan. With a sword at his side, any puppet looks good, I'm sure I would cut a ridiculous figure. Don't upset yourself, you might escape this curse, and if you don't, like Rigoletto, you can always hope that they will pull your statue down one day, as in the case of Pinheiro Chagas, and transfer it to a quiet spot or store it in some warehouse, it is happening all the time, some people are even demanding that the statue of Chiado be removed. Chiado too, what do they have against Chiado. They say he was a scurrilous buffoon and is not fit for the elegant site where his statue stands. On the contrary, Chiado could not stand in a better place, one cannot imagine Camões without Chiado, besides they lived in the same century, if there is anything that needs changing it is the position in which they put the friar, he should be turned to face the epic poet with hand outstretched, not a begging hand but an offering, giving hand. Camões needs nothing from Chiado. Camões is no longer alive, therefore we have no idea what he needs or doesn't need. Ricardo Reis went to the kitchen to get some coffee, returned to the study, sat opposite Fernando Pessoa, and said, It always feels strange not being able to offer you a cup of coffee. Pour another cup and put it in front of me, I'll keep you company while you drink. I cannot get used to the idea that you do not exist. Seven months have passed already, enough time to engender a life, but you know more about that than I do, you are a doctor. Is there some veiled hint in that last remark. What veiled hint should I make. I'm not sure. You are touchy today. Perhaps it's this business of removing statues, this proof of how fickle human loyalties can be, the Discus Thrower is another example. What discus thrower, The one on the Avenida, Now I remember, that naked youth pretending to be Greek, Well, he too has been removed. But why. They said he looked effeminate, they spoke of moral health and protecting the eyes of the city's inhabitants from shameful displays of nudity. If the youth was not exaggerated in any of his physical proportions, what harm was he doing. Those so-called proportions, although neither exaggerated nor excessive, were more than sufficient to illustrate certain details of the male anatomy. But I thought they said the youth looked effeminate, is that not what they said. Yes. Then surely he offended because he was found wanting, not because there was too much of him. I am only repeating as best I can the rumors circulating in the city. My dear Reis, are the Portuguese gradually taking leave of their senses. If you who lived here ask this question, how can a man who lived abroad for so many years be expected to answer it.

Ricardo Reis, finishing his coffee, now debated whether or not to read the poem he had dedicated to Marcenda, the one beginning, *Already impatient for the summer*. When finally he made up his mind and began to rise from the sofa, Fernando Pessoa pleaded with him with a sadly vacant smile, pleaded, Distract me, you must have other scandals to confide. Whereupon Ricardo Reis, without needing to pause for thought, announced in seven words the biggest scandal of all, I am about to become a father. Fernando Pessoa looked at him in astonishment, then burst out laughing, he could not believe it, You're joking. Ricardo Reis said somewhat stiffly, I am not joking, besides I fail to understand your surprise, if a man regularly sleeps with a woman, in all likelihood she will conceive, that is what happened in my case. Who is the mother, your Lydia or your Marcenda, or is there a third woman, with you one never knows. There is no third woman, and I did not marry Marcenda. Ah, so you would have a child with Marcenda only if you were married to her. Well, obviously, you know the strict morality observed in traditional families. And chambermaids have no such scruples. Sometimes they do. True, remember when Álvaro de Campos told us how he was mocked by a hotel chambermaid. Not in that sense. In what sense, then. A hotel chambermaid is also a woman. The things one learns after one is dead. You don't know Lydia. My dear Reis, I shall always treat the matter of your child with the greatest respect, nay, veneration, but having never been a father myself, I know not how to translate these metaphysical feelings into the tedious reality of everyday life. Stop being ironic. Your sudden paternity must have dulled your senses, otherwise you would perceive that there is nothing ironic in what I am saying. Irony there most certainly is, though it may go under the guise of something else. Irony, rather, is the disguise. A disguise for what. Perhaps for grief. Don't tell me that it grieves you never to have had a child. Who knows. Have you regrets. I am the most regretting of persons and today do not even have the heart to deny it. You regret that you regret. That habit I had to give up when I died, there are certain things on this side that are not permitted. Fernando Pessoa stroked his mustache and asked, Are you still thinking of going back to Brazil. There are days when I seem to be back there already, and there are days when I have the impression that I was never there at all. You are floating, in other words, in midocean, neither here nor there. Like the rest of the Portuguese. But this gives you an excellent opportunity to make a new life for yourself, with a wife and child. I have no intention of marrying Lydia, and I still haven't decided whether I will acknowledge the child as mine. If you will allow me to express an opinion, my dear Reis, you are a cad. Perhaps, but Álvaro de Campos took loans he never repaid, He was a cad too, You never really got along with him, I never really got along with you, We never really understood each other, That was inevitable, since each of us was a multitude of different people. What I do not understand is this high moral tone of yours, this conservatism. A dead man by definition is a conservative, he cannot bear any tampering with order. You once fulminated against order. Now I fulminate on its behalf. If you were alive and found yourself in my shoes, with an unwanted child, its mother from a lower class, you would have the doubts I have. The very same. The doubts of a cad. That's right, dear Reis, of a cad. I may be a cad, but I have no intention of abandoning Lydia. Perhaps because she is making things easy for you. True enough, she told me there was no need for me to acknowledge the child as mine. Why are women like this, Not all of them, Agreed, but only women can be like this. Anyone listening to you would think you had a great deal of experience with women. The only experience I have is that of a spectator, an observer. No, one has to sleep with them, make them pregnant, even if it ends in abortion, one has to see them when they are sad and happy, laughing and weeping, silent and talkative, one has to watch them when they do not know that they are being watched. And what does an experienced man see at such moments? An enigma, a labyrinth, a charade. I was always good at charades, But a disaster when it came to women, My dear Reis, that is not kind, Forgive me, my nerves are humming like a telephone wire in a strong wind. You are forgiven. I have no job and no interest in looking for one, I spend my days sitting here in my apartment, sitting in some restaurant, or on a bench in the park, as if I had nothing to do but sit and wait for death. Let the child be born. It isn't up to me, and a child wouldn't solve anything, I feel that it does not belong to me. You think someone else might be the father. No, I'm certain I'm the father, that's not the problem, the problem is that only the mother truly exists, the father is an accident. A necessary accident. Undoubtedly, but dispensable once the necessity has been provided, so dispensable that he could die at once, like a praying mantis. You are as frightened of women as I was, Perhaps even more. Did you ever hear from Marcenda again, Not a word, but I wrote a poem to her several days ago, Are you serious, Well, to be frank, it's only a poem in which her name appears, would you like me to read it to you. No. Why not. I know your poetry by heart, both the poems you have written and the poems you will write, the only novelty would be the name Marcenda. Now it is your turn to be unkind. Nor can I ask to be forgiven on the grounds that my nerves are bad, go ahead, then, and read me the poem. *Already impatient for the summer.* And the second line could be, *I also weep for its flowers.* That's right. As you can see, we know everything about each other, or at least I about you, Is there anything that belongs only to me, Probably not. After Fernando Pessoa left, Ricardo Reis drank what remained of the coffee in his cup, it was cold but tasted good.

A few days later the newspapers reported that twenty-five Hitler Youth students from Hamburg, visiting our country in order to study and promote National-Socialist ideals, were guests of honor at the Teacher Training College. After an extensive tour of the Exhibition to Mark the Tenth Anniversary of the National Revolution, they wrote the following in the Roll of Honor, We are nobody. This meant, as the clerk on duty hastened to explain, that the people are indeed nobody if not guided by the elite, the cream, the flower, the chosen few of our society. Note that the word *chosen* derives from *choice* which implies *election*, for we would have our people guided by the chosen few if they can choose them, whereas to be guided by a flower or by a cream is ridiculous, at least in the

Portuguese language, so let us use the French word *élite* until such time as we find something better in German. Perhaps with this in mind the creation of the Portuguese Youth Movement has been decreed, in October its activities will start in earnest, the Movement will have a membership of two hundred thousand youths, the flower or cream of our youth, from which, hopefully, the elite will emerge, destined to govern us when the present regime comes to an end. If Lydia's child is born and survives, in a few years' time he will be able to take part in parades, enroll in the junior ranks of the Portuguese Youth Movement, don the green and khaki uniform, display on his belt the letter S, which stands for Serve and Salazar, or Serve Salazar, therefore a double S, SS, extending his right arm in Roman-style salute. And Marcenda, with her aristocratic background, will enroll in the Women's Organization for National Education, she too will raise her right arm, since it is only the left that is paralyzed. To show how our patriotic youth is shaping up, representatives of the Portuguese Youth Movement will travel to Berlin in uniform, let us hope they will have an opportunity to repeat that celebrated phrase, We are nobody. They will also attend the Olympic Games, where, needless to say, they will make a splendid impression, these proud and comely youths, the glory of the Lusitanian race, the mirror of our future, a blossoming tree that extends its branches in Roman salute. My son, Lydia tells Ricardo Reis, will have nothing to do with such a farce, and with these words we could start an argument that would last ten years, if we live that long.

Victor is nervous. This mission is one of enormous responsibility, not to be compared with the routine job of tailing suspects, bribing hotel managers, interrogating porters who spill the beans immediately. He puts his right hand to his hip to feel the reassuring presence of his pistol, then takes from the inside pocket of his jacket, very slowly, with the tip of his fingers, a peppermint lozenge. He unwraps it with infinite care, because in the silence of the night the sound of rustling paper can be heard ten paces away, this is unwise of him, an infringement of security regulations, but the smell of onion, perhaps because of his nervousness, has become intense and there is the danger that at the critical moment his prey might flee, being downwind of him. Hidden behind tree trunks, concealed in doorways, Victor's henchmen are waiting for the signal, they gaze steadily at the window from which filters an almost invisible thread of light, the fact that the inside shutters are closed in this heat is itself an indication of conspiracy. One of Victor's henchmen hefts the crowbar with which he will prize open the door, another slips the fingers of his left hand into an iron knuckle-duster, both men, much experienced, will leave a trail of shattered hinges and broken jaws. On the sidewalk opposite stands another policeman, behaving like an innocent passerby or rather a law-abiding citizen returning home to this building, but he does not rap with the knocker for his wife to come and open up, What kept you so late. In less than fifteen seconds the door is opened just as effectively by crowbar, the first obstacle overcome. The policeman waits on the staircase, his job is to listen carefully, to give warning if he hears anything, to let Victor know, for Victor is the brains behind this operation. In the doorway the shadowy form of the policeman appears, he lights a cigarette, which means that all is well, no suspicions have been aroused on the floor they have surrounded. Victor spits out the peppermint, he is afraid of choking at the height of the action, should there be hand-to-hand combat, he breathes through his mouth, relishes the freshness of the peppermint, he no longer seems the same Victor. But he has barely taken three steps before that telltale effluvium again rises from his stomach, its one advantage, considerable, is that the henchmen, following their leader, will not lose him. Only two remain behind, watching the window for any attempt to escape, in which case they have been given orders to shoot without first calling out. The squad of six men ascends Indian file, like a procession of ants, in the total silence, and the air grows close and electric with tension. The men have all become so nervous, they do not even notice their chief's stench, you could almost say that everything now smells the same. Having reached the landing, they begin to wonder if there is really anyone in the building, the silence is so deep that the entire world appears to be asleep. If Victor's information were not so reliable, he would give everyone orders to return to the usual snooping, shadowing of suspects, asking questions, paying for answers. Inside the apartment someone coughs. The tip-off has been confirmed. Victor aims his flashlight at the door, like a wise cobra the cleft crowbar advances, introduces its fangs between the jamb and the door, and waits. Now it is Victor's turn, with his knuckle-duster he strikes the door with the four blows of destiny, yells, Police, the crowbar gives the first wrench, the jamb splinters, the lock grates, inside there is uproar, chairs overturned, the sound of rapid footsteps, voices. No one move, Victor shouts in a commanding voice, his nervousness gone, and suddenly the lights go on on all the landings. The neighbors, wanting to join the fun, dare not enter the stage but have illuminated it. Someone must have opened a window, because three shots can be heard from the street. Changing position, the crowbar tries the crack at the lower hinge, the door splits from top to bottom, gapes open, and with two mighty kicks the henchmen bring it to the ground. The door first crashes against the facing wall of the corridor, then collapses sideways, making a large gash in the plaster. A great silence has descended on the apartment, there is no escaping now. Victor advances with pistol in hand, Nobody move. Flanked by two henchmen, he enters the room, which looks onto the street, the window is open and outside, below, the men are keeping watch, while here in the room are four men on their feet, their hands in the air, their heads lowered, defeated. Victor smiles with satisfaction, You are all under arrest, you are all under arrest. He gathers up some papers, which lie scattered on the table, orders the search to begin, calls the policeman over, the one with the knuckle-duster who is looking very sorry for himself because there was no resistance and thus no chance to land a single blow, and tells him to go to the back and see if anyone escaped. They hear him call out from the kitchen hatch, then from the fire escape, to his colleagues who were covering the other exits, Did you see anyone escape. They replied that one escaped, in the report to-morrow it will be written that a man was seen climbing over the walls of the courtyard or jumping from rooftop to rooftop, the versions will vary. The policeman with the knuckle-duster returns, looking very sour, Victor does not need to be told, he starts bel-lowing, livid with rage, the last trace of peppermint gone, What a bunch of idiots. And when he sees that the arrested men cannot suppress a smile of triumph, however wan, he realizes that it was none other than the ringleader who gave them the slip, now he is foaming at the mouth, uttering dire threats, demanding to know the fugitive's name, his destination, Speak or you all die. His hench-men aim their pistols, the one with the knuckle-duster raises his arm, fist clenched, then the director says, Cut. Still beside himself with rage, Victor cannot calm down, for him this is no laughing matter, ten men needed to capture five, and they allowed the ring-leader, the brains behind the conspiracy, to give them the slip, but the producer intervenes good-naturedly, the filming has gone so well that there is no need for a retake, Forget it, don't let it upset you, if we had caught him, that would have been the end of the film. But dear Senhor Lopes Ribeiro, the police are made to look such fools, the corps is brought into disrepute, seven men sent to kill a spider and the spider escapes in the end, that is to say the fly, because we are the spider. Let it escape, there is no lack of spiders' webs in the world, from some you escape, in others you die. The fugitive will find shelter in a boardinghouse under an assumed name, thinking he is safe, he has no idea that his spider will be the daughter of the landlady, according to the script a very serious young woman, a dedicated nationalist who will regenerate his heart and mind. Women are a powerful force, real saints, and the producer is clearly an intelligent man. They are engaged in this conversation when the cameraman, a German newly arrived from Germany, approaches, and the producer understands him, for the man practically speaks Portuguese, A *gross* plan of the *Polizei*. Victor too understands, gets into position, the cameraman's assistant claps the boards, bang, May Revolution second take, or some other phrase in a similar jargon, and Victor, brandishing his pistol, reappears at the door with a menacing and derisive smirk, You're all under arrest, you're all under arrest. If he now shouts it with less force, it's to avoid choking on the peppermint lozenge he has just popped into his mouth in order to purify the air. The cameraman declares himself satisfied, *Auf Wiedersehen, ich habe keine Zeit zu verlieren, es ist schon ziemlich spät*, Good-bye, I've no time to waste, it's getting late. Turning to the producer, *Es ist Punkt Mitternacht*, It is midnight on the dot, to which Lopes Ribeiro replies, *Machen Sie bitte das Licht aus*, Turn off the light. The translation is supplied because our German is still rudimentary. Victor has already descended with his squad, who lead their captives away handcuffed, so conscious of their duty as policemen that they take even this masquerade seriously, an arrest is an arrest even if it is only make-believe.

Other raids are being planned. Meanwhile Portugal prays and sings, because this is a time of festivities and pilgrimages, for much chanting of mystical psalms, for fireworks and wine, folk dances from Minho and open-air concerts, processions of angels with snow-white wings and floats carrying religious figures. All this under a blazing sky, heaven's reply to those long days of miserable winter, but heaven will continue to send us scattered showers and thunderstorms, because they too are the fruits of the season. And at the

Teatro de São Luís, Tomás Alcaide is singing in *Rigoletto, Manon,* and *Tosca,* and the League of Nations has decided once and for all to lift the sanctions against Italy, and the English are objecting to the flight of the zeppelin Hindenburg over factories and other strategic locations in Britain, and people are still saying that the German annexation of the Free City of Danzig is imminent, but that need not concern us, because only a sharp eye and the finger of an experienced cartographer would be able to find that tiny dot and barbaric word on the map, and the world will certainly not come to an end on that account. When all is said and done, the peace and quiet of our own hearth and home is not helped by interfering in the affairs of our neighbors. They make their own lives, let them unmake them. A rumor has been circulating, for example, that General Sanjurjo plans to enter Spain covertly to head a monarchist movement, though he tells the press that he has no intention of leaving Portugal, he and his entire family live in Monte Estoril in the villa Santa Leocádia, with a view of the sea and his conscience at rest. Some of us might say to him, Go, save your country, while others might say, Leave well enough alone, don't get involved in these problems. Because are we not all obliged to be good hosts, as we were with the dukes of Alba and Medinaceli, who not a moment too soon found refuge at the Hotel Bragança, where they say they intend to remain for some time. Unless all this is nothing more than another police raid with the script already written, the cameraman at the ready, and everyone waiting for the director to say, Action.

Ricardo Reis reads the newspapers. He remains unperturbed by the world news that reaches him, perhaps because of his temperament, or perhaps because he believes in the popular superstition which says that the more one cries doom, the less doom occurs. If this is true, then man should embrace pessimism as the surest road to happiness, and perhaps by persevering in his fear of death he may attain immortality. Ricardo Reis is not John D. Rockefeller, the newspaper he buys is the same as all the other newspapers the boy carries in his satchel or displays on the sidewalk. The world's threats are universal, like the sun, but Ricardo Reis takes shelter under his own shadow, What I do not wish to know does not exist, the only real problem is how to play the queen's knight. But reading the newspapers, he forces himself to worry a little, Europe is seething and perhaps will boil over, and there is no place for a poet to rest his head. The two old men, on the other hand, are very excited, so much so that they have decided to make the great sacrifice of buying a newspaper every day, one will buy it one day, the other the next, they can no longer wait until late afternoon. When Ricardo Reis appeared in the park to perform his customary act of charity, they were able to respond with the arrogance of the pauper who is ungrateful at heart, We already have a newspaper. They unfolded the large pages with noisy ostentation, proving yet again that one cannot trust people.

Having reverted, after Lydia's vacation, to his habit of sleeping practically until lunchtime, Ricardo Reis must have been the last person in Lisbon to learn of the military coup in Spain. Bleary-eyed, he went to pick the morning newspaper off his doormat and returned to his bedroom yawning. Ah, the pretense of calling the tedium of life serenity. When his eyes met the headline, Military coup on Spanish mainland, he was overcome by vertigo, a feeling of hurtling through the air. He should have foreseen this. The Spanish army, the guardian of the nation's virtues and traditions, was about to speak with the voice of military force, the merchants would be expelled from the temple, the altar of the Fatherland would be rebuilt, and the immortal glory of Spain, which a few of her degenerate sons had brought into decline, would be restored. On an inside page Ricardo Reis came across the text of a telegram which had been intercepted, In Madrid there are fears of a Fascist revolution. The adjective bothered him. Granted, the telegram comes from the Spanish capital where the left-wing government is installed, and one expects them to use such language, but it would be much clearer if they said, for example, that the monarchists have struck a blow against the republicans. That way, Ricardo Reis would know where the line is drawn, for he himself is a monarchist, as we may recall or should remind ourselves. But General Sanjurjo has issued a formal denial of that rumor circulating in Lisbon that he was planning to head a monarchist movement in Spain, so Ricardo Reis need not take sides, this battle, if it should become a battle, is not his, the disagreement is between republicans and republicans. Today the newspaper has printed all the news at its disposal, tomorrow it may tell us that the revolution has failed, that the rebels have been vanquished, that peace reigns throughout Spain. Ricardo Reis does not know whether this would cause him relief or distress. When he goes out for lunch, he pays close attention to people's faces, to what they are saying, there is tension in the air but the tension is kept under control, perhaps because there is still little news, or perhaps because people are keeping their feelings to themselves. Between his apartment and the restaurant he sees some expressions of triumph, a few of gloom, and realizes that it is not a question of a skirmish between republicans and monarchists.

We now have a fuller picture of what happened. The insurrection began in Spanish Morocco and its leader appears to be General Franco. Here in Lisbon, General Sanjurjo has declared that he is on the side of his comrades in arms but repeats that he does not wish to play an active role. Any child can see that the situation in Spain is serious. Within forty-eight hours the government headed by Casares Quiroga fell, Martinez Barrio was entrusted with forming a government, Martinez Barrio resigned, and now we have a cabinet formed by Giral, we'll see how long that lasts. The military boasts that the revolution has triumphed, if things progress in this way the days of Red domination in Spain are numbered. Even if the abovementioned child does not read, he will know the truth of this statement just by looking at the size of the headlines and at the bold exuberance of typefaces, which will spill over into the small lettering of the editorials within the next few days. Then tragedy struck. General Sanjurjo, en route to take his seat on the military directorate of the revolution, met a horrible death. His airplane, either because it was carrying too many passengers or because there was insufficient power in the engine, if that does not amount to the same thing, was unable to climb and collided with a few trees and then a wall, in full view of the Spaniards who had come to watch the takeoff. Under an implacable sun both plane and general burned in one great bonfire. The lucky pilot, Ansaldo by name, got away with nothing more serious than minor bruises and burns. The general had sworn he had no intention of leaving

Portugal, but we must understand that deception is the very substance of politics, though God may not approve of it. Perhaps this was divine punishment, because everyone knows that God does not castigate with sticks and stones but tends to favor fire. Now, while General Queipo de Llano is proclaiming military dictatorship throughout Spain, vigil is being kept over the corpse of General Sanjurjo, also known as the Marquês de Riff, in the Igreja de Santo António do Estoril. When we say the corpse, we mean what is left of it, a charred stump, a man so corpulent in life now reduced in death to sad ashes, his tiny coffin could be that of an infant. How true it is that we are nothing in this world, yet no matter how often we repeat these words and though we see them confirmed every day, they are always hard to accept. Members of the Spanish Falange form a guard of honor for the great warlord, wearing their full uniform of blue shirt, black trousers, a dagger in a leather belt. Where did these people come from, I ask myself, because they were certainly not dispatched in haste from Morocco to attend the solemn funeral rites. But the abovementioned illiterate child could tell us, and the *Pueblo Gallego* reports, that there are fifty thousand Spaniards in Portugal. Obviously besides a change of underwear they packed their black trousers and blue shirts and daggers, little dreaming that they would wear their uniforms in public and in such sad circumstances. But on these faces marked by a virile grief there is also a gleam of triumph, for death is the eternal bride whose arms welcome the man of valor, death is an unblemished virgin and she prefers Spaniards among all men, especially if they are soldiers. Tomorrow, when the mortal remains of General Sanjurjo are transported on a horse-drawn gun carriage, the news will hover overhead, like angels bringing fair tidings, that motorized columns are advancing on Madrid, that the siege has been consummated, that the final assault will be made in a matter of hours. People are saying that there is no longer any government in the capital, they also say, contradicting themselves, that the government in the capital has authorized members of the Popular Front to take whatever arms and ammunition they need. But this is only the death rattle of the demon, the day is at hand when the Virgin of Pilar will crush the serpent beneath her immaculate feet and the crescent moon will soar above the graveyards of iniquity. Thousands of Moroccan troops have already landed in southern Spain, and with their help we shall restore the empire of the cross and rosary over the odious symbol of the hammer and sickle. The regeneration of Europe is making giant strides, first there was Italy, then Portugal, then Germany, and now Spain, this is the good land, this the best seed, tomorrow we reap the harvest. As the German students wrote, We are nobody, and those same words were muttered by the slaves to each other as they built the pyramids, We are nobody, the masons and drovers of Mafra, We are nobody, the inhabitants of Alentejo bitten by the cat infected by rabies, We are nobody, the recipients of the alms distributed by charitable organizations and relief agencies, We are nobody, those flood victims of Ribatejo for whose benefit a gala day was held at the Jockey Club, We are nobody, the national unions which paraded in May with their arms outstretched, We are nobody. Perhaps the day will come when we will all be somebody, this is not a quote, it is merely a feeling.

To Lydia, who is also nobody, Ricardo Reis speaks of the events in the neighboring nation. She tells him that the Spaniards in the hotel celebrated the latest news with a great party, not even the general's tragic death dampened their spirits, and now not an evening passes without bottles of French champagne, Salvador is as happy as a clam, Pimenta talks in Castilian to the manner born, and Ramón and Felipe could not contain their joy upon learning that General Franco is Galician, a native of El Ferrol. Only the other day someone had the idea of hoisting a Spanish flag on the hotel verandah to mark the Hispano-Portuguese alliance. And you, Ricardo Reis asked, what do you think of Spain, of what is happening there. I am not educated, you are the one who ought to know, Doctor, with all the books you've read to get where you are today, the higher one goes, the farther one can see. Therefore the moon shines on every lake. Doctor, you say the prettiest things. The situation in Spain had been going from bad to worse to utter chaos, it was about time someone came along to put an end to all the squabbling, the only hope was for the army to step in, just as happened here, it's the same everywhere. I know nothing about these things, but my brother says. I already know what your brother says. How can you know, Doctor, you and my brother are such different people. What does he say then. He says that the military will not win because all the people will be against it. Let me assure you, Lydia, that the people are never all on one side, but I'm curious to know what you mean when you say the people. The people are like me, a hotel chambermaid who has a revolutionary brother and sleeps with a doctor who is against revolutions. Who taught you to say these things. When I open my mouth to speak, the words are already there, it's just a matter of letting them come out. Generally, one thinks before he speaks. Well perhaps in my case it is like having a baby, which grows without our noticing it and is born when the time comes. How have you been feeling lately. If it weren't for missing my periods, I wouldn't believe I was pregnant. You are still determined, then, to have the child, My baby boy, Your baby boy, Yes, and I am not likely to change my mind, Think about it carefully, But I don't think. With these words Lydia gave a contented laugh, and Ricardo Reis was left without a reply. He drew her to him, kissed her on the forehead, then on the corner of her mouth, then on her neck, the bed was not far and soon both serving maid and doctor were on it. No more was said about her sailor brother. Spain is at the other end of the world.

Les beaux esprits se rencontrent, as the French say, a remarkably subtle race. Ricardo Reis speaks of the need to preserve order, and in an interview given to the Portuguese newspaper *O Século* General Francisco Franco has just declared, We desire order in our nation. This prompted the newspaper to print in bold letters, The Spanish Army's Task of Redemption, thus showing how numerous those *beaux esprits* are, if not indeed innumerable. A few days later, the newspaper raises the question, When will a First International of Order be organized against the Third International of Disorder. The *beaux esprits* are already giving their reply, the initiative is under way, Moroccan soldiers continue to land, a governing junta has been set up in Burgos, and there is a rumor that within a matter of hours the final confrontation will take place between the army and the forces of Madrid. As for the fact that the population of Badajoz has taken up arms to resist the military advance, we should not attribute any special importance to that, it provides only an interesting footnote to our discussion about what the people are or are not. Men, women, and children armed themselves with rifles, swords, cudgels, scythes, revolvers, daggers, and hatchets, whatever came to hand, perhaps this is the way the people arm themselves, but the philosophical question of what the people are, if you will forgive my presumption, remains a moot point.

The wave swells and gathers. In Portugal, volunteers are flocking to enroll in the Portuguese Youth Movement, these are patriotic youths who decided not to wait for the inevitable conscription. With a hopeful hand and neat lettering, under the benevolent gaze of their fathers, they sign the letter and vigorously march to the post office, or, trembling with civic pride, they deliver the letter personally to the doorman at the Ministry of National Education. Only their respect for religion prevents them from declaring, Here is my body, here is my blood, but it is clear for all to see that they long for martyrdom. Ricardo Reis runs his eye down the lists, trying to visualize faces, postures, ways of walking that might give substance, meaning to the abstraction of these proper nouns, which are the emptiest words of all unless we put human beings inside them. In years to come, twenty, thirty, fifty years, what will these grownup men or old men, if they live that long, think of their ardent youth, when they heard or read the clarion words of the German youths who said, We are nobody, and rallied like heroes repeating, We, too, we, too, are nobody. They will use such phrases as, The foolishness of youth, A mistake made in my innocence, I had no one to turn to for advice, I have repented at leisure, My father ordered me to sign up, I sincerely believed in the movement, The uniform was so impressive, I would do it all over again, It was one way of getting on with my life, The first to enlist were much admired, A young man is so easily persuaded, so easily deceived. These and similar excuses are offered, but now one man gets to his feet, raises his hand, requesting to be heard. Ricardo Reis nods, anxious to hear a person speak of one of the other people he once was, to hear age describing youth, and this is the speech the man made. You have to consider the individual motives, whether the step we took was taken out of ignorance or malice, whether of our own free will or because we were compelled. The judgment, of course, will vary, depending on the times and on the judge. But whether we are pardoned or condemned, our life must be weighed on the scales of the good and evil we did, let everything be taken into account, if that is possible, and let the first judge be our conscience. Perhaps we should say once again, though for a different reason, that we are nobody. At that time a certain man, loved and respected by some of us, I will say his name to spare you the trouble of guessing, Miguel de Unamuno, then rector at the University of Salamanca, no mere fourteen- or fifteen-year-old stripling like us but a venerable gentleman in his seventies, the author of such highly acclaimed books as *Del sentimiento trágico de la vida, La agonía del cristianismo, En torno al casticismo, La dignidad humana*, and many others, a guiding spirit from the first days of war, pledged his support to the ruling Junta of Burgos, exclaiming, Let us save western civilization, I am here at your disposal O sons of Spain. These sons of Spain were the insurgent troops and the Moors from Morocco, and he made a personal donation of five thousand pesetas to what was even then called the Nationalist Spanish Army. Since I cannot remember the prices of those days, I cannot say how many bullets one could buy with five thousand pesetas. Unamuno urged President Azaña to commit suicide, and a few weeks later he made further statements that were no less vehement, My greatest admiration, my deepest respect goes to those Spanish women who held the communist rabble at bay and long prevented it from seizing control of Spain. In a transport of ecstasy he called them holy women. We Portuguese have also had our share of holy women, two examples will suffice, Marília, the shining heroine of *Conspiracy*, and the innocent saint of *The May Revolution*. If the Spanish women have Unamuno to thank for their sainthood, let our Portuguese women give thanks to Senhor Tomé Vieira and Senhor Lopes Ribeiro, one day I should like to descend into hell and count for myself the holy women there. But about Miguel de Unamuno, whom we admired, no one speaks now, he is like an embarrassing wound one tries to conceal, and only his words, almost his last, spoken in reply to General Milan d'Astray, the one who shouted in that same city of Salamanca, Long live death, have been preserved for posterity. Doctor Reis will never learn what those words are, but life is too short for a man to learn everything, and so is his. Because those words were spoken, some of us reconsidered our decision. It was good that Unamuno lived long enough to see his mistake, although only to see it, because he did little to correct it, having little time left, and perhaps too he wished to preserve the tranquillity of his final days. And therefore all I ask is that you wait for our last word, or the next to last, if on that day our minds are still clear and yours is too. I am finished. Some of those present vigorously applaud this hope of salvation, but others protest, indignant at the malicious distortion of Unamuno's Nationalist doctrine, because it was only out of senility, with one foot in the grave, or pique or capriciousness, that Unamuno dared question the magnificent battle cry of the great patriot General Milan d'Astray, who only had wisdom to impart, none to receive. Ricardo Reis does not know what Unamuno will say to the General, he is too shy to ask, or afraid to penetrate the veil of the future, *How much better to pass in silence, without anticipation,* this is what he once wrote, this is what he tries to achieve each day. The old soldiers leave, discussing as they go the words of Unamuno, judging those words as they themselves would like to be judged, for everyone knows that the accused, in his eyes, is always absolved.

Ricardo Reis reads the news he has already read, the call by Unamuno, the rector of Salamanca, Let us save western civilization, I am here at your disposal O sons of Spain, and the five thousand pesetas paid out of his own pocket for Franco's army, and the exhorting of Azaña to commit suicide, but he hasn't got to the holy women yet, not that we need to wait to know how he will express it. Only the other day we heard a simple Portuguese film producer say that on this side of the Pyrenees all women are saints. Ricardo Reis slowly turns the pages, distracts himself with the latest news, items that might as easily have come from there as from here, from this decade or any other, past, present, and future, weddings and baptisms for example, departures and arrivals. The problem is that we cannot choose the news we want to read, like John D. Rockefeller. He runs his eye down the classified advertisements, Apartment to let, he already has one. But wait, here is the steamer *The Highland Brigade* due to leave Lisbon for Pernambuco, Rio de Janeiro, Santos, what news will she bring, persistent messenger, from Vigo. And it appears that all Galicia has united behind General Franco, he is after all a native son of that region. The reader, restless, turns the page and once again encounters the shield of Achilles, which he has not seen for a long time. It is the same display of pictures and captions, a prodigious mandala, a kaleidoscopic universe in which all movement, suspended, offers itself to our contemplation. At last it is possible to count the wrinkles on the face of God, more commonly known by the name of Freire the Engraver, here is his portrait with the implacable monocle, here the necktie he uses to strangle us, even though the physician says we are dying from some disease or bullet wound. Freire's wares are illustrated below, testifying to the infinite wisdom of their creator, who has lived an unblemished and honorable life and received three gold medals, the ultimate distinction conferred by the Deity, who does not however advertise in the *Diário de Notícias*. At one time, Ricardo Reis saw this advertisement as a labyrinth, now he sees it as a circle from which there is no escape or exit, like an endless desert without paths. He adds a small goatee to the portrait of Freire the Engraver and doubles the monocle into spectacles, but not even this makes Freire look like the Don Miguel de Unamuno who also became lost in a labyrinth, from which he managed to emerge, if we give credence to the Portuguese gentleman who stood up to address the assembly, only on the eve of his death, leaving us in doubt as to whether Unamuno held to those almost-last words or instead relapsed into his initial complacency if not complicity, concealing his rage, suppressing his defiance. The yes and no of Unamuno disturbs Ricardo Reis, he is divided between this present, which is common to both their lives, the two linked by news items in the press, and the obscure prophecy of the soldier-orator who, knowing the future, did not reveal everything. A shame Ricardo Reis did not have the courage to ask the man what Don Miguel said to the general, but then he realizes that he kept silent because it had been clearly hinted that he would not be in this world on the day of that repentance, You never learn what those words are, but life is too short for a man to learn everything, and so is yours. Ricardo Reis begins to see the direction the wheel of destiny is turning. Milan d'Astray, who was in Buenos Aires, passed through Rio de Janeiro on his way to Spain, the paths of men do not vary much, and now comes sailing across the Atlantic, glowing with excitement and eager for battle. Within the next few days he will disembark at Lisbon, the ship is the *Almanzora*, then proceed to Seville and from there to Tetuán, where he will replace Franco. Milan d'Astray approaches Salamanca and Miguel de Unamuno, he will shout, Long live death, and then the curtain falls. The Portuguese soldier-orator again asks leave to speak, his lips move, the black sun of the future shines, but the words are inaudible, we cannot even guess what he is saying.

Ricardo Reis is anxious to discuss these matters with Fernando Pessoa, but Fernando Pessoa does not appear. Time drags like a sluggish wave, it is a sphere of molten glass on whose surface myriad glints catch one's eye and engage one's attention, while inside glows the crimson, disquieting core. Days and nights succeed each other in oppressive heat that both descends from the sky and rises from the earth. It is late afternoon before the two old men appear on the Alto de Santa Catarina, they cannot take the burning sun which surrounds the sparse shadows of the palm trees, the glare on the river is too much for their tired eyes, the shimmering air leaves them gasping for breath. Lisbon opens her spigots but there is not a drop of running water, her inhabitants have become caged birds with open beaks and drooping wings. As the city sinks into torpor, the rumor circulates that the Spanish Civil War is nearing its end, which is probable if we bear in mind that the troops of Queipo de Llano are already at the gates of Badajoz, with the divisions of the Civil Guard, which is their Foreign Legion, eager for combat. Woe to him who opposes these soldiers, so great is their desire to kill. Don Miguel sets off from home for the university, taking advantage of the fringe of shade that skirts the buildings along the route. The sun bakes the stones of Salamanca, but the worthy ancient can feel a military breeze in his face, in his contented soul he returns the greetings of his countrymen, the salutes he receives from the soldiers at headquarters or in the street, every one of them the reincarnation of El Cid Campeador, who in his day also said, Let us save western civilization. Ricardo Reis, leaving his apartment early one morning before the sun became too hot, also took advantage of the fringes of shade while waiting for a taxi to appear and take him, panting, up the Calçada da Estrela as far as Prazeres. The visitor does not need to ask the way, he has not forgotten the location or the number, four thousand three hundred and seventy-one, not the number of a door, so there is no point in knocking or inquiring, Is anyone home. If the presence of the living is not in itself enough to dislodge the secrets of the dead, these words serve no purpose. Ricardo Reis reached the railing, placed his hand on the warm stone, the sun, though still not high, has been hitting this spot since dawn. From a nearby path comes the sound of a brush sweeping, it is a widow cutting across at the far end of the road, her face hidden behind a crepe veil. There is no other sign of life. Ricardo Reis descends as far as the bend, where he pauses to look at the river, the mouth of the sea, a most appropriate word, because it is here that the sea comes to quench its unassuageable thirst, sucking lips pressed to the land. Such an image, such a metaphor would be out of place in the austere structure of an ode, but it occurs to us in the early morning, when the mind submits to feeling.

Ricardo Reis does not turn around. He knows that Fernando Pessoa is standing beside him, this time invisible, perhaps forbidden to show himself in the flesh within the precincts of the graveyard, otherwise the place would be too crowded, the streets congested with the dead, the thought makes one want to smile. The voice of Fernando Pessoa asks, What brings you here at this early hour, my dear Reis, is the view from the Alto de Santa Catarina, where Adamastor stands, not enough for you. Ricardo Reis replies without replying, From here we can watch a Spanish general sailing to join the Civil War, are you aware that civil war has broken out in Spain. Go on. They tell me that this general, whose name is Milan d'Astray, is destined to meet Miguel de Unamuno one day, and he will exclaim, Long live death, to which there will be a reply. Go on. I would like to know the reply given by Don Miguel. How can I tell you before he gives it. It might interest you to know that the rector of Salamanca has sided with the army, which intends to overthrow the government and the regime. That is of no interest to me whatsoever. I once thought that loss of freedom might be natural and right in flourishing societies, now I do not know what to think, I was counting on you, you have let me down. The most I can do is to offer a hypothesis. What hypothesis. That your rector of Salamanca will reply by saying that there are circumstances in which to remain silent is to lie, I hear a morbid cry, Long live death, a barbarous and repugnant paradox, General Milan d'Astray is crippled, no insult intended, Cervantes was also crippled, unfortunately today in Spain there are far too many cripples, it pains me to think that General Milan d'Astray might try to start a popular psychology, a cripple who does not possess the spiritual wealth of a Cervantes usually takes consolation in the harm he can cause others. You think he will give this reply. Out of an infinite number of hypotheses, this is one. It does jibe with what the Portuguese soldier said. It is important when things jibe and make sense. What sense can there be in Marcenda's left hand. You still think of her, then. From time to time. You needn't look so far, we are all crippled.

Ricardo Reis is alone. On the lower branches of the elm trees the cicadas begin to chirr, mute but inventing their own voice. A great black vessel enters the straits, only to disappear into the shimmering reflection of the water. The panorama seems unreal.

Ricardo Reis now has another voice in his apartment. He owns a small radio, the cheapest on the market, the popular Pilot model with an ivory-colored Bakelite case, chosen because it occupies little space and can easily be transported from the bedroom to the study, the two rooms where the somnambulist who lives here spends most of his time. Had he decided to buy one before the pleasure of living in new quarters wore off, he would now possess a superheterodyne receiver with twelve vacuum tubes and enough power to rouse the neighborhood and draw a crowd beneath his window. Eager to enjoy the music and listen to the broadcasts, all the housewives in the district would be there, including the two old men, friendly and polite once more because of this latest novelty. But Ricardo Reis only wants to keep up with the news, discreetly, in privacy, the radio lowered to an intimate whisper. He does not explain to himself or try to analyze the restless feeling that brings him to the set, he does not wonder about the hidden message in that dim eye, the dying Cyclops that is the light of the minuscule dial, its expression showing neither joy nor fear nor pity. And he cannot say whether it is the victories of the revolutionary army in Spain that delight him or the resounding defeats of the forces that support the government. Some will argue that the two are the same, but they aren't, no sir, the human soul is more complicated than that. To be pleased that my enemy is beset doesn't mean that I applaud the besetter. Ricardo Reis does not investigate his inner conflict, he leaves his uneasiness alone, like one who, lacking the courage to skin a rabbit, asks another to do the job for him while he stands watching, annoyed at his own squeamishness. Standing close enough to breathe in the warmth released by the skinned flesh, a subtly pleasant smell, he conceives in his heart, or wherever such things are conceived, a loathing for the man capable of the great cruelty of skinning. How can he and I possibly belong to the same human race. Perhaps this is why we hate the hangman and refuse to eat the flesh of the scapegoat.

Lydia was delighted when she saw the radio, How pretty, how nice to be able to hear music at any hour of the day or night. An exaggeration on her part, because that time is a long way off. She is a simple soul able to rejoice at the smallest thing, unless this is a pretext to conceal her distress that Ricardo Reis has become so slovenly in his ways, no longer caring about his appearance, no longer looking after himself. She told him that the dukes of Alba and Medinaceli had left the hotel, to the great disappointment of Salvador, who cherishes a real affection for his clients, especially if they are titled, though in this case they are not, because the idea of calling Don Lorenzo and Don Alonso dukes was nothing but a joke of Ricardo Reis, which it is time to drop. He is not surprised. Now that the day of victory is approaching, they live their final moments of exile in sweet luxury, which explains why the hotels in Estoril are now frequented by what the gossip columns refer to as a select Spanish colony, with plenty of dukes and counts there on vacation. Don Lorenzo and Don Alfonso followed the scent of the aristocracy, and in their old age they will be able to tell their grandchildren, In the days when I was exiled with the Duke of Alba. For the benefit of these Spaniards the Portuguese Radio Club recently introduced a Spanish broadcaster, a woman with a voice like a soubrette in an operetta. She reads the news of the Nationalist advances in the graceful language of Cervantes. May God and the Portuguese Radio Club pardon us this sarcasm, it is provoked by an urge to weep rather than any desire to smile, which is exactly how Lydia feels, who tries valiantly to be merry and lighthearted though weighed by her anxiety for Ricardo Reis in addition to the terrible news from Spain, terrible from her point of view, which as we have seen coincides with that of her brother Daniel. Upon hearing, on the wireless, that Badajoz has been bombarded, she begins to cry like a Mary Magdalene, strange behavior for her, considering that she has never been to Badajoz and has neither family nor possessions there that might have suffered in the bombing. Why are you crying, Lydia, Ricardo Reis asks her, but she has no reply, perhaps it was something Daniel told her, but who told him, what was his source of information. The war in Spain must be much discussed aboard the *Afonso de Albuquerque*, as the sailors scrub the decks and polish the brass, they pass on the latest news among themselves, nor is all the news what the newspapers and radio would have us believe. Aboard the *Afonso de Albuquerque* there is not much confidence in the reassurances of General Mola, who belongs to the quadrille of the matador Franco and has promised that before the month is out we shall hear him address us over Radio Madrid. That other general, Queipo de Llano, says that for Madrid it is the beginning of the end, the revolution is barely three weeks old and almost over. Rubbish, replies the sailor Daniel. But Ricardo Reis, awkwardly trying to console Lydia and dry her tears, and still hoping to win her over to his way of thinking, repeats the news he has read and heard, There you are weeping for Badajoz, don't you realize that the Communists cut an ear off one hundred and ten landowners and then defiled their womenfolk, in other words, raped the poor creatures. How do you know. I read it in the newspapers and also read, in an article written by Tomé Vieira, a journalist and the author of several books, that the Bolsheviks gouged out the eyes of an elderly priest, then poured gasoline on him and set him on fire. I don't believe that. It's in the newspapers, black on white. My brother says one shouldn't always believe what the newspapers say. I'm not in a position to go to Spain to see for myself, I have to believe that they are telling the truth, newspapers don't lie, that would be the greatest crime imaginable. Doctor, you are a learned man while I can scarcely read or write, but I've learned one thing in life, there are lots of truths and they often say different things, we won't know who is lying until the fighting starts. And what if it is true that they gouged out a priest's eyes and poured gasoline on him and burned him alive. Then it's a horrible truth, but my brother says that if the church were on the side of the poor and helped them on this earth, then the poor would be the first to give their lives for the church. And what if they cut the ears off the landowners and raped their wives. That would be another horrible truth, but my brother says that while the poor are suffering on this earth, the rich are already enjoying paradise without going to heaven. You always answer with your brother's words. And you, Doctor, always speak with the words of the newspapers. True enough.

Now there have been disturbances in Funchal and in other places on the island, with crowds looting public offices and dairy farms, and people have been killed or wounded. The situation must be serious, because two warships have been sent out, along with a fleet of airplanes and squads of hunters with machine guns, a military force capable of waging a civil war Portuguese-style. Ricardo Reis does not fully grasp the reason for the uprising, which need not surprise either us or him, because he has only the newspapers to rely on for information. He turns on his ivory-colored Pilot radio. Perhaps the words we hear are more believable than the words we read, the only drawback is that we cannot see the announcer's face, because a look of hesitation, a sudden twitch of the mouth will betray a lie at once, let us hope that someday human inventiveness will make it possible for us, sitting in our own homes, to see the face of the announcer, then at last we will be able to tell the difference between a lie and the truth, and the era of justice will truly begin, and let us say, Amen. The arrow on the dial points to the Portuguese Radio Club, and while the tubes are heating up, Ricardo Reis rests his weary forehead on the radio case. From inside comes a warm odor that makes him feel a little giddy, a distracting sensation, then he notices that the volume knob is switched off. He turns it, at first hears only the deep hum of the carrier wave, then a pause, a sudden burst of music, the song *Cara al sol con la camisa nueva*, the anthem of the Falange for the pleasure and comfort of the select Spanish colony in the hotels of Estoril and at the Bragança. At this very moment in the casino they are having a dress rehearsal for the Night of Silver, to be presented by Erico Braga, and in the hotel lounge the guests glance suspiciously at the green-tinted mirror. The Radio Club announcer then reads a telegram sent by veteran Portuguese legionnaires who served in the fifth division of the Spanish Foreign Legion, they greet their former comrades who are taking part in the siege of Badajoz, a shiver goes up our spine as we listen to those military sentiments, the Christian fervor, the fraternity of arms, the memory of past triumphs, the hope in a bright future for the two Iberian fatherlands united in one Nationalist cause. After listening to the final news bulletin, that three thousand soldiers from Morocco have landed in Algiers, Ricardo Reis switches off the Pilot and stretches out on the bed, desperate at finding himself so alone. He is not thinking about Marcenda, it is Lydia who occupies his thoughts, probably because she is closer at hand, one might say, although there is no telephone in this apartment, and even if there were one, he could hardly call the hotel and say, Good evening, Senhor Salvador, this is Doctor Ricardo Reis speaking, do you remember me, we haven't spoken to each other in ages, I say, those were extremely happy weeks I spent in your hotel, no, no, I don't need a room, I simply wanted to speak to Lydia, could you ask her to come around to my apartment, excellent, how very kind of you to let her off for a couple of hours, I am feeling very lonely, no, it isn't for that, all I need is a little company. He gets up from the bed, gathers together the pages of the newspaper lying all over the floor and on the bedspread, and runs his eye down the list of entertainments, but nothing stirs his interest. For a moment he wishes he were blind, deaf, and dumb, thrice the cripple Fernando Pessoa says we all are, then among the news items from Spain he notices a photograph that had escaped him previously, army tanks bearing the Sacred Heart of Jesus. If this is the coat of arms they are using, then there can be no doubt that this will be a war waged without mercy. He remembers that Lydia is pregnant, with a baby boy, as she constantly tells him, and this baby boy will grow up and go to the wars that are now in the making. One war leads to another, let us do some calculations, the baby comes into the world in March of next year, if the average age when youths go to war is twenty-three or twenty-four, what war will we have in nineteen sixty-one, and where, and why, and over what wasteland. With the eyes of imagination Ricardo Reis sees the boy riddled with bullets, dark and pale like his father but only his mother's son, for his father will not acknowledge him.

Badajoz has surrendered. Spurred by the rousing telegram from the veteran Portuguese legionnaires, the Spanish Foreign Legion achieved miraculous victories, whether at a distance or in hand-to-hand combat, and singled out for special honor were the brave Portuguese legionnaires of the new generation who were anxious to prove themselves worthy of their predecessors, one should add that it always helps to feel that one's native land is not far away. Badajoz has surrendered. Reduced to ruins by continuous bombardment, swords broken, scythes blunted, clubs and hatchets smashed, the city has surrendered. General Mola declared, The hour has come to settle accounts, and the bull ring opened its gates to receive the militiamen taken captive, then closed them, the fiesta is under way, machine guns shout *olé, olé, olé*, the noise is deafening in the bull ring of Badajoz, and the minotaurs dressed in cheap cotton fall on top of one another, mingling their blood in mutual transfusion. When not a single monster is left standing, the matadors will liquidate with their pistols those who were simply wounded, and if any escape this mercy, it is only to be buried alive. All that Ricardo Reis knew about this event was what he read in the Portuguese newspapers, but one newspaper accompanied its report with a photograph of the bull ring in which bodies could be seen scattered here and there, a wagon looked completely out of place, was it meant for deliveries or removals, for bulls or minotaurs. Ricardo Reis learned the rest from Lydia, who had been told by her brother, who had been told by who knows whom, perhaps it was a message from the future when all will finally be resolved. No longer crying, Lydia tells him, Two thousand lost their lives, her lips are trembling, her cheeks flushed. Ricardo Reis tries to console her, takes her by the arm, but she pulls away, not out of any rancor but simply because today she cannot bear it. Later, in the kitchen, as she is washing the dirty dishes that have accumulated, she begins to cry again, and for the first time she asks herself why she comes to this apartment. Is she the doctor's maid, his cleaner, she is certainly not his lover, because that word implies equality, no matter whether male or female, and they are not equal.

Then she does not know if she is crying for the dead of Badajoz or for her own death, which is the death of feeling that she is nobody. Sitting in his study, Ricardo Reis has no idea what is going on. To take his mind off the two thousand dead, a truly incredible number, if Lydia was telling the truth, he reopened *The God of the Labyrinth*, to continue where he had left off, but could get no meaning from the words. He realized that he had forgotten the narrative, so he went back once more to the beginning, The body, discovered by the first chess player, occupied with its outstretched arms the squares of the King and Queen's pawns as well as the next two squares in the direction of the enemy camp. Reaching this point, Ricardo Reis again lost the thread, seeing the chessboard as a desert and the sprawled corpse as a young man who was no longer a young man, then he saw a circle inscribed in that huge square, an arena strewn with bodies crucified on their native soil, and Sacred Hearts of Jesus went from one to the other making sure that there were no survivors. When Lydia walked into the study, done with her chores, Ricardo Reis was sitting with the book closed in his lap, he appeared to be sleeping and looked, caught unawares like this, almost old. She stared at him as if he were a stranger, then left without making a sound. She begins to think, I won't come back here, but she cannot be certain.

Now that General Milan d'Astray has finally arrived, another proclamation is issued from Tetuán, war without mercy, war without truce, war unto death against the Marxist vermin while observing humanitarian principles, As one can gather from the words spoken by General Franco, I have not yet occupied Madrid because I do not wish to sacrifice innocent citizens. Now here is a considerate fellow, someone who would never order the massacre of innocents as Herod did, no, he will wait until they grow up rather than have such a burden on his conscience and overcrowd heaven with angels. It is inconceivable that these fair winds from Spain should not produce similar events in Portugal. The bids have been made, the cards placed on the table and dealt, the time has come to know who is for us and who is against us, let us make the enemy show his face, betray himself by his own duplicity, and let us count as ours all who out of cowardice or greed or fear of losing the little they have seek refuge in the shade of our flag. Therefore the national unions have decided to stage a rally opposing Communism, and as soon as this news is announced, the furor that accompanies all great moments in history grips the entire community. Petitions are signed by patriotic associations, women, either individually or in various committees, demand representation, and in order to put their members into the right frame of mind, some unions hold special meetings, the union of shop assistants, for example, or master bakers, or hotel workers, and in the photographs those present can be seen saluting with stiff raised arms, each rehearsing his role as he awaits the opening ceremony. During these meetings, the manifesto of the national unions is read out and applauded, it is an impassioned declaration of their political allegiance and their confidence in the nation's destiny, as becomes clear from the following excerpts taken at random, There can be no doubt but that the national-corporative workers are Portuguese through and through and staunch Roman Catholics, The national unions call upon Salazar for drastic remedies to great evils, The national unions acknowledge private enterprise and the individual's right to acquire property as the only foundation for every social, economic, and political organization, and for social justice. Since they are struggling for the same cause and fighting the same enemy, members of the Spanish Falange speak to the entire nation on the Portuguese Radio Club, applauding Portugal for wholeheartedly joining this crusade, which actually is historically inaccurate, because everyone knows that we Portuguese have been fighting this crusade for years. But that is typical of the Spaniards, they are always ready to take over, and have to be constantly watched.

Ricardo Reis was never at a political rally in his life, an omission that must be attributed to the peculiarities of his temperament, to his upbringing, to his love of the classics, and also to a certain personal shyness, which should not surprise anyone familiar with his verse. But this national outcry, the civil war in neighboring Spain, perhaps too the unusual venue as demonstrators begin to assemble here in the bull ring of Campo Pequeno, ignite in him a tiny flame of curiosity. What will it be like watching thousands of people gathered together to listen to speeches. What phrases will they applaud and why, how much sincerity will there be on the part of those who speak and those who listen, what will the expressions be on their faces, what gestures will be used. For one who is by nature so incurious, this is an interesting change. Ricardo Reis set out early in order to be sure to get a seat, taking a taxi to arrive more quickly. The night is warm as August draws to a close. Special trams go by, packed to overflowing, the passengers chat amiably, while a few on foot, more inflamed with Nationalist zeal, cry out, Long live the New State. There are union flags, which in the absence of any breeze the standard bearers wave vigorously to display their colors and emblems, here is a heraldic corporative still contaminated with republican traditions, there a guild, to use the word for an artisan association in an earlier age. Entering the arena, Ricardo Reis is swept along by this great torrent of humanity and finds himself among bank employees all wearing a blue armband inscribed with a crucifix and the initials SNB. It is indeed true that the virtue of patriotism pardons all sins and reconciles all contradictions, including this one, because the bankers have taken as their emblem the Cross of Christ, who in His time drove the merchants and money changers, the first branches of this tree, the first flowers of this fruit, from the temple. Just as well for them that Christ was not like the wolf in the fable, because the wolf slaughtered the gentle lambs instead of waiting for them to turn into obstinate sheep. Before, it was all much simpler, now we spend our time asking ourselves if the waters were muddy at their source or became polluted en route.

The arena is practically full, but Ricardo Reis has succeeded in finding a good spot on a bench in the sun, not that it matters today, for all is shadow and darkness. The good thing about his seat is that it is close enough to the platform to see the speakers' faces yet not so close as to prevent him from having a good view of the whole arena. Flags and union banners continue to file in, the latter are all national but many of the flags are not, and understandably, because we do not need to exaggerate the sublime symbol of the Fatherland in order to see that we are among Portuguese and, let it be said without boasting, among the best. The tiers are full, the only room left is in the center, where the banners can be seen to best advantage, which explains why there are so many down there. Acquaintances greet each other, the assembled acclaim the New State, and they are numerous, they stretch forth their arms in a frenzy, jumping up every time a new banner is carried in, saluting in Roman style. Forgive this constant repetition on their part and ours, *O tempora, O mores*, Viriathus and Sertorius fought so hard to expel the imperial occupiers from their country, but despite the struggle of those two heroes Rome returns in the image of her descendants, clearly the easiest domination of all is to buy men, who sometimes offer themselves so cheaply, in exchange for a strip of cloth to wear on their arms, or for the right to adopt the crooked crucifix as their emblem. A brass band plays popular tunes to help pass the time while people wait. At last the officials take their places on the platform and the crowd goes wild with excitement, the air shakes with patriotic cries, Portugal Portugal Portugal, Salazar Salazar Salazar. Salazar is not present, he appears only at his convenience, but Portugal is here, since it is everywhere. To the right of the platform, to the chagrin of the local residents, seats which had remained empty were now taken by Fascist delegates from Italy, dressed in their black shirts and decorations, and to the left now stood the Nazi delegates from Germany, with their brown shirts and armbands bearing the swastika. They all saluted the crowd with outstretched arms, and the crowd responded, rather less disciplined but eager to learn. At this point members of the Spanish Falange made their entrance, dressed in their familiar blue shirts, their uniforms in three different colors but united by a single ideal. To a man, the crowd is on its feet, its cheers filling the air in that universal language known as roaring, and Babel is unified at last by gestures. The Germans speak no Portuguese or Castilian or Italian, the Spaniards speak no German or Italian or Portuguese, the Italians speak no Castilian or Portuguese or German, the Portuguese, however, speak Castilian extremely well, *Usted* if addressing someone, *quanto vale* if buying something, *gracias* if thanking someone, but when souls are in harmony one mighty shout is good enough in all languages, Death to Bolshevism. Silence is restored with some effort, the band finishes its military march with three drumbeats, and now the first speaker of the evening is introduced, Gilberto Arroteia, a shipyard worker from the Navy Arsenal, how they persuaded him remains a secret between himself and temptation. Then a second speech by Luís Pinto Coelho, who represents Portuguese youth, and one begins to see what this is all about, because with words that could hardly be more explicit he calls for the creation of a Nationalist militia. The third speaker is Fernando Homem Cristo, the fourth Abel Mesquita, both from the national unions of Setúbal, the fifth is António Castro Fernandes, who one day will be a government minister, and the sixth Ricardo Durão, whose strong convictions are in keeping with his rank of major. In a few weeks' time he will repeat his speech in Évora, once again in a bull ring, We are gathered here, united by the same patriotic ideal, to declare and show the government of our nation that we are loyally pledged to carry on the traditions and achievements of our Lusitanian ancestors who gave new worlds to the world and spread faith and empire, let us also declare to a fanfare of horns and trumpets that we have gathered here as one man around Salazar, this genius who has dedicated his life to the service of the Fatherland. Finally, seventh in order but first in terms of political influence, Captain Jorge Botelho Moniz from the Portuguese Radio Club reads a motion urging the government to create a civic legion that will dedicate itself entirely to the service of the Fatherland, just as Salazar has, for it is only right that we should follow his example as far as our weak ability permits. This would seem an opportune moment to cite the parable of the seven twigs which are easily broken when separate but when tied together form an unbreakable fasces. Upon hearing the word legion, the crowd rises to its feet once more, always to a man. To say legion is to say uniform, to say uniform is to say shirt, all that remains to be decided is the color, but this is not a matter we can settle here. In any case, rather than be accused of behaving like monkeys we will not choose black or brown or blue, white gets dirty very quickly, yellow is the color of despair, as for red, God forbid, and purple evokes Christ on the road to Calvary, the only color left is green, so the gallant young men of the Portuguese Youth Movement agree that green is fine and dream of nothing else as they wait to be given their uniforms. The rally is drawing to a close, the unions have done their duty.

As one expects of the Portuguese, the crowd leaves the arena in an orderly fashion, some people still cheering but on a subdued note. The more meticulous of the standard bearers roll up their flags and slip them into protective sheaths. The main floodlights in the bull ring have been turned off and there is just enough light for the demonstrators to find their way out. Outside, special trams are filling up, there are also trucks for those who have to travel some distance, and lines waiting to board both. Ricardo Reis, though he was out in the open all through the rally, feels the need for fresh air and declines the taxis, which are snapped up at once by others. He sets out on foot to cross the entire city, walks where there is no sign of the patriotic crusade, these trams belong to other lines, the taxis doze in the squares. From Campo Pequeno to the Alto de Santa Catarina it is almost five kilometers, quite a distance for this doctor who is usually so sedentary in his ways. He arrived home with sore feet, exhausted. As he opened a window to clear the stuffiness in the room, he realized that during the long walk home he had not thought once about what he had seen and heard in the arena. He could not remember a single idea, reflection, comment, it was almost as if he had been carried on a cloud, or transformed into a cloud hovering in midair. Now he wanted to think, to turn it all over in his mind, to reach conclusions, but he tried in vain, all he could see were those black, brown, and blue shirts defending western civilization, the Greeks and Romans. What speech would Don Miguel de Unamuno have made if invited. Perhaps he would have appeared between Durão and Moniz, would have shown himself to the multitude, Here I stand before you, sons of Portugal, nation of suicides who do not cry out, Long live death, I have nothing to say to you, for I myself am old and weak and need someone to protect me. Ricardo Reis contemplates the deep night, anyone with the power of seeing signs and omens would say that something is brewing. It is very late when Ricardo Reis closes the window, and in the end all he can think is, No more political rallies for me. Starting to brush his jacket and trousers, he found himself inhaling the smell of onion, how strange, he could have sworn he had been nowhere near Victor.

The following days bring a spate of news, as if the rally at Campo Pequeno has triggered events throughout the world. A group of North American financiers informed General Franco that they were prepared to back the Spanish Nationalist Revolution, the idea must have come from the influential John D. Rockefeller, because it would be a mistake to keep him completely in the dark, *The New York Times* reported the military coup in Spain, taking every precaution not to injure the old man's weak heart, but there are some risks that cannot be avoided. In the dioceses near the Black Forest, the German bishops announced that the Catholic Church and the Reich will fight shoulder to shoulder against the common foe. In order not to fall behind in this show of strength, Mussolini has warned the world that he is capable of mobilizing eight million men at a moment's notice, many of them still glowing from their victory over that other enemy of western civilization, Ethiopia. But to return to our paternal nest. In addition to the growing number of volunteers joining the Youth Movement, thousands have also enrolled in the Portuguese Legion, as it will come to be known, and the Undersecretary of the Corporations has drafted a statement in which he praises the national unions in the most eloquent terms, their patriotic initiative of holding a political rally, a crucible where Nationalist hearts are forged, now nothing stands in the way of building the New State. It has also been announced that the President of the Council is visiting military installations, touring the munitions factory at Braço de Prata, and inspecting the armaments depot of Beirolas, any subsequent visits, tours, or inspections will be duly reported.

From the newspaper Ricardo Reis learns that the *Afonso de Albuquerque* has sailed to Alicante to pick up refugees. He feels sadness in his heart because of his tie to the fortunes of this ship, though Lydia did not tell him that her sailor brother left for sea on a humanitarian mission. Lydia, for that matter, has not appeared lately, the dirty clothes are piling up, the dust is gathering on the furniture, and things are gradually losing their outline, as if tired of existing, which may also be the effect of eyes tired of seeing. Ricardo Reis has never felt so lonely. He sleeps nearly all day, on top of his unmade bed or on the sofa in the study. He even fell asleep on the toilet, but only once, because he woke then with a terrible fright, dreaming that he had died on the toilet, his trousers down, a corpse with no self-respect. He wrote a long letter to Marcenda, page upon page, mining a whole archaeology of remembrance beginning with that first evening in the hotel, the words flow without interruption from memory to memory, but when he comes to the present, Ricardo Reis cannot find anything to say, to ask for, to offer. So he collected the pages, tapped them straight, flattened out some corners that had been folded over, then tore up the letter methodically, page by page, until it was reduced to pieces so small, not a single word was readable. He did not throw the pieces into the wastebasket, but waited until the early hours of the morning, when everyone was asleep, and went and threw his sad carnival shower of confetti over the park railing. The dawn breeze carried them over the rooftops, and an even stronger wind will pick them up and carry them far away, but not as far as Coimbra. Two days later he copied his poem onto a sheet of paper, Already *impatient for the summer*, knowing that this truth was now a lie, because he felt no impatience, only an infinite weariness. He addressed the envelope to Marcenda Sampaio, poste restante, Coimbra, if she does not claim it in six months, the letter will be destroyed. And that conscientious and prying employee we mentioned earlier, if he takes the letter to Doctor Sampaio's office, no harm will come of it. Upon arriving home, having exercised his paternal prerogative and opened the letter, the father will say to his daughter, You appear to have an unknown admirer, and Marcenda will read the poem, smiling to herself. It does not even occur to her that it is from Ricardo Reis, because he never told her he was a poet, though there are certain similarities in the handwriting.

I'm not coming back, Lydia has said, yet here she is knocking at the door. The key to the apartment is in her pocket, but she does not use it, she has her pride, she said she would not come back, it would look bad now if she used the key as if this were her own home, which it never was, and today even less so, if it is possible for something to be less than never. Ricardo Reis opens the door, concealing his surprise. Since Lydia appears to hesitate as to which room she should go to, he moves to the study, she can follow if she wishes. Her eyes are red and swollen, perhaps she has finally decided, after a great struggle with the joy of anticipated mother-hood, to have an abortion, because the expression on her face doesn't seem to have been caused by the fall of Irun or the siege of San Sebastian. She says, You must excuse me, Doctor, I wasn't able to come. But immediately, in the same breath, she corrects herself, Not because of this, I just thought you didn't need me anymore. She corrects herself again, I was feeling tired of this life, and having said this, she stands there waiting. For the first time she looked straight at Ricardo Reis, and thought, Perhaps he is ill. I missed you, he said, then fell silent, he had nothing more to say. Lydia took two steps, she will start with the bedroom, make his bed, then go to the kitchen and wash the dishes, then soak his clothes in the washtub, but this is not the reason she came, although she may do all these chores later. Ricardo Reis asks her, Why don't you sit down, then says, Tell me what's wrong, and Lydia begins

347

to sob. Is it because of the child, he asks, and she shakes her head, even manages a glance of rebuke amid her tears, before blurting out, It's because of my brother. Ricardo Reis remembers that the *Afonso de Albuquerque* has returned from Alicante, a port still under the control of the Spanish government, he puts two and two together and finds they make four. Has your brother deserted and stayed behind in Spain. No, he came back with the ship. So then. There's going to be a disaster, a disaster. Look, tell me what this is all about. The sailors, she stopped to dry her tears and blow her nose, are about to mutiny and sail out to sea. Who told you this. Daniel, he told me to keep it a secret but I had to talk to someone I can trust, I came here, Doctor, I have no one else to turn to, my mother has no idea. Ricardo Reis is surprised to find that he is devoid of feeling, perhaps this is fate, we know what will happen, know it is inevitable, yet we remain silent, onlookers only, watching the spectacle of the world even as we leave it. Are you sure, he asked. She nodded, tearful, waiting for the right questions, those to which a simple yes or no can be given, but such questioning requires an act of courage beyond human powers. For the want of anything better let us make do with, for example, What are their plans, surely they don't believe that their going out to sea will bring down the government. Their idea is to make for Angra do Heroísmo, free the political prisoners, take possession of the island, and then wait for riots to break out here. And if nothing happens. If there are no riots, they will go to Spain and join forces with the government. They're mad, they won't even get beyond the straits. That's what my brother said, but they refuse to listen. When is this to take place. He didn't tell me, but it will be within the next few days. And the ships, which ships are involved. The *Afonso de Albuquerque*, the *Dão*, the *Bartolomeu Dias*. They're mad, Ricardo Reis repeats, but he is no longer thinking about the conspiracy which has been revealed with such innocence, what he is recalling is the day of his arrival in Lisbon, the torpedo boats in the dock, their flags drenched like soggy rags, their lifeless hulks painted a deathly gray, The *Dão* is that one nearest you, the porter had told him, and now the *Dão* was about to sail out to sea in defiance. Ricardo Reis took a deep breath, as if he himself were on the prow of the ship, the salt wind in his face, the biting spray. He repeated, They're mad. Can there be a note of hope in his voice, surely not, an absurd illusion on our part, for he cherishes no hope. But everything may turn out all right in the end, who knows, they may even abandon their plan, and if they don't, who knows, they may even make it to Angra, we will see what happens, but you must stop crying, tears won't help, the sailors may change their mind. No, Doctor, you don't know them, as sure as my name is Lydia they won't change their mind. Having spoken her name, she suddenly realized that she should not be here, I can't do any cleaning for you today, I must get back to the hotel at once, I only came to unburden myself, I hope no one has noticed I am missing. Can I do anything to help. It's those sailors who need help, with all that way to go before they reach the straits, the one thing I beg of you, on the souls of your dear ones, is to keep this a secret, even though I wasn't able to keep it myself. Don't worry, my lips are sealed. But they parted enough for a kiss of consolation, and Lydia moaned because she felt so unhappy, although one could detect another deep sound in that moan, we humans are like this, feeling many things at the same moment. As Lydia descended the stairs, Ricardo Reis, most unusual for him, went out on the landing. She looked up, he nodded, they both smiled, certain moments in life seem perfect and this was such a moment, like a page on which there was writing but is now blank again.

When Ricardo Reis went out to lunch the next day, he lingered in the park to gaze at the warships before the Terreiro do Paço. He knew little about ships in general, only that dispatch boats were bigger than torpedo boats, but at a distance they all looked exasperatingly alike. He could not tell which was the *Afonso de Albuquerque* and which the *Bartolomeu Dias*, but the *Dão* he knew, because the porter had told him, The *Dão* is the one nearest you. Lydia must have been dreaming, or her brother had frightened her with a joke, this incredible story of conspiracy and ships heading for sea. Three of them are moored along the quay, as calm as can be in the breeze, and the frigates going upriver, and the ferries for Cacilhas ceaselessly plying to and fro, and the seagulls in the cloudless blue sky, and the sun shining brightly on the expectant river.

What Daniel told his sister is true after all, a poet can sense the fear that trembles in these waters. When do they leave, Within the next few days, Lydia replied, and Ricardo Reis's throat tightens and his eyes cloud with tears, this was how Adamastor's great weeping began. He is on the point of leaving when he hears voices call out in excitement, Over there, over there. They belong to the two old men, and other people are asking, Where, what is it, and children playing leapfrog interrupt their game and call out, Look at the balloon, look at the balloon. Ricardo Reis wiped his eyes with the back of his hand and saw rising into the air, on the other side of the river, an enormous airship, it must be the Graf Zeppelin or the Hindenburg, arriving to drop off mail for South America, on the rudder is a swastika in white, red, and black, like a kite launched by children into the sky, a hovering symbol that has lost its original meaning, a threat rather than a shooting star. The links between men and symbols are curious, we need only think of St. Francis of Assisi joined by blood to the cross of Christ, and the cross of Christ on the armbands of the bank employees at the political rally, it is a miracle that a person does not get lost in this maze of associations. The Hindenburg, its engines roaring, flew over the river in the direction of the castle, then disappeared behind some houses, and the roar gradually died away. The airship is about to drop the mail at Portela de Sacavém, perhaps *The Highland Brigade* will then transport the letters, for in the world there are many recurring paths. The old men return to their bench, the children go back to their leapfrog, the currents of air grow still again, and Ricardo Reis is no wiser. The ships sit in the accumulating heat of the afternoon, their prows facing out to sea, the sailors must be having their lunch, today as every day, unless today is their last day. In the restaurant, Ricardo Reis filled his glass with wine, then the glass of his invisible guest, and as he raised his glass to take the first sip, he made a gesture as if offering a toast. Since we cannot look into his thoughts to see whom or what he was toasting, let us follow the example of the waiters in this establishment, who pay no attention, because this customer may be a little odd but by no means is he the oddest.

The afternoon was most agreeable. Ricardo Reis went down to the Chiado, to the Rua Nova do Almada, to observe the ships at close quarters. On the quay, and as he was crossing the Terreiro do Paço, he recalled that in all these months he had not been to the Café Martinho da Arcada. Fernando Pessoa, on the last occasion, had felt that it would be unwise to challenge the memory of those familiar walls, and somehow they had never gone back, neither of them giving it another thought. For Ricardo Reis there is some excuse, with so many years abroad the habit of going there, if ever a habit, has been broken. Nor will he go there today. Seen from the middle of the square, the ships afloat on that luminous water look like toy boats displayed in a window, on mirrors to give the effect of a fleet in harbor. But when one draws closer, one sees very little, only the sailors going back and forth on deck. At this distance they seem unreal, if they are talking we cannot hear them, and what they are thinking remains a secret. Ricardo Reis was lost in reverie, having forgotten why he came here, he was simply gazing, nothing more, when suddenly he heard a voice beside him, So you've come to see the ships, Doctor. He recognized that voice, it belonged to Victor. His first reaction was puzzlement, where was the smell, then it became clear, Victor was downwind of him. Ricardo Reis felt his heart beat faster, did Victor suspect, had the sailors' plan to mutiny been discovered. The ships and the river, he replied, but could also have mentioned the frigates and the seagulls, also that he was about to take the ferry to Cacilhas just for the pleasure of the crossing, of watching the dolphins leap, but he merely repeated, The ships and the river, and withdrew brusquely, telling himself he had acted foolishly, he should have kept up a natural conversation, if Victor knows there is something afoot, he must surely have found it suspicious to see the doctor there. Then it occurred to Ricardo Reis that he should warn Lydia, was obliged to do so. But he immediately changed his mind, What could I tell her, that I saw Victor in the Terreiro do Paço, it might have been a coincidence, even the police enjoy looking at the river, and Victor could have been off-duty, simply yielding to the seafaring impulse that is common to all Portuguese, and spotting the doctor there, it seemed only natural to greet him, for old times' sake. Ricardo Reis passed the entrance of the Hotel Bragança, went up the Rua do Alecrim, where engraved on stone steps were the words *clínica de enfermedades de los ojos y quirúrgicas, A. Mascaró, 1870,* there is nothing that tells us whether this Mascaró graduated from a medical faculty or was a simple practitioner, in those days the rules regarding diplomas were less strict, even today they are not that strict, we need only recall that Ricardo Reis treated heart patients without any special qualifications. He followed the itinerary of the statues, Eça de Queirós, Chiado, D'Artagnan, poor Adamastor viewed from behind. Pretending that he was admiring the statues, he walked around each slowly, three times, feeling that he was playing cops and robbers, but he soon calmed down, Victor was not following him.

The afternoon passed and darkness fell. Lisbon is a tranquil city with a wide river of legendary fame. Ricardo Reis did not go out to dinner, he scrambled two eggs, folded them into a bread roll, accompanying this meager fare with a glass of wine, and even this he found difficult to swallow. On edge and restless, he went down to the park after eleven o'clock to take another look at the ships. All he could see were the mooring lights, and now he could not even tell the difference between the dispatch boats and the torpedo boats. He was the only soul on the Alto de Santa Catarina, one could no longer count Adamastor, now completely petrified, the screaming throat forever silent, the face terrifying to behold. Ricardo Reis went home, the ships won't leave in the night, because of the risk of running aground. Half-dressed, he lay on his bed, slept, woke up, and went back to sleep, calmed by the great silence throughout the apartment as the first light of day filtered in between the slats of the shutters. When he woke up, nothing had happened, and now that another day had dawned it seemed impossible that anything could happen. He felt ashamed of himself, appalled that he had removed only his shoes and jacket and tie. I'll have a bath, he decided, and was bending down to look for his slippers under the bed when he heard the first cannonade. But perhaps he was mistaken, perhaps a piece of furniture had fallen in the apartment downstairs, perhaps the landlady had fainted with a thud, but another explosion rang out, the windowpanes shook, the ships are firing on the city. He opened the window, on the street, people were in a panic, a woman shouted, God help us, it's a revolution, and ran for dear life toward the park. Ricardo Reis pulled on his shoes, slipped on his jacket, just as well that he had not taken off his clothes, almost as if he had known what would happen. The neighbors were already on the stairs, wrapped in their dressing gowns. When they saw the doctor appear, and a doctor can be relied upon to know everything, they asked in great distress, Are there people hurt, Doctor. His leaving in such haste must mean that someone has called him out to deal with an emergency. Covering their bare necks, they trail after him, standing at the entrance to the building where out of modesty they are partially concealed. When Ricardo Reis arrived at the park, a crowd had already gathered. The residents of this neighborhood are privileged, because there is no better vantagepoint in Lisbon for watching vessels enter and leave. The warships were not firing on the city, the fortress of Almada was firing on the warships. On one of them. Ricardo Reis asked, Which ship is that. Fortunate for him, he asked someone who knew, It's the *Afonso de Albuquerque*. So it was the ship on which Lydia's brother was serving, the sailor Daniel, whom he had never met. He tried to picture his face, but could see only the face of Lydia. At this very moment she must be looking out of a window at the Hotel Bragança, or she has gone into the street in her maid's uniform, she is running to the Cais do Sodré, and now stands at the quay, her hands pressed to her bosom, perhaps weeping, perhaps with dry eyes and flushed cheeks, suddenly letting out a scream because the *Afonso de Albuquerque* has been hit by a shell, then another. Someone on the Alto de Santa Catarina is clapping his hands, at this moment the two old men appear, their lungs bursting, how did they manage to get here so quickly, living as they do at the bottom of the hill, but they would rather die than miss this, and that is certainly possible, considering the effort they have made. It all seems like a dream. Drifting slowly, the *Afonso de Albuquerque* has probably been struck in some vital organ, perhaps the boiler room, the rudder. The fortress of Almada continues to fire, and the *Afonso de Albuquerque* appears to answer, but we are not sure. From this side of the city new booms can be heard, louder, less frequent, That's the fortress of the Alto do Duque, someone remarks, they are lost now, they'll never get away. And at that very moment another ship emerges, a torpedo boat, the *Dão*, almost certainly the *Dão*, trying to shield herself with the smoke of her own stacks and skirting the southern bank in order to escape the guns of the fortress of Almada, but if she gets past Almada she will not escape the Alto do Duque. Shells explode near the shore, this is to get the range, the next volley will strike the ship, and yes, there is a direct hit. A white flag is already being unfurled on the *Dão*, but the firing continues, the ship begins to list, then white sheets, shrouds, funeral shrouds, the end is near, the *Bartolomeu Dias* will not even have time to leave her berth.

It is nine o'clock. One hundred minutes have passed since the hostilities began, the dawn mist has dispersed and the sun shines from a clear sky. They must be searching now for the men who jumped into the sea. From this belvedere there is nothing more to be seen. As the veterans explain what happened to some latecomers, Ricardo Reis sits down on a bench. The old men join him, eager to start up a conversation, but the doctor says nothing, he sits with his head lowered, as if he were the one who had tried to sail out to sea only to be caught in the net. While the adults talk, their excitement subsiding, the children start to play leapfrog and the little girls sing, *I went into Celeste's garden, what did you go there to do, I went there to look for a rose*. More appropriate would be the ballad from Nazaré, *Don't go to sea Tonho, you might drown Tonho, ah Tonho, poor Tonho, what an unfortunate fellow you are*. Lydia's brother is not Tonho, but when it comes to misfortune there is little difference. The old men, indignant, turn away when Ricardo Reis gets to his feet. He finds some comfort when he hears a woman say, out of pity, Poor souls, she is referring to the sailors but Ricardo Reis feels those words as if someone were caressing him, placing a hand on his forehead or gently stroking his hair. In his apartment he throws himself on the unmade bed, covers his eyes with his arm, and weeps freely, weeps foolish tears, because this was not his revolution, *Wise is the man who contents himself with the spectacle of the world*, I must repeat that phrase a thousand times, what should all this matter to one who no longer cares who wins and who loses. Ricardo Reis gets up and puts on his tie, he is about to go out, but passing his hand over his face, he feels his stubble, he need not look in the mirror to know that there are white hairs glistening there among the black, the harbinger of old age. The dice have been thrown, the card played has been covered with the ace of trumps, no matter how fast you run you cannot save your father from the gallows, these are popular sayings to help ordinary men bear the blows of fate. Ricardo Reis, an ordinary man, sets about shaving and washing himself, while he is shaving he doesn't think, he concentrates on the razor scraping at his skin, one of these days he must sharpen the blade. It was half-past eleven when he left his apartment for the Hotel Bragança, and why not, no one should be surprised to see a former guest who stayed for almost three months, who was so dutifully served by one of the chambermaids, a chambermaid whose brother took part in the mutiny, she herself had told him, Yes, Doctor, I have a brother at sea, he is serving on the *Afonso de Albuquerque*, no one should be surprised that Ricardo Reis has come to make inquiries, to see if he can help, poor girl, how she must have suffered, some people are born unlucky.

The buzzer sounds much hoarser, or has his memory started to deceive him. The figurine of the page mounted on the baluster raises its extinguished globe, even in France there were such pages, but he will never find out where this page came from, there is not time to know everything. At the top of the stairs Pimenta appears, about to descend, thinking a client has arrived with luggage, then he stops, not yet recognizing who is coming up. He could have forgotten, so many faces enter and leave the life of a hotel porter, and we must take the poor lighting into account as well. But now the new arrival is so close that even though he keeps his head lowered, there is not a shadow of doubt. Well upon my word, if it isn't Doctor Reis, how are you, Doctor. Good day Pimenta, that chambermaid, what is she called again, Lydia, is she here. Ah, no, Doctor, she went out and hasn't returned, I believe her brother was involved in the mutiny. Pimenta has barely finished speaking when Salvador appears on the landing, pretending to be surprised, Why Doctor, how delighted I am to see you back. Pimenta tells him what he already knows, The doctor would like to speak to Lydia. Ah, Lydia isn't here, but if I could be of any assistance. She had spoken to me about a brother who was serving in the navy, I only

355

came to see if I could offer my services as a doctor. I understand, Doctor Reis, but Lydia went out as soon as the shooting began and she hasn't returned. Salvador always smiles when he is giving information, he makes a good manager, and let us repeat once more, the last time, that he has cause for complaint against this former guest, who slept with one of the chambermaids and perhaps still does, and who now turns up, playing the innocent, if he thinks he is deceiving the manager, he is much mistaken. Do you know where she might have gone, Ricardo Reis asked. She must be around somewhere, she could have gone to the Naval Ministry, or to her mother's house, or to the police station, because the police are always involved in such matters, but do not trouble yourself, Doctor, I will tell her that Doctor Reis was here, and she is sure to go looking for you. Salvador gave another smile, like one who has set a trap and can already see his prey caught by the leg, but Ricardo Reis answered, Yes, do tell her to come and see me, here is my home address, and he wrote the futile directions on a sheet of paper. Annoyed at this response, Salvador stopped smiling, but Ricardo Reis never learned what he was about to say, because two Spaniards came down from the second floor, engaged in heated discussion. One of them asked, *Señor Salvador los ha llevado el diablo a los marineros.* Yes, Don Camilo, the devil has taken them. Good, the hour has come to say *Arriba España, Viva Portugal, Arriba*, exclaimed Don Camilo, and Pimenta added on behalf of the Fatherland, *Viva*. As Ricardo Reis went downstairs, the buzzer sounded, there had once been a bell here, but the guests complained, they said it was like the bell at the gates of a cemetery.

Lydia did not come that afternoon. Ricardo Reis went out to buy the late edition of a newspaper. He scanned the headlines on the front page, then turned to the double center page. At the bottom, Twelve Sailors Killed, and their names and ages followed, Daniel Martins, twenty-three years of age. Ricardo Reis stopped in the middle of the street, holding the newspaper wide open, submerged in silence. The city has come to a standstill, or walks on tiptoe, its forefinger pressed to sealed lips, suddenly there was a deafening noise, the horn of an automobile, a quarrel between two lottery-ticket vendors, a child crying because his mother had cuffed his ear, Any more of that and I'll give you a good hiding. Lydia was not waiting for him, nor was there any indication that she had called. It is almost night. The newspaper reports that the arrested men were taken before the district attorney, then to Mitra, and that the bodies of the dead, some of whom still have to be identified, are in the morgue. Lydia must be searching for her brother, or else she is at her mother's house, both women weeping over this great and irreparable calamity.

A knock at the door. Ricardo Reis ran to open it, his open arms ready to embrace the tearful Lydia, but it was Fernando Pessoa, Ah, it's you. Were you expecting someone else. If you know what has happened, you must realize that yes, I am, Lydia, I believe I told you once, had a brother in the Navy. Is he dead, Yes, he is dead. They were in the bedroom, Fernando Pessoa seated at the foot of the bed, Ricardo Reis in a chair, the room now in total darkness. Half an hour passed in this way, and they heard a clock chiming on the floor above. How strange, Ricardo Reis thought to himself, I don't remember ever having heard that clock before, or perhaps I heard it once and then put it out of my mind. Fernando Pessoa sat with his hands on one knee, his fingers clasped, his head lowered, without stirring he said, I came to tell you that we will not see each other again. Why not. My time is up, do you remember my telling you that I had only a few months left. Yes, I remember. Well, that is the reason, those months have come to an end. Ricardo Reis tightened the knot in his tie, got to his feet, put on his jacket. He went to the bedside table, took *The God of the Labyrinth* and put it under his arm. Let's go then, he said, Where are you going, With you. You should stay here and wait for Lydia. I know I should. To console her after the loss of her brother. I can do nothing for her. And the book, what do you want that for. Despite the time granted me, I never managed to finish it, You won't have time, I will have all the time I could possibly want. You are deceiving yourself, reading is the first faculty one loses, remember. Ricardo Reis opened the book, saw meaningless marks, black scribbles, a page of blotches. The faculty has already left me, he said, but no matter, I'll take the book with me just the same. But why. I relieve the world of one enigma. As they left the apartment, Fernando

Pessoa told him, You forgot your hat. You know better than I do that hats aren't worn where we're going. On the sidewalk opposite the park, they watched the pale lights flicker on the river, the ominous shadows of the mountains. Let's go then, said Fernando Pessoa. Let's go, agreed Ricardo Reis. Adamastor did not turn around to look, perhaps afraid that if he did, he might let out finally his mighty howl. Here, where the sea ends and the earth awaits.

José Saramago

THE GOSPEL ACCORDING TO JESUS CHRIST

Translated from the Portuguese by Giovanni Pontiero

"His greatest book . . . Saramago's novel is an extraordinary, eloquent heretical text, filled with deep compassion for humanity's suffering"   JAMES WOOD, *New Republic*

"A moving and even a profound book . . . It manages to fill out the simple, sparse narratives while retaining the authentic mysteriousness of life itself, a remarkable achievement . . . It sends us back to the Bible with renewed sense of its depths"   GABRIEL JOSIPOVICI, *Independent*

José Saramago

BLINDNESS

Translated from the Portuguese by Giovanni Pontiero

"José Saramago always has been audaciously inventive as a novelist. *Blindness* is his most surprising and disturbing book. It is a fantasy so persuasive as to shock the reader into realising how fragile and contingent our social conditions always have been and will be. This is a novel that will endure" **HAROLD BLOOM**

"Saramago writes a prose of particularly luminous intensity, brilliantly rendered into English by Giovanni Pontiero. The themes he chooses are sweepingly ambitious . . . The works recall García Márquez for their epic reach and Primo Levi for their insight into the fragility of human nature under adversity" **LISA JARDINE,** *The Times*

Julio Cortázar

HOPSCOTCH

Translated from the Spanish by Gregory Rabassa

"Anyone who hasn't read Cortázar is doomed . . . something similar to a man who has never tasted peaches. He would quietly become sadder, noticeably paler, and probably little by little he would lose his hair"   **PABLO NERUDA**

"*Hopscotch*, a superb work, should establish Cortázar as an outstanding writer of our day . . . The dialogue is brilliant, whether the subject is literature, love, Mondrian, jazz or the fallibility of science. Individual scenes are superbly alive . . . the rapid-fire invention of the language makes every page sparkle, thanks to the translation by Gregory Rabassa, which gives a dazzling parallel to Cortázar's stylistic magic"   **DONALD KEENE**, *New York Times*

Giuseppe Tomasi di Lampedusa

THE LEOPARD

Translated from the Italian by Archibald Colquhoun

"Every once in a while, like certain golden moments of happiness, infinitely memorable, one stumbles on a book or writer, and the impact is like an indelible mark. Lampedusa's *The Leopard*, his only novel, and a masterpiece, is such a work"　**BRUCE ARNOLD,** *Independent*

"A novel of exceptional stature. One may claim for it classic status"　**FRANK KERMODE**

"Perhaps the greatest novel of the century"　**L. P. HARTLEY**

"The poetry of Lampedusa's novel flows into the Sicilian countryside . . . a work of great artistry"　**PETER ACKROYD**

Boris Pasternak

DOCTOR ZHIVAGO

Translated from the Russian by
Manya Harari and Max Hayward

"A book that made a most profound impression upon me and the memory of which still does . . . not since Shakespeare has love been so fully, vividly scrupulously and directly communicated . . . The novel is a total experience, not parts or aspects: of what other twentieth-century work of the imagination could this be said?"

ISAIAH BERLIN, *Sunday Times*

"The first work of genius to come out of Russia since the Revolution" V. S. PRITCHETT

Mikhail Bulgakov

THE MASTER AND MARGARITA

Translated from the Russian by Michael Glenny

"A masterpiece . . . a classic of twentieth-century fiction"
New York Times

"A superb, stunning allegorical novel in which the Devil and his retinue invade modern Moscow and wreak havoc. The book rockets between outlandish fantasy, deadpan realism and sombre moments of religious meditation. The reader is swept along towards an optimistic assertion of love over cynicism, conformism and cant . . . In the West, in the theatre and literature, he is relished as one of the greatest modern Russian writers, perhaps the greatest"
NIGEL JONES, *Independent*

The Peak District

CONTENTS

PREFACE

This is the third revised edition of the Geologists' Association Guide No. 26 to the Peak District, the first having been published in 1957 and the second in 1972.

Over the forty years since the first edition was written there have been very considerable changes in the classification of the rocks exposed in the Peak District, and the systematic work by the British Geological Survey along with that by private research workers has added immensely to a better understanding of the geology of the area. The rocks themselves have not changed, of course, but in general exposures are not as good as they used to be, more especially in the limestone area where trees, especially willows, have grown apace.

Users of the Guide should note that a large part of the Peak District lies within the oversight of the Peak District National Park Authority. Whilst this may make access somewhat easier it does impose certain restrictions upon the collection of specimens in several specific areas, such as the picnic area in Tideswell Dale where the collecting of plants and rocks is strictly forbidden. The policy of the Authority, however, does not preclude serious geological work, and it will give sympathetic consideration to any application to carry out specific research. The address of the Authority is Aldern House, Baslow Road, Bakewell, Derbyshire DE4 1AE.

Most of the itineraries in this Guide have specific localities marked on accompanying sketch-maps. Where greater precision of siting is essential grid references are given. As all localities lie within the SK area of the Ordnance Survey maps these initials have been omitted from the grid references.

The relevant O.S. Landranger 1:50,000 maps are nos. 110 and 119.

Figures 14 and 30 are based partly upon the maps of the Geological Survey and are Crown Copyright, being reproduced by permission of the Controller, Her Majesty's Stationery Office.

Grateful thanks are due to Mr Colin Stuart of University College London for his excellent work in finalising the illustrations.

This Guide has been partly financed by the Nature Conservancy Council for England (English Nature) and the Geologists' Association is very grateful for the assistance in this of Dr. Jonathan Larwood, and to Dr. David Evans for his contribution on conservation in the Peak District. A substantial grant from the Curry Fund of the Association has covered other costs.

LIST OF FIGURES

Introduction

INTRODUCTION

The Peak District is an area of outstanding natural beauty. Situated at the southern end of the Pennines in north Midland Britain, it lies mainly in the county of Derbyshire with some parts extending into the adjacent counties of Cheshire, Staffordshire and Yorkshire. It is an upland region with large areas standing at or above 300 m AOD, whilst some parts of the north and west extend above the 500 m contour-line.

Geologically and physiographically the Peak District is an area of two contrasting types. A large central limestone area is surrounded on all sides except the south by extensive peat-covered moorlands based upon sandstones and shales younger than the limestone. The limestone area supports some mixed farming; it is cut by numerous deep valleys or dales, many of which are dry though they have obviously been formed by stream erosion. On the uplands, water supply can pose a problem but, generally speaking the annual rainfall is sufficient to sustain many crops and to supply food for livestock. The country is criss-crossed by limestone walls and there are scattered spinneys mainly of ash or beech.

Outside the limestone area sometimes referred to as the 'White Peak', the sandstone-shale country, especially to the north and west has been called the 'Dark Peak' and has an entirely different character. It includes the highest points in the Peak District such as Kinder Scout in Derbyshire at 632 m AOD and Shining Tor the highest point in Cheshire at 558 m AOD. These are above the tree-line and support a cover of heather and bilberry. At lower levels the sandstones which may be partly peat-covered are relatively dry and support the growth of gorse and heather. Intervening areas underlain by shales and mudstone, unless they have not been artificially drained, tend to be swampy and marked by the growth of sedges and rushes.

The disposition of different types of rock, the presence or absence of fossils and the occurrence of deposits of economic importance in the Peak District are due to a long and complex geological history. Parts of this history are virtually unknown but, for convenience, it can be broken into several parts.

Figure 1. Geological sketch-map of the Peak District and the country around showing the distribution of Triassic and Carboniferous rocks, the location of deep boreholes and some of the localities mentioned in the text.

Introduction

1. *Pre-Carboniferous:* This is an immense period of time extending to the beginning of the Carboniferous Period about 360 Ma ago. No rocks formed during this time span are visible at the surface in the Peak District though some representatives can be examined not far away in Charnwood Forest, Shropshire and North Wales. The only evidence of the nature of the pre-Carboniferous rocks is provided by three boreholes (Figure 1). The Woo Dale borehole east of Buxton (09587248) proved volcanic rocks beneath a cover of 273.6 m of Lower Carboniferous limestones which gave a radiometric age (K/Ar) of 382 ± 6 Ma indicating a Devonian or older age. It is thought that the volcanic rocks have suffered considerable argon loss, and it is quite conceivable that they are actually of Precambrian age (Cope, 1979). The Eyam borehole in the north of the limestone area (20967603) proved marine rocks of Ordovician age under a cover of 1851.05 m of Lower Carboniferous rocks (Dunham, 1973). At Caldon Low, north of Ashbourne (08044822) a borehole proved red sandstones beneath a thick cover of Lower Carboniferous rocks, and it is thought that these may be of Devonian age (Inst. Geol. Sc. 1978). As yet, there is no direct evidence of the presence of rocks of Cambrian or Silurian age beneath the Lower Carboniferous cover. The pre-Carboniferous surface could have been quite complex as the Lower Palaeozoic rocks had been strongly folded and faulted in the course of the Caledonian orogeny at the end of the Silurian Period, to produce extensive mountain chains. During Devonian times these were greatly reduced by erosion, much of it under arid conditions.

2. *Lower Carboniferous (Dinantian):* The subdivision of the Lower Carboniferous is shown in simplified form in Table I.

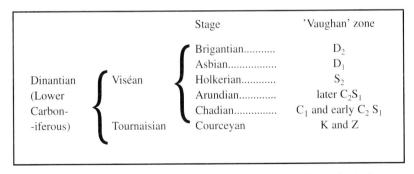

	Stage	'Vaughan' zone
	Brigantian...........	D_2
	Asbian.................	D_1
Dinantian (Lower Carbon-iferous) — Viséan	Holkerian............	S_2
	Arundian.............	later C_2S_1
	Chadian..............	C_1 and early $C_2 S_1$
Tournaisian	Courceyan	K and Z

Table I. In order to provide easy reference to previous literature a rough equation is shown between modern Stages and earlier Zones based solely on brachiopod-coral faunas.

In early Carboniferous times the sea advanced from the south or southwest gradually encroaching upon the largely peneplained land surface and completely

Introduction

covered the Peak District area by Holkerian times, though it failed to submerge an upstanding peninsula, the Brabant-Welsh Massif, to the south. The latter persisted, though in gradually diminishing size, until very late in Carboniferous times. The ancient rocks over which the sea advanced were not only folded but were affected by northwest to southeast and northeast to southwest faults. Tensional conditions in the Crust led to the production of half-grabens and relative movements of the fault blocks. Some sank relative to others and received thick sedimentation. Upstanding blocks, which have been called 'high's, received little terrigenous sediment but provided environments of shallow tropical waters in which corals could flourish and limestone could accumulate. The central parts of the Peak District lay on one of these highs, the fault-bounded margins of the "rigid block" corresponding very roughly with the present boundary of the limestone area. The climate was tropical and the area lay to the south of the Equator. Limestone deposition, accompanied by volcanic eruptions of lava and ash continued through Asbian and Brigantian time. One can envisage the Peak District block as a fault bounded area of fairly shallow sea in which limestone was accumulating at the same rate as the block subsided. Outside it, deeper marine conditions prevailed and a great deal of land-derived material was deposited. The faunas of the two areas were distinct so that whilst, for example, goniatites were present in the deeper waters outside the block they rarely migrated into the shallower waters on the block. In Asbian and Brigantian times in particular, a distinctive type of limestone with its own suite of fossils (a different facies) accumulated on the slope between block and basin. This facies is referred to as 'reef' (perhaps an unfortunate term because in modern parlance the term 'reef' is associated with coral, animals whose remains are rarely found in Carboniferous reefs).

Towards the end of Brigantian time, either through accelerated sinking of the block or to uplift of land to the north and east, from Scotland to Scandinavia, or indeed to a combination of both, terrigenous sediment was brought on to the block thus marking the end of Dinantian time and the beginning of the Namurian. The upper limit of Dinantian is taken at the base of the succeeding Namurian which is arbitrarily marked by a widespread marine band with the goniatite *Cravenoceras leion* Bisat. On the eastern side of the Peak District there was probably continuous sedimentation from the Dinantian to the Namurian, but on the western side there is evidence of considerable earth movement and erosion in that time interval, no doubt caused by movement along the western boundary fault in the basement and by tilting of the block.

3. *Upper Carboniferous (Silesian):* Throughout the Pennines the Upper Carboniferous is marked by the incoming of a great deal of sandy material to form 'grits' in the Namurian and sandstones in the succeeding Westphalian (Coal Measures). Argillaceous sediments, shales and mudstones, are also widespread in the Namurian and become more dominant in the Westphalian. Thin coal seams

appear in the Namurian and these become more common and thicker in the Westphalian (hence the old term 'Coal Measures'). The boundaries of the Namurian are fixed at widespread thin shaly bands with goniatites (marine bands), the *Gastrioceras subcrenatum* band above and the *Cravenoceras leion* band below. The Namurian rocks are classified on the basis of the goniatites present in the marine bands as follows:

Stage	Goniatite Zone	Selected marine band
WESTPHALIAN		
....*Gastrioceras subcrenatum*		
YEADONIAN	G_1	*Gastrioceras cancellatum*
MARSDENIAN	R_2	*Reticuloceras superbilingue*
KINDERSCOUTIAN	R_1	*Reticulocereas reticulatum*
ALPORTIAN	H_2	*Hudsonoceras proteus*
CHOKERIAN	H_1	*Homoceras subglobosum*
ARNSBERGIAN	E_2	*Eumorphoceras bisulcatum*
PENDLEIAN	E_1	*Eumorphoceras pseudobilingue*
....*Cravenoceras leion*		
DINANTIAN		

Table II Stages and Goniatite Zones of the Namurian.

The extremely widespread occurrence of specified marine bands points to a fairly even surface over which sedimentation occurred, only just above sea-level, so that the slightest excess of subsidence over sedimentation or eustatic changes of sea-level resulted in the sea sweeping over large areas relatively quickly. The Namurian sediments of the Peak District comprise alternations of 'grits', shales or mudstones with a thin coal and a marine band above the coal, the total thickness being not less than 2 km.

The Namurian grits are generally coarse quartz sands with a varying but high proportion of feldspars and scattered mica flakes. They and the associated argillaceous rocks vary considerably in thickness from place to place suggesting that the faults in the basement were still influencing sedimentation (Collinson, 1976) but not to the same extent as in Dinantian times.

The mineralogical make-up of the grits strongly suggests derivation from a granitic source. Within the grits, cross-bedding indicates that more were derived from the north but there were minor contributions from the west and south (Brabant-Welsh Massif).

The northerly derived granitic debris was carried southwards to culminate in large deltas together forming an immense lobe concentrated in the southern Pennine area, but with thinner developments beyond. The moving sand bodies were redistributed on the delta tops and, more especially in Pendleian and Kinderscoutian times, water-logged masses of sediment, turbidity currents, rolled down the delta fronts into deeper water where they gave rise to repeated fining-upwards sequences. When the sandbanks rose above water-level tropical plants migrated on to them and, in some cases, formed enough peat to become coal after burial, possibly beneath marine mud. Many of the shales and mudstones were deposited in quiet lagoons on the delta top.

In later Silesian times (Westphalian-Stephanian) subsidence of the basement continued but sedimentation, though heavy enough to keep up with downward movement of the basement, was less tumultuous than in Namurian times. Sands and muds were deposited and frequently built up to extend to or above water-level. Immense tropical swamps were formed and beds of peat accumulated, on occasion up to a thickness of 10 m before further sediments were washed in. Marine incursions, marked by the occurrence of goniatites, became less frequent than in the Namurian. Freshwater molluscs such as *Anthracosia* spp. lived in some of the lagoons and these have been found useful as marker horizons. Fossil plants which occur in profusion above some coal seams are also useful in equating (correlating) coal seams from one coalfield to another. Coal very rarely exhibits recognisable plant structures but plant spores, which can be extracted from coal, are also valuable markers. Only very thin remnants of Westphalian rocks survive in the Peak District, some thousands of metres of highly productive sediments having been removed by denudation in pre-Triassic times.

In end-Carboniferous times the British area became one of north-south compression and the Peak District area underwent folding and extensive faulting, some of the latter being related to faults in the basement. These powerful stresses are to be referred to the Asturic phase of the Hercynian orogeny.

4. *Mesozoic Era:* During the Permian and more especially during the Triassic Period the Peak District area along with many others was subject to intense erosion. The high mountains formed by the Hercynian movements probably reached an altitude of at least 5,000 m AOD. In the Triassic an immensely thick mantle of Upper Carboniferous rocks was removed from the central part of the Peak District so that the Dinantian limestones were uncovered. It seems likely that many of the major features of the landscape were initiated at this time.

Introduction

There is no direct evidence as to what happened in the area during the long Jurassic and Cretaceous Periods, but evidence outside the area points to marine conditions as well as dry land at various times (Cope *et al.*, 1992) and it is believed that the district was once covered by a mantle of Cretaceous chalk. All the evidence points to a movement of the area into higher latitudes during the Mesozoic Era.

5. *Cenozoic Era*: Apart from the so-called 'Pocket Deposits' in the southeast of the Peak District, which are now known to be of Pliocene age, no deposits of Tertiary age are known. From outside evidence it would appear that the area underwent uplift during Tertiary times, but there is no evidence of contemporaneous igneous activity as in the adjacent Staffordshire area (Cope, 1996).

There are no very extensive areas of glacial deposits such as till ('Boulder Clay') or fluvio-glacial sands and gravels except in the most western part of the area around Macclesfield and Leek. Several glacial erratics in the limestone area are attributed to the Wolstonian glaciation and some very small patches of till are thought to be of Devensian age. On the fringes of the Peak District there are several good examples of glacial overflow channels. In recent (Holocene) times thick peat has accumulated in some areas, particularly on the Namurian moorlands, but this is now being actively eroded. Flint flakes of Mesolithic age have been found at the base of the peat at several localities.

Structure and Mineralisation: The limestone area of the Peak District has been likened to a dome. A west-east section across the northern part of the area, roughly along the line of the River Wye, displays a marked anticlinal component (Figure 2) which could very roughly be repeated in various other directions. However, there are several other broad anticlinal and synclinal areas, especially in the east and

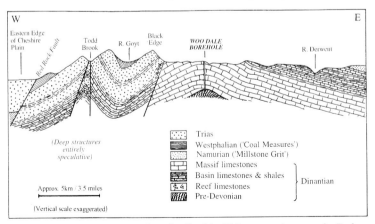

Figure 2. Diagrammatic section from the Cheshire Plain eastwards across the Peak District. The length of the section is about 40 km and the vertical scale is exaggerated about ten times in order to portray the gross structures, consequently the angles of dip are much higher than on the ground.

south as around the rivers Dove and Manifold, which are superimposed upon the flanks of this main anticline.

The surrounding Namurian rocks are generally folded on predominant north-south axes, an outstanding example being the Goyt Trough or Syncline to the west of Buxton which can be traced for many kilometres. In the north, around the Kinder Scout plateau, the stratal dips are low and the folding is very broad.

Faults are very variable in direction but the more powerful ones are usually on north-south lines. In the limestone area many of the faults give evidence of a tear component, and many such faults have later served as conduits for hydrothermal solutions. The old idea of mineral deposits such as those of galena (PbS), sphalerite (ZnS) and chalcopyrite ($Cu\,Fe\,S_2$) having had a magmatic source has long since been abandoned. It appears more likely that these minerals, along with the common gangue associates of calcite, fluorite and barite, were transported by brines permeating through deeply buried sediments.

The Valley of the River Wye

ITINERARY I

The Valley of the River Wye from Buxton to Miller's Dale

Aims: To examine the succession of Dinantian limestones of massif facies and contemporaneous igneous rocks; to visit a number of fossil localities and to examine some important sedimentological and structural features.

Maps & Memoirs: Ordnance Survey Sheet 119, 1:50,000 Landranger Series.
Geological Survey Sheet 111 (Buxton) 1 : 50,000.
Geological Survey SK07 (Buxton), SK17 (Miller's Dale) 1: 25,000.
Stevenson, I.P. & G. D. Gaunt, 1971, Geology of the country around Chapel-en-le-Frith. *Mem. Geol. Surv.*

Transport: This itinerary and that for Itinerary II can be followed, though rather sketchily, in one day if private transport is used. Should two days be available then the first could profitably be spent on this route described as far as Miller's Dale, the return to Buxton being made by bus. On the second day, Miller's Dale would be reached by bus from Buxton and the valley of the Wye traversed by foot from Miller's Dale to Monsal Head. It is important for users of private vehicles to note that the A6, Buxton to Bakewell, road between Buxton and Calton Hill, a distance of about 10 km is a Clearway. The following places can be used for parking, though space may be very limited during holiday periods and summer week-ends: - Buxton, public parking ground adjacent to the railway viaduct at the east end of Spring Gardens; Devonshire Arms Hotel, Ashwood Dale (permission needed); junction of Cunning Dale with A6 road, limited and unsafe if travelling westwards; foot of Topley Pike 5 km east of Buxton on the north side of the A6; viewpoint on left of A6 road at summit of Topley Pike (113275); Miller's Dale old station yard.

General Geology: What may be regarded as the type-section of the Lower Carboniferous (Dinantian) rocks in the massif facies is sporadically exposed along the valley of the River Wye and in the abandoned cuttings of the former L.M.S. railway (the tunnels are inaccessible) (Figure 3). The Wye, rising on the Namurian rocks to the southwest of Buxton, enters the western flank of a low irregular dome in the limestone at Buxton and cuts through the structure so that the section shows a duplicate, but in fact more complete succession, on the eastern side. Owing to pre-Namurian denudation of the limestone the western succession is incomplete and, because of this and gaps between exposures, is best regarded as complementary.

The total thickness of beds exposed from the base of the Namurian on the eastern side where the junction with the Dinantian is probably a conformable one, to the base of the section near Topley Pike, 5 km east of Buxton, is approximately 450 m

The Valley of the River Wye

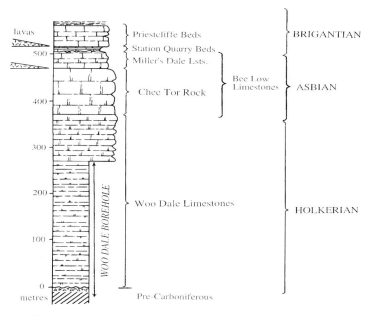

Figure 3. General succession in the Dinantian (Holkerian, Asbian & Brigantian) in the Miller's Dale area.

(Cope, 1933). To this must be added the 270 m of Dinantian limestones proved in the Woo Dale borehole to obtain a total thickness of about 700 m for the whole of the Dinantian in this part of the Peak District. All three Dinantian stages, represented by predominantly shallow water sediments, lavas and tuffs, were deposited between 350 Ma and 315 Ma ago on a fairly stable fault-bounded block of ancient rocks in warm shallow seas at about latitude 19° S.

Route: This begins in Buxton. The town is situated at more than 300 m above sea-level. At one time, and particularly during the nineteenth century, it was noted as a spa especially beneficial for the treatment of rheumatic conditions; its thermal waters which issue at a constant temperature of 38° C were recognised by the Romans as therapeutic. Buxton water is now bottled for sale throughout the country; though its purity is not doubted it is questionable whether any bottled water is any better for consumption than the average tap-water. The lower part of the town is built on Namurian shales; these were well exposed some years ago when a deep trench was excavated along the length of Spring Gardens, the main street. The higher reaches of the town are founded on the Carboniferous Limestone which is exposed in various places such as Holker Road. There, the Namurian rocks occur at a lower altitude than the older Carboniferous Limestone,

The Valley of the River Wye

not on account of the amount of dip but because the Namurian shales were deposited upon a highly eroded limestone surface (an example of an unconformity).

The valley of the River Wye changes its name several times. The part nearest to Buxton is Ashwood Dale. At the supermarket (formerly the site of the gas-works) one kilometre southeast of the railway viaduct in Spring Gardens, well-bedded light coloured limestones were formerly visible in the old railway cutting. They dip westwards at a low angle and include a thick layer of brown-weathering rock, a vesicular basaltic lava. Fossils found in the limestone about 10 m below this lava include the brachipod *Davidsonina septosa* and show that the lava is part of the Lower Miller's Dale Lava. It follows that the limestones between the supermarket and the viaduct are the Miller's Dale Limestones.

Proceeding eastwards down the valley we are moving in a direction contrary to the dip of the rocks and consequently into lower and older strata. Almost as far as the Devonshire Arms in Ashwood Dale (close to the first railway bridge over the A6 road : 082726) mural cliffs in the Chee Tor Rock, the lower member of the Bee Low Limestone, are to be seen on both sides. They are not accessible for examination except at Lover's Leap, a chasm on the south side of the road about 1 km east of the supermarket, and in a small roadside quarry a little east of that. These limestones of Lower Asbian age are called the Chee Tor Rock after the impressive bastion of Chee Tor farther down the valley. They are here over 100 m thick and consist of very pure thickly-bedded limestones (with over 98% $CaCO_3$) which have been quarried extensively particularly for use in the chemical industry.

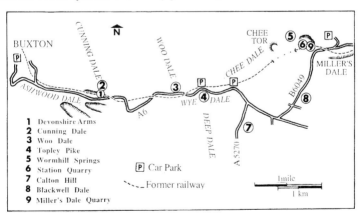

Figure 4. Sketch-map showing the localities in Itinerary I.

In the railway cutting to the north of the Devonshire Arms, most easily reached by climbing the embankment to the east of the bridge, and then crossing the latter, the base of the Chee Tor Rock can be seen (LOCALITY 1, Figure 4). It is underlain by dark coloured limestones, the Woo Dale Limestones of Holkerian (S_2) age which are seen to contain numerous large shells of the brachiopod *Daviesiella llangollensis* (Dav.) (Figure 5). The underlying limestones exposed on the south side of the road opposite the inn are crumbly brown dolomitic limestones. The brachiopod *Davidsonina carbonaria* (McCoy) has been found in these limestones just to the east of the bridge and in the adjacent Cunning Dale on the north side of the A6 road, giving evidence of the Holkerian age (S_2) of these beds.

Just beyond the bridge enter Cunning Dale on the left; a short distance ahead on

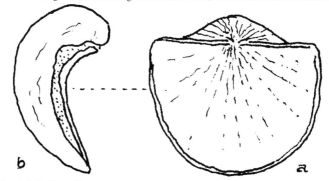

Figure 5. Daviesiella llangollensis (Dav.). A Holkerian brachiopod. a. Brachial valve and umbo of pedicle valve, b. Median section. Half natural size.

Figure 6. Plane of normal fault, Cunning Dale, Buxton. Chee Tor Rock on downthrown (left) side, Woo Dale Limestones on the upthrown side. Scale given by Figure (left).

The Valley of the River Wye

the left is a ramp road giving access to an abandoned quarry. This shows, on its eastern face (LOCALITY 2), an excellent exposure of a fault plane (Figure 6). The fault throws down to the west so that the Chee Tor Rock on the west abuts against Woo Dale Limestones on the east. This fault, a component of a fault complex, can be traced for several kilometres. It passes through Pig Tor, a wooded limestone eminence a little farther down the valley.

As far as, and indeed just beyond the next railway bridge across the road, scattered exposures of the Woo Dale Limestones, including many dolomitized beds, indicate that the gentle westerly dip experienced so far is continuing. A little to the east of that railway bridge the lowest beds seen in the section are exposed around the entrance to Woo Dale, which joins Wye Dale from the north. Beyond this point a gentle easterly dip sets in. The small building near the bridge over the river (LOCALITY 3) houses a pump for lifting water from the Woo Dale borehole. This borehole was put down in 1948 by Imperial Chemical Industries Limited as a site chosen by the writer for purely scientific purposes. The borehole went to a depth of 270.5 m through Viséan Limestones, most of them intensely dolomitized. These rested upon a thin basal breccia grading down into purplish-brown and green altered volcanic rocks with highly inclined partings. Unfortunately, the altered volcanic rocks have not proved very favourable for age determination, partly on account of argon loss. The maximum age so far proved is 382 Ma (Cope, 1979) which indicates Devonian or older. It seems quite possible that the volcanic rocks could be Ordovician or even of Precambrian age. However, the important fact provided by this borehole is that an ancient land mass was not inundated by a Lower Carboniferous sea until Holkerian times.

Proceed to the foot of Topley Pike just beyond the next railway bridge (103725). There is a good parking ground on the left of the A6 road with an entrance immediately opposite Deep Dale. Walk a few metres into Deep Dale on the south side of the main road. Woo Dale Limestones exposed on the right side of the main road ahead will be seen behind a clump of trees on the left (LOCALITY 4), and a few metres farther south in the cliff they are seen to be cut off by a fault throwing down to the south and bringing the Chee Tor Rock down to dale level. The fault shows some mineralization, mainly calcite.

A considerable thickness of Woo Dale Limestones, though becoming much overgrown is exposed on the south wide of the A6 road to the east of this point, but close examination is not recommended here on account of the traffic conditions.

It will now be necessary to decide upon the route to be taken for Miller's Dale:-

(a) From the eastern end of the car park take the well pronounced path leading alongside the Wye, across the entrance to Great Rocks Dale into Chee Dale and down to the impressive Chee Tor (124734), the type-locality for the Chee Tor

Rock. The most striking thing about the Chee Tor Rock is that it is extremely thickly bedded or even massive. Some of the bedding planes are accentuated by the presence of clay partings; these are more readily visible in freshly cut quarry faces than in natural outcrops where they tend to be squeezed or washed out. The clay bands are very variable in thickness, 20 mm being an average figure. When fresh the clays are blue-grey in colour and carry some finely disseminated iron pyrites, but weathering reduces them to a greyish-brown colour. The clays are decomposed volcanic ashes probably originating from dust clouds formed outside the area. The dust fell into the sea and for the time-being at least, limestone deposition ceased. Walkden (1972) regards some of these clay partings (wayboards) as having been raised above sea-level where, for a considerable time, they formed palaeosols.

The walking distance from the Topley Pike car park to Miller's Dale is about 4 km and a little over an hour should be allowed for this. After 3 km Wormhill Springs will be passed on the left. These originate at the junction of the Miller's Dale Limestones with the underlying Miller's Dale Lower Lava which behaves as an impervious body (LOCALITY 5). The same lava, affected by faulting, will be seen where the footpath ascends to the level of the former railway (131734). Enter Miller's Dale Station Quarry (LOCALITY 6) on the left and refer to the description at the end of the alternative route (b).

(b) Follow the A6 road eastwards, climbing the whole time. Pull into the small lay-by on the left near the top of the hill (113725). This is excavated out of basal Chee Tor Rock (Bee Low Limestones) which succeed the Woo Dale Limestones visible when ascending the road. There is a splendid view looking northwards across the Wye from this point, covering the confluence of Great Rocks Dale with Chee Dale. Immediately to the east of the confluence is the old East Buxton Quarry showing a section of Woo Dale Limestones with the basal part of the Chee Tor Rock just visible at the summit of the hill. The limestones in the higher part of the quarry face are relatively light coloured and are calcite-mudstones or calcilutites. The right bank (western side) of Great Rocks Dale is marked by the now abandoned Tunstead Quarry which once held the record for the longest limestone quarry face in Europe. Over a period of 60 years or so many millions of tons of high grade limestone were removed from this quarry.

Not far from the lay-by is the well known Calton Hill Quarry (119713) long since abandoned. It was designated as a SSSI by English Nature. Prior permission to visit this quarry must be obtained from the owners, Derbyshire County Council via the County Planning Officer, County Offices, Matlock, Derbyshire DE4 3AG. Just ahead of the lay-by on the right of the A6 road, take the A5270 signposted 'Brierlow Bar'. After about 600 m parking is available near the sharp bend on the left. The exposure (LOCALITY 7) is poor and limited as compared with the

situation when the quarry was working in the 1920's and a little later. The geology
of Calton Hill was well described by Tomkeieff (1928) and more recently by Miller
(1988) who, however, was not able to observe many of the outcrops available to
the first author. There seemed to have been two phases of igneous activity at
Calton Hill, first the eruption of basaltic lavas with tuffs and agglomerates. Any
possible relationship with the Miller's Dale Lower Lava is uncertain but the
activity was certainly within Asbian times. This was followed by an intrusion of
basanitic magma, seen on the south side of the pond. The basanite (an olivine-
bearing basic rock containing feldspathoids) is remarkable for the occurrence of
small nodules of ultrabasic rock which may be fragments from the outermost part
of the Mantle. At one time small geodes filled with amethyst crystals were quite
common in the lava but the writer has not seen one for many years.

Regain the A6 and after 1 km take the B6049, signposted 'Sheffield' on the left.
The road junction is on Miller's Dale Limestones and to the south the rising ground
includes the Upper Miller's Dale Lava capped by the Priestcliffe Limestones on the
eastern limb of the Priestcliffe Anticline. Descend Blackwell Dale. Just beyond
minor cross-roads an inlier of the Lower Miller's Dale Lava is visible on both sides
of the road (LOCALITY 8). With a low northerly dip the lava passes below
road-level just south of where the road was obviously cut through a cave. A low
northerly dip is observable in the Miller's Dale Limestones and a small patch-reef
in these limestones was formerly visible (Cope, 1972). Where the road bends
sharply to the right, on the right-hand side, is a mineral vein coinciding with a
northerly-throwing fault. On the downthrown side of this fault are dark grey to
black thinly-bedded limestones with abundant *Lithostrotion junceum.* These are
the Station Quarry Beds of Brigantian (D_2) age which lie immediately below the

*Figure 7. Formerly exposed section across a channel or pit in the Miller's Dale Limestones,
old Miller's Dale station yard, north side. Scale given by 40cm hammer.*

The Valley of the River Wye

Upper Miller's Dale Lava. The position of the lava, Station Quarry Beds and Miller's Dale Limestones can also be seen in the large disused quarry across the valley of the Wye to the north. There the lava forms an outlier culminating in the prominent Knot Low. Descend the hill and cross the Wye by the minor road to the left.

Proceed to the former railway goods yard, now a car park, at the site of the former Miller's Dale Station. Formerly, the tree-covered cliff on the north side of the car park showed an excellent section of dark coloured Station Quarry Beds resting upon an irregular surface of Miller's Dale Limestones (Figure 7). This includes a section across the deep pit or channel in the lower limestones displaying a large waterworn boulder (Cope, 1972). Walk westwards along the footpath and after about 300 m veer up the slope into the abandoned Miller's Dale Quarry (LOCALITY 6 and 9;136734). The junction between the Miller's Dale Limestones and the overlying Station Quarry Beds may be examined here. The base of the lava is not as readily discernible as it was some years ago when the precise thickness of the Station Quarry Beds was established as 7.6 m.

On palaeontological grounds the junction between the Asbian Stage and the younger Brigantian Stage is taken at the base of the Station Quarry Beds.

ITINERARY II

Miller's Dale to Monsal Head

Aims: to continue the examination of the succession of Asbian and Brigantian limestones and contemporaneous lavas and tuffs noting, in one place, the actual dying out of a lava flow; to visit several fossil localities and to examine a typical Brigantian coral band.

Maps and Memoirs: Ordnance Survey Sheet 119, 1: 50,000 Landranger Series.
Geological Survey Sheet 111 (Buxton), 1: 50,000.
Geological Survey SK 17SW (Miller's Dale), 1: 25,000.
Stevenson, I.P. & G.D. Gaunt, 1971. Geology of the Country around Chapel-en-le-Frith. *Mem. Geol. Surv.*

Transport: This itinerary involves walking from the car park at the former Miller's Dale station or from the bus stop in the valley below, a total distance of about 6 km. There is very limited parking for vehicles at the confluence of Tideswell Dale with Miller's Dale (152732) and vehicles cannot be taken beyond this into the hamlet of Litton Mill. There is parking space in Tideswell Dale approached only from the Miller's Dale-Tideswell road, where there is also a public convenience.

Miller's Dale to Monsal Head

General Geology: From Miller's Dale the gentle easterly dip continues on what can be regarded as the eastern limb of the main anticline. Beds above the Upper Miller's Dale Lava known as the Monsal Dale Limestones having a total thickness of about 200 m are exposed on both sides of the valley of the Wye and its tributaries as well as in the now rather overgrown cuttings of the former main-line railway. They are mainly grey to dark grey limestones, often with lenticular or nodular chert, occasional bands with a profusion of giganteid productids and occasional rather spectacular beds made up of compressed and waterworn large productid valves. The Monsal Dale Limestones which are of Brigantian (D_2) age are succeeded by the Eyam Beds, a series of limestones with an upwardly-increasing shale component and in some areas with a development of reefs at the base; these beds carry a P_2 fauna including the goniatite *Goniatites granosus* indicating a bathymetric change in conditions of deposition. These beds are exposed in the Headstone Cutting to the east of Monsal Head which, unfortunately, is no longer accessible. The Eyam Beds, the base of which probably lies within the Headstone Tunnel, are succeeded by 20-30 m of mainly Lower Carboniferous shales (the Longstone Mudstones) but carrying a basal Namurian goniatite *Cravenoceras leion* Bisat. They are present in the old railway

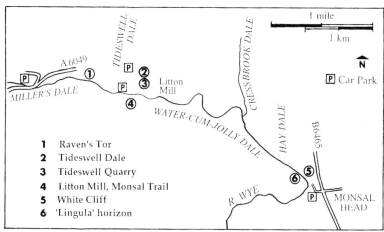

Figure 8. Sketch-map showing the localities in Itinerary II.

cutting due north of the Home Farm of Thornbridge Hall (Little Longstone; 197712); it would seem that on the eastern side of the Peak District sedimentation was continuous from the Dinantian to the Namurian, depicting rather different conditions from those which operated in the west.

Miller's Dale to Monsal Head

Route: Walk eastwards from the bridge in Miller's Dale and just beyond the railway viaduct fork right to Litton Mill (Figure 8). Passing the Angler's Rest Hotel the valley side first shows outcrops of Miller's Dale Limestone. The Lower Miller's Dale Lava then appears in a long narrow inlier and a good section of the

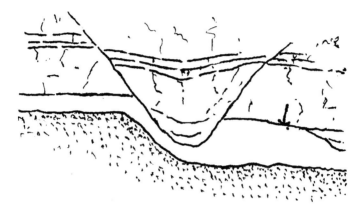

Figure 9. Solution hollow between Miller's Dale Limestones above and Lower Miller's Dale Lava below. Ravenstor. Scale given by 40cm hammer (right).

lava can be seen at the foot of Ravenstor (157732) where a shallow cave has been eroded at the lava-limestone junction (LOCALITY 1 and Figure 9). The lava is a blue grey amygdaloidal basalt representing a gaseous extrusion. It may have been erupted on the sea-floor (Cope, 1997) though this is difficult to prove. Some years ago at Ravenstor the lava was seen to incorporate some well preserved specimens of an orthocone nautiloid.

Whilst walking down the valley observe the hillside to the south of the river. In the lower part some 15 metres above the line of the old railway is the outcrop of the Upper Miller's Dale Lava dipping gently eastwards. The large abandoned quarry at the Miller's Dale end is in thickly bedded whitish limestones, the Priestcliffe Beds (Cope, 1933) about 36 m in thickness, succeeded by dark grey limestones and chert with a Brigantian fauna, including such typical species as *Pugilis pugilis*. A small quarry at 133734 formerly showed the base of the lava resting upon 7.6 m of Station Quarry Beds some of which showed a profusion of the eye-visible foraminiferid *Saccaminopsis* sp. but, unfortunately, this is now no longer accessible owing to the uncontrolled growth of willows.

From Ravenstor to the first house in Litton Mill the roadside exposures are now in Miller's Dale Limestones.

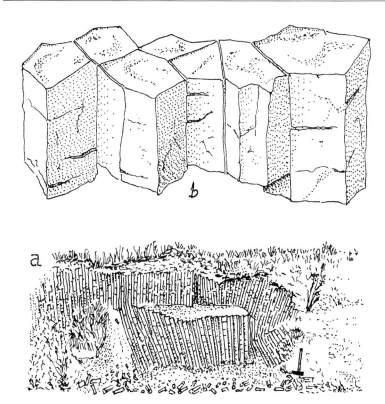

Figure 10. Clay made columnar through contact metamorphism by an overlying lava flow, south end of Tideswell Dale,. a. Temporary section (hammer for scale), b. Close-up of some columns.

If time permits, make a short deviation up Tideswell Dale on foot and enter the old quarry on the east (LOCALITY 2; 153734). This shows not only the Upper Lava but also a dolerite intrusion which has converted the limestone on the quarry floor into marble. If weathering and recent erosion have been suitable a volcanic tuff at the southern limit of the quarry (LOCALITY 3) will be seen to have a prismatic structure (Arnold-Bemrose, 1899 and Figure 10).

From Miller's Dale to the south side of the Wye Valley opposite Tideswell Dale the Upper Miller's Dale Lava appears to maintain a constant thickness of about 30 m, but in an old railway cutting at 152731 south of the Wye the lava is seen to be dying out rapidly eastwards (Figure 11) (LOCALITY 4). Access to the old cutting, now part of the Monsal Dale Trail, is by a path almost opposite the small provision shop in the hamlet of Litton Mill, across the river by the footbridge and then

Miller's Dale to Monsal Head

westwards along the south bank of the river, climbing a rough path to the level of the old rail track and then continuing westwards to the end of the deep cutting. A better exposure of the lava is on the south face of the cutting (153730). At Miller's Dale Station, where the lava is slightly over 30 m thick, the overlying beds are massive white limestones succeeded by dark coloured limestones with chert. Where the lava is seen to die out in the cutting and, on the north side of the Wye at Hammerton Hill, the eroded lava front is succeeded by thinly-bedded dark

E   W

Figure 11. Nose of the Upper Lava flow at Litton Mill, Miller's Dale. Spade (bottom right for scale).

coloured limestones with chert. The latter misled early workers, such as Arnold-Bemrose (1907) and Sibly (1908), who concluded that the dark limestones above the Priestcliffe Beds at Miller's Dale had been brought down by a 60 m - throw fault to abut against the lava in the cutting. This was re-interpreted by Cope (1933) with the elimination of the proposed fault.

Return to the road in Litton Mill, turn right and continue through the mill gates at Litton Mill. Follow the well-marked footpath through Water-cum-Jolly Dale. Having just cleared the buildings there is an indifferent exposure of the Lower Lava at water-level in the mill-leat on the left. The cliffs along the dale are in Miller's Dale Limestone and they border deeply incised meanders which may be connected with the sudden change in direction of the Wye at Monsal Head.

Proceed to Cressbrook Mill (disused) and join the road. Cressbrook Dale entering from the left gives a good section of the succession above the Upper Lava. There is a poor exposure of this lava at the confluence of the dales, and this has given rise to a difference of opinion. The British Geological Survey (1985) and Butcher & Ford (1973) have expressed the view that this lava rests directly upon light coloured Miller's Dale Limestone, whilst Walkden (1972) thought that this lava was not the Upper Lava at all. The writer holds strongly that the Cressbrook Dale Lava is a tongue of the Upper Miller's Dale Lava and that it rests upon the Station Quarry Beds for, up to the end of World War II, at least 1 m of black limestones were exposed beneath the lava on the left bank of Cressbrook Dale, and more were exposed in the side of the road opposite the Cressbrook Mill Gates.

The Monsal Dale Limestones show considerable lateral variation not only in the thickness of specific parts of the sequence but also in the lithology and fossil content. For example, the thickly bedded, almost white, Priestcliffe Beds, which succeed the Upper Lava around Miller's Dale and around Taddington, further to the south, pass into more thinly bedded generally darker limestones with chert as they are traced eastwards. Fortunately, there are several marker beds which can be traced over short distances and are useful for local correlation. The main markers are coral bands, the most important of which in stratigraphical order are the following:

> The White Cliff Coral Band
>
> The Hob's House Coral Band
>
> The Upperdale Coral Band

None of these bands can be identified in the north part of the Dinantian limestone country although certain faunal components of the bands, such as *Lonsdaleia floriformis* and *L. duplicata,* occur sporadically.

About 42 m above the Miller's Dale Limestone is the Upperdale Coral Band; it shows about 1 m of massive limestone with silicified *Lithostrotion junceum, L. martini* and *Diphyphyllum lateseptatum.* It is well seen at the site of the former Monsal Dale station (177720), at the base of the dark limestones above the Priestcliffe Beds at Miller's Dale Quarry, and just below the lip of the lowest scarp in Hay Dale (178722).

The Hob's House Coral Band is indifferently exposed just above a landslipped area on the slope immediately south of the former Monsal Dale station. The best exposures of this band will be seen at the slipped limestone stacks of Hob's House included in Itinerary III (Page 24).

The best exposure of the White Cliff Coral Band is at the type locality to the north of the old Monsal Dale station (LOCALITY 5). It is rather inaccessible, but it seems to be over 1 m thick with *Lithostrotion* spp below and clisiophyllid corals above; these corals are obviously in the growth position but the prostrate attitude of many of them suggests that water currents had influenced growth.

There was formerly an excellent exposure of the White Cliff Coral Band in a small quarry 140 m WSW of the Crosdale Head Mine on the west side of Castlegate Lane, Great Longstone but, unfortunately, this has now been removed by quarrying.

Crossing Monsal Dale near the old station is one of the master mineral veins of the district, the Putwell Hill Vein. In the past it was worked for galena, but more recently it has produced spar (calcite) though operations have now ceased.

The exposures in the cuttings along the old main-line railway have deteriorated considerably largely due to uncontrolled tree growth since the line was closed.

Scattered exposures near the site of the Old Monsal Dale Station show slump structures in some of the limestones, supporting the idea of an easterly palaeoslope. Some dark limestones contain a very small *Lingula* sp; the most reliable exposure for these is on the roadside (183717) below White Cliff (LOCALITY 6).

In the northern part of Cressbrook Dale a thick volcanic tuff, the Litton Tuff occurs 20-47 m above the Cressbrook Lava. It crops out over a wide area to the west of Longstone Edge and extends to Litton, but it dies out on Hay Top near Cressbrook and so cannot be identified in the Wye Valley section.

ITINERARY III

Monsal Dale and Ashford-in-the-Water

Aims: To view the remarkable change in the direction of the River Wye adjacent to Monsal Head, to study a well developed coral band at Hob's House, two thin lava flows with a doleritic intrusion, and to examine the occurrence of the Ashford Black Marble.

Maps & Memoirs: Ordnance Sheet 119 , 1: 50,000.
Geological Survey Sheet 110 (Buxton), 1: 50,000.
Aitkenhead, N., J. I. Chisholm & I. P. Stevenson, 1985. Geology of the country

Monsal Dale and Ashford-in-the-Water

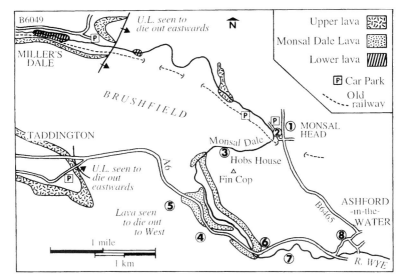

Figure 12. Sketch-map showing the localities in Itinerary III and lava outcrops.

around Buxton, Leek and Bakewell. *Mem. Geol. Surv.*

Transport: The itinerary begins at the Monsal Head Hotel, Little Longstone, which is easily accessible from Buxton, Matlock or Sheffield. There is a good car park adjacent to the hotel overlooking Monsal Dale well occupied during week-ends and at any time during the summer months. There is a private parking ground behind the hotel. Note: there is no through road from Monsal Head westwards up the valley of the Wye though vehicles can be taken as far as Cressbrook or through Hay Dale. There is a car park close to the foot of Hay Dale (177723).

Route: The view from the Monsal Head car park is one of the most entrancing in the whole of the Peak District (LOCALITY 1). In the distance upstream, with trees around the river, is Upperdale and Water-cum-Jolly Dale where the Wye flows in deeply entrenched meanders, Over to the right is the impressive White Cliff whilst, to the left in the middle distance is a linear scar up the hillside marking the worked outcrop of the Putwell Hill Vein which was originally worked for galena. To the left downstream the river makes a remarkable change in its direction. For more than 15 km the River Wye has followed a general easterly course, apart from some deviation around Chee Tor. From the confluence of Cressbrook Dale with the River Wye, the latter flows in a southeasterly direction as far as Monsal Head where it swings through more than 90° to flow in a southwesterly direction as far as the entry of Taddington Dale, whence it resumes its general easterly direction of flow. This sudden change of direction of the River Wye has never been satisfactorily explained. It may well date back to a Triassic erosion surface when resistant scarps of Namurian sandstone extended farther west than they do today.

Monsal Dale is that part of the River Wye extending from Cressbrook Mill to Ashford-in-the-Water. To gain access to the lower part of Monsal Dale proceed from the Monsal Head Hotel in a southerly direction to the top of the steep unfenced road descending into the valley. On the right at the top of the hill (LOCALITY 2) are massive limestones with chert and occasional corals including *Lonsdaeia floriformis* (please do not hammer these). Pass through the narrow stile on the opposite side of the road and follow the footpath along the steep hillside on the left bank of the Wye. The scattered exposures of dark limestone with chert are in the upper part of the Brigantian Stage (D_2); they dip eastwards at a low angle.

The path passes high above the western portal of the Headstone Tunnel. About 1 km WSW of the hotel the limestone stacks of Hob's House (LOCALITY 3) are reached. These are landslipped stacks of dark limestone with chert. The bedding is conspicuous, the average thickness of the beds being just under a metre. Here, the Hob's House Coral Band is clearly visible in the lower part of several stacks. The coral band is about a metre thick; the lower part is made up of colonies of species of *Lithostrotion* especially *L. junceum* together with *Syringopora* sp. The upper part of the band is crowded with large simple corals, mainly dibunophyllids and many of these lie in a prostrate position as through they had been broken by wave or current action. Closer examination, however, show that the corals actually grew recumbently; this may have been a reflection of the direction of currents and food supply.

The corals of the Hob's House band were originally secreted as calcium carbonate ($CaCO_3$) but they are now made of silica (SiO_2). The precise cause and date of the transformation is not known, but it is likely to have been shortly after deposition of the limestone and contemporary with the formation of the chert nodules and bands.

Arnold-Bemrose (1907) observed, in the valley below Hob's House, two lava flows, each about 10 m thick and separated by about 50 m of limestone. He did consider that they might be eastern extensions of the Lower and Upper Miller's Dale lavas, but abandoned this view because the upper of the two lavas was succeeded by limestones with chert rather than by the light coloured chert-free Priestcliffe Beds of Miller's Dale. It has been seen that that the Miller's Dale Upper Lava dies out eastwards along a line about 3 km east of Miller's Dale. However, it has been seen too that the lava near Cressbrook Mill may represent an easterly extension of the Upper Lava. The lavas in Monsal Dale noted by Arnold-Bemrose are now poorly exposed, His general section might suggest another easterly extending tongue of Upper Lava under Brushfield, the piece of relatively high ground between Taddington and Monsal Head. This indeed has been postulated by Butcher & Ford (1973). Flow-fronts of this lava are seen at

Monsal Dale and Ashford-in-the-Water

LOCALITY 5 in Great Shacklow Wood facing westwards and at LOCALITY 4 (168705) between Taddington Dale and Dimmins Dale. Father south at New Bridge (LOCALITY 6) a dolerite sill is closely associated with the lava. There is an excellent section of the intrusion on the left bank of the river and on the roadside at New Bridge Corner (180698) where about 6 m of hard compact ophitic olivine dolerite showing spheroidal weathering can be examined. This exposure is now partly obscured by a fence and vegetation. However, the true horizons of the two Monsal Dale lava flows remain problematical. The British Geological Survey concluded that the upper lava below Fin Cop is not to be correlated with the Upper Miller's Dale Lava because the limestone separating it from the lower flow yields Brigantian fossils (Aitkenhead, N. *et al*, 1985).

The Hob's House Coral Band can be traced along the western side of Fin Cop and is also seen on the right bank of the Wye in the northwestern part of Great Shacklow Wood (LOCALITY 7) at (172702) and at the foot of Nettler Dale (184696).

Beyond New Bridge the Wye resumes its normal easterly direction of flow which roughly coincides with the direction of dip of the limestones.

Proceed downstream to the western edge of Ashford-in-the-Water, well known geologically for the Ashford Black Marble of Brigantian age. This is not a true marble because it has not been produced by thermal metamorphism of limestone. It is a dark grey to black fine grained limestone containing a considerable amount of argillaceous carbonaceous material, which takes a high polish. When polished the rock appears to be almost black with light flecks produced by comminuted crinoid and shell debris. The Ashford Black Marble occurs in well defined beds generally about 0.5 m thick, and it was exploited mainly by shallow mining to the immediate west of Ashford. The marble has worked in the Rookery Mine (190696) to the north of the River Wye, and south of the river at the hill called The Arrock (192694), as well as in Kirk Dale (184688) and Nettler Dale (180694; 177693) where old quarries and mines can still be entered. The marble was worked around Kirk Dale certainly as early as the 16th Century. During Victorian times in particular the marble was used for table tops, washstand tops, clock cases and jewellery and it was employed in churches for floors and statuary pieces. Several good examples may be seen in Ashford Church. The marble was frequently inlaid with other Peak District limestones, often fossiliferous ones, and minerals such as Blue John; this gave rise to an industry which flourished almost to the outbreak of World War I.

If you wish to investigate a little bit of industrial archaeology and see what old lead mine surface buildings look like, make a small detour from Ashford southwards up Kirkdale to the Magpie Mine, south of Sheldon (Figure 13; 173682).

The village of Ashford-in-the-Water lies adjacent to the A6 road and there are frequent bus services to Buxton, Bakewell and Chesterfield.

Figure 13. The Magpie Mine surface buildings, Sheldon.

ITINERARY IV

Castleton and Mam Tor

Aims: To study the relationship between the Dinantian limestones and the succeeding Namurian sediments and to examine the different facies of the Dinantian Stage with particular reference to their included fossils.

Visitors wishing for a more detailed account of the geology, cave systems and mineral deposits should consult the companion G.A. Guide No. 56, Ford, T.D. 1996, *The Castleton Area, Derbyshire.*

Maps & Memoirs: Ordnance Survey Sheet 110, 1: 50,000, Landranger Series. Geological Survey Sheet 99 (Chapel-en-le-Frith), 1: 50,000. Geological Survey SK 18 (Castleton), 1: 25,000. Stevenson, I.P. & G.D. Gaunt. 1971. Geology of the country around Chapel-en-le-Frith. *Mem. Geol. Surv.*

Transport: There are several small car parks in the Castleton area but space is at a premium owing to the popularity of the district. There is a good parking area on part of the abandoned A625 road, now a cul-de-sac, on the edge of the Mam Tor landslip and that has a metalled turning circle for vehicles (132835). It is recommended that vehicles are parked here whilst the itinerary is covered entirely on foot. the total distance is about 12 km.

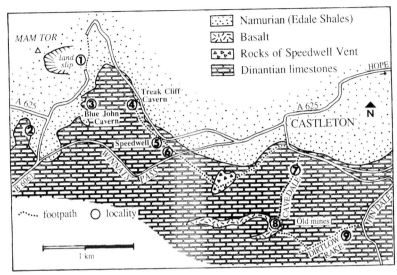

Figure 14. Geological sketch-map of the Castleton area showing localities in Itinerary IV.

Route: The easterly facing landslip of Mam Tor the 'Shivering Mountain'

Figure 15. The landslip scar of Mam Tor viewed from the south.

(LOCALITY 1, Figure 14 and Figure 15) lies close to the car park. Landslipping has occurred here for centuries and is still active, witness the damage caused to the former A625 main road which, after years of expensive maintenance, had to be closed in 1977. The instability is due to the pervious Mam Tor Sandstone of which at least 100 m thickness can be seen in the upper part of the scar where it rests upon the friable and easily lubricated Edale Shales. Slipping is caused in part by springs issuing from the base of the sandstone.

In the valley bottom, beyond the mounds of landslipped material, goniatites have shown that the lowest horizon in the Edale Shales is E_2 whilst the overlying Mam Tor Sandstone is in subzone R_1. The Castleton borehole close by showed basal Namurian in E_1 resting upon Dinantian shales of P_2 age. This demonstrates the extent of the Dinantian / Namurian unconformity in the area between Mam Tor and the Blue John Cavern to the south. There are several marine bands exposed in the Edale Shales of Mam Tor; they are difficult of access but flint-hard bullions, sometimes with solid goniatites, can be found in the talus covering the lower part of the scar.

Proceed to Windy Knoll Quarry in the angle between the Sparrowpit road and the A625 road along Rushup Edge (LOCALITY 2) (126830). This is a very old quarry and possibly the site of a sink-hole. It shows several metres of pale grey limestone with sparse fossils but including *Davidsonina septosa* and, rather surprisingly, the coral *Palaeosmilia murchisoni*, both indicative of an Asbian (D₁) age. Some distance away the crudely-bedded reef limestones show dips of the order of 20°. The Asbian limestones show several Neptunean dykes containing blocks of a dark limestone similar to the Eyam limestones which are not now present in the immediate area, together with breccia and oil-impregnated shale. The whole is covered unconformably by Edale Shales and, at the junction and extending down into the dykes, is a viscous sticky hydrocarbon mixture called elaterite. This is possibly the residue of an oil accumulation trapped beneath the Edale Shales. The latter appear to be of E_2 age at this point.

Cross the main road and proceed to the Blue John Cavern which is readily seen. The cavern is open to the public and is well worth a visit. Follow the footpath leading eastwards from the cavern and pass through a stile in the wall. Leave the path and follow the contour along the left side of the gully in front of the crags (LOCALITY 3; 133835). These crags are in highly fossiliferous fore-reef limestones; they yield a variety of brachiopods, pelecypods, gastropods, bryozoa and occasional trilobite fragments . Lower down the slope the limestone contain fossils which show a partial infilling with lime sediment, the rest of the void being occupied by coarser calcite deposited at a later date. They act as natural spirit-levels, for the junction between the sediment below and the calcite above indicates the plane of the horizontal at the time of burial (Broadhurst & Simpson, 1967). These observations show that the present dip of the fore-reef limestones is largely primary so that the sediments must have accumulated on a sloping surface having a gradient as high as 1 in 2.

Regain the footpath and walk to Treak Cliff Cavern (LOCALITY 4). This cavern is open to the public and has considerable geological interest. The outer part of the entrance roadway to the cavern is lined because it has been cut through a spectacular conglomerate at the local markedly discordant base of Edale Shales. This consists of large blocks of limestone in a shale matrix (Simpson & Broadhurst, 1969). Inside the entrance, stairs and a footway lead to what is called the "old series" of caverns. These expose the boulder bed of limestone in a shale matrix. Blue John, a striped purplish-blue variety of fluorite (CaF_2) is exposed and, further in, veins of the mineral are seen cutting the limestone beneath the boulder bed.

Continue down the path to the car park on the south side of the road and examine the richly fossiliferous limestone overlain unconformably by the Edale Shales, noticing the absence of the boulder bed. Return to the path and continue to LOCALITY 5 where there are some limestone outcrops, one of them surmounted by a bush. The boulder bed is again visible here. There are blocks of all sizes up to many metres across embedded in the shale matrix, muddy limestone and crinoid debris. The crag bearing the bush is one of the clasts within the boulder bed. Return to the footpath and continue southwards to the Speedwell Mine (LOCALITY 6). This is open to the public. Entrance is artificial; a flight of steps leads downwards to the Grand Canal, a flooded straight mine drivage about 900 m long. A boat takes visitors to a platform from which to view the so-called Bottomless Pit in a lofty cavern. Dye tests have shown that water from here reappears in the Russet Well in Castleton about 1 km away.

You are now at the foot of the spectacular Winnats Pass through which now passes a narrow road carrying the traffic previously using the old A625 road. This limestone gorge has not yet been satisfactorily explained. It has been described as a series of collapsed caverns or, more recently, as an exhumed Dinantian sea floor chasm. At the rear of the car park adjacent to the Speedwell Mine are exposures of the so-called 'Beach Beds', limestone made up of broken and abraded brachiopod valves. These 'Beach Beds' are thought to be of P_2 age, but their mode of origin is quite obscure. If time permits, a short diversion could be made into Winnats Pass to see the passage of bedded massif limestones into fossiliferous apron-reef limestones.

A short distance eastwards down the road from the Speedwell Mine is a footpath leading in a southeasterly direction. Over to the right is a marked depression in the steep slope known as Cow Low Nick which offers an excellent section across the steeply sloping apron-reef. A pocket in the limestone here, about two thirds of the way down the apron-reef has yielded solid goniatites indicating a B_2 (upper Asbian) age. The goniatites are abraded which suggests the action of currents. Follow the path until just before it veers to the northeast. At this point there is a slight eminence in the ground to the right of the path. This is the site of the Speedwell Vent (Arnold-Bemrose, 1907) (Figure 14). There is now very little surface evidence of a volcanic nature but occasional specimens of basaltic and pyroclastic material can be unearthed. More recently, it has been suggested that this is not a vent but represents material from the Cave Dale Lava to the south which spilled down the steep submarine slope formed by the accumulating apron-reef (Broadhurst & Simpson, 1973). The lava appears to be on the same horizon as the Lower Miller's Dale Lava, 19 km further south (see Itinerary I).

Continue into Castleton. On the southern edge of the village at the foot of a vertical cliff is Peak Cavern noteworthy because the entrance, 20 m high and 33 m wide, is the largest cavern entrance in Britain. Close by is the entrance to Cave Dale, below and immediately to the east of Peveril Castle (LOCALITY 7). Below the castle pale coloured limestones are seen to be poorly bedded with a high dip of 25-30° towards Castleton. These rocks belong to the fore-reef which has shown high dips throughout the area. The fore-reef limestones on the eastern side of the dale are highly fossiliferous, the brachiopod *Pungnax pugnus* being especially abundant. Proceed up the dale to a point where it narrows and the path is confined by limestone crags on each side. A fault crosses the dale here and the fault rock accompanied by mineralization can be examined on both sides of the dale. Further up the dale beyond a stile the bed of the dale becomes level and outcrops of an amydaloidal lava (the Cave Dale Lava) can be studied. Columnar joining of the basalt can be examined but this should not be hammered as it provides such a splendid example (LOCALITY 8). From the lava outcrop climb the south side of the dale and proceed southeastwards until the old workings along the Dirtlow Rake are reached. The openworks should be followed in a northeasterly direction. Specimens of fluorite, barite (barytes) and calcite can be collected. On meeting the road which runs parallel to Pin Dale on its northern side note the large masses of silicified limestone adjacent to the road. These are probably from a wall of the rake (LOCALITY 9) and observe the limestones in the in the old quarry on the south side of Pin Dale. There the limestone is well bedded and almost horizontal and clearly belongs to the massif or shelf facies. To the left, the beds are seen to bend over and dip sharply towards Hope as the reef limestones are approached.

The return can be made via Castleton, noting the sparse exposures of dark coloured basin limestones on the roadside just beyond the village. The Mam Tor car park is now ahead.

ITINERARY V

Glutton Dale, Parkhouse Hill, Dowel Dale and Chrome Hill

Aims: To examine exposures of the reef facies of the Dinantian noting the passage of standard or massif bedded limestones of Asbian (D_1) age into unbedded

Glutton Dale, Parkhouse Hill, Dowel Dale and Chrome Hill

fossiliferous reef limestones of B_2 age, and study an exhumed Namurian topography.

Maps & Memoirs: Ordnance Survey Sheet 119, 1: 50,000, Landranger Series.
Geological Survey Sheet 110 (Buxton), 1: 50,000.
Aitkenhead, N. & J.I. Chisholm. 1985. Geology of the Country around Buxton, Leek and Bakewell. *Mem. Geol. Surv.*

Transport: From Buxton the outward journey could be started by bus to Brierlow Bar on the Ashbourne road (A515) or to Earlsterndale. In the latter case the bus should be left near Jericho Farm on the B5053, just before Earlsterndale is reached. The total walking distance is 16-20 km involving a good deal of rugged country. Note: the itinerary outlined below can not be followed in full if private transport is used, but the more essential part can be undertaken. There is limited parking space in the roadside quarry at Jericho cross-roads and, for a very brief stop, in Glutton Dale just before the road bridge over the River Dove is reached (084666).

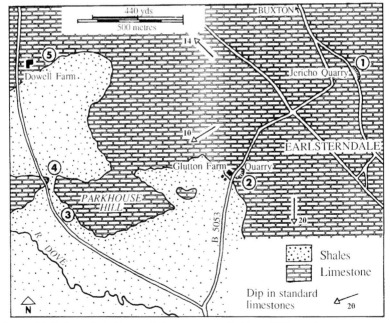

Figure 16. Geological sketch-map of the area around Parkhouse Hill, near Earlsterndale, showing localities in Itinerary V.

Glutton Dale, Parkhouse Hill, Dowel Dale and Chrome Hill

Route: The Journey from Buxton to Brierlow Bar is entirely over gently dipping Asbian (D_1) limestones; these are mainly in the Chee Tor Rock, the lower member of the Bee Low Limestones, and just below the Lower Lava Flow horizon. On the outskirts of Buxton detached outcrops of the lava at Staden Low to the north of the A515 road and at Fox Low to the south have been correlated with the Lower Miller's Dale Lava by the finding of a *Davidsonina septosa* Band in the limestones a short distance below them.

At Brierlow Bar turn right along the road towards Earlsterndale and Longnor. Climb the hill past limestone quarries on the left and note the poorly fossiliferous

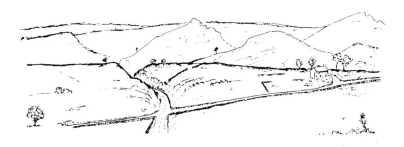

Figure 17. View from Jericho Quarry looking westwards over Glutton Dale.

pale grey limestones exposed as narrow gently dipping outcrops especially on the left . These limestones dip towards the west at a low angle to pass beneath the Namurian rocks which can be seen in the distance as you look west.

At the road bifurcation at Jericho Farm take the minor road to the left leading to Earlsterndale. Jericho Quarry (disused) lies on the left (LOCALITY 1 and Figure 16), a few metres beyond the junction. This quarry affords an indifferent exposure of the *Davidsonina septosa* Band, the best place for seeing it being just above the quarry floor at the northern end. Evidence of turbulent conditions at the time of deposition is provided by a few compound coral coralla which are in an inverted position. This quarry is important because it provides evidence of the Asbian age of the massif limestones. Visitors are asked not to remove any specimens from the quarry face.

There is a splendid view looking to the west from Jericho Quarry with the sharp wave-like Parkhouse Hill on the left and the more distant Chrome Hill over to the right, a view which justifies the name 'Peak District' for this particular area (Figure 17).

Glutton Dale, Parkhouse Hill, Dowel Dale and Chrome Hill

The limestones at Jericho Cross-roads dip westwards at about 15°. Descend to Glutton Dale either via the village of Earlsterndale where refreshments may be had at the Quiet Women, or by descending the field by the old limekiln. The head of Glutton Dale is at the cross-roads; in the corner, which is on the northwest flank of Hitter Hill, well bedded light grey limestones are well exposed. These yield a sparse Asbian fauna of productids and spiriferids, the latter not at all common in the massif facies at this horizon and here suggesting an approach to the reef to the west. Continuing southwestwards down the dale it is noticeable that the limestone still shows bedding at the point where the road exhibits a sharp increase in gradient. A little father down the dale the bedding planes disappear rather abruptly and the limestone merges into an almost non-bedded reef limestone. This is well exposed in a small disused quarry on the left of the road (LOCALITY 2) at the bottom of the dale. It was here that Wolfenden (1958) found a discrete algal zone in the reef. An interesting fauna is present in this quarry; there are solid goniatites of P_2 age along with the Asbian (D_1) coral *Palaeosmilia murchisoni*. Without doubt, this Glutton Dale section, discontinuous though it is, demonstrates the lateral passage of normal bedded massif limestones in to virtually non-bedded reef limestones, and the transition takes place over such a short distance.

Descend to the vicinity of Glutton Grange Farm on the right. If the ascent of Parkhouse Hill is contemplated, permission should be sought at the farm. It is not recommended that the ascent should be made from this point but rather by a scree slope near LOCALITY 3. There is, however, an impressive view of Parkhouse Hill from this point. It is a mass of reef limestone rising through blue and black Namurian shales with a fault on its precipitous southern side (see Front Cover). Hudson (1931), impressed by the very uneven sub-Namurian surface, pointed to this as a very likely Namurian topography in the process of exhumation.

Continue down the road past the old cheese factory and then right along a very narrow lane just before reaching a road bridge over the River Dove (084666). Shallow sections of Namurian shales may be seen in isolated outcrops along the river banks and these shales can be traced well up the southern flank of Parkhouse Hill. Proceeding along the lane, the reef limestones at the foot of Parkhouse Hill can be examined on the right where they appear from beneath the unconformable cover of Namurian shales. A particularly good locality for fossils is at LOCALITY 4 beneath a large limestone pinnacle at the northwestern end of the hill. The ascent of the hill is best made just south of this locality by entering a shale-filled depression on the west of the hill and climbing a narrow path. Fossils, such as the brachiopod *Dielasma saccula*, even show traces of the original colour-banding. From the summit it is evident that the upstanding reef mass of Parkhouse Hill is almost completely surrounded by Namurian shales. Where these have been removed by erosion we are looking at an exhumed Namurian topography. There is an extensive hollow or valley in the reef limestone filled with Namurian shales to the south of Dowall Hall, once known as Dowel Farm (076675).

Return to the cart-track and proceed to Dowall Hall. The lower B_2 algal reef is exposed in the gorge north of the hall (LOCALITY 5) (076677).

Shortly after passing the hall and entering Dowel Dale, fossiliferous reef limestones are seen on both banks of the dale. On the eastern bank these reef limestones can be seen to pass laterally into well bedded light grey limestones which include a *Davidsonina septosa* Band. Traced towards the reef this band becomes more and more unfossiliferous until fossils fail entirely at a position where the limestones cease to be bedded and can be recognised as of reef facies.

Chrome Hill (070673), also famed for its reef fossils, may be ascended from the northeast by striking across country for 600 m from Dowel Dale. It is bounded on its eastern side by the Chrome Hill Fault, probably a continuation of the fault which determined the steep slope of Parkhouse Hill on its southern side. Namurian shales pass well up the slopes of Chrome Hill on all sides. Looking westwards from the summit of Chrome Hill it is evident that the conspicuous sandstone capping Hollins Hill to the west once abutted against the flanks of Chrome Hill and so there is, in this area too, evidence of extensive pre-Namurian or Namurian denudation of the Dinantian rocks.

Wherever a trace of bedding can be observed in the reef, dips of the order of 30° W can be measured. Highly fossiliferous pockets of fossils are present near the summit and discontinuous masses of upper B_2 algal reef occur to the north of the summit.

ITINERARY VI

Eyam and Stony Middleton

Aims: To study the stratigraphy and palaeontology of the massif limestones and reef limestones in the the higher Dinantian so well displayed in the cliffs and quarries of Middleton Dale and around Eyam.

Maps & memoirs: Ordnance Survey Sheet 119, 1: 50,000. Landranger Series. Geological Survey Sheet 99 (Chapel-en-le-Frith), 1: 50,000. Stevenson, I. P. & G. D. Gaunt. 1971. Geology of the country around Chapel-en-le Frith. *Mem. Geol. Surv.*

Eyam and Stony Middleton

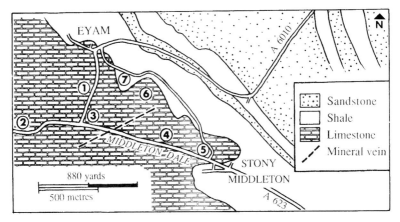

Figure 18. Geological sketch-map of Stony Middleton area showing localities in Itinerary VI.

Transport: Stony Middleton and Eyam are accessible by bus from Buxton, Manchester and Sheffield. In using private vehicles great care should be taken over parking alongside the busy A623 road through Middleton Dale. There are convenient car parks in Eyam village, one in the main street outside the church for short stays, but the better one is on the east side of the street at the northern end of the village. The latter has an adjacent museum largely given over to the history of lead mining and to the Great Plague of 1665.

Route: The village of Eyam is built upon the Eyam Limestones of P_2 age of which a thickness of about 40 m is present. At the top, about 12 m of flat reef are developed. In Cucklet Dale, a short distance from the main car park, a small knoll reef in the Eyam Limestones can be seen on the left. From the car park proceed eastwards, past the church, and at the road bifurcation turn southwards along the road through Eyam Dale which joins the A623 in 1 km. Along this traverse the Dinantian limestones are dipping in a northwesterly direction to pass beneath the Namurian, the scarp of which was evident in the car park. The road passes from the flat reef to the underlying dark Eyam Limestones (LOCALITY 1; Figure 18) and then on to the older Monsal Dale Beds. There are scattered exposures of the Upper Shell Bed and of the *Orionastraea* Band. At the road junction turn westwards along the A623. After 1 km enter Furness Quarry on the right (21007608) (LOCALITY 2). At Furness Quarry the Geological Survey put down a deep borehole in 1970-72. It reached a final depth of 1,851m. Starting in Brigantian (D_2) limestones it proved limestones, lavas and tuff bands of Brigantian and Asbian age, limestones partly dolomitized with fossils indicating an Holkerian (S_2) age, and a very thick sequence of shallow water limestones to the base of the Viséan at a depth of 1,730 m. The borehole continued downwards into dolomites, mudstones with anhydrite nodules and bands, then into greenish-grey and red sandstones to a depth of 1,803 m. On palaeontological grounds this last group of

Eyam and Stony Middleton

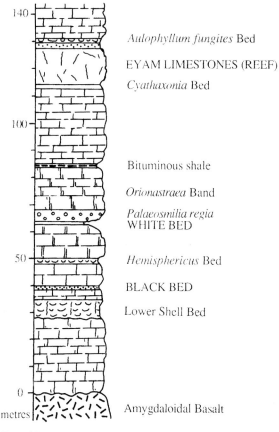

140

Aulophyllum fungites Bed

EYAM LIMESTONES (REEF)

Cyathaxonia Bed

100

Bituminous shale

Orionastraea Band

Palaeosmilia regia
WHITE BED

50

Hemisphericus Bed

BLACK BED

Lower Shell Bed

0

metres

Amygdaloidal Basalt

Figure 19. Typical Dinantian succession in Middleton Dale (after T.O. Morris).

beds was accepted as a thin Tournaisian sequence. This rests with marked unconformity on mudstones with purple staining which are of Ordovician age (Dunham, 1973).

Furness Quarry provides an excellent section of more than a 50 m thickness of Monsal Dale Limestones surmounted by several metres of Eyam Limestones, the junction being marked by a clay-band on an eroded surface. The section of the Monsal Dale Limestones exhibits a number of marker and fossiliferous bands which can be traced through the length of Middleton Dale to the east. The lowest exposures are in crinoidal limestone with scattered giganteid productids below the Lower Shell Bed (Figure 19). The amygdaloidal basalt shown at the base of the figure was proved in a borehole at Hanging Flat (20527600) but it is not exposed. The Lower Shell Bed (the Lower Giganteus Bed of Morris, 1929) is about 2 m thick and crowded with *Gigantoproductus edelburgensis*, and is succeeded by the Black Bed, a 1.5 m stratum of dark bituminous limestone which includes the '*Lonsdaleia* Bed' of Morris. About 20 m above the Black Bed is the White Bed, up to 2 m of white weathering calcilutite with chert nodules which weathers differentially to give a bedding-cleft conspicuous throughout Middleton Dale. About 8 m above this is the *Orionastraea* Band with *O. indivisa*. About 12 m higher is the 'Bituminous Shale' of Morris. This is a thin coal with blue shale carrying fish debris. This is clearly an emergent surface which was later inundated by a shallow sea in which the flat reefs of the Eyam Limestone, visible in the top left of the quarry, were deposited.

Return to the junction of the Eyam road with the A623, Just to the east of this on the north side of the road is Shining Cliff (218756) (LOCALITY 3). This quarried cliff affords the best section in Middleton Dale and gives access to about 60 m of the lower part of the succession and was the type-section of Morris (1929). The beds are almost horizontal. The Lower Shell Bed lies near the base of the section close to the quarry floor at its southern corner; it is about 3 m thick and crowded with *Gigantoproductus edelburgensis*. Below this are thickly bedded crinoidal limestones which probably rest upon the amygdaloidal lava referred to in the Furness Quarry section. Above the Lower Shell Bed are limestones with scattered colonies of corals including *Lonsdaleia floriformis*, a typical upper Brigantian species.

The White Bed of calcilutite with chert is a conspicuous marker horizon which appears high in the cliff face. This is overlain by the 'Hackly Bed' so called on account of its close joining, and a coral band with *Palaeosmilia regia* and *Dibunophyllum* aff. *muirheadi*. The *Orionastraea* Band so well seen in Furness Quarry does not seem to be present in this section. The higher beds are accessible from the top of the cliff; they contain pockets of productids.

From Shining Cliff walk eastwards towards Stoney Middleton village. About 300 m down the dale the Dirty Rake is crossed. Open works (22077571) show it to be nearly 7 m wide at the top but it narrows downwards. Barytes is seen on a tip close by.

The Shining Cliff succession can be followed in the north wall of the dale past Castle Rock (LOCALITY 4) where the Upper Shell Bed is about 25 m below the base of the Eyam Limestones, to 'The Cliff' (227757) where the White Bed can be seen to be cut out by the pebbly base of the Hackly Bed. There is an increase of dip so that the flat reef of the Eyam Limestones is brought down. These thick beds can be observed to thin out eastwards in the vertical cliffs in the village. Overlying them are some very fossiliferous limestones. A coral band rich in *Aulophyllum fungites* is visible at the side of the road to the left of the fork at the old Toll House

(LOCALITY 5). Follow this road for a short distance and turn along Mill Lane which turns sharply left back to Eyam. About 200 m along this lane is a small quarry (LOCALITY 6). This exposure is in thinly bedded limestones with zaphrentids and numerous spiriferids. The lane continues in a northwesterly direction along the feather-edge of the Dinantian dip slope which swings into an almost east-west direction. On the right is a hollow occupied by Edale Shales and beyond which rises the landslipped escarpment of the Shale Grit. At a bend in the lane (LOCALITY 7), 400 m from Eyam, there is an exposure of black shales which have yielded *Eumorphoceras bisulcatum* indicating an E_2 age; this is only a few metres above the base of the Edale Shales.

ITINERARY VII

Matlock, Via Gellia and Griffe Grange

Aims: To observe some of the main points of geological interest along the valley of the River Derwent from its confluence with the River Wye near Rowsley, through Matlock Bath to Cromford, then along the Via Gellia and the Griffe Grange valley to Grangemill.

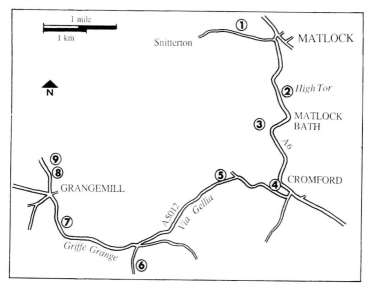

Figure 20. Sketch Map of Matlock - Cromford area showing localities in Itinerary VII.

Maps & Memoirs: Ordnance Survey Sheet 119, 1: 50,000, Landranger Series. Geological Survey Sheets 111 & 112, 1: 50, 000.

Matlock, Via Gellia and Griffe Grange

Transport: Good roads, very narrow in places, but numerous small spaces for short term parking of a single vehicle. Especial care must be exercised along the Via Gellia as it is narrow with numerous bends and carries a great deal of heavy traffic.

Route: Between Haddon Hall and Rowsley the River Wye receives the combined waters of the River Bradford and the River Lathkill on the right bank. At Rowsley the Wye joins the Derwent coming from the north. The Derwent then follows a southernly course through Darley Dale. It has a wide flood plain. The high ground to the east of this is formed by the Ashover Grit (the equivalent of the Roaches Grit to the west). The valley runs down through Darley Dale along the line of a powerful north-south fault to the west of which are lower Namurian rocks around Stanton-in-Peak involved in the west-east Stanton Syncline. Further west the Dinantian limestones rise gently from beneath the Namurian cover around Alport and Elton. On entering Matlock from the north take the right hand turn for the A6 road to Cromford and almost immediately turn right again for the minor road to Snitterton (Figure 20). On the right is the disused Cawdor Quarry (LOCALITY 1; 287605); it shows the succession in the upper part of the Dinantian. The Upper Lava of the Matlock area is seen to be succeeded by about 30 m of light grey limestones with typical Brigantian (D_2) fossils including the coral *Lonsdaleia floriformis*. These beds have been called the Upper Lathkill Limestones and they are similar to the higher Brigantian strata of the Wye Valley section (p. 10). Resting unconformably on these beds are grey and dark grey, irregularly bedded limestones which are seen to pass laterally into thinly bedded limestones and shales. They yield a rich brachiopod fauna including *Spirifer striatus* (Martin) and *Pugilis pugilis* (Phillips) and, most importantly, in a thin bed of limestone, the goniatite *Goniatites granosus* Portlock. This enables a correlation of this group of dark limestones and shales, the Cawdor Limestones, with P_2 sub-zone thin limestones and shales (Longstone Mudstones) of the Headstone cutting in the Wye Valley section (p. 17).

To the north of Cawdor Quarry the basal beds of the Namurian succeed the Cawdor Limestones. It was in this area that Whitehurst, nearly 200 years ago, first used the term 'Millstone Grit' for a coarse sharp-grained sandstone used in the making of millstones. The term was rendered invalid as a lithlogical type when Hull and Green of the British Geological Survey used the term 'Millstone Grit' as a formation name to include not only sandstones but shales, mudstones and fireclays which make up the Namurian.

At Matlock the valley of the Derwent narrows abruptly to become a gorge entrenched in the limestone which continues through Matlock Bath southwards to Cromford, a distance of about 5 km. The origin of this gorge is at present unknown. Matlock Dale, as the gorge is called, carries the main A6 road and the railway, the latter traversing a tunnel beneath High Tor (LOCALITY 2), a precipitous cliff of

Matlock, Via Gellia and Griffe Grange

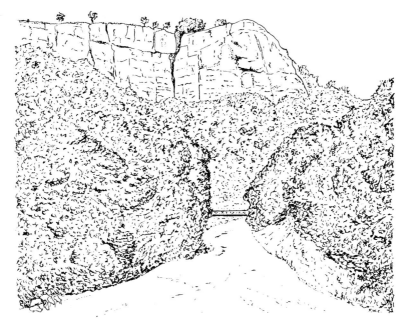

Figure 21. High Tor, Matlock from the west. A lenticular mass of reef limestone is visible near the top of the main face.

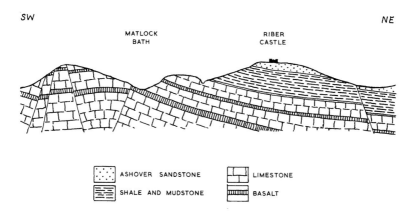

Figure 22. Diagrammatic section through Riber Castle and Matlock Bath area. Length of section about 4 km.

Matlock, Via Gellia and Griffe Grange

limestone over 100 m in height between Matlock and Matlock Bath (Figure 21). It seems likely that the presence of thermal springs led to baths being built here by the Romans, for masonry reputed to be Roman has been found during excavation work at Matlock Bath. The water of these thermal springs has a constant temperature of 20°C.

On the Heights of Abraham to the west of Matlock Dale there are many old lead mines and several caverns. The Rutland Cavern (LOCALITY 3) is well worth a visit; it is the largest of the local caverns. In a gallery called the Roman Hall traces of Roman handicraft dating back 2,000 years have been found. In the Masson Cavern there is a large inner cavern measuring 70 m in length, 15 m in width and 30 m in height; this was accidentally discovered by lead miners many years ago. The Cumberland Cavern at Matlock Bath is also quite extensive.

In various parts of Matlock Dale and especially on the lower slopes of the Heights of Abraham there are deposits of calcareous tufa, precipitated from warm spring waters.

The Mining Museum at Matlock Bath should be visited; there are instructive displays of the various methods formerly used in the mining of lead and other local minerals. Matlock Bath lies to the east of a large limestone area with a long history of lead mining.

At High Tor the Cawdor Limestones, which vary rapidly, are almost completely calacareous and include a reef mass over 30 m thick (Figure 21). This can be seen clearly from the main road. These limestones continue southwards to Cromford and are succeeded by Numurian shales dipping gently eastwards. The steeper slopes above these shales are produced by the Ashover Grit and it is upon this that Riber Castle is situated (Figure 22). The well known beauty spot 'Black Rock' just over 1 km south of Cromford (293557) is also part of the Ashover Grit.

The Bonsall Fault, master fault of the Matlock district striking NW-SE, passes through Cromford. The average southerly throw of this fault is about 100 m; it does not appear to be mineralized although it is in an area criss-crossed by mineral veins.

Travelling south from Matlock Bath turn right at the traffic signals and after 250 m turn right on to the A5012 road. At the Pig of Lead Inn (284575) bear left for the Via Gellia (not, in spite of its name, a Roman road; it was built by John Gell of Carsington). Beginning at Cromford the junction between the Cawdor Limestones of P_2 age with the underlying thickly bedded light grey Brigantian (D_2) limestones is exposed behind a building on the side of the road south of the mill pond at Cromford (LOCALITY 4; 292571). The Bonsall Fault can be seen

Matlock, Via Gellia and Griffe Grange

Figure 23. Polished surface of Hopton Wood 'marble'. Specimen measures 20 cm along the top.

in the cliff at the Cromford Garage and its position is also clear further to the northwest in the road near the centre of Bonsall village. The Brigantian limestones rest upon a thin lava flow which can be traced high up on both sides of the Via Gellia. Below this lava flow the thickly bedded Via Gellia Limestones crop out. About 1 km west of the Pig of Lead, and on the north side of the Via Gellia (LOCALITY 5; 275573), a dark grey grey bed of limestone yields typical Asbian (D_1) fossils such as *Palaeomilia murchisoni* (Ed. & H.) and *Davidsonina septosa* (Phillips) similar to those in the *D. septosa* Band in the Wye Valley (p.11).

Certain beds of the Asbian Via Gellia Limestones have been quarried for many years for use as 'marble'. This is a limestone which will take a polish and is a marble in a mason's sense but, as it has not been metamorphosed, it is not a marble in a geological sense. The best known quarries for this attractive marble are at Hopton Wood about 700 m south of the junction of the Via Gellia with a minor road leading to Wirksworth (LOCALITY 6; 263557). These limestones are thickly bedded to massive, light grey to oatmeal coloured and frequently highly crinoidal; they take a good polish (Figure 23).

Dovedale

The Via Gellia Limestones are of Asbian age and roughly equivalent to the Bee Low Limestones of the Wye Valley. They are about 150 m thick in the Via Gellia and their base may be seen in the Griffe Grange Valley, the western extension of the Via Gellia at LOCALITY 7 (254565). The underlying Woo Dale Limestones are visible on the roadside. They are dark coloured limestones and yield occasional specimens of *Daviesiella llangollensis* (Dav.) regarded by the writer as indicating a Holkerian (S_2) age.

Proceed northwestwards along the Griffe Grange Valley for about 2 km to Grange Mill where there are several large quarries in Asbian limestones. This area was made famous through the discovery by Geikie (1897) of two Lower Carboniferous volcanic necks later mapped by Arnold - Bemrose (1907). The larger of the two necks having a maximum diameter of about 700 m extends northwards from the Grangemill crossroads (LOCALITY 8). It is poorly exposed but may be seen in a disused quarry at LOCALITY 9 (24425783). The smaller neck lies a short distance to the north alongside the Winster road (B5056). It gives rise to a low mound but is very poorly exposed. Each vent shows an outer ring of tuffs with lapilli and an inner basaltic core.

ITINERARY VIII

Dovedale

Aims: To examine the relationships of the various facies of Dinantian limestones to one another, to study some of the very fossiliferous reef limestones in the valley of the River Dove, and to enjoy some of the most breathtaking scenery in Britain.

Maps & Memoirs: Ordnance Survey Sheet 119, 1: 50, 000 Landranger Series. Geological Survey Sheet 124 (Ashbourne), 1: 50, 000.

Transport: With Buxton as a centre the journey to Hartington via the A515 and B5054 can be made by bus. At the end of the day the return to Buxton from Ilam can be made by going through Thorpe Village to the Ashbourne-Buxton road for the bus service. Assuming these transport arrangements, the total walking distance is about 18 km. If using private transport from Buxton, take the A515 (Ashbourne) road to a point about 5 km north of Ashbourne with Tissington village on the left. Turn right at the signpost marked 'Thorpe'. After sharp left hand and right hand bends go straight ahead at the crossroads into Thorpe. Turn right in village. After 1 km turn right for car park with Izaac Walton Hotel on left. The car park (146508) is a spacious one but it tends to be fully occupied especially in the summer months. Walk upstream and cross River Dove by stepping stones. Note: the traverse of the dale starting from the hotel takes the route described below in reverse.

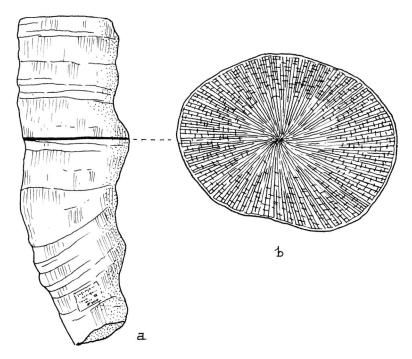

Figure 24. Palaeosmilia murchisoni (Edwards & Haime). A typical Asbian coral. a. Corallum, b. Transverse section, 5 cm across.

General Geology: All three major facies of Dinantian limestones are present in the area but the reef limestones are the most prominent, especially from a scenic point of view. The area is affected by a broad anticline, the Dovedale Anticline, which has a steady axial plunge to the north-northwest. All the main topographical features have been carved out of reef limestones.

Route: In Hartington take the minor road southwards opposite the church, follow it through a sharp left hand bend and then turn right along the lane leading southwards to Beresford Dale. This lane passes over fairly thickly bedded light coloured limestones which are poorly fossiliferous. The Asbian (D_1) coral *Dibunophyllum bourtonense* may occasionally be found and on this basis these beds may be regarded as Asbian massif limestones, the approximate equivalent of the Chee Tor Rock of the Wye Valley area. All around Wolfscote Hill (138584) there are bedded limestones breccias and there is a good exposure of these in the field to the north of Frank's Rock just above the incised Wolfscote Dale. The dale itself is excavated in reef limestones containing shell beds and local limestone breccias. The fauna includes the massif D_1 fossil *Palaeosmilia murchisoni* (Ed. & H.) (Figure 24) together with the goniatite *Beyrichoceras castletonense* which denotes the B_2 subzone. Clearly, this part of Wolfscote Dale was very close to the western edge of the massif in Asbian times. Narrowdale Hill (11755724) lies just over 1 km to the southwest of Frank's Rock. The B_2 reef limestones of this hill have yielded many beautiful specimens of brachiopods.

The country immediately to the west of Beresford Dale is underlain by Numurian shales. A slight eastward extension of their outcrop brings these shales into Beresford Dale to the northwest of Frank's Rock and it can be seen that the Namurian beds rest unconformably upon the limestone. The outcrop of the shales in Beresford Dale extends just eastwards of the river for a short distance, and on the right bank their impermeability accounts for the swampy state of the ground near the river.

Proceeding southwards along the flood plain from Frank's Rock, well bedded light grey and purplish grey limestones are seen along the left bank. These beds belong to the Wolfscote Dale Limestone; they dip upstream at a low angle and disappear beneath the Alsop Moor Limestones.

Southwards from Frank's Rock, on the right bank of the Dove, is Drabber Tor (138569), a high bluff composed of fairly thickly bedded limestone without chert, which has been referred to as the Iron Tors Limestone on account of its good exposure at Iron Tors a little farther south on the left bank. The Iron Tors Limestone must be older than the Wolfscote Dale Limestone, but owing to the paucity of fossils the main hope of dating it must be through the dating of the Dove Dale Limestones, father south, into which they seem to pass.

At a point where the River Dove swings sharply to the west and then back to the southeast (145558) there are some excellent exposures of the Iron Tors Limestone, and a little father south these limestones can be seen to merge insensibly into the Dove Dale Limestone which is of reef facies.

Walk along the path to the main road at Lode Mill and then proceed southwestwards to Milldale . Along the roadside are good exposures of grey to black limestones with lenticular and nodular chert. There is a bed of dolomite about a metre thick which can be followed for several hundreds of metres along the hillside south of Milldale . Fossils are infrequent but fossils from the same beds near Nab's Spring father south in Dovedale include *Pustula nodosa* Thomas suggesting that these beds are of Chadian (C_2) age. The Milldale Limestone beds, about the same age as the Dovedale Limestone reef limestones, can be seen at the high bluff known as Raven's Tor on the right bank about 1 km south of Milldale.

Dovedale

Standing on the footpath on the left bank it will be seen that there is a gradual transition between reef and basin facies limestones.

Close to the entry of Nab's Dale from the east are the Dove Holes (Figure 25), two impressive caves in the reef limestone. South of Dove Holes, the rising ground on the right bank of the river appears to be mainly on basin facies, but on the left bank, which carries the footpath, somewhat higher reef limestones are splendidly exposed in the massive cliffs from Pickering Tor to Reynard's Cave and southwards to Tissington Spires. The lower reef limestones in this area yield *Levitusia humerosa* (J. Sowerby) which suggests a Chadian (C_2) age.

To the south of Lover's Leap the valley of the Dove is marked out by the conical hill of Thorpe Cloud on the east and the almost equally impressive Bunster Hill on the west. Both these hills appear to be reef knolls, that is immense piles of light grey, very fine grained calcareous almost calcilutitic material, which can be likened to that forming the reef knolls in the Clitheroe area of Lancashire and are of Chadian age. There is a considerable amount of fine crinoid debris at some horizons. There are nests or pockets of beautifully preserved fossils in numerous places. The fine calcareous mud must have been trapped in a network of organisms such as algae, sponges, bryozoa, etc. (Contrary to what the term 'reef' might suggest in modern parlance, these limestones very rarely contain corals): Only in this way could a mound of calcareous mud have continued to stand under water

Figure 25. Dove Holes in Dovedale.

with surface gradients far in excess of that would be permitted for such fine material. On Thorpe Cloud a semblance of crude bedding can sometimes be seen, especially on the western slope of the hill, but none of these surfaces can be traced very far. Bands of reef breccia appear to lie parallel to the present surface, but such bands probably occupy penecontemporaneous erosion hollows in the reef.

The summit of Thorpe Cloud (152510) has been known as an excellent locality for fossils for more then a century. Some of the reef limestone is very shelly, of a type little known in reefs at this horizon of the Dinantian elsewhere in Britain. The fossils are well preserved, easily extracted and can be collected in large numbers should this be required for statistical research. The fauna is extensive but mainly of brachiopods, the commonest being *Spirifer bollandensis* Muir-Wood, *Reticularia lobata* Muir-Wood and *Pugnax* spp. The highest beds yield occasional specimens of the tabulate coral *Michelinia megastoma* (Phillips).

Thorpe Cloud and Bunster Hill were formerly covered by the higher Dinantian limestones but a great deal of this cover was probably removed by pre-Namurian denudation and later by Triassic denudation.

ITINERARY IX

The Valley of the River Manifold

Aims: To see some of the swallet holes in the bed of the River Manifold which carry the whole of the river into its underground course after a dry spell of weather; to examine the acutely folded limestones at Apes Tor near Hulme End, the impressive Thor's Cave, the spectacular reef limestone features and some of the spoil-heaps of the old Ecton Copper Mine.

Maps and Memoirs: Ordnance Survey Sheet 119, 1: 50, 000 Landranger Series Geological Survey Sheet 111 (Buxton), 1: 50, 000.
Aitkenhead, N., J. I. Chisholm & I. P. Stevenson, 1985. Geology of the Country around Buxton, Leek and Bakewell. *Mem. Geol. Surv.*

Transport: The best starting point for this excursion is Hartington on the B5054 which has bus services from Ashbourne, Buxton and Bakewell. Private vehicles can be used in the Manifold Valley as far as Redhurst Crossing (096561) to the northwest of Wetton; there is parking space near Wettonmill and a small parking plot at Redhurst Crossing . There is another small car park at Weag's Bridge (100543) which may be reached from Wetton or Grindon; this lies approximately midway between Thor's Cave and Beeston Tor.

Manifold Valley

General Geology: The River Manifold rises within a kilometre of the River Dove in a field behind the Travellers'Rest Inn at Flash some 12 km away to the NW on the eastern flank of Axe Edge. From its source to Hulme End the Manifold has cut a valley in Lower Namurian rocks roughly parallel and to the west of the Dove. Close to the bridge at Hume End on the B5054 the Manifold enters Dinantian limestone terrain and pursues a deeply entrenched meandering course southwards. At Beeston Tor to the south of Wetton the Manifold receives its main tributary, the Hamps, on its right bank. The Manifold, and to some extent the Hamps, has a well developed underground course from the vicinity of Wettonmill so that, after a spell of dry weather, the whole of its water flows underground to reappear on the surface at Ilam where it joins the River Dove. The rocks exposed in the valley of the Manifold are all limestones, some with very thin shale partings, probably deposited

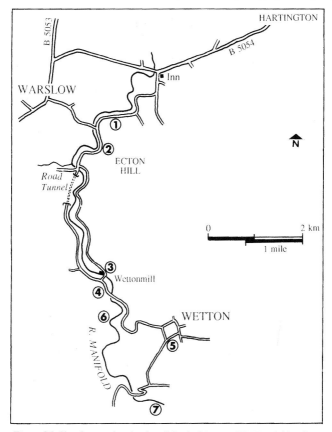

Figure 26. Sketch-map showing localities in Itinerary IX, Manifold Valley.

Manifold Valley

in a marginal position between block and basin. There are also conspicuous large masses of reef limestone attributed to the marginal or reef facies of the Dinantian. This main section of the Manifold Valley has been eroded through a very broad anticline, but the detailed and local structure is often complex. In particular, the immense masses of reef limestone which give rise to spectacular cliffs bordering the river have suffered very little during folding, some of which was pre-Namurian. They have acted as immense bastions with the result that the less competent thinly-bedded limestones and shales have yielded to produce complex folded and fault structures.

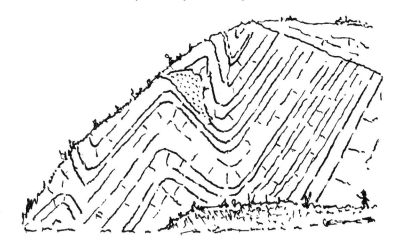

Figure 27. Folded limestones at Ape's Tor, Manifold Valley. Scale figure, bottom right.

Route: Take the Hulme End -Warslow road (B5054) from the southwest end of Hartington village (Figure 26). In 1 km the road crosses the River Dove. After a further 1.5 km, and just short of a road bridge over the River Manifold, turn sharply southwards at the Manifold Inn (106593). Follow the Alstonefield road for about 400 m and turn right down a narrow lane; this turns to the left between farm buildings at West Side. Beyond the next right hand bend we reach a series of small disused quarries on the left. This is the famous Apes Tor Section (LOCALITY 1) (100585) which is protected under the aegis of the National Trust. (Note: a vehicle can be parked for a short time on the road verge towards the western end of the section). The well-bedded dark grey limestones with occasional chert and some thin carbonaceous partings are folded into zig-zag series of slightly asymmetric anticlines and synclines. The crests and troughs of the folds are acute (Figure 27) and the plunge can be measured. The fold axes trend NNW-SSE. At the western end of the section, at the top of the cliff face, a low-angle thrust is visible. The limestones are poor in identifiable macro-fossils but, on the basis of the contained foraminifera, they are thought to be of upper Holkerian or lower Asbian age.

Manifold Valley

Further down the valley at Ecton a steep narrow road negotiable by vehicles enters on the right from Warslow.

To the south, on the left, is Ecton Hill renowned for the amount of copper ore it produced from its extensive mines from the 17th Century through to the 18th Century, at a time when ships were being copper-bottomed. At that time the Ecton mines were the richest copper-producing ones in the whole of Britain. Production fell off rapidly during the 19th Century and had ceased by 1890. The Ecton mineralisation is unique in many ways. In Derbyshire mineralisation generally occurs towards the top of the limestone succession where the succeeding Numurian shales have behaved as an impermeable cap, preventing percolation of the hydrothermal solutions to higher levels. This is also the case at Ecton. However, in Derbyshire copper mineralisation, with fluorite as one of the main gangue minerals, is generally confined to the eastern part of the area. Ecton is unusual in being a copper/fluorite occurrence on the western edge of the area and in being in the fluorite zone. The main copper ore at Ecton is chalcopyrite ($CuFeS_2$) which was mainly deposited in large near-vertical pipes as well as in flats corresponding roughly to bedding planes in the limestone. Other sulphide ores such as galena (PbS) and sphalerite (ZnS) also occur in quantity and there is an extraordinarily wide range of secondary minerals formed by the oxidation of primary sulphides in the zone above the water-table. These include the colourful hydrated copper carbonates malachite and azurite. The gangue minerals are fluorite, barite and calcite, very large scalenohedra of calcite having been found in the past whilst the fluorite may be colourless or blue.

It is now difficult to obtain mineral specimens on the surface, but scattered waste hillocks in the central part of Ecton Hill about 600 m south of Apes Tor are worthy of examination from this point of view. Permission to visit various parts of Ecton Hill should be sought from Mr G. Cox of Ecton House and, in so far as spoil heaps are concerned, from the owners of farmhouses on the eastern side of the hill. Underground exploration of the old workings is possible, but this should only be undertaken with expert guidance and with the knowledge of landowners. In view of the possibility of underground exploration taking place visitors are requested not to throw any materials down the shafts.*

There is an old spoil heap on the hillside above the road (098584); this has long been exhausted of readily accessible mineral specimens and railings have been placed around it. On the left of the road below this is a small quarry (LOCALITY 2) in calcrete, a limestone scree in which angular limestone fragments have been

---

* Those wishing for further details of the Ecton Copper mine are recommended to consult R.S.W. Braithwaite's 'Itinerary XV. The mineralisation of Ecton Hill, Staffordshire'in Eager, R.M.C. and F.M. Broadhurst, 1991, Geologists' Association Guide No. 7, Geology of the Manchester Area.

cemented together by calcium carbonate deposited from groundwater when the annual rainfall was higher than today, probably in late Pleistocene times.

Continue along the road for about 1 km; just before the road crosses the river a gate on the left (093578) gives vehicular access to the lower reaches of the River Manifold. The cart-track with two further gates, which must be closed after use, leads along the western flank of Ecton Hill and the Sugarloaf to Wettonmill. An alternative route to Wettonmill is to follow the road beyond the river bridge and, first moving to the right then swinging sharply to the left, use the former railway tunnel which is about 600 m long. It is a straight but narrow tunnel without passing places. Headlights should be used and a halt made at the tunnel entrance in case another vehicle has already entered at the other end.

At Wettonmill (LOCALITY 3) there are exposures of reef limestones which lie below the bedded Ecton Limestones seen at Apes Tor, and which may be of Holkerian age. An exposure showing the junction between reef and bedded limestones can be seen behind the farm buildings at Wettonmill (09585612).

Close to Wettonmill, after moderately dry weather, the water of the River Manifold can be seen sinking through the river bed. The best point for seeing this is to the south of Wettonmill. Follow the narrow lane coming southwards from the road tunnel, cross a shallow ford and stop near the hump-backed bridge (LOCALITY 4). River water can be seen to go underground at the base of the low cliff on the right bank of the river (this may be marked by an iron grating). Close by (096557) is Ossom's Cave which has yielded an interesting post-Pleistocene fauna including Przewalski's horse *Equus caballus przewalski*. The lane and the tarmac road from Wettonmill (course of the former light railway which was closed in 1933) meet at Redhurst Crossing (095561) where there is a small but muddy parking space on the left. A gate lies across the course of the old railway track which continues down the valley, but vehicles can not be taken beyond the gate. From Redhurst Crossing it could be useful, if time permits, to visit the village of Wetton, 2 km east up the narrow steep lane on the left (a few passing places have recently been made). The church at Wetton is worthy of a visit if only to see the grave, near the east window, of Samuel Carrington (LOCALITY 5) for many years the village schoolmaster and an assiduous collector of local fossils, many of which are now preserved in various museums, including the British Museum (Natural History). The tombstone is decorated with carvings of Dinantian fossils including *Productus* and *Nautilus*, all somewhat stylised.

Return to Redhurst Crossing. In the course of the descent there are splendid panoramic views across the Manifold Valley with the church spires in the villages of Butterton and Grindon to the west standing out beyond Ossom's Hill and with Thor's Cave in the middle distance.

Manifold Valley

Figure 28. Thor's Cave, Manifold Valley, viewed from the north.

Having reached the restricted parking area at Redhurst Crossing proceed on foot beyond the gate for about 800 m. Thor's Cave is situated high above the river on the left bank (LOCALITY 6) (Figure 28). Cross the footbridge and follow the path to the cave. The interior of the cave receives light from another entrance called the West Window. The cave has been dissolved out of reef limestone which forms a large discrete mass. The deposits on the cave floor were excavated many years ago; they were not removed systematically and consequently the fauna recorded is a composite one covering many thousands of years; it includes bear, hyena, sabre-toothed tiger and more recent inhabitants, including Man.

As in Dovedale so in the Manifold Valley the most conspicuous elements in the landscape are due to reef limestones. The upstanding masses of reef limestone at Thor's Cave and nearby Beeston Tor and Nanny Tor, contrast strongly with the bedded limestones and mudstones out of which they seem to rise. Each mass of reef limestone appears to be dome-shaped with a rounded top and very steep or vertical sides. Each may reach a height of 30 m or more. The bedded limestones around each mass or reef dip outwards and, on account of shearing during folding, it is difficult to study in detail any passage there may be between reef and bedded limestones. However, if we proceed downstream to Beeston Tor (LOCALITY 7), another prominent reef mass, the junction can be examined in the bed of the river below the Hamps confluence and about 50 m from Beeston Tor Cottage. Observation is easier when the river is coursing overground than when the limestones are dry. The Beeston Tor reef yields a scattered but extensive fauna with some brachiopods in a remarkable state of preservation, a specimen of *Pericyclus fasciculatum* (McCoy) has been found here and this may well indicate Chadian age for the lowest reef and bedded limestones in the valley of the River Manifold.

ITINERARY X

Mam Tor, Edale and Kinder Scout

Aims: To study the stratigraphy and palaeontology of the Namurian rocks in the Mam Tor - Edale area and to note the relationship between these rocks and the underlying Dinantian limestones.

Maps and Memoirs: Ordnance Survey Sheets 110 & 119, 1: 50, 000 Landranger Series.
Geological Survey Sheet 99 (Chapel-en-le-Frith) 1: 50, 000.
Stevenson, I. P., & G. D. Gaunt, 1971. Geology of the Country around Chapel-en-le-Frith. *Mem. Geol. Surv.*

Transport: Edale may be reached by train from Sheffield and Buxton and there is a bus service from Buxton to Castleton. For private transport there is a car parking ground on the abandoned A625 road in the Mam Tor landslip, and also near Edale railway station.

Route: It is assumed that this will begin at the Mam Tor car park from which the landslipped face of Mam Tor may be viewed (see Itinerary IV). The upper part of Mam Tor consists of the Mam Tor Sandstone, a repetitive series of sandstones and shales of Kinderscoutian (R_1) age; there is a marine band carrying the goniatite *Reticuloceras reticulatum* at its base (Figure 29). Each cyclic unit or cyclothem consists of massive sandstone at the base followed above by laminated sandstone and then by shale and mudstone. The thickness of a cylothem varies from one to three metres. The base of each sandstone unit is sharp and exhibits sole-markings the orientation of which indicates the action of currents flowing from the north. The laminated sandstones frequently exhibit low-angle cross-bedding and ripple drift cross-lamination.

Graded bedding is also to be seen and it is thought that this kind of evidence indicates rapid deposition of sand by turbidity currents moving down the slopes of a delta which was being built out into a deeper marine environment . In many localities the shale and mudstone unit in a cyclothem yields poor goniatite and bivalve faunas which inhabited the sea.

In the Mam Tor landslip scar the Mam Tor Sandstones are seen to be underlain by the Edale Shales, a thick series of blue and black shales which extend down to rest upon the Dinantian limestones. There is evidence that the Mam Tor Sandstone - Edale Shale junction is not everywhere at the same horizon, in other words the junction is a diachronous one. The base of the Edale Shales is very irregular and wherever it is seen it is best described as an unconformable one. Immediately

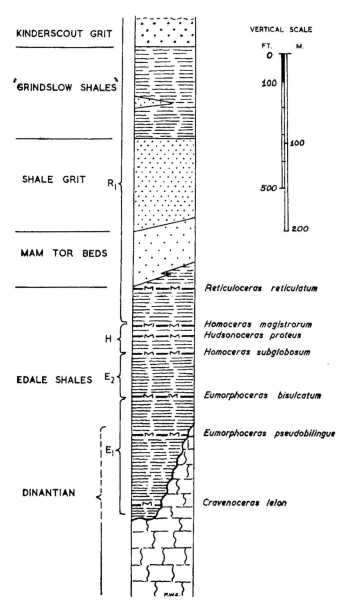

Figure 29. Generalised vertical section of the Namurian rocks in the Mam Tor - Edale area. Only selected marine marker horizons are shown.

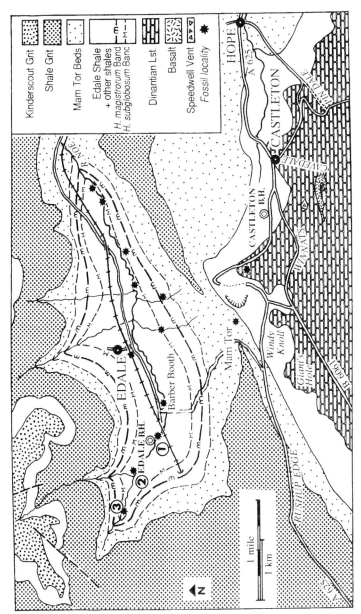

Figure 30. Geological sketch-map of the Edale - Castleton area, showing localities in Itinerary X

below the landslip a marine band with the goniatite *Eumorphoceras bisulcatum*, marking the base of the E_2 subzone has been found a short distance above the Dinantian limestones whilst at the Castleton borehole, a short distance to the east, the Edale Shales with E_1 subzone goniatites were found just above the limestone. There are numerous marine bands in the Edale Shales but it is not possible to study these in the face of the landslip, though slipped hard bullions with solid goniatites and other marine fossils can be found in the scree in several places. These bullions (concretions) are extremely hard and splintery and care should be exercised in hammering them. The wearing of goggles is recommended if this operation is undertaken.

In order to examine some of the marine bands in the Edale Shales it is necessary to go to the Vale of Edale where there are good exposures along the course of the River Noe and its tributaries (Jackson, 1927) (Figure 30).

From the Mam Tor car park return to the A625 road along Rushup Edge and take the narrow lane running northwards through a col (Mam Nick;135835) in the Mam Tor Sandstone and leading steeply down to Barber Booth. The ground immediately to the north of Mam Nick is much affected by land-slipping.

The flanks of the Vale of Edale are deeply dissected by small streams, tributaries of the River Noe, which cut down through beds below the Kinderscout Grit. Their courses expose the sequence in the Namurian from the R_1 subzone down through the *Homoceras* (H) Zone and from the E_2 to the E_1 subzones. The lowest *Eumorphoceras* (E) beds can be examined towards the western end of the Noe valley near the Barber Booth railway viaduct (LOCALITY 1; 107848) where some 25 m of shale are exposed. Fossils are numerous and include the goniatites *Cravenoceras malhamense* Bisat, *Neodimorphoceras scaliger* (Schmidt) and lamellibranchs, including unusually large individuals of *Posidonia membranacea* McCoy. The succeeding beds of E_2 age are well exposed around Upper Booth to the northwest of the confluence of the Crowden Brook with the River Noe (LOCALITY 2; 103853) Higher up the valley near Lee House (LOCALITY 3; 097856) sediments of *Homoceras* (H) Zone age are present and the fossils include species of *Homoceras* and *Homoceratoides*. Above Lee House R_1 beds are present and these include a band of shales with *Reticuloceras reticulatum* (Phillips).

Above the Edale Shales the Mam Tor Sandstones around Edale and in the Alport and Ashop valleys further to the north are about 70 m thick; this compares with a thickness of almost 150 m at Mam Tor. This is a measure of the diachronous nature of the upper and lower limits of the sandstone unit.

The Mam Tor Sandstone covers large areas to the north of Edale and Rushup Edge and around Kinder Scout and, together with the succeeding Shale Grit, is largely covered by peat. The upper and lower boundaries of the Shale Grit are also diachronous so that its thickness is about 200 m in the west of the Vale of Edale; it thins considerably eastwards towards Hathersage.

The country occupied by the Shale Grit and the succeeding Kinderscout Grit can be seen in the northern tributaries of the River Noe. The main valley from Upper Booth to Edale Head and Jacob's Ladder affords useful traverses through typical Shale Grit country. Extensive outcrops of the Shale Grit and of the overlying Kinderscout Grit can also be examined by following the Grindslow Brook northwards from Edale along one of the Pennine Way routes.

The Kinderscout Grit, is responsible for many of the striking topographical features in the northern part of the Peak District, more especially the Kinder Scout plateau and the eroded stack-like outcrops such as Crowden Tower (095872), Wheel Stones on Derwent Edge to the east and strong scarp features as at Kinder Downfall (082888) and Bamford Edge, also to the east.

Usually the Kinderscout Grit is developed in two leaves with a total thickness approaching 200 m, but there are wide variations within short distances. The lower leaf of the Kinderscout Grit is coarse, feldspathic and usually pebbly. On the western side of Kinder Scout it is nearly 100 m thick but it appears to thin rapidly to the north. There are outliers of this lower leaf at Crook Hill (184868) and Win Hill (187852), a short distance to the east. The top of this lower leaf is often a poor quality ganister with Stigmarian rootlets. Ganisters are a more siliceous variety of sandstone and sometimes represent the lower parts of old soil profiles.

The upper Kinderscout Grit is also very variable in thickness, 25 m to 30 m being the norm in the Edale area. It is a medium grained sandstone with coarser bands and with bands containing shale pellets. The top of the upper Kinderscout Grit is often ganisteroid and there may be a thin coal succeeded by shales which include the *Reticuloceras gracile* marine band.

To the north of the Peak District the shales between the two leaves of the Kinderscout Grit include the Butterly Marine Band which carries a benthonic mollusc and brachiopod fauna, but this band has not been found south of Hayfield (036868).

Unless visitors are thoroughly experienced in fell-walking they are strongly advised to confine their attention to outcrops along and close to the first 3 km of the Pennine Way leading northwards from Edale. The terrain which is peaty and very swampy in places can be difficult to traverse, and impenetrable mists can descend without warning at any time of the year.

Ramshaw Rocks, the Roaches and Goldsitch Moss

ITINERARY XI

Ramshaw Rocks, the Roaches and Goldsitch Moss

Aims: To study the relationship between structure and scenery; to examine Namurian 'grits' (sandstones) and a typical cyclothem including a goniatite-bearing band (marine band).

Maps and Memoirs: Ordnance Survey Sheet 119; 1: 50, 000 Landranger Series.
Geological Survey Sheet 111 (Buxton), 1: 50, 000.
Geological Survey SK06 (Roaches and Upper Dove Valley), 1: 25, 000.
Aitkenhead, N., J. I. Chisholm & I. P. Stevenson. 1985. Geology of the country around Buxton, Leek and Bakewell. *Mem. Geol. Surv.*

Transport: There is a bus service from Buxton to Leek via the A53 and useful stops are at the Travellers' Rest Inn, near Flash (032678), and the Royal Cottage Inn, near Ramshaw Rocks. There are limited parking spaces for private vehicles along the route and there is a large car park for customers at the rear of the the Travellers' Rest.

General Geology: The unconformable junction between the Dinantian limestone and the overlying Namurian (formerly known as the Millstone Grit) runs roughly north and south through Buxton. To the west of this line the alternating Namurian sequence of thick sandstones (grits) and shales gives rise to a large area of peat-covered moors cut by irregular stream courses. To the immediate west of Buxton it includes the two highest points in Cheshire, the Cat & Fiddle Inn on the A537 Buxton Macclesfield road at 515 m AOD and, a little to the northwest of this, Shining Tor at 558 m AOD.

The Namurian and, in places, a thin overlying remnant of Westphalian (Coal Measures) rocks, are folded on north-south axes. The most prominent of these folds, the Goyt Trough or Syncline, lies nearest to the Namurian-Dinantian junction. It can be traced from Ludworth (a few km SW of Glossop) in the north almost to Leek in the south with a possible extension westwards into the Cheadle Coalfield. The angle of the dip of the rocks on the two limbs of the syncline is variable, 10° to 20° being the usual amount. In various parts of the fold there is also a measurable plunge, usually to the north.

The term 'Millstone Grit' was coined by Whitehurst (1778, p. 147) for a coarse sharp-grained sandstone used in the Peak District for making millstones. However, that use as a lithological term was completely invalidated when the pioneer Survey geologists, Hull and Green (1887), extended the term to give it a temporal/stratigraphical meaning for the whole of what we now call the Namurian, so including shales and mudstones.

Ramshaw Rocks, the Roaches and Goldsitch Moss

The Goyt Syncline in the area covered by this itinerary provides one of the most spectacular demonstrations of the close relationship between structure and scenery in the British Isles. This is mainly due to the alternation of thick sandstones with equally thick more easily eroded rocks, such as shales and mudstones. Strong contrasting surface features result. That part of the Namurian succession covered by this itinerary extends from below the base of the Roaches Grit to the relatively thin remnant of Westphalian (Coal Measures) rocks shown in Figure 31.

At the time of formation of the Namurian rocks, 320-310 Ma, the area of the present British Isles lay in the tropics possibly in a southern latitude. Immense rivers brought debris mainly from the north building up extensive deltas, with braided streams and lagoons, outwards into a marine area to the west and south. Eustatic changes of sea-level possibly correlated with the vicissitudes of a southern hemisphere glaciation led to periodic transgression of the sea across the alluvial flats inland of the delta fronts, the evidence lying in the thin distinct marine bands of shale carrying goniatites and marine pelecypods as well as occasional trilobites, fish, crustacea and radiolaria, which we shall see in the course of this excursion.

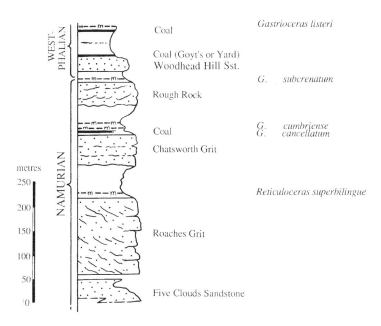

Figure 31. Generalised vertical section of Upper Carboniferous (Silesian) rocks in the Goyt Syncline area.

Ramshaw Rocks, the Roaches and Goldsitch Moss

Route: Leave Buxton by St John's Road or Macclesfield Road and proceed through Burbage southwards. At the road fork take the A53 (Leek). The road climbs steeply and roughly follows the base of the Roaches Grit for several kilometres.

On the left (east) the lower ground is occupied mainly by Dinantian limestones which appear from beneath the Namurian. Axe Edge forms the main watershed between streams such as the Goyt and the Dane running westwards to the Irish Sea and other streams such as the Wye, Dove and Manifold ultimately emptying into the North Sea via the Trent and Humber.

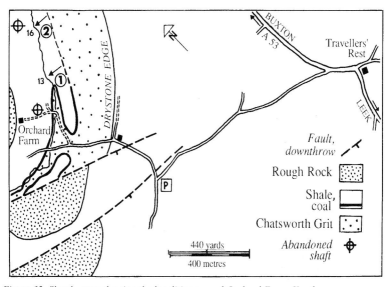

Figure 32. Sketch -map showing the localities around Orchard Farm, Knotbury.

About 5 km south of Burbage the Derbyshire-Staffordshire county boundary is reached (031685). This is marked by the headwater of the River Dove which appears as a spring at the base of the Roaches Grit scarp on the right of the road. Just before reaching the Travellers' Rest Inn (032678) and a sharp right hand bend, take the second turning to the right, signposted 'Knotbury', and stop at the next second turning to the right in 1 km. There is limited parking on a wider part of the road here. Walk up the road on the right for about 300 m to a farmstead on the right (023686). On the right is the dip-slope of the Roaches Grit succeeded by shales. Rising up just beyond the farm is an escarpment of the higher Chatsworth Grit called Drystone Edge. Turn and pass through the first gate.

Ramshaw Rocks, the Roaches and Goldsitch Moss

On the right is the dip-slope of the Chatsworth Grit. A thin coal seam was proved by boring on the lower part of this slope. Follow the cart-track bearing to the right

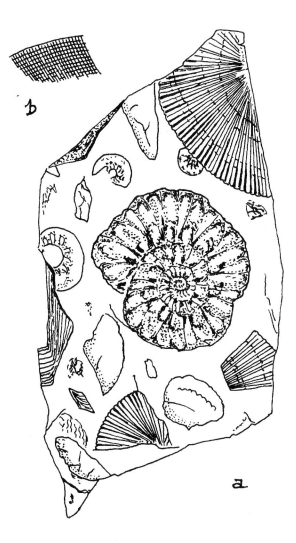

Figure 33. Gastrioceras cancellatum Bisat. a. Crushed specimen in shale, 2 x natural size, b. Characteristic ornamentation x 20.

Ramshaw Rocks, the Roaches and Goldsitch Moss

and just beyond a second gate descend into the stream by the wall, On the left, Orchard Farm (020689) built on the higher Rough Rock is conspicuous. Proceeding northwards up the stream gorge (LOCALITY 1, Figure 32), excavated in shales above the Chatsworth Grit, is a prominent bed of disturbed shales. This contorted band, visible on both sides of the ravine, is believed to have been produced by bedding-plane-slip during the folding of the rocks (Cope, 1946). The marine band characterized throughout the area, and indeed throughout the Pennines, by the goniatite *Gastrioceras cancellatum* (Figure 33) will be found a short distance below the contorted band. The sequence "sandstone - seat - earth - marine band - non-marine shales" known as a cyclothem is repeated many times in the Namurian (Figure 34).

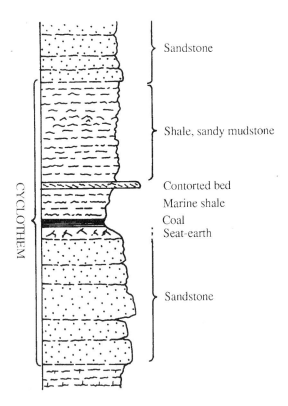

Figure 34. A typical Namurian rhythmic unit of sedimentation (or cyclothem). Vertical scale variable.

A little father upstream, close to a cascade on the right bank of the stream, the next higher marine band with *Gastrioceras cumbriense* is present, though a little difficult to locate and impossible if the stream is in flood (LOCALITY 2). Return to the first gate. In the summertime with good weather, a worthwhile deviation of little over 2 km can be made by walking westwards down the main valley to Three Shires Head (020689), where the counties of Cheshire, Derbyshire and Staffordshire meet. This attractive walk is mainly over the Chatsworth Grit which, crossed by several faults and showing some excellent examples of cross-bedding, forms a wide outcrop at Three Shires Bridge.

Regain the Buxton-Leek A53 road and proceed southwards past the Travellers' Rest Inn and the Royal Cottage Inn (636640). The road is now overlooked on the right by the impressive Ramshaw Rocks escarpment in the Roaches Grit (Back cover, upper). About 2 km south of the Royal Cottage is a small inconspicuous stone house on the right. Turn sharply to the right here on the minor road and climb the escarpment. There is limited space for parking vehicles (not coaches) on the left of the narrow lane shortly after a sharp right-hand bend (LOCALITY 3, Figure 35). This is an excellent viewpoint from which to appreciate the relationship between structure and scenery. The lane at this point is situated on the dip-slope of the Roaches Grit.

This rises eastwards to culminate at the top of its escarpment, the grit showing some remarkable weathering profiles which may have been produced by a weathering regime very different from the present one. Over to the west the skyline marks the rim of the same grit escarpment on the other limb of the Goyt Syncline. The two escarpments converge southwards with the south-directed point of the V being through Hen Cloud (009617) where it is affected by faulting. This V-shaped outcrop of the Roaches Grit indicates a northerly plunge of the fold. The axis of the fold is clearly marked by the remarkable V-shaped outcrop of the next higher resistant sandstone, the Chatsworth Grit, which can be seen in the middle distance to the west (Figure 36).

The Roaches Grit can be examined in the numerous exposures towards the top of the Ramshaw Rocks. The sandstones are seen to be pale buff to purplish-brown in colour with coarse sharp grains of quartz, a considerable amount of feldspar and scattered subangular to rounded quartz pebbles. Some of the massive beds of sandstone show pene-contemporaneous channels incised in their tops and a study of the cross-bedding shows that the material had a generally northerly source (Collinson, 1976). That much of the sand was deposited quickly is evident from the occasional fossil plant branches which may be found, lying almost perpendicularly to the normal bedding. The detritus making up the sandstone must have been derived from a granitic terrain lying far to the north, from the Scottish

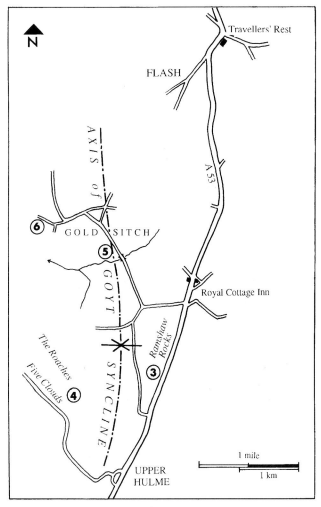

Figure 35. Sketch-map showing localities in Itinerary XI for the Roaches-Goldsitch Moss areas

area or even from Scandinavia. It was transported southwards by powerful rivers which became anastamosed or braided and deposited in shifting sandbanks over large areas at a very low height above sea-level. In the shales immediately succeeding the Roaches Grit and coal is a marine band marked by the occurrence of the goniatite *Reticuloceras superbilingue* (Figure 37). The Pecten-like

Figure 36. V-shaped outcrop of the Chatsworth Grit, Ramshaw Rocks, Staffordshire due to northerly plunge of the Goyt Syncline. View from dip-slope of Roaches Grit on east limb. Skyline formed by Roaches Grit on west limb.

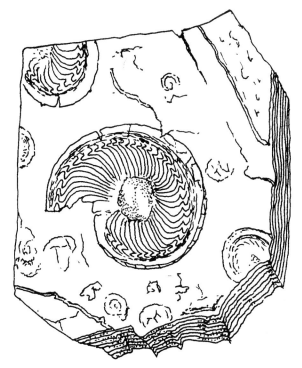

Figure 37. Reticuloceras superbilingue Bisat. Crushed specimen in shale showing typical ornamentation. 2 x natural size.

Dunbarella sp. is also common. In order to see the Roaches Grit at its maximum development together with the underlying Five Clouds Sandstones it will be necessary to return to the main road, turn southwards and descend part way down Cat Tor (Figure 35) then take a turning to the right to the village of Upper Hulme and follow the minor road leading NW for about 3 km. The Roaches Grit will be seen to form an immense bastion-like escarpment, first at Hen Cloud then at Five Clouds, on the western limb of the syncline (LOCALITY 4).

Another excellent section across the Goyt Syncline can be examined a little farther north at Goldsitch Moss (Figure 35). Return to the main road at Ramshaw Rocks, turn northwards and, after 2.5 km, take the turning to the left at a minor cross-roads (026637). In 1 km take the right fork towards Newstone Farm coinciding with a feature marking the base of the Roaches Grit. Descend the hill and attempt to park at the bridge over a small stream (LOCALITY 5) (015644). This stream affords a section across the syncline. The latter is assymetric, dips on the eastern limb being 30° or higher whilst those on the western limb rarely exceed 10°. The exposed sequence extends from below the Roaches Grit to the top of the Namurian and the lowest part of the Westphalian. Upstream from the bridge are outcrops of the Roaches Grit with the *Reticuloceras superbilingue* marine band just above it, and the Chatsworth Grit surmounted by a thin coal beneath the *Gastrioceras cancellatum* marine band. The bridge is situated on the westerly dipping Rough Rock, which is unusually soft here and gives rise to a weak feature to the north and south of the stream. The top of the Rough Rock can be located on the left bank of the stream just below the bridge and the contorted band can be seen to overlie the marine band with *Gastrioceras subcrenatum*, the accepted boundary between the Namurian and the Westphalian. Farther down the stream, now known as the Black Brook, is the Woodhead Hill Rock, a well-developed sandstone not far above the base of the Westphalian. This and associated shales are here stained red; this is thought to be the result of water percolation from a former cover of Triassic rocks. It seems likely that the present landscape is largely a Triassic one, modified by the Pleistocene glaciation.

The *Gastrioceras subcrenatum* marine band on the western limb of the syncline can be seen at LOCALITY 6 (002648).

Beds above the Woodhead Hill Rock are poorly exposed, but in the past several thin coals in the lowest Westphalian were worked on Goldsitch Moss. There are many small spoil heaps from these ancient workings scattered over the area.

The headwaters of the River Goyt and the River Wye

ITINERARY XII

The headwaters of the River Goyt and the River Wye

Aims: To examine the relationship between the Dinantian limestones and the overlying Namurian sandstones and shales, and to study the Namurian succession to the southwest of Buxton together with a glance at the lowest Westphalian beds in the outlier of the Goyt's Moss coalfield (Figure 38).

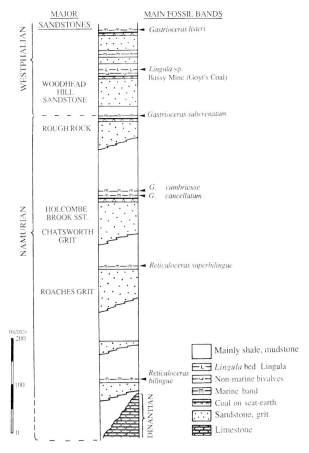

Figure 38. Generalised vertical section of the Namurian and basal Westphalian rocks of the Goyt Syncline or Trough.

The headwaters of the River Goyt and the River Wye

Maps & Memoirs: Ordnance Survey Sheet 119, 1: 50, 000, Landranger Series.
Geological Survey Sheet 111 (Buxton), 1: 50, 000.
Aitkenhead, N. & J. I. Chisholm, 1985. Geology of the country around Buxton,
Leek and Bakewell. *Mem. Geol. Surv.*

Transport: If Buxton is used as a centre, vehicular transport is not essential, the
total walking distance being no more than 16 km including some rough ground.

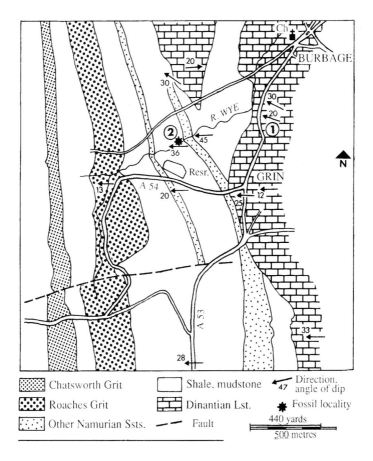

Figure 39. Geological sketch-map of the area to the southwest of Buxton showing localities 1 and 2 in Itinerary XII.

The headwaters of the River Goyt and the River Wye

Route: Leave Buxton either by St John's Road or Macclesfield Road and proceed to Christ Church, Burbage. Continue along the A53 road. The rising ground on the left is underlain by light coloured well bedded Dinantian Limestones of massif facies, whereas to the right (west) is the elevated ground of the Namurian (see Figure 38 for the generalised succession of the area).

About 1 km south of the church a small disused quarry on the left (LOCALITY 1, Figure 39) (043723) shows these limestones dipping steeply westwards. Sparse corals and brachiopods indicate an Asbian (D_1) age and place the limestones below the horizon of the Lower Miller's Dale Lava. The low-lying ground to the right of the road through which one of the headwaters of the River Wye courses is occupied by Namurian shales. Exposures are poor and no fossils have been found, but it is clear that Namurian sediments occupy a hollow excavated in the limestone, for limestone is again conspicuous in the rising ground to the north of the stream. Upon reaching the A53/A54 road bifurcation a useful diversion can be made to the Old Grin Quarry (048722) in order to see a 30 m section of the Chee Tor Rock (lower Bee Low Limestone) showing several clay partings (wayboards) on eroded bedding planes and a *Davidsonina septosa* Band near the top of the quarry face. In order to reach this quarry take the Leek A53 road for about 300 m and turn left along the road signposted 'Harpur Hill'. After about 700 m take the track on the left marked by the Caravan Club sign. The old quarry is now an official Caravan Club site and permission to view should be obtained from the warden. The site is closed during the winter months. A well-marked *Davidsonina septosa* band occurs a few metres below the top of the face. A 2 m wide calcite vein can be seen in the northeast corner at the top of the quarry; this appears to follow a north-south fault throwing down to the west. It appears to be coursing through woodland towards Poole's Cavern about 300 m to the north. By continuing southeastwards along the Harpur Hill road for another 1.5 km, it is possible to see a splendid section at Countess Cliff (054709) through well-bedded calcilutites (very fine grained limestones). These are lower in the succession than the limestones at Locality 1, and are Holkerian (S_2) in age (see Back cover, lower).

Regain the A53 Leek road and, moving westwards, after a short distance locate the site of a former railway bridge over the road. From here it is easy to appreciate that, beyond the River Wye to the N, an outcrop of limestone measuring about 1.5 km from north to south appears as an inlier in the Namurian area. A study of the dips is sufficient to demonstrate that the Namurian succeeds the Viséan limestones unconformably and that the basal Namurian beds were deposited upon a very uneven limestone surface. Some measure of the unconformity, and of the overlap associated with it, can be gained by examining the Wye section just to the north of the Burbage Reservoir which lies close to the Congleton-Macclesfield A54 road (036723). A bed of grey micaceous sandstone dipping upstream at 45° is

The headwaters of the River Goyt and the River Wye

succeeded by a marine band with the goniatite *Reticuloceras bilingue* (Cope, 1946) (LOCALITY 2). The grey sandstone can be traced northwards until it appears to rest upon the limestone in the inlier. This shows that the whole of the lower part of the Namurian is missing, a state of affairs contrasting sharply with the succession 15 km to the northeast near Castleton.

Continue westwards along the Congleton-Macclesfield main road for just over 1 km. At this point a small water pumping station will be reached on the right of the road (033714) (Figure 40). The stream course on the south side of the road shows a section of the beds above the Roaches Grit, for on the right of this stream 275 m south of the main road, the grit is seen to be succeeded by a marine band of dark blue shale with *Reticuloceras superbilingue*, and on the left bank the base of the succeeding Chatsworth Grit (the equivalent of the Holcombe Brook Grit of Lancashire) can be seen about 30 m above the marine band, forming the so-called

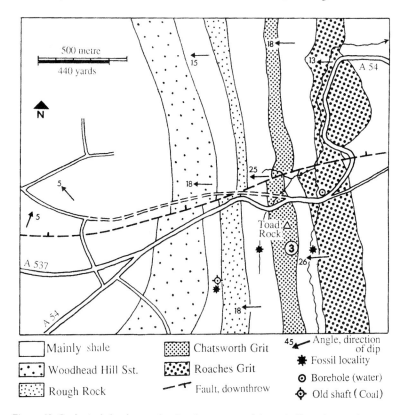

Figure 40. Geological sketch-map showing the outcrops of the main Namurian sandstones on Axe Edge Moor, along the Buxton-Macclesfield (Congleton) road and locality 3.

Toad Rock (LOCALITY 3).

Climb the scarp of the Chatsworth Grit noting the subarkosic (feldspathic) nature of the rock and descend the peat-covered dip-slope of the sandstone to the next stream to the west. A coal seam succeeding this sandstone was proved by several old trial holes and may have been worked on a small scale. Old spoil heaps alongside the stream yield pieces of shale with crushed marine fossils including the goniatite *Gastrioceras cancellatum.* A considerable tonnage of the Holcombe Brook Coal was hauled from the Old Axe Edge Colliery during the 19th Century for use mainly in lime-kilns.

All these beds are dipping westwards as they are on the eastern limb of the Goyt Trough or Syncline which is the first important structural feature to the west of the limestone outcrop. To the west of the stream a surface feature is evident; this is due to the outcrop of the succeeding Rough Rock, the uppermost sandstone of the Namurian. The Rough Rock is barely seen owing to the presence of thick peat.

Regain the main road by walking over the peat hags in a northerly direction. Going westwards along the road we reach the peat-covered outcrop of the Woodhead Hill Sandstone (basal Westphalian or 'Coal Measures') and descend its gentle dip-slope to the point where the road bifurcates for Macclesfield (A537) and Congleton (A54). Take the A537 right fork and after 250 m turn right, following the unfenced road which descends into the valley of the River Goyt (Figure 41). At the T-junction turn to the right and enter the valley of the Goyt. Until recently it was possible to walk alongside the stream immediately to the north to see the ganinsteroid top of the Woodhead Hill Sandstone, together with the shaly Goyt's Coal and succeeding shales carrying non-marine lamellibranchs, such as *Carbonicola* sp., typical of this lower part of the Westphalian. Unfortunately, a strong fence, crossing the stream about the top of the sandstone, now precludes any examination of these higher beds. The Goyt Coal, sometimes exposed on the right bank of the stream where it bends sharply northwards (017716) is of poor quality, consisting of about 1.5 m of bands of bright coal separated by laminae of black carbonaceous shale. It was worked many years ago and was used for lime-burning near Buxton. The coal is succeeded by about 4 m of blue shales and mudstones with ironstone nodules yielding several species of the non-marine bivalve *Carbonicola* including *C. fallax* and *C. rectilinearis* (Eagar, 1956). Four metres above the coal is a prominent bed of tough, black and blue laminated shale about 180 m thick, yielding in its lowest few millimeters *Lingula* sp. which denotes a return to marine conditions (Cope, 1949b).

In the roadside cutting, where both the stream and the road bend northwards (016718), is an erosional feature within the Westphalian. A thin conspicuous hard sandstone band marking the base of the post-erosional deposits varies greatly in its distance above the *Lingula* band, which occurs in the bank of the stream below the road (Cope,1949).

The headwaters of the River Goyt and the River Wye

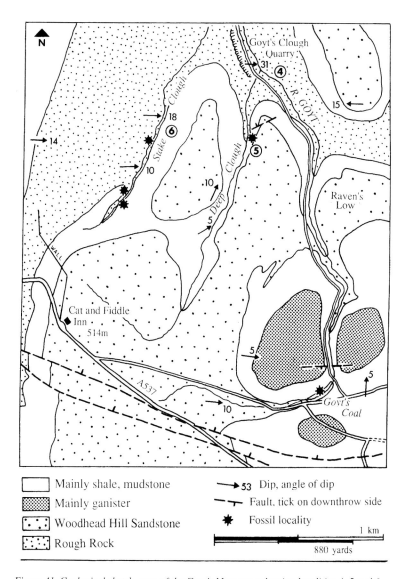

Figure 41. Geological sketch -map of the Goyt's Moss area showing localities 4, 5 and 6.

The headwaters of the River Goyt and the River Wye

In order to see a good exposure of the Rough Rock and immediately overlying beds it will be necessary first to walk to Goyt's Clough Quarry (LOCALITY 4; Figure 41). (Note: vehicles are not permitted to travel downstream along the road through the valley). This lies roughly 1.5 km north of the last exposures described. Goyt's Clough Quarry is situated on the left at the confluence of the stream in Deep Clough with the Goyt (012735). This part of the route lies approximately along the axis of the Goyt Syncline and, in the course of this walk through an area of considerable beauty, a descent is gradually made from horizons above the Goyt's Coal on to the underlying Woodhead Hill Rock, then through shales into the Rough Rock which is well exposed in the quarry.

The top of the Rough Rock and immediately overlying strata are exposed from time to time at a point in Deep Clough about 340 m south of the quarry (LOCALITY 5). The following section was measured some years ago:

	metres
Current-bedded sandstone (Woodhead Hill Sandstone)	- -
Blue and grey shales	15.0
Contorted shale..	0.5
Marine Band *(Gastrioceras subcrenatum)*	0.4
Shale	0.3
Coal	0.05
Fireclay and ganister	1.5
Pale grey sandstone (Rough Rock)	- -

The bed of contorted shale is one of several beds at different horizons in the Upper Carboniferous of the Peak District attributed to shear brought about by bedding-plane-slip during folding and known to be present in other areas where the stratal dip is appreciable.

If conditions are such that the exposures in Deep Clough are not available it will be necessary to add 2 km of rough walking if it is desired to see the succession immediately above the Rough Rock. There are excellent exposures in Stake Clough (LOCALITY 6).

CONSERVING THE EARTH HERITAGE RESOURCE OF THE PEAK DISTRICT

The geological character of a region has a profound influence on the development of its natural features and wildlife as well as the nature of human land use, The Peak District may be regarded as a particularly good example, dividing as it does into distinctive areas of topography, vegetation and pattern of land use. These areas are (1) the limestone dominated White Peak, (2) the high sandstone and peat covered plateau of the Dark Peak, (3) the sandstone scarp land of the western area, together with (4) the fringe of the Peak District and the Derwent valley in the southeast.

The limestones of the White Peak (1) comprise marginal reef facies, bedded platform carbonates with occasional interbedded lava flows. These limestones, capped by shales, acted as a host to lead mineralisation and are the medium for the development of karst-like topography. The product of a complex delta and floodplain, the Dark Peak (2) exposes the Edale Shales and above, the sandstones and shales (with their characteristic rocky scarps) of the high peat moorland. West of White Peak (3) the more variable landscape exposes the Lower Coal Measures in the synclinal trough of the Goyt Valley, whilst in the southeastern margins of the area (4) the marginal Carboniferous Limestones are important because of their mineralisation; the landscape is dominated by the deeply incised Derwent valley.

A RESOURCE FOR EVERYONE

Since Roman times the Peak District has been a major mineral resource. Galena for lead, barytes, fluorite and coal have all been actively exploited. Both the Carboniferous Limestone and Millstone Grit have been an important source of building stones and the limestones continue to be a source of high quality calcium carbonate and aggregate.

Since the 18th century the Peak District has served as a field laboratory for the study of Natural History. Many aspects of the Peak District geology remain the subject of active research and will continue to do so into the future. It is a valuable education resource being within easy reach of several densely populated centres in England and is visited by students of all levels, and geologists both professional and amateur. Perhaps most significant today, however, is the attraction of the landscape to the wider public; as well as walkers, climbers and cavers tourism brings the general public in vast numbers to enjoy the spectacular scenery and attractions, such as the Blue John Mine and the exhibition caves around Castleton, in one of the world's most visited National Parks.

The diverse geology of the Peak District reflects its complex geological history. Extensive reef development, migrating rivers, coal swamps, and volcanic eruptions are all part of the Carboniferous 'picture' now represented in the rocks of the area. The landscape has evolved via erosional events first initiated in Namurian times. It is this complex story of the evolution and interaction between geology, landscape, habitat, wildlife and land use that we are conserving for future generations.

CONSERVING THIS RESOURCE

The importance of the Peak District within the context of British geology and the range of pressures placed upon this resource make its careful conservation essential, ensuring that future generations can continue to learn from and enjoy the region.

As part of the conservation process the most important geological localities in the Peak District are afforded protection as Sites of Special Scientific Interest (SSSIs). There are 38 geological SSSIs in the Peak District ranging in size from the extensive Castleton SSSI which covers several aspects of Dinantian and Namurian Stratigraphy, Carboniferous Volcanism, Caves and Mass Movement to small sites, such as disused quarries with only a single interest. These sites have been selected on a national (UK) basis as part of the Geological Conservation Review (GCR) the philosophy of which is to identify those sites of national importance which most clearly represent our current understanding of geology (Ellis [ed], 1996). Complimentary to the SSSI series are Regionally Important Geological Sites (RIGS), selected by local groups reflecting regionally and locally important geology.

In a new initiative English Nature and the Countryside Commission have produced a map which depicts the natural and cultural dimensions of the landscape *'The Character of England; landscape, wildlife and natural features'* which identifies areas of similar landscape character. In the Peak District they correspond to the four mentioned areas. Such an approach to conservation complements the site-based system, placing SSSIs and RIGS in a wider context based on locally identifiable landscapes and features with which everyone is familiar.

FIELDWORK AND CONSERVATION

The Peak District contains a large and valuable Earth heritage resource. The purpose of conservation is not to 'mothball' this resource but to ensure that the way in which the resource is used guarantees its presence for future generations. An essential part of Earth heritage conservation is the practical use of Earth heritage sites, geology is, after all, a field based subject.

A responsible approach to field work should be adopted for all sites whether large or small, extensive or restricted in resource. Clear and straightforward guidelines have long been established by the *Geologists' Association* and *English Nature.* Both form a framework of principles regarding access permission, responsible approach to site and the need for all to follow such guidelines.

By following this advice, the value and interest of the localities discussed in this guide

Further reading

as well as the many other sites in the Peak District may be sustained for the education and enjoyment of everyone.

FURTHER INFORMATION

The Geologists' Association *Code of Conduct for Fieldwork* is available from The Geologists' Association, Burlington House, Piccadilly, London W1V 9AG (0171 434 9298)

English Nature's *Position statement on fossil collecting* as well as further advice and information regarding SSSIs and RIGS is available from English Nature's Peak District and Derbyshire Team at Manor Barn, Over Haddon, Bakewell, Derbyshire DE45 1UJ (01629 815095)

The character of England: landscape, wildlife and natural features (1996) available from: English Nature, Northminster House, Peterborough, PE1 1UA and the Countryside Commission, John Dower House, Crescent Place, Cheltenham, GL50 3RA.

REFERENCE

Ellis, N. V., Bowen, D. Q., Campbell, S., Knill, J. L., McKirdy, A. P., Prosser, C.D., Vincent, M.A. and Wilson, R. C. L. (1996). *An Introduction to the Geological Conservation Review*. Geological Conservation Review Series 1, Joint Nature Conservation Committee, Peterborough, 113pp.

FURTHER READING

AITKENHEAD, N, & CHISHOLM, J. I. 1982. A standard nomenclature for the Dinantian formations of the Peak District of Derbyshire and Staffordshire. *Institute of Geological Sciences.* 82/8.
ALLEN, J. R. L. 1960. The Mam Tor Sandstones: a 'turbidite' facies of the Namurian deltas of Derbyshire, England. *Journal of Sedimentary Petrology, 30,* 193-208.
ARNOLD-BEMROSE, H. H. 1894. On the Microscopical Structure of the Carboniferous Dolerites and Tuffs of Derbyshire. *Quarterly Journal of the Geological Society, London,1,* 603-644.
ARNOLD-BEMROSE, H. H. 1899. On the sill and faulted inlier in Tideswell (Derbyshire). *Quarterly Journal of the Geological Society, London, 55,* 239-250.
ARNOLD-BEMROSE, H. H. 1907. The Toadstones of Derbyshire; their Field Relations and Petography. *Quarterly Journal of the Geological Society, London, 63, 241-281*
BROADHURST, F. M. & SIMPSON, I. M. 1973. Bathymetry on a Carboniferous reef. *Lethaia, 6,* 367-381.
BUTCHER, N. J. D. & FORD, T. D. 1973. The Carboniferous Limestone of Monsal

Further reading

Dale, Derbyshire. *Mercian Geologist, 4*, 179-196.

COLLINSON, J. D. 1968. Deltaic sedimentation units in the Upper Carboniferous of Northern England. *Sedimentology, 10*, 233-254.

COLLINSON, J. D. 1976. Deltaic evolution during basin fill, Namurian of the Central Pennines, England. *American Association of Petroleum Geologists Bulletin (Abstract), 60*, 52.

COPE, F. W. 1933. The Lower Carboniferous Succession in the Wye Valley Region of North Derbyshire. *Journal of the Manchester Geological Association, 1*, 125-145.

COPE, F. W. 1936. The *Cyrtina septosa* Band in the Lower Carboniferous succession of North Derbyshire. *Summary of Progress of the Geological Survey, 2*, 48-51.

COPE, F. W. 1939. The mid-Viséan (S_2-D_1) succession in North Derbyshire and north-west England. *Proceedings of the Yorkshire Geological Society, 24*, 60-66.

COPE, F. W. 1946. Intraformational contorted rocks in the Upper Carboniferous of the Southern Pennines. *Quarterly Journal of the Geological Society, London, 101*, 139-176.

COPE, F. W. 1949a. Woo Dale Borehole near Buxton, Derbyshire. *Quarterly Journal of the Geological Society, London, 105*, iv.

COPE, F. W. 1949b. Correlation of the Coal Measures of Macclesfield and the Goyt Trough. *Transactions of the Institute of Mining Engineers, 105*, 466-483.

COPE, F. W. 1966. The Butterton Dyke near Keele and Butterton, Staffordshire. *North Staffordshire Journal of Field Studies, 2*, 25-37.

COPE, F. W. 1972. Some stratigraphical breaks in the Dinantian massif facies in North Derbyshire. *Mercian Geologist, 4*. 143-148.

COPE, F. W. 1973. Woo Dale Borehole near Buxton, Derbyshire. *Nature Physical Science, London, 243*, 29-30.

COPE, F. W. 1979. The age of the volcanic rocks in the Woo Dale Borehole, Derbyshire. *Geological Magazine, 116*, 319-320.

COPE, F.W. 1997. An igneous dyke complex in the Carboniferous Limestone of north Derbyshire and its significance. *Proceedings of the Yorkshire Geological Society, 20* 1-5.

COPE, J. C. W., INGHAM, J. K. & RAWSON, P. F. 1992. *Atlas of Palaeogeography,* Geological Society of London, Memoir 13.

DUNHAM, K. C. 1973. A recent deep borehole near Eyam, Derbyshire. *Nature Physical Science, London, 241*, 84-85.

EAGAR, R. M. C. 1956. Additions to the non-marine fauna of the Lower Coal Measures of the north-Midlands coalfields. *Liverpool & Manchester Geological Journal, 1*. 328-369.

EAGAR, R. M. C. & BROADHURST, F. M. 1991. *Geology of the Manchester Area. Geologists' Association Guide No. 56*, 118 pp.

FORD, T. D. 1996. *The Castleton Area, Derbyshire.* Geologists' Association Guide No. 56, 93 pp.

HUDSON, R. G. S. 1931. The pre-Namurian knoll topography of Derbyshire and Yorkshire. *Transactions of the Leeds Geological Association, 5*, 49-64.

HULL, E. & GREEN, A. H. 1864. On the Millstone Grit of North Staffordshire and the adjoining parts of Derbyshire, Cheshire and Lancashire. *Quarterly Journal of the Geological Society, London, 22*, 242-267.

Further reading

INSTITUTE OF GEOLOGICAL SCIENCES. 1978. I. G. S. boreholes 1977. *Report of the Institute of Geological Sciences, 78/21.*

JACKSON, J. W. 1927. The succession below the Kinderscout Grit in North Derbyshire. *Journal of the Manchester Geological Association,* **1**, 15-32.

MILLER, G. D. 1988. The Calton Hill SSI - an update. *Amateur Geologist,* **12/2**, 31-39

MORRIS, T. O. 1929. The Carboniferous Limestone and Millstone Grit Series of Stony Middleton and Eyam, Derbyshire. *Proceedings of the Sorby Scientific Society,* **1**, 37-67.

SADLER, H. E. 1964. The Origin of the Beach Beds in the Lower Carboniferous of Castleton, Derbyshire. *Geological Magazine,* **101**, 360-372.

SIBLY, T. F. 1908. The faunal succession in the Carboniferous Limestone (upper Avonian) of the Midland area (north Derbyshire and north Staffordshire). *Quarterly Journal of the Geological Society, London,* **64**, 34-82.

SIMPSON, I. M. & BROADHURST, F. M. 1969. A boulder bed at Treak Cliff, Derbyshire. *Proceedings of the Yorkshire Geological Society,* **37**, 141-151.

TOMKEIEFF, S. I. 1928. The volcanic complex of Calton Hill, Derbyshire. *Quarterly Journal of the Geological, London,* **84**, 703-718.

WALKDEN, G. M. 1972. The mineralogy and origin of interbedded clay way-boards in the Lower Carboniferous of the Derbyshire Dome. *Geological Journal,* **8**, 143-160.

WHITEHURST, J. 1778. *An enquiry into the original state and formation of the Earth.* London.

WOLFENDEN, E. B. 1958. Paleoecology of the Carboniferous reef complex and shelf limestones in north-west Derbyshire, England. *Bulletin of the Geological Society of America,* **69**, 871-898.